# STRANGE GODS

## ALISON KIMBLE

Immortal Works LLC
1505 Glenrose Drive
Salt Lake City, Utah 84104
Tel: (385) 202-0116

© 2021 Alison Kimble
https://www.authoralisonkimble.com

Cover Art by Ashley Literski
http://strangedevotion.wixsite.com/strangedesigns

This book is a work of fiction. Names, characters, businesses, organizations, places, events and incidents either are the product of the author's imagination or are used fictitiously. Any resemblance to actual persons, living or dead, events, or locales is entirely coincidental.

ISBN 978-1-953491-14-5
ASIN B097NXK362

*For Mom, who gave me belief in myself.*

# CHAPTER I
## SPKY

Up until this exact moment, Spooky hadn't been sure whether or not Luke liked her. Now it seemed improbable there was any other reason he was holding her hand under the table. She stiffened as he curled his fingers around the edge of her palm. She wasn't sure if she wanted his hand on hers, but she didn't want to get caught with it there.

Then his touch was gone, and in its place, a piece of paper. Spooky shifted her eyes to the closest counselor, but no heads turned. No one had noticed the exchange.

She crinkled the contraband in her hand: a note. Pens were restricted-use items, so notes were rare. More importantly, notes were risky—you couldn't change your story once it was in writing. She wanted to read Luke's face as much as the words he had put on the paper, but she kept her chin pointed at the front of the cafeteria.

"Remember, there is no such thing as your true self, only unlimited potential for growth and change," Izeah Dodgson continued into the mic. "I want you to reflect on those words when you're tucked into your bunks tonight." He scanned the room over the top of his glasses. His bald head shone in the fluorescent lighting. "To close us off, I have an announcement. Yesterday evening, patrol spotted a large animal inside the fence. Now, now." Izeah put up his hands as if to quiet the room of silent campers. "I don't want anyone to be alarmed. This is exactly why we have the fence in the first place."

The fence wasn't really designed to keep things out. Spooky had seen the exposed chain-link exterior when the cab dropped her off on orientation day. The plastic sheeting that made it impossible to climb only ran along the inside. But the illusion of trust was a core part of Izeah's philosophy of rehabilitation, so he insisted the fence was keeping animals out rather than keeping two hundred delinquents in. The fence kept things out, just like the motion-activated floodlights "scared off raccoons," and the foam spork she had just used to eat her runny chili "saved on dishwater."

"A thorough search of the camp tells us our visitor didn't stay, but we want to be cautious. If you see anything, anything at all, please alert a counselor." The mic whined. "We are on the edge of a wilderness. We must respect that we aren't the only ones out here."

The second Izeah dismissed the crowd to their post-dinner duties, Spooky glanced down at the scrap of paper in her hand: *Meet tonight.*

There were no other instructions, but Spooky knew Luke's plan. That didn't mean she thought it was a good idea. She tried to make eye contact during post-dinner cleanup, but work duty ended before she could give Luke so much as a head shake.

He was going, whether she joined him or not.

When the last bell rang and the cabin lights went out, Spooky kept her eyes open and began counting. After she reached sixty for the fortieth time, she folded back the blanket, rolled off the bunk, and tucked the pillow in her place. With sneakers in hand, she crept past heavy-breathing campers to the entrance. Not a single floorboard creaked. She had earned her nickname, at least in part, because of her talent for passing through life quietly.

The trick to avoid the motion detectors, Luke had told her, was to do three things at once: jump the lower sensors, duck the upper sensors, and don't set foot inside the circle. Spooky didn't trust herself to jump and duck anything, so she squatted and swung a leg around the cabin's open side. Izeah insisted a circle of open cabins inspired "community," but the formation also ensured anyone could look out and see her dangling from the doorway. Gripping the wall for balance, she found the ground next to the cabin with her toe. Arms shaking, she transferred her weight and set both feet outside.

She crouched and scanned the night. Her sleep shirt was twisted and stuck to her body with sweat. Her heartbeat should have been loud enough to wake all ten cabins. But nothing stirred.

She had done it. She had snuck out. This was a teenage rite of passage. Even if someone had invited her, she wouldn't have had the nerve to attempt this at home. She wasn't sure she had the nerve for it now, but she certainly wasn't ready to try to reverse the process and get back inside the cabin. Her hands quivered as she put on her sneakers. After a few more moments watching the silent dark, she started across the field toward the back of the main lodge.

Even though Spooky had been at Dodgson for over a month, she had never been outside after the last bell. It was like the world had flipped upside down; the field around her was flat black, while all the light and life played out in the sky above her. Bright points and brilliant clusters and tiny pinpricks twinkled. She had to rely on her feet more than her eyes to find each step.

She exhaled for the first time since she read the note, or maybe for the first time that summer. It was as if the darkness put her at an unreachable distance from the sleeping campers and counselors. Even her limbs felt far away.

Only now, in the quiet, did it occur to Spooky she might be walking into a trap.

Although they had been at Dodgson together all summer, she had only known Luke since he was assigned to cafeteria duty two weeks ago. He'd come up to her while she was setting up the buffet, tucked a hair back into her hairnet, and asked about her nickname. And he kept finding her, in between serving and mopping and scrubbing. He had even started saving a seat for her at meals.

It was unfamiliar territory to have anyone, much less a guy, show interest in getting to know her. She had thought they were becoming friends. Maybe even a little more. And since he'd held her hand longer than strictly necessary to pass the note, almost definitely more. But she shouldn't let herself forget this wasn't some guy from English class—every camper at Dodgson was here for a reason. Luke was here for a reason.

Spooky pictured Luke's straight, pointy nose and white-blond hair. His half smile. She couldn't imagine that face leering out of the night, ready to inflict violence. But it was possible that Luke had set her up to meet someone else. Someone who wanted to have a private word without the watchful eyes of counselors. She wasn't aware of any enemies. Unfortunately, it didn't take much to set off one of two hundred delinquents. There were plenty of stories of accidental offenses leading to nasty consequences.

And Luke had been distant during post-dinner cleanup. While she'd been spraying down tables on one side of the cafeteria, he'd been stacking chairs on the other. When she started collecting serve ware, he began mopping. He'd ducked her attempts to make eye contact. She hadn't seen him come back from taking out the trash at all.

He'd been avoiding her.

Spooky stopped walking. Why had Luke bothered to write her a note? The forethought seemed sweet at first, but the risk was impractical. Counselors were attentive during announcements; it was the worst possible time to communicate. He could have waited until after dinner was over and whispered the words.

But he'd already tried to do that, hadn't he? Luke had asked her to sneak out twice this week. The note hadn't given her a chance to say she was too tired, or she couldn't risk the scuffs. A note only gave her the choice to show up or leave him waiting.

Spooky rubbed her arms through her long-sleeve flannel. She should turn around and get back in bed. She didn't even know how many scuffs she would get if she was caught out here. It was a big camp, and Luke said patrols only went around once or twice a night, but she should have tried to do the math. The image of Luke standing alone in the cold had been on her mind instead.

She sighed through her nose and kept walking. Spooky liked

Luke, or at least, she thought she might start to. She definitely didn't want him to stop talking to her. And he would have every right to if he took the risk of coming out here and she didn't show. Going back now would put a quick end to the only good thing happening at Dodgson.

Still, Spooky approached the dumpsters behind the lodge like a ghost. She had come back here dozens of times on garbage duty, but the shape of things changed at night. The lodge had lost its edges. Every shadow was a void. Her ears twitched. Luke had told her to meet him at the door, but it seemed like she had arrived first. She huddled behind one of the rusty bins to wait.

Her toes had just started to go numb when footsteps brushed the dirt nearby. A white-blond head bobbed into view.

"Luke!" He was alone. A laugh bubbled up. Dodgson really did something to your faith in people.

"Sorry I'm late." He jogged over to her. He didn't bother to keep his voice low, but they were far from any sleeping quarters. "I had to wait for my cabin-leader to snore."

"I wasn't here long," Spooky said.

He took a step closer. She took a step back and jumped when her shoulder brushed the dumpster. She was relieved it was just him, but just him, alone in the dark, gave her plenty of new reasons to be nervous.

"So, what's up?" she blurted.

"Oh, you know, out for a midnight stroll." She could hear his smile more than see it.

"A stroll, huh? Aren't you worried about the animal that got inside the fence?"

"It was a bear. A huge one."

"Really? How do you know?" At least there weren't any grizzlies in Colorado.

"Animal control told me when I showed them where I saw the snake."

"You saw a snake?" Spooky dropped the casual tone she'd been attempting. "Where?"

"Between the dumpsters. I saw it when I was taking out the trash after dinner. I'm surprised you didn't hear me yelling." He chuckled and edged closer. "But don't worry. They checked everywhere. It's gone."

"Was it a rattlesnake?" She picked up one foot then the other, eyeing the shadowy ground.

"Don't worry." Luke closed the distance between them. "I'll protect you."

"But what if it's still..."

He put his hands on the dumpster behind her and leaned in.

It was a strange sensation having somebody else's lips against hers. Things touched her mouth every day, but another set of lips felt different somehow, like she was trying to use her left hand for something she usually did with her right.

She couldn't tell Luke how strange it was. She couldn't let anybody at Dodgson find out she was having her first kiss only two weeks after her eighteenth birthday. She would become an instant target for that kind of quaint, teenage naiveté.

But privately, she could celebrate her second milestone of the night. She had pictured this moment for a long time. While she never could have guessed who, where, or when, she had imagined a slow, inevitable, folding together. Lips slightly open, arms entwined, and bodies close.

This was turning out to be a much more thorough exploration of her mouth than she had imagined. And it was getting more thorough by the second.

Luke mimed a slow chew, then a few quick guppy gasps. She tried to catch his rhythm. If he noticed she was doing something wrong, he didn't pause to address it. She pursed her mouth when his opened, and he gave her lower lip and a decent part of her chin a lick.

Spooky pushed him away. He barreled back in faster than she could wipe her face.

"Luke, hold on..."

The words became garbled as he mashed her lips around. Her hair slid all over the bin as he guided her head this way and that with his mouth. A sticky spot clung to her shirt.

Enough. This midnight tryst was over.

Spooky hitched her foot up to push herself off the dumpster. Her knee slid between Luke's legs and slammed into his groin.

"Oof!"

Spooky gasped as he doubled over. He backed away from her with a high keen.

"Oh, sorry!" Spooky reached for him. "I'm sorry!"

"What the..." he whimpered. "What's wrong with you?"

A beam of light swung around the corner of the lodge. Footsteps and voices drifted through the chill.

Counselors on patrol.

"Luke," Spooky muttered. "Luke, we have to leave."

A trio of figures rounded the building, flashlights swaying. Spooky jumped behind the dumpster. Luke was doubled over in the open. If he would just move a few feet toward her, the bin would be between him and the oncoming counselors.

"Luke, come here," she hissed.

He groaned. A beam landed on his platinum hair. He spared one hand from his crotch to block his eyes.

"Hey! Stop right there!" a counselor called.

The voices picked up. The light stayed on Luke. If she didn't move now they would catch her too.

"Sorry," she whispered.

Spooky bowed her head and dashed to the nearest tree. The trunk wasn't wide enough to conceal her shoulders, so she darted to the next one. She scrambled around it and pressed her back against the bark. It wouldn't take much searching to find her, but there was nowhere left to sneak. Between this pine and the forest was the fence, complete with twenty-foot-high, unscalable plastic sheeting. To "keep out the animals."

"Any other campers out here making choices that don't reflect their true potential?" Counselor Jackie called.

"Come on out," another counselor she knew, Mark, commanded. "Let's start rebuilding."

The words didn't sound natural, but they were familiar from daily speeches and role plays. Unlike Izeah Dodgson, the rest of the staff delivered their canned lines about trust with varying levels of conviction.

The third counselor spoke in a low voice. Spooky heard "slip in behavior" and "initiate the reparation process."

"...but before we begin rebuilding," the counselor said. "I want you to choose to be your best, most trustworthy self and tell us: are you out here alone?"

Spooky might not be Luke's favorite person right now—she could still feel the spot where her knee met his pelvis—but if there was one thing that guaranteed every pyro, bully, and druggie here would turn on you, it was ratting someone out to the counselors.

"I was just checking to make sure I locked the dumpsters after dinner. Animal control came and I got distracted. I wasn't sure," Luke whined.

He was talking too much. He sounded like he was lying. She tried to melt into the tree trunk.

"I trust you," the counselor said in a monotone voice. "But if there were someone out here with you, and you were to tell us now, I would recommend you get thirty scuffs. I'll talk to Mr. Dodgson about that personally." He paused. "Otherwise, you're looking at fifty, minimum."

Fifty scuffs? Only the rough bark stopped Spooky from sliding to the ground. She had known being out of bounds was a multiplier for whatever else you were caught doing. She should have gone to examine the scuff board after dinner instead of trying to catch Luke's eye. She should have done the math before leaving her bed instead of counting the seconds.

Fifty scuffs was bad. Fifty scuffs, plus her existing twenty-three, would put her at a serious risk of maxing out before the summer was over. A rise that fast would land her back in Adam Dodgson's office, in a seat she had vowed she wouldn't return to after day one.

From the second she stepped out of the cab, everything at Dodgson had been jarring. Her bags were whisked away to be searched. She had to swap the clothes she came in for rough gray pajamas. She had a schedule with building names and times, but no clock or map. She wandered around in loaner flip flops, trying to follow the crowd without getting too close. The other campers looked at her like she was food. The counselors looked right through her.

But nothing at the camp was more jarring than the Dodgson brothers and their conflicting approaches to delinquent rehabilitation.

"Exploratory teens," Izeah began in his welcome speech, "fall into a pattern of behavior slips and mistrust that feed each other. They make a mistake, and their community implements new restrictions. Parents, teachers, and friends treat them like they are going to misbehave again. So they break more rules. Blame, rules, and offenses pile up until, eventually, they conclude they can't do anything right. So why try? They'll always mess up anyway, right? Wrong!" He yelled the answer to his own question so loudly the grass around her could have rippled. "We know you can be better. We'll give you the trust you need to break the cycle of negative thinking. Here at Dodgson, we give you the freedom to be your best selves. In a controlled environment, of course."

"Do you know why you're here?" Adam Dodgson asked as soon as she sat down across from him. It seemed like a silly question. Spooky knew what she had done. His dim office and quiet attention were the stark opposite of Izeah's blustering speech on the field. Elaborate promises of trust and rehabilitation swirled in her head.

"Err. Because I made a mistake, and I can do better?"

"No. Because you were insufficiently motivated to behave." Adam had all the hair Izeah lacked. His sandy mane was just graying at the temples. "Outside these walls, the fallout of your actions wasn't enough to constrain your behavior. Breaking rules didn't affect you, personally, in a way that mattered to you. I'm going to change that."

Adam Dodgson reached into the filing cabinet beside his desk and pulled out a red folder with her name on it.

"When you break rules, you get scuffs. When you get scuffs, there are consequences. With the appropriate consequences, you will choose not to break rules."

Izeah's speech had mentioned scuffs. The word was meant to evoke something temporary, like a bit of grime that could be wiped away. After all, Izeah said to the field of teens in gray pajamas, he believed each and every one of them had endless potential to do better. Two minutes into their meeting, Spooky had a feeling Adam Dodgson didn't share his brother's optimism.

"I've talked to your parents, and I'm impressed." His voice was even and deliberate. "To motivate you to behave this summer, they already had their own consequences in mind. I helped them add a few additional details."

Adam opened the red folder and repositioned it to face her. Inside were her scuff levels: predetermined punishments for every ten scuffs, up to one hundred.

Spooky had assumed if she was caught sneaking out, she would spend the rest of the summer shoveling chicken shit, or maybe even bunking in the closed cabins with campers who were a little more stabby. Working in the cafeteria and sleeping in an open cabin were privileges of her good behavior. There was Dodgson, and then there was Dodgson.

But the scuff level punishments at camp weren't what scared her. At eighty scuffs, consequences started bleeding through the fence and into her life outside. Adam Dodgson would take out his horrible red folder and make sure misery followed her through the gates. Spooky hadn't just left for Dodgson with her suitcases. Her parents had put her in the cab with an ultimatum. If she got one hundred scuffs, the bleak and lonely years so far would be the best of her life.

And now she was about to hit seventy-three scuffs with almost half her time at Dodgson remaining.

"No one under the dumpsters," Jackie called.

"I'm alone," Luke whined again.

"Sure you are," Mark said.

He was close. Too close. The beam of his flashlight waved on either side of the tree. She squeezed her eyes shut. His footsteps grew louder.

A sizzling *crack* echoed, and her vision blazed red.

# CHAPTER 11
# THE CHANGE

Spooky opened her eyes to bright light and long shadows. A buzz reverberated through the air. The floodlights were on. Someone else was out of bed. Someone who didn't know to avoid the upper and lower motion detectors for the five-foot-tall "raccoons."

"Seems like we have another camper making choices that don't reflect their full potential," Jackie said.

"Waiting to meet a friend?" Mark asked.

"This is Patrol," the unknown counselor said. "Where was the trip? Over."

"Confirm Patrol," a crackling voice responded. "Motion tripped at the girls' cabin circle. Over."

"Jackie and Mark will report and assist search. Karl taking out-of-bounds camper, Luke Jenson, to the holding cabins. Over." The radio released static and a click. "Looks like those fifty scuffs are yours. Your life is about to get very uncomfortable. But we trust you will do better next time."

Luke grumbled as their steps crunched away.

Spooky cringed. Everyone got the same number of scuffs for breaking a rule, but the scuff level consequences were always customized. You couldn't threaten a slob with a messy work duty, but you sure could motivate a germaphobe. Adam Dodgson knew that. And as the levels went up, the repercussions became more severe. She had heard whispers of other campers' maximum scuff level punishments: getting kicked out of a dream sports program, going to rehab, or being sent to military boarding school.

She didn't know what was in store for Luke, but sailing up five levels at once was sure to be painful. He had started the night with about thirty scuffs, so at least he wouldn't max out.

"Wasn't that where last night's patrol saw the bear?" Mark asked. His voice was farther away, but the lights seemed to give everyone permission to speak at full volume.

"Yeah," Jackie replied. "They said it was massive. Fast too. It disappeared before they could radio for the tranq gun."

Mark whistled. "Maybe it'll come back and eat some of these little shits."

Jackie's retort faded with their footsteps.

After a few moments of silence, Spooky peered around the tree. Fluorescent rays reflected off swirling pollen and dirt in the air. Jackie and Mark were swaying silhouettes a quarter of the way across the field. The blue dumpsters cast long shadows, abandoned.

Spooky crept into the open and jogged low to the first bin. She gripped the rusty edge and peeked over the top. Every camper was supposed to stay in bed, without moving or talking, until they caught whoever tripped the sensors. Her pillow and wadded up clothes would be following instructions perfectly. Once they identified the culprit, the lights would go out, and she could sneak back into her cabin. The unlucky camper would be carted off with Luke.

Luke. She sagged against the dumpster. Ever since boys in middle school had started calling her ears "handles" and trying to grab them while making fishy faces, she hadn't put herself in a position for a first kiss to happen. But Luke hadn't seemed to mind her stringy hair or her big ears or the long silences when she couldn't think of anything else to say to him. He had still smiled and saved her a seat.

Their late-night encounter hadn't gone like she expected—it had gone horribly, actually. But for a brief moment, she had let herself hope that her maybe-more-than-a-friendship with Luke was the start of something.

At the beginning of every school year, as far back as she could remember, Spooky had felt hopeful. She'd use mousse to arrange her hair over her ears and wear her brightest shirts. She'd buy fresh note-books or steal a few from Victoria's room. She'd write down a neat list of classes with her teachers' names and room numbers. And she'd keep her eyes open for The Change: that one thing that would come along and start her life.

It might be a guy, who would find her fascinating and become her first everything. It might be a friend, with whom she could share the kind of secret language that made everyone else an outsider. It might even be a disaster—a classmate choking in the cafeteria, or a fire—some moment when she could step out of the shadows, jump into action, and make everyone reevaluate that spooky girl.

But after a week or two, she'd settle back into grays. She'd stop taking notes in her new notebooks and let classes happen to her. She'd slump over her lunch with the same group of stragglers in the corner. She'd realize that no transformative person was going to emerge from the familiar names and faces.

The beginning of freshman year, sophomore year, and junior year had come and gone with no Change in sight. Halfway through junior year, she accepted The Change wasn't going to happen in high school. It wasn't going to happen until she was walking the paths of some distant college with a leather bag over her shoulder and a thick sweater protecting her from the autumn chill. What hours would she keep if she lived in a dorm, without having to worry about disturbing her parents? What would she say in class, without teachers who still talked about her sister's perfect papers? How would she act if she were a stranger entering a room of strangers? Would she still intro-duce herself as Spooky? Or would it be Laurel Specki, unassociated with any other local Speckis?

Just for a second, against the dumpster, when Luke first leaned in —before the slobber and the accidental knee in the groin—it had almost felt like The Change.

But it wasn't time for The Change yet. She had to survive the summer, get through senior year, graduate, and start over somewhere new. Dodgson wasn't a destination. Dodgson was a slippery steppingstone. She could grip it with her toes and leap to the far shore or slide off into a current that would drag her down. And a risk like this, a fifty-scuff risk, could threaten her chances of making it to the other side.

She hadn't been caught, but she wasn't in bed yet either. She would be ready to run for the cabin as soon as they shut off the lights. She hopped in place, then crouched to re-tie her laces.

Motion made her glance up. Something under the dumpster was moving.

She leapt back, eyes flitting over the shadows. It looked like a trash bag undulating in nonexistent wind. Then it uncoiled.

Hot pins rolled over her skin.

Snake.

It darted out from beneath the bin and struck at her foot. She shot straight up, full of searing adrenaline. It feinted at her legs as she jumped and stomped and twisted away. Foot after foot of tan length emerged, winding after her. Colorado had rattlesnakes, but this looked more like an anaconda. She shrieked as it made contact.

There was pressure but no pain. She glanced down; the snake had no head. The impossible thing was all body, and it was coiled around her ankle.

It wrenched her leg, knocking her onto her stomach. She gasped and coughed. Before she could catch her breath, it started dragging her over the dirt toward the dumpsters. Gravel grated her front as it pulled her between the bins. She scrambled to get ahold of the metal sides, but only splinters of rust caught under her fingernails. She screamed.

Bright light flared up. The ground disappeared. Her body floated.

She was hovering in nothingness. There was endless white in every direction. The stars that should have been above her, the dumpsters, the lodge...all of it was gone. The only matter in the whiteness was her. Her, and the snake around her ankle. Now it looked more like a rope, towing her through a cloud.

She kicked her legs and waved her arms, but she only bobbed in place. She screamed until her throat strained, but it was like yelling into cotton.

The snake must have bitten her, or maybe she'd hit her head. Spooky ran her hands over her stomach and sides, then up to her neck and through her hair to her skull. She couldn't find the source of the injury. Maybe evidence of what had happened in the real world hadn't carried over to this dream place. She brushed bits of gravel off her front, and they drifted away like asteroids.

If she was unconscious by the dumpsters, nobody would find her until the main lodge opened in the morning. Maybe not until after breakfast.

"I'm here!" she hollered. Her pulse pounded louder than her voice in her ears. "Help, I'm here!"

She couldn't die yet. She had barely even lived.

Then the world turned black. Her stomach lurched and she grabbed at nothing. Gravity slammed her onto her front.

She wheezed, her ribs vibrating. The whiteness was gone. She hauled herself to her knees, waiting for the spots in front of her eyes to swim away.

This was the first and last time she would ever sneak out to meet a boy.

Spooky clambered to her feet. She stood in the center of a clearing surrounded by dark trees. The sky was charcoal and starless. She swayed in place, waiting to recognize something.

Across the expanse sat a cabin. Or a house. Or a barn. It didn't match the institutional-log-cabin style of most of the buildings at Dodgson. It was like a wooden circus tent, with a huge circular body, and a roof that sloped more and more sharply until it converged in a point. Splintering, crooked planks covered the entire structure top to bottom. Light emanated from a few haphazard holes punched in the walls. The orange glow made shadows around the clearing shudder.

Spooky hadn't been everywhere on the Dodgson grounds. There were plenty of restricted areas, like the dumpsters, the counselors' quarters, and the closed cabins. It was possible a building this big was nestled in some corner of the camp. But surrounding the clearing, all she could see were trunks and treetops. There was no space at Dodgson for this much forest.

The longer she stood there, the more certain she became she was no longer inside the fence.

There were exits in the fence, of course. There had to be, in case one of the pyros developed primitive survival skills and started a fire. Day one, when drop-offs were finished and all the parents had gone, Adam Dodgson had demonstrated the emergency exits. The entire camp had sat in the dirt near the fence line, still wearing their gray welcome pajamas. The schedule listed this timeslot as "Camp Rule Review," and with her scuff levels fresh in her mind, Spooky was ready to listen. On this section of fence, metal bars broke up the plastic sheeting, outlining a doorway. Adam Dodgson drove up on a golf cart, got out, and walked over to it.

"You may not follow all of my rules," he said. "But there is one that you will follow, and it is this: you will not leave Camp Dodgson."

There was no lock on the door, just a metal latch. He lifted it.

Spooky reeled back, smacking her hands against her ears. The campers around her were in a similar state of distress, grimacing and holding their heads. The alarm was so loud she couldn't think. She wanted to run.

Adam Dodgson watched them writhe another second, then tapped something into his phone. The alarm stopped.

"Leaving the camp," he said, his voice muffled, "will guarantee immediate maximum scuff level consequences. No negotiation, no second chances."

Then he got back in his golf cart and drove off. Izeah took over and instructed them to go to the cafeteria, so he could review the full set of rules on the scuff board.

Watching Adam Dodgson drive away, Spooky had resolved that even if the camp was burning, she would stay inside the fence. She would let the flames scorch her heels before she would lift that latch. She wouldn't give him the excuse.

But something had happened tonight, something beyond her control. Spooky had never joined the group in the high school parking lot who passed around a murky bottle, lifted in drops and tablespoons from their parents' liquor cabinets, but she could only describe what had happened to her as a blackout. Or a whiteout. In whatever stupor had made her think she was floating through clouds, it was possible she had wandered through one of the emergency exits and into the woods. She couldn't hear the alarm, but it was possible.

The house looked inhabited. Asking for a phone seemed like a better idea than wandering off into the forest. Spooky didn't want to knock on the door of whoever had decided to live out here alone. Maybe she could peek in a window first.

She tried to take a step and stumbled. The living rope was still looped around her left ankle. It drew a straight line across the clearing and disappeared into the trees opposite the house.

None of this made any sense.

A bang rang out. She whirled to face the house as it strained out a creaking, thumping rhythm. A section of the planks swung outward. A figure filled the arched doorway.

"At last!" a man's voice boomed. "You've arrived!"

# CHAPTER III
# CARCASS

The speaker was only a silhouette. Spooky froze, unsure if he had seen her, or who he'd meant to call out to. Before she could move or reply, he leapt from the doorway and thumped onto the dirt in front of her.

The figure was bigger than anyone she had ever seen. If she held her arms out to either side, she would barely get her hands around the edge of him. If she reached straight up, she only might have been able to tap his brow. Even for his height and girth, his head was massive. Two curling points rose out of the top. They could have been a head-dress, but they looked a lot more like horns. His facial features suggested one of his parents was a toad. Round, front-facing eyes framed a flat nose. A wide mouth curved over many chins that spilled halfway down his chest in rolls. Robes covered the rest of him, flowing from rounded shoulders to a connected point on his middle, where his hands were tucked into his sleeves.

Her mind kept trying to interpret his bulk as a coat and his facial features as a trick of the light. No matter how long she stared, the creature before her wasn't human.

"Human," he purred, as if he had read her mind. His eyes roved over her.

"Stay back." The sound of her voice jolted her. Lightning raced from her stomach to every limb. "Stay back!" The bolts reached her legs. She whirled and fled.

Hurdling off every footfall, Spooky crossed the clearing in seconds. She leapt across the tree line and skidded to a stop at the edge of murky water. Mush slid beneath her feet, and she threw her arms around a trunk. A swampy landscape stretched into the gloom. The whole area was flooded. Only twisted trees, hanging vines, and islands of muck broke the glassy surface.

"Human," said a deep voice in her ear.

A chill ran over her whole body.

Her leg jerked out from under her. She flew up into the air, whipped upside-down so fast her fingertips brushed the ground. She clambered to reach the snake-like thing around her ankle. It looked like every other vine draped from the swamp canopy. She scratched at it, but even with her adrenaline pumping, her fingernails were no match for the fibrous plant.

Her abs gave out and she swung upside down. The monster was standing in front of her. She was up high enough that they were eye-to-eye.

"Let me down! Get away from me!"

Spooky threw wild punches at the broad face. The creature chuckled, and the folds of his chin vibrated. He didn't retreat, but he didn't come any closer either. After a few more jabs, she gave up and let herself dangle. Her head pounded with the influx of blood.

"I haven't seen one of your kind up close in millennia." His round eyes followed her as she swung to and fro. "I have waited so long for this moment."

"Please let me go," Spooky stammered. "I don't know what you want. I didn't mean to bother you. Just, please, let me go..."

He lifted one hand out of his robes, revealing nine long fingers tipped in black. Spooky couldn't breathe as the wide hand extended toward her. He folded all but his pointer finger into his palm, as if to quiet her. The number of digits had shut her up already.

"You have confused my meaning. I do not want you to leave." He tucked his hand back into the opposite sleeve. "I am the one who brought you here."

Spooky couldn't swallow properly. She shook her head. "Please, I have to leave... I have to get back."

"You will remain here as long as I have a use for you."

"This can't be real." Now her whole body was shaking. Hot tears slid out of the corners of her eyes. "Monsters aren't real."

He arched one thin eyebrow. "I am not a monster. I am a god. And I prefer to converse by the fire. Follow me inside, and you will come to no harm. Otherwise, I won't promise painless treatment."

He turned his back. Her breath hitched as she descended. She managed a handstand before the vine deposited her on her head. By the time her feet reached the ground and she looked up, her captor was halfway across the clearing. He moved too smoothly, as if he was gliding on a track. He disappeared into the wooden house.

Spooky forced herself to stand. Her foot was numb, and her elbows stung, and her head throbbed. She pinched herself, and that hurt too. Maybe she was lying between the dumpsters unconscious, and she was experiencing pain from real injuries as a part of a strange dream. She pinched herself in a different spot. It still hurt.

Spooky didn't know if this was a dream or a hallucination. She only knew she had to get away from this monster. Straight pines rose on either side of the swamp's gnarled canopy and surrounded the rest of the clearing. If she followed the waterline, she could disappear into the forest.

She kicked and wriggled her trapped leg. The vine was flexible, looped in a pile. She took a step toward the forest, and its grip tightened. She tried to take one more, and it pulled her hopping back.

The monster wanted her to follow him inside. Apparently, she didn't have a choice.

The vine stayed slack and approving as she shambled toward the house. Wooden fences and crates peppered the clearing, casting shadows. An animal in a pen stamped its feet and snorted. It smelled like a horse. Spooky couldn't remember if she had ever smelled anything in a dream before.

A thirty-foot tunnel jutted out from the building, like a massive entrance of an igloo. She hovered at the open door. The arched interior was lined with woven straw. Birds, puffed up with their eyes squeezed tight, clung to the weave. Compartments along the walls held sleeping chickens. It was an aviary.

She stepped across the threshold. The door swung shut behind her, trapping her with sweet and putrid smells. The floor was strewn with feathers and droppings. She picked her way around the mess. A few of the chickens ruffled their feathers but slept on.

Not all the aviary's inhabitants were sleeping. Halfway down the corridor, a row of nine little birds lined up at attention on a rafter. Five fat chickens sat on a shelf beneath them. Their shining eyes stayed fixed as she approached. There was something on the little ones' stomachs.

Holes. Where their guts should have been, the nine birds were hollowed out and filled with seeds. The top of each chicken's round body was spilling over with kernels, like popcorn coming out of a bowl. They were all dead.

Spooky jumped back and collided with the woven wall. The living flock twittered and squawked.

Half of the monster's face appeared at the end of the tunnel, like a grotesque mask. "What is taking so long?"

She glanced between him and the dead birds, her mouth flapping. "What the...what are those?"

His eye rolled to the rafter. "The bird feeders. That is how I separate the corn for the chickens and the seed for the starlings."

"I...didn't realize. I didn't realize those birds would eat different things." She couldn't think of anything else to say to smooth over her reaction.

"Do not dally," he growled. "I've been waiting eight thousand years. I won't wait a moment longer."

She didn't want to find out what a monster who made bird-corpse birdfeeders had planned for her, but she also didn't want to make him angry. She cupped her hand to her temple to block out the starlings' lifeless stares. She forced herself to take one step, then another, until she had followed the monster inside.

Spooky emerged into a cylindrical room. It looked like an ode to the Iron Age: all wood and fire and dark metal. Baskets lined the walls, piled high with gourds, potatoes, and withered corn. One basket held what appeared to be squirrel tails. On the far side of the room, a pot big enough to be a Jacuzzi sizzled in a stone hearth. The monster sat on a stump beside it, watching the contents bubble.

Spooky took new stock of her host in the firelight. What her eyes had pieced together in the dark was now clear: he was definitely not human. Horns sprouted from either side of his head and twisted over his crown. The ivory things stood in contrast to his skin, which she could now see was a ruddy shade of orange. Froggy eyes bugged beneath finely arched eyebrows. Thin nostrils slanted in a flat nose. A broad mouth rested above chins and jowls, which emphasized the effect of his oversized head. He looked like a chimera of a giant, a toad, a ram, and a carrot.

With one of his nine-fingered hands, he beckoned her toward a table made of a halved log.

Spooky inched toward a stump at the far end of the table and took a seat. It hadn't been cold outside, exactly, but she had felt exposed and awake. In here, the light and warmth from the fire made everything feel hazy. More dream-like. The monster rose from the hearth and settled himself across from her. He folded his hands on the tabletop, exposing eighteen long fingers from his sleeves.

"State your name."

"Spooky. No, uh, I mean, it's Laurel. Laurel Specki."

"Which of your names shall I call you?"

"Spooky is fine."

"Very well, human I shall call Spooky. I am the god known as Carcass." Spooky wasn't great with names, but this one she thought she would remember. "I have brought you to my world to entertain me."

"Uh, what?"

"I have brought you to my world to entertain me."

"Right...but what does that mean?"

"When last I visited Earth, humans told each other stories around their fires. I would often visit their camps at night to listen." Carcass watched her over steepled fingers. "Perhaps you have heard of me?"

"Uh, no. I haven't."

"Ah well, to be expected. It has been eight thousand years." He smacked his lips. "An occasional appearance fueled new legends, but if I revealed myself too often, the humans wouldn't congregate after dark. It was a delicate balance."

"Uh, okay."

"When I returned to Earth last night, I was pleased to see an encampment of humans still lived near the door. However, I found no gathering, no campfires, no stories. So I thought, why not bring a human here? Replace the campfire with my own fireside?"

"Um, sure." Her hands twitched as she folded and unfolded them in her lap. "But I'm not very good at telling stories."

"You are human." Carcass blinked. "Humans are exceptional storytellers."

"Other people are much better at it."

"But you were the one who was there. Next to the door. Alone." He leaned over the table. "I don't care if you aren't the premier orator of your generation. I have waited eight thousand years. I will not wait another moment. Begin."

"Just...tell you a story? Any story?"

"A story, a folk tale, a myth, a legend... I know the old ones, but I am sure you humans have come up with a few more in the last eight thousand years, mmm? And if not, invent one. All your kind shares this gift."

His tawny eyes reflected the firelight. Her mind was empty. She had done a pretty good job of playing along so far, but she couldn't engage with him as if what he wanted from her was real, when none of this could be. She rocked and shook her head. This wasn't real.

"Tell me a story or I will find another human."

"Could you?" She exhaled a laugh. "That would be great. Please, please, go find someone else..."

"...and I will hollow out your body to hold grubs for the starlings."

She jerked. "You'll what?"

"Starlings eat both plants and insects, you see. My little birdies will enjoy the challenge of picking grubs out of your eye sockets. And not to worry." He smiled, revealing blunt yellow teeth. "I'll find another human who can entertain me. Almost any one of you would do."

Spooky pictured another confused girl coming down the tunnel and passing her corpse. She couldn't stop herself from imagining white grubs wriggling out of her face.

"No!" She gripped the edge of the stump. "I'll tell you a story."

"Then begin."

"Okay. Okay, a story..." She searched for a complete narrative, tracing the grain of the table with her gaze. *Tell the table a story, Spooky.*

"Okay. How about this: once upon a time, there was a ship called the Titanic. On the ship, there was a rich girl named Rose and a poor boy named Jack. They met one night when she uh, well she was engaged and didn't want to be. So she tried to jump into the ocean..."

She forgot the finer points of the plot but got through the major ones. All too suddenly, the ship was sinking, main characters were dying, and the story was over. She had distilled a three-hour movie to about five minutes.

"Err...the end." She ran her eyes along the table and up to her host. He was watching her over his folded hands.

"Is that it?" he asked.

"That's the end of Titanic."

"A metaphor for hubris, a cautionary tale. Universal themes of love and loss—a new story, to be sure, but the themes are consistent with the ones sung about long ago." He shrugged. "You are not a strong orator, but I will endure it. Next story."

At least he hadn't threatened to turn her into a bird feeder. She looked back at the table and cleared her throat.

"Umm, okay. So once upon a time there was...a girl named Juliet and a boy named Romeo. And their families, their families didn't like each other, and they regularly met up to brawl and duel...but also, they were both at a party. I mean, Romeo and Juliet were."

She sounded like an idiot. Somehow, she made it through the duplicity and murder and got most of the names of the major characters. Carcass sat still, only blinking as she did her best rendition of Juliet. She stabbed herself in the heart with an invisible knife, hoping to add visual interest to what she struggled to illustrate in words.

Then Juliet was dead, Romeo was dead, and the story was over.

"Next," Carcass said.

She moved on to other memorable plotlines. The Matrix. Scream. Predator. Lord of the Rings. Lord of the Flies. After she reached the end of each story, she waited, and each time, he asked for another. The fire in the corner burned so brightly it hurt her eyes. Spooky wiped her forehead. She kept talking.

Batman Begins. Superman Returns. Buffy the Vampire Slayer-Season One, main plot arch. She glanced up from time to time, just to make sure Carcass hadn't moved from his seat.

"Is that enough?" she asked after she woke Sleeping Beauty with a magic kiss. She wasn't sure how much time had passed, but it felt like hours.

"Enough?" Carcass asked.

"Have you heard enough stories?"

"No. It will be 'enough' when you have told me every story that humans have amassed over the last eight thousand years."

Spooky laughed. "That's impossible." Giddiness at the ridiculousness of his request made her bolder. "I'm sorry, but I can't do that."

"Maybe not, but I know humans are adept at making up stories. When you run out and can neither remember nor come up with another tale, I will find a new use for you."

He bobbed his head toward the tunnel of birds.

She couldn't tell another story. Her voice was hoarse, and the sharp edge of the stump had dug into her legs, and she needed fresh air. She touched the pocket of her sweatpants where she would have kept her phone, before remembering she hadn't had her cell phone for over a month. Dodgson had almost eradicated her habit of reaching for it.

"If I just had my phone this would be a lot easier."

Carcass tilted his head. "Your 'phone'?"

"It's a device that...it's like a little box. I can use it to look up stories." She could also use it to call for help. She sat straight up, almost bouncing off the stool. "Better stories. Way better stories than I can tell from memory."

"Hmm. And where is this phone?"

"It's at Dodgson."

"I presume that 'Dodgson' is the place from which I took you?"

"Yes!"

Maybe if she could get back to Dodgson this would all be over. Maybe the sun would come up, and Carcass would disappear, and it would all turn out to have been the strangest damn dream. At the very least, she could get help.

"Very well. I will let you return to 'Dodgson' to fetch your phone." Carcass unfurled his folded hands and gestured toward the tunnel.

"Okay! Great, fantastic."

Spooky rose from the table. Carcass made no move to stop her as she backed out of the room. The door at the end of the tunnel was open. She dashed past birds dead and alive and burst out into the fresh air. The sky was lighter now.

A whinny directly to her right made her jump. She turned and found herself facing a horse's rear end.

"Sorry!" she said, stumbling back. Its tail swished, revealing three holes where there should have been one.

Somewhere between the sentient vine, the god with eighteen fingers, the bird-corpse bird feeders, and the horse with three assholes, Spooky had decided she really didn't like it here.

But she didn't know which way to go to get back. Twisted trees across from the house marked the entrance of the swamp. The rest of the clearing was bordered in straight gray pines, which looked more like the trees around Dodgson. She would rather get lost in the forest than stay here. She picked a direction and lopped toward the tree line.

The vine yanked her leg, slamming her onto her front. She screamed as it dragged her away from the house. The world turned white.

# CHAPTER iv
# EIGHT THOUSAND YEARS

Spooky floated in the embrace of an endless cloud. She was back in the strange white space. She couldn't tell if the whiteness was pressing in on her or was a thousand miles away. There was no information for her to gather. It was just blank.

The vine drifted innocently past her face, miniature leaves waving at her like it hadn't just dragged her screaming across the earth. She would have thought she was hovering in place, but she had a point of reference: one end of the vine disappeared above her head. It was like she was sinking in water and the vine was a rope crossing the surface. Her dark hair spread across her vision as the point got ten, then twenty, then thirty feet away.

As suddenly as the whiteness had appeared, she fell in darkness. Her hip bashed something sharp as she landed on her side.

"Ow," she whimpered, tearing up. She had reached her limit for being pulled, dragged, bruised, and beaten.

Glowing patches blocked her vision, but after a few seconds, her eyes adjusted. She was spilling halfway out of the space between the dumpsters. The area behind the lodge was as still and quiet as it had been while she waited for Luke. The counselors were gone, the floodlights were off, and the stars were still out.

She was back at Dodgson.

Spooky dropped her forehead to her hands and let the tears run down her face.

She hated it here, but she was so glad to be back.

She hoped a counselor would come by on patrol so she could hug them and whisper sweet nothings into their uniform about how wonderful it was to see them. She would take the scuffs for physical contact just to have another person to cling to. She would take the scuffs for being out of bed, just to see a flashlight cut through the shadows.

Her mouth felt dusty, and her body ached. Was any of what she had just experienced real? If she could get near other humans, she would be safe. If she got back in bed and put the covers over her head, monsters named Carcass wouldn't be able to find her.

Spooky crawled out from between the bins. One leg refused to cooperate. She moaned. The vine, which should have stayed behind with the other impossible things, still held her ankle in a vice grip. It wound between the dumpsters and disappeared. It anchored her in this nightmare.

She tried to dig her fingers under it, but she couldn't create a gap between vine and skin. She scanned the area for something, anything, she could use to cut it off her. Sharp items were hard to find at Dodgson, and it would take an axe to hack through this overgrown tree-branch. Still, she had to try. She leveraged it around the corner of one of the bins and grated it back and forth.

A white dot appeared between the dumpsters, like a hole burned in a photograph. It stretched into a glowing line. Worms emerged from the light. No, not worms. Eighteen long fingers, which curved and pulled apart to reveal a huge eyeball. It rolled around the scene and settled on her.

The fleshy eyelashes retracted and the eye vanished. For a moment, the area stayed shadowed and still. Her forearms burned and her leg was twisted at an angle that cramped her hip, but she sawed the vine faster, wheezing through her teeth.

An orange face appeared, outlined in white. With froggy eyes rolling up toward the sky, Carcass squeezed through the corridor between the dumpsters. His head glided toward her, suspended a foot above the ground, dragging his body like a fish on a line. He inflated, bit by bit, as parts of him emerged from between the bins.

Once the end of his robes was through, he pivoted upright, horns reaching toward the sky. He settled onto the dirt with a slight poof of fabric.

"No, no, no." Spooky dropped the vine, which she hadn't even dented, and hid her face in her hands. She pressed her palms into her eyes hard enough to see spots of light. She was back in the real world now. The monster shouldn't be here.

"Now, where do we find your 'phone'?" he asked.

She heard the question but wasn't ready to open her eyes yet. "You aren't supposed to be real," she whispered.

"I gave you a choice. You may serve me in one way or another."

"There are other people here." Spooky climbed to her feet, gesturing to the silent camp. "And a lot of them are probably better storytellers than I am. Can't you go find someone else?"

He shrugged. "A new human will go through the same cycle of disbelief, panic, anger, and denial that you are still working through. It's amusing, but hardly the coherent storytelling I came for."

"I'll start screaming." She balled her fists at her sides. "I'll bring every person in this camp running. With tranq guns."

Carcass snorted. "The humans who spotted me last night tried to pursue me. No human can find me if I don't want to be found. And they won't find you either."

Her fists loosened. Maybe a huge bear hadn't been walking the grounds of Dodgson. Maybe the counselors had spotted a silhouette they couldn't explain any other way. The snake and the bear— Carcass seemed to be the cause of both strange animal sightings.

"Produce your phone now, or you will make a fine bird feeder."

They stared at each other. Screaming her head off would only guarantee her a spot in his aviary. Unless there happened to be a second patrol near the lodge, she couldn't even be sure anyone would hear her. The cabins full of sleeping campers and counselors were on the other side of the grounds. Even if she did manage to wake up a counselor, what could they do to help her? Any interruption would probably only encourage him to drag her back to the clearing with the house.

Spooky couldn't think of anything else to threaten or bribe him with. She had no leverage.

"The phone is in there." She pointed at the back door of the main lodge.

Carcass looked at the door and then at her. "So go get it."

"I don't have a key." Spooky didn't consider herself to have a temper, but right now being obtuse felt like control, and anger felt better than fear. "It's locked."

Carcass raised one of his massive hands. The door crashed inward. The deadbolt burst through the frame and hinges that weren't meant to bend that way screeched. Spooky jumped, fear tinging the anger she was trying to cling to. He hadn't even touched it.

"Now it isn't," Carcass said.

Her heart thumped faster. Counselors with tranq guns couldn't save her from a telekinetic monster. Hopefully, the sound had been brief and distant enough to let the camp sleep on.

Even if she couldn't stop herself from feeling it, she didn't have to show him she was afraid. She glared at the ground and stalked past him.

"Is this the way humans speak to gods these days?" he muttered behind her. "No wonder your world is in this position."

Spooky marched inside. The camp didn't advertise where they kept confiscated items, but Luke had told her where the counselors took the razor they had wrestled off a camper during a dramatic lunchtime scuffle: the locked cabinet in their break room. According to Luke, he had seen bags of contraband inside, probably collected from suitcases at the beginning of camp.

It was too dark in the break room to see the cabinet. The window on the door was laced with wire, so no one could reach through it if the glass shattered. More evidence of the camp's trust in its wards.

Carcass had entered the hallway behind her, his body filling it from wall to wall. He was hunching, but his horns still scraped the ceiling.

"The phone is in there. It's also locked," she added before he could tell her to go get it. "Can you break it open? Quietly?"

At least now that they were inside, they were out of sight, and the sound of any further destructive telekinesis would be muffled.

He rolled his eyes and flicked his wrist. The door clunked open with a little less violence.

Spooky flipped on the light. The room had a TV, a couch, a computer, and a refrigerator. The cabinet was bolted to the back wall. Carcass broke the padlock open for her. Plastic bags, each marked with a camper's name, were stacked inside. They held all the forbidden objects deemed dangerous or distracting to rehabilitation. Pills, blades, and cigarettes were interspersed with more mundane items like curling irons and pencils. She ripped open one bag and took out a hefty pair of scissors. She almost started hacking away at the vine then and there, but scissors wouldn't help her against Carcass. She put them on the desk, just in case a moment arose when she might be able to run.

Finally, she found the bag labeled "Specki, Laurel." All it held was a pair of jeans with holes at the knees, her wallet, her phone, and her phone charger.

"Do not linger," Carcass said, sounding bored.

"Hold your horses." The vine jerked her leg and she fell onto her already bruised hip.

"Hey!" she snapped. Carcass took a sudden interest in examining a calendar on the wall.

Cupping her swollen hip, she plugged in her phone and pressed the "on" button. After a few painful moments of darkness, the screen lit up.

"Yes!" she gasped. A phone in her hand gave her power. She could call the police, or the national guard, or the air force; anybody with enough firepower to take on a monster. Or at least, if they couldn't take him down, anyone with enough strength to take her from him.

Carcass cocked his head. "Is that your phone?"

"Yeah, this is it," she replied, pulled out of her fantasy of clinging to a ladder as she was airlifted out of the camp.

"Then begin telling me a story immediately." He bent somewhere in the middle of his robes and settled onto the couch.

"Let me find one..." The rescue operation would have to wait. She would appease him now and wait for an opening to escape.

Spooky slumped into the computer chair and opened a browser. The reception wasn't bad for a camp in the woods. She searched for short stories and clicked the first result: *One Hundred Classic Bedtime Stories*.

"Okay, here we go. This one is called The Letter from the Queen. 'He wrote the first of his letters in black ink, and the second in silver. The third he illuminated with gold...'" Her mind didn't even really follow the plot of the story. It had the repetitive style of a German fairytale—something about a prince who wanted to seize power from his elder brother. But it was much easier to sit in the office chair than on the rough stump, and it was much easier to read than to think.

"'...The final letter came with a vial," she croaked. "The poison the queen had sent tasted sweet. It was a message of forgiveness. The End.'"

She glanced up at Carcass. His hands were folded in front of his mouth, and his eyes were wide.

"Do you want me to start another one?" she asked. Her vocal cords felt frayed.

He put up a finger and the phone floated out of her grasp.

"Hey!"

It arched across the room and hovered above his fingertip. He brought it close to one eyeball.

"What is this?" he muttered.

"My phone." Spooky was too tired to be anything but literal.

"Are there more?"

"More what?"

"More stories in this phone."

"Oh yeah. You can search for anything." She put her hand out and it drifted back to her. She snagged it out of the air and clicked to the search page. Blue links teased reservoirs of literature, both amateur and established. She held it to face him and scrolled. Carcass leaned forward, eyes darting over the screen.

Carcass did say he hadn't seen a human in eight thousand years. He had no idea what modern technology could do. He might not be afraid of people, but had he ever seen a tank? Or a plane? Or a rocket launcher? He didn't even know she could use the phone to call for help.

"Modern Short Stories–America's Best in the Last Hundred Years," Carcass said.

"Huh?"

"I would like to hear a story from America's Best in the Last Hundred Years.'"

Spooky looked at her phone. The words he had just spoken were linked at the bottom of the screen. Through the fog of exhaustion, her synapses fired.

"You can read!" she blurted.

"I can understand any language gathered through the common sixteen senses." He raised his eyebrows. "How did you think I was speaking to you?"

Her mind made the leap it probably should have as soon as she turned on the light and saw the TV and the computer.

"You don't need me at all!" Spooky laughed, rocking back in the chair. "You can read these stories to yourself! Or watch TV!" He blinked. "Oh, right, TV, that's new. Well, TV is like..."

"A series of images and sounds transmitted through a screen. Again, I understand the words you say. But that doesn't sound very entertaining."

Spooky paused. How could she explain the progression of media over the last eight thousand years?

"You came here looking for humans telling stories around a fire, and you didn't find any. That's because we don't do that very often anymore. We have more modern ways of sharing stories... We write them in books or act them out on TV shows or in movies. And you can access almost everything online. That's what I used my phone for."

He sat in silence another moment. "Show me."

She tapped out a number of searches. She presented the first chapter of an eBook. His eyes grew rounder as she started the first episode of a mini-series on King Arthur and his court.

"Here, just take my phone!" She thrust it toward him. "You search here, and click on the link for the story you want, like this. Nonfiction, fiction...anything! The stories from all of humanity!"

She held her breath as he plucked the phone up between two sharp nails. He drew it to one eye, then the other. He raised a long, orange finger and pressed. The screen snapped and crackled. It went black.

"Oh..." The smile faded from her face. "You have to be more gentle. That's okay, there are other phones here. There's even a..."

She spun around in the chair and pushed the power button on the computer. She twitched when Carcass's massive head appeared over her shoulder.

"What is this?"

"A computer. It does all the same things as my phone, but bigger."

The screen switched from black to blue, then showed a "password" field over a picture of happy campers lined up in front of the main lodge. It had to have been photoshopped.

She tapped the desk. "It's locked."

"What part of it needs to open?" Carcass raised his hand.

"Not that kind of locked!" she squealed before he smashed it. "It's password protected! But there are a lot of other phones in the cabinet. I can give you someone else's."

"The phones are too small and very delicate," he said with a sniff. "I presume this is not the only computer on Earth?"

"No."

"You wish to be free of me, mmm?"

She gripped the armrests. "Yes."

"Then I will strike a bargain with you. You may either return with me to my world and operate a phone on my behalf, searching for stories and reading to me from it until you die..."

"Or?" she interjected, not liking her first option.

"Or give me the capability to do so myself on one of these computers." He gestured toward it. "If you do that, I will leave you here, unharmed."

She was stuck at Dodgson. It wouldn't be easy to get him a computer. She eyed Carcass from robe to horn, trying to come up with some other way out of this. She had thought of his skin as the color of a carrot, but the wrinkled folds of his face reminded her more of a pumpkin. A huge, telekinetic pumpkin, who she definitely wouldn't be able to outrun.

"It's not just the computer you need. You'll need Wi-Fi or a router, and a power outlet."

He blinked.

She tried to rephrase. "Stories aren't just in the computer. You have to stay connected to the internet. You'll have to use it here. In this room."

"In this tiny, ugly space?" He added one more wrinkle to his face, above his nose. "No, I wish to sit beside my fire. But do not worry." He grinned. "You are fully mobile and transportable to my world even if a computer isn't."

Not an option. "Where is your world exactly?"

"Through the mist that separates all worlds. Through the void. There is a door between our worlds outside. You've passed through it twice already."

Spooky opened her mouth to explain Wi-Fi and electricity, but she thought it might be easier to learn about a magical portal instead. "Can you show me how the door works?"

Carcass led her back out into the night. The stars along the horizon were fading. Her wallet bulged in her pocket, along with one of the other campers' phones. She had turned it on straight out of the bag without charging it, and the battery was low. But she wanted to have an option to call for help, just in case she couldn't figure out how to give him a working internet connection in another world.

"The door is there." He pointed between the dumpsters. The vine disappeared at the spot he indicated. "That is but one of the doors to my world."

"How does it work?"

Carcass smiled. "Perhaps, a demonstration?"

She was only able to hop once before the vine wrenched her off her feet. She shrieked as it pulled her between the bins. A corner of the dumpster passed way too close to her eye. Suddenly, she was zooming through whiteness. It was nothing like the peaceful drift from earlier; the vine towed her like it was attached to a speed boat. In a matter of seconds, she skidded to a stop on her back. She sat up. She was in the middle of the clearing where she'd first met Carcass. In front of her was the house, behind her was the swamp, and all around were trees. The gray horse had emerged from its pen, thankfully, headfirst. It whinnied and stomped.

A section of the vine reversed direction and she flew back into whiteness.

She hit the ground between the dumpsters with her hair flying and teeth clacking.

"That is how you go from my world to yours," Carcass said. He was smiling. Of course he was.

"Was that necessary?" she snapped. She lugged herself out of the narrow space.

"As a brief reminder of your choices, yes. Give me a computer, and access to all the internet holds, or you will never escape me."

Her bruises and scrapes sang with the temptation to shout at him.

But he had made his point. She would never get away if he didn't let her go. Even if she called the police, or the army, all he had to do was yank her through the invisible door between the dumpsters. No one would ever find her.

"I'm trying to figure out how to make the internet work in your world," she said through clenched teeth. "Explain to me—in words— how this door works."

"Very well. This is the entrance to what you might think of as a tunnel between our worlds. A tunnel through the void. It exists in a fixed place, but it can be opened to accommodate whatever needs to pass through."

He picked up the vine. As he lifted, it drew a white line in the air. The edges smoked, like he was slicing open an envelope full of clouds. He put his hand into the line and pulled on one side, stretching it into a glowing triangle. Spooky leaned forward as far as she dared. The vine extended at least fifty feet into the emptiness, before it disappeared.

"Once something enters the door in your world, it will flow through the tunnel and come out on the other side."

"So if I hold a wire, and let the other end go to your world, it won't get warped or broken going through?"

"Did you get warped or broken going through?"

Maybe mentally. "No," was all she said.

He dropped the vine, and the whiteness shrank around it. "As long as something is in the door, it will stay open, connecting our worlds."

"Okay." Spooky stood up straighter. "Then I'll do it. I'll get you what you want, but then you have to set me free. Deal?"

The skin around his eyes crinkled. "Deal."

# CHAPTER V
# GODS AND CREATIONS

"We had always intended for you to graduate and go to college. Maybe that's just not in the cards for you."

"You'll turn eighteen this summer. A legal adult."

"We can't be expected to share our space with someone who doesn't respect our values. If this is how you're going to act..."

"We've contacted the camp and let them know our position. It's hard for us to have you here. We need a break."

"But if you can make amends this summer, we are willing to try again."

"You have to show us."

"We need a break."

Her parents weren't like the parents in any of the stories she had told Carcass. They weren't villains who beat or berated, or nurturers who supported and advised. They didn't yell but mean well. Their love wasn't layered. Children in the Specki household were one of two things: proof of their parents' excellence, or a legal dependent. And Spooky had never had to wonder which daughter fit into which category.

Spooky had heard the story many times: her parents hadn't planned to pause their journeys up the ladder toward two illustrious law careers to have children. Victoria had been a surprise. They regularly spouted this to company as they led them past certificates and awards to the one, stiff-collared family portrait hanging in the hallway. What was wrong with calling a child accidental when in the same breath you could coo about her acceptance to enrichment programs, AP classes, and then Harvard? What was a break in your career to produce a perfect protégé to follow in your footsteps?

Victoria gave them something to talk about with the partners at their law firms, another point of connection like golf or tennis. Their doll-like, down-haired seven-year-old complimented their polished image, and they outsourced the time-consuming work of childcare. So they got pregnant again. Of course, Spooky had been planned based on Victoria's blueprint. Creating a child as perfect as Victoria on accident was a point of pride. Having Spooky on purpose wasn't something they mentioned to company.

They had high hopes for Spooky at first, of course, back when she was little Laurel. At five, when she was still quiet and scrawny, they decided to keep her out of school an extra year. She didn't remember much about that time, except receiving more educational toys than she could figure out how to operate and attending playdates with more kids than she could learn the names of. They had been hoping she would mature, academically and socially. At six, even though she hadn't changed, they followed the letter of the law and enrolled her in school.

She didn't excel. She was often behind. That was the beginning of the sideways looks. The end of the questions about her day. The click of closed office doors. The shift from being a potential addition to a burden. They somehow never returned to the studio to update the family portrait.

From seven to seventeen, Spooky had stayed within the bounds of an unspoken agreement: they would take care of her basic needs, provided she didn't cause trouble or ask for more. They made sure she was fed, clothed, and in school. They signed permission slips and checks for the necessities. They let her borrow their cars for her job at the yogurt shop. Beyond that, they didn't interact much.

But then she had gone and done something her parents could neither tolerate nor forgive. And they had shipped her off to Dodgson with two suitcases and an ultimatum: fall back in line over the summer, or don't expect to come home at the end of it. Unlike many of the other bags in the cabinet, her bag of confiscated belongings didn't contain a house key.

If she maxed out, she was kicked out. She would have nowhere to live for her senior year of high school, and no one to cosign on a loan for college. And now, she was going to have to risk her maximum scuff level consequences.

She was going to have to leave the fence.

Wilderness bordered Dodgson on three sides. The trees on the fourth side parted for a two-lane highway, which ran past Dodgson and through the town of Root Park. The pamphlet Spooky had read on the cab ride referred to Root Park as a hub for surrounding areas. The word choice was probably meant to soothe parents' concerns about access to emergency services. Spooky suspected the fence had been a condition to soothe the town's concerns about being a mile down the road from a camp full of troubled teens.

Spooky used the borrowed phone to search for a place she could buy a computer in Root Park. A warning about the low battery flashed. Luckily, there weren't many roads to memorize in the forty-two-minute walk to an electronics store called Office Shack. The description advertised TVs, computers, microwaves, and device repair. She would only have to make two turns to get there.

The phone screen went black. Spooky's hands tingled as she slipped it into her pocket next to her wallet. She didn't have much money in her checking account, but this qualified as an emergency use of her credit card. She would get Carcass a computer, finish out the summer at Dodgson, go home for her senior year of high school, and then set off to college where The Change would be waiting for her. She clapped as if her palms could seal that series of events.

She turned to Carcass. "I am going to Office Shack to get you a computer. It's a long walk to town. Am I going to have enough slack?" She wiggled the leg the vine held captive.

Carcass didn't move, but after a beat, the vine uncurled.

Spooky gasped, then let out an unsteady laugh. It didn't mean she was safe, but losing this physical shackle felt like the first step toward freedom. She finally had some leverage. She had a plan.

She lifted her pant leg to assess the damage. The vine had left a white spiral where the blood had been squeezed out, rimmed in young, red bruises.

"Lead the way," Carcass said.

"You're coming?"

"Nothing else tempts my attention at the moment." He smacked his lips. "And I wouldn't want you to forget your choices and lose your way."

Spooky opened her mouth to object, but she couldn't think of a reason to insist he stay behind. Besides, she would need at least a little magical help to get out of the camp.

She limped over to the fence line. The sky was an inky gray. If anyone happened to be walking across the field, or circling the main lodge, they would see the silhouette of a giant monster and a camper out of bed. They were still sheltered from most sightlines by the lodge itself, but Spooky scanned the area.

She could be late for her morning cafeteria shift, or even missing for a few hours. That number of scuffs would have horrified her yesterday, but today she could accept it. What she couldn't do, under any circumstances, was let anyone catch her outside the fence.

She eyed the plastic wall. One person standing on another person's shoulders couldn't reach the top of it. Carcass appeared beside her.

"Can you give me a boost? Lift me over with your mind, or whatever?"

He nodded.

"Okay," she said. "Let's go."

Carcass grabbed the back of her shirt and jumped. She was airborne. Her legs flew up and she hollered as they soared over the top of the fence. Her stomach hit her ribcage as they plummeted down the other side. Carcass landed with a boom, flattening until his eyes bugged out. His grip on her shirt swung her body like a puppet. He dropped her on her hands and knees.

Spooky staggered to her feet, straightening her stretched flannel. "Humans are breakable, you sadist!"

He didn't turn his head, but one wide eye rolled to look at her. He turned away with an equally wide smile. "Stop squawking. Which way?"

She hated that smile.

She stomped through the pine needles along the outside of the fence. After a few minutes, her feet dragged. Fatigue muffled her fury. By the time they made it to the dirt road at the front of the camp, she had stopped picturing him getting tangled in his robes and falling on his froggy face. When they made their first turn off the dirt road onto the two-lane highway, curiosity sprouted in the space panic and anger had vacated.

Spooky watched Carcass out of the corner of her eye. He didn't glide the way he had before; his robes rustled with what seemed like individual steps. He appeared as real and solid as the pavement. Something about his profile—the set of his mouth, or perhaps his half-lidded eyes—seemed serene. Contemplative, even. Less like a monster. Although, he had never called himself a monster.

"Are you really a god?" she blurted.

The pace of his steps didn't change. "Yes, I am a god."

Spooky hadn't given religion much thought. Her parents had never pointed her in a spiritual direction, and she'd never felt a compulsion to go anywhere special on Sundays. Now, she wished she had some basic theological framework to help her understand what Carcass claimed to be.

Then again, Carcass was not a member of any pantheon she had ever heard of. At the very least, there was something large and orange missing from the major religions' account of the universe.

"But what does that mean? What does it mean to be a 'god?'"

"Gods can turn their desires into reality. What I wish to exist, I can create."

"You can make whatever you want appear? Out of thin air?"

"Yes."

That sounded like divinity, but something didn't add up. "Then why are you doing this to me?"

"Self-pitying, aren't you? I already told you—you happened to be near the door when I sent a feeler."

"No, I mean, if you can make whatever you want appear, why did you need me to keep you entertained? To tell you stories?"

He looked down at her. "How do you know I did not create you to tell me stories?"

"Oh...oh." That thought had not crossed her mind, and now that it had, she wanted to send it back. "Did you?"

He turned his gaze forward. "No."

"Well, why don't you make yourself a computer? Or someone to tell you stories by the fire? Then you won't need me at all."

Carcass snorted. "My creation would only tell me stories I had invented to come out of its mouth."

"Well why not make something that comes up with its own stories?" She wanted to end this expedition right now. By her estimation, there were still a few hours left before the first bell. She could get back in bed.

"Before I came to Earth, it never would have occurred to me to want stories, or to make something that could tell them."

"Okay, but now that it has..."

"I don't know how."

"So you can't create whatever you want." She winced at her own blunt assessment. He raised an eyebrow at her.

"I did not think the obvious needed to be stated," Carcass enunciated. "Gods can create whatever they want, within the bounds of what they know. To create something, I have to know it fully, through and through, down to its smallest particle and its tiniest wavelength. And its nonphysical properties as well, if it has them.

"But my earlier statement wasn't baseless: when I was born in the void, my desire, knowledge, and power were in perfect alignment. I could, at that time, create everything I wanted. But this balance is unique to each god. Visiting other worlds, I have come to want things I have neither the knowledge nor the power to create. I cannot make a thing to tell me stories like humans on Earth do."

"That's too bad." She tried to sound sympathetic to soften her earlier tone.

"It's not so bad. I can visit Earth and have the locals assist me." He smiled at her, his teeth as large as bricks. "Isn't that fortunate?"

She rolled her eyes. A sprinkling of houses had appeared on either side of the highway. In the distance, signs for gas stations and fast food replaced the trees.

Something else clicked. "Are humans gods, then?"

"Humans?"

"Well, we make roads, houses, computers..." The forest transitioned into front yards, as if to illustrate all man had made out of wilderness. "But we can't make everything we want. Only what we know how to make."

Carcass scoffed. "Reorganizing what already exists based on laws you cannot control is hardly what I meant by my use of the word 'creation.'" He turned to her. "And do not lie to me and tell me you fully understand the laws you obey, or even what you rearrange within their bounds."

"It just sounded like what you described."

"Then you were not listening. In a void of nothing, what would you create? You would want for things, most certainly. You are born wanting—for air, for food, for love. Yet, none of those things would appear."

"Fine, fine. I get it."

"The only thing you would produce in the void is stories. Uncontrollably, of course. Your mind would hallucinate sensations and invent narratives to give them meaning. Your kind really does seem to be made for it."

She kicked a pebble and it bounced down the road. "Why do you care so much about stories anyway?"

"Does that strike you as a strange thing to want?" He frowned and looked at the sky. "You probably haven't ever imagined what a world would be like without them."

"Uh, no, I guess not."

"And I had never imagined a world with them. Until I came to Earth and encountered humans interpreting themselves and the world around them, and then reinterpreting everything, again and again. Forming narratives and explanations for every leaf, every mood, every storm. Out of the smoke from their fires. Out of nothing."

Spooky's chest tightened. She might be more interested in his musings on humanity if he wasn't justifying the reasons he had kidnapped her. No matter how boring his world was, stories weren't worth the ordeal he was putting her through. Instead of the ration of sleep Dodgson's schedule allowed her, she had been chased, pummeled, and threatened. Her future was on the line for his amusement.

"I don't care about stories," she snapped. "It doesn't matter. It's just for entertainment."

"You think stories don't matter to you?" He blinked at her. "From what I've observed, you don't even know when you are telling one."

She didn't know what he meant by that and didn't care. Spooky took a few slow breaths, waiting for the fist in her chest to loosen. She couldn't antagonize him now. She needed him happy enough to keep their agreement. He could say whatever he wanted. She didn't even know if anything he was telling her was true.

Still, another question tugged on her brain. They made the second turn, off the highway onto a side street.

"If humans aren't gods, it sounds like you're saying a god made us."

"Then the way 'it sounds' is accurate."

"Then who is he? She?"

Carcass shrugged. "I don't know the god of Earth personally. But I can guess some things, from having observed the creation." He gazed at the sky. "This is a High Order world. Few gods would have the power or knowledge to create a pale imitation."

Spooky glanced around as if she could see what Carcass saw in the molecules of the air. She didn't know what a High Order world was, but it sounded fancy.

"I myself take a great deal of inspiration from Earth, when I can," Carcass continued. "You might have noticed some familiar things in my world?"

"The swamp and the house...that's your world?"

"Indeed. I have been able to understand many objects fully enough to recreate them. I've even imitated a few life forms." He smiled. "With my own improvements on the original designs, of course."

Spooky pictured the abominable anatomy of the horse with the swishing tail and grimaced. Clearly, they had a different view on what constituted an improvement. She tried to think of something, anything, else.

"What about other gods? Are there others? Do they come to Earth, like you do?"

"Office Shack."

"What?"

Carcass extracted a hand from his sleeve and pointed. "Office Shack. We've arrived."

# CHAPTER VI
# OFFICE SHACK

Office Shack nestled into a row of boxy storefronts between a nail salon and a cafe. Gods, stories, creations—Spooky felt like the ground was listing as they crossed the empty parking lot. Even for more answers about the universe, she didn't want to keep Carcass with her for any longer than necessary. Unfortunately, waiting was now their only option. The red decal on the window displayed the store hours: 9:00 a.m. to 5:00 p.m. The sun wasn't even over the horizon yet.

Spooky would definitely be counted as missing if she didn't appear until after nine, but she could still sneak back into the camp and pretend to have fallen asleep behind a tree. It wasn't that far-fetched; Dodgson kept them all on the brink of exhaustion. She didn't even need them to believe her. She just needed to make sure no one would figure out she had left the camp.

"The computer is in there," Spooky said. "But there won't be anyone to let us in for a few hours."

Carcass narrowed his eyes.

She took the phone out of her pocket. "I can tell you stories while we wait." She clicked the power button before remembering it was dead.

In the reflection of the front window, Spooky saw Carcass raise his right hand.

The pane exploded in a shower of glitter. Spooky screamed. The store alarm blasted a trilling note.

"That is annoying!" Carcass exclaimed.

He pulled his index finger into his palm. Something inside the store crunched. The alarm stopped.

Spooky clamped her hand over the high-pitched whine coming out of her own mouth. She didn't want to be the next thing to go crunch. She glanced up and down the street, half expecting to see heads popping out of doors and windows. The commercial district was deserted. For now.

Carcass was already inside, wandering through aisles of shelving that only came halfway up his chest. Spooky hopped on her toes and shook out her hands. She had to get what they came for and get out of there as soon as possible. She checked the rubber edge of the window frame for shards of glass and hoisted herself in after him.

Office Shack's stock matched the needs of the middle-of-nowhere community it served. The shelves contained as many walkie-talkies, radios, and GPS's as TVs, computers, and phones. She picked the most rugged, heavy-duty laptop she could find. The box said it was drop tested and approved for outdoor use. She grabbed a mouse and some coiled cords from a bin before seeing a sign for longer ones in the back.

Carcass broke the lock on the stock room door for her, and it swung open to reveal more shelves and crates. She found a hundred-foot Ethernet cable and an outdoor Ethernet extender, as well as extension cords long enough to connect Christmas lights from gutters to living rooms and back again.

Arms laden, Spooky dragged her haul to the register and loaded up four jumbo shopping bags. She eyed the blank screen of the register. She had intended to wait for the store to open and buy everything on credit, but that plan had been destroyed with the front window. Her hand shook as she pulled her wallet out of her pocket. It only held her debit card, her credit card, her driver's license, her yogurt shop stamp card, and a few crumpled bills. She sighed. Something was better than nothing. She smoothed out the money.

"What are you doing?" Carcass asked, coming up behind her.

"You can't just take things without paying for them."

She almost laughed at the idea that Carcass would care about taking something that didn't belong to him, but she was too tired. She was in the presence of a god, but he couldn't care less about piety.

He leaned closer to the bills. "And that is modern tender?"

"Yeah, but not enough of it." She placed the money on the counter.

He plucked the five-dollar bill up with two fingers and brought it close to his left eye. Then he popped it into his mouth. He swallowed and smacked his lips.

"Hey!" After everything, this final injustice was a step too far. "That's for the store!"

"A visual assessment would only tell me what it's supposed to look like, not what it's made of." He gazed at the ceiling. "This is a simple thing to know fully."

He opened his left hand. The worn five-dollar bill he'd just eaten lay in the center of his palm.

"What was that, a magic trick?"

"Not a trick. A creation." He put his left hand flat on the counter. "Now, how many of these pieces of this tender do you require to 'pay'?"

"Um." She hadn't checked price tags. The broken window was huge. "Maybe a thousand?"

He lifted his hand toward the ceiling. A stack of identically wrinkled five-dollar bills grew taller beneath it.

"Wow," Spooky said. "That's actually really useful."

Carcass shrugged. "Inanimate objects are often a simple arrangement of atoms and not so difficult to copy. Living things tend to be a bit mushier."

Spooky wished her mind didn't carry her so smoothly to the next conclusion: "So the things from Earth you recreated in your world... did you...did you eat all of them? Did you eat a horse?"

Carcass glided toward the window, robes barely ruffling the powdered glass that coated the floor. "Are we finished here? I am not a being of unlimited patience."

"Never mind." Spooky grabbed the shopping bags. "Let's go."

As soon as they jumped the fence again, Spooky exhaled. She had done it. She had left the camp and returned without anyone even noticing she was gone.

Still, she couldn't let any counselors interrupt her now that she was so close to getting rid of Carcass. They didn't have the cover of night any longer. She hurried them both into the lodge. According to the clock on the desktop, it was 5:19 a.m.—less than two hours until the first wake-up bell.

She spread the instruction manuals on the couch for Carcass to read. She had covered as much as she could on the walk back, but there was still a lot to explain to someone who had never touched an electronic device before. Carcass held each page up to a softball-sized eye for a few moments, before flipping to the next. Meanwhile, Spooky charged the borrowed phone and the new laptop, working through the setup wizards and necessary downloads. All she needed was power, an internet connection, and a browser. Everything else was extraneous. She plugged extension cord into extension cord, creating a long, white worm that wound its way through the mess on the break room floor. She plugged the Ethernet cord into the dusty router under the desk, scaring away a few spiders.

She turned to Carcass, who was eye-to-page with another booklet.

"All set. Now we have to get the wires outside." She eyed the cheap carpet. Carcass's destructive powers had been on display all evening. "Do you think you could make a small hole in the floor here? Small. Think small. This big." She held her fingers a few inches apart.

He nodded. She clasped the router to her chest as Carcass pointed at the floor. A three-inch chunk of carpet and wood popped up like a cork. She shone the phone's flashlight into the crawl space.

As much as she didn't want to let her former captor within grabbing distance, Spooky knew the perfect tool to thread the wires beneath the lodge.

"I think we need that vine back."

She fed the Ethernet and extension cords into the hole while the vine pulled foot after foot through the foundation. When there was no slack left, she yelled for it to stop, and tucked the router back in place.

With the scissors set to one side and the borrowed phone in her pocket, just in case, she collected the bags of contraband and stacked them back in the cabinet. The padlock popped together and sealed the forbidden items inside. It looked like it had never been touched. Spooky turned around. The splintered door frame and mangled hinges told a different story. The Dodgsons would turn the camp upside-down if they thought campers had broken into the lodge.

Spooky seized the scissors and started hacking the break room door.

"You don't have to cut it," Carcass said. "That door is already open."

"Very funny." She wiggled one of the blades free from where she had stabbed it into the vinyl. "If the counselors think a camper broke in here, they might search the room, and they could find the wires. They already think they saw a bear last night." She gestured with the scissors. "I'm adding claw marks."

Carcass raised an eyebrow at her handiwork. The blades hadn't left more than superficial scratches.

"Very well."

He folded four fingers into his hand and slashed the door. Five deep gouges painted a clear picture of the recent presence of a beast.

"Yeah, that's a lot better," Spooky said. "Um, could you put a couple of those in the hallway? And the outside door, too."

Spooky plucked bags of chips and cookies from the top of the refrigerator. She ripped them open and sprinkled them around the room. The claw marks really sold it, but the combined effect was impressive. It looked like a hungry bear had gone on a rampage at the back of the main lodge. It would be practically impossible for the Dodgsons to conclude a camper could have been behind the damage.

She ran outside with the laptop in one hand and shopping bags full of tech packaging in the other. The vine lay still next to Carcass. It had pulled the cords through a hole in the siding and deposited them in a jumble.

"Uh, thanks," she said to the vine. She lifted her laden arms. "Here. A working computer for you to take to your world."

"You will assist me until I am using the computer beside my fire. You will be free of me after. Not before."

He pointed between the dumpsters, and a misting line appeared. The vine twisted around the ends of the cords and slithered toward it. Spooky stepped on the ends near the lodge to keep them steady as loop after loop of slack unwound from the pile.

"Follow," Carcass said. He squished between the dumpsters, his body compressing like a gummy candy between fingers. His frame lit up in white and disappeared.

Spooky kicked dirt, gravel, and pine needles over the wires, then shuffled after him. She held the shopping bags behind her and inched into the rusty corridor. The white line was like a tear in the universe; the camp behind it was visible on either side. She balanced on one leg and stuck the other toward it. Her foot vanished, her ankle rimmed in brightness.

One more step, and she'd be rid of Carcass forever.

She wiggled her invisible toes, took a breath, and leaned forward.

All she could see in front of her was white. It filled her peripheral vision, then surrounded her. She knew what to expect this time, but the words "void between worlds" echoed in her mind. She clutched the laptop tighter, focusing on the warm whirring against her chest.

Then she was falling. She managed to land on her feet, but she stumbled and spilled half the contents of her shopping bags in the dirt. Just as dawn had come on Earth, the sky here was light, but the tone was different somehow. Or maybe it was the brown and gray landscape itself that seemed discolored, like a photograph filtered in sepia, black, and white. Scraggly shrubs transitioned into a forest of pine trees behind the circular house. Carcass stood beside the threshold.

Spooky followed the Ethernet and power cords' trail across the clearing, into the tunnel, past the chirping birds, to the circular interior. The fire had gone down, and the coals glowed.

She set the laptop on the wooden table, plugged in the cables, and pressed the "On" button. The screen turned blue. Carcass rustled in behind her. She checked the connection and opened a search browser. She typed in "stories," then faced the laptop screen toward him.

He sat down on a stump and draped one orange finger over the mouse. He clicked on a link. The page opened and the first line of text said, "Once upon a time."

"Are we done?" Spooky asked.

Carcass waved his hand, round eyes fixed on the screen. "The door is open for your return. Goodbye, Spooky."

Spooky bounded through the tunnel and out of the house. A sliver of white mist shimmered above the spot where the wires ended. She ran toward it and jumped back into the void.

# CHAPTER VII
# THE LIGHT OF DAY

The blaring, clanging, ear-splitting wake-up bell was, for once, a blessing. It knocked Spooky out of her spinning thoughts and back into her skin. Self-preservation and sanity demanded she stop thinking.

Her work duty in the cafeteria required her to start the day both clean and early, so she was always among the first to face the icy morning air. It had only been an hour since she snuck into bed, but she creaked out of it like she hadn't moved in a thousand years. Everything hurt. She hobbled out of the cabin before Cabin-leader Lucy had even lifted her head. She only had fifteen minutes to shower before the next bell.

The grime covering her would have been suspicious, but no one on the first bathroom shift looked up from their own dragging feet. A female counselor took her post on one side of the open-air showers. Spooky limped to the furthest stall, hung her soap, tucked the phone and scissors into her towel, and threw her ruined pajamas on the ground. She wished the wood and concrete box was tall enough to cover her face but settled for ducking her head and crying, hot tears mixing with the shower water and dirt.

The second bell rang. Clocks were one of the many amenities Dodgson denied campers; if you knew how much time you had, you knew how much time you had to waste. Her work duty in the cafeteria started at the third bell. She pulled down her sweatshirt to hide the phone and scissors in her waistband.

Spooky trudged along the path to the front of the main lodge. She had until the fifth bell to complete her pre-breakfast tasks, or she would get a scuff. She would give this to the Dodgsons: constantly racing against punishment did take one's mind off darker things.

Counselor Trevor greeted her at the door to the kitchen.

"Camper Laurel," he barked. "Camper Luke won't be joining us. He's been reassigned to another work duty."

Spooky tried not to show any reaction to Luke's "reassignment." He was probably knee deep in chicken poop right now. Or cleaning toilets with a toothbrush.

"Until another camper is given the responsibility of cafeteria duty, we'll make do," Trevor continued. "You mop. I'll take the garbage—"

"No!" she said a little too quickly. She didn't want a counselor taking a close look at the dumpsters before she did. What would she see in the light of day? Would everything have evaporated in the morning sun?

He raised his thick eyebrows.

"I want to handle all of it myself," she said. "I feel like...I feel like I'm ready to take on more responsibility."

There were no mirrors in the camp, but Spooky couldn't imagine she looked ready to take on anything except an early grave. At least her sweatshirt and jeans hid her bruises and scrapes.

But Trevor just shrugged. "If you're late, it'll be scuffs. Now get to work."

A few bells later, Spooky adjusted her hairnet and took her place at the oatmeal station. Campers rushed in through the double doors to claim seats. Even though the food was often bland and strangely wet, and it meant sitting through Izeah's speeches, meals were the only activity anyone could look forward to.

"Campers! Good morning!" Izeah Dodgson called, taking the mic on the foot-high platform at the front of the cafeteria. "Good morning! I know this will be a productive day, where each of you will shine and succeed under the trust we have placed in you! We have some important announcements."

He paused. His words lingered in the silent room. Even without the threat of scuffs for disrupting announcements, no one would speak. All of the screamers and talkers had been beaten into submission by their fellow campers. No one got away with delaying food.

"But we are going to save those for your small group meetings. Fuel up! Today is your day to be the best possible you!" He stepped down from the platform. Only then did chairs scrape back. It was a mercifully short speech today.

Everyone lined up at the buffet or oatmeal station. Spooky concentrated on the serving spoon as she plopped oatmeal into bowls, but she couldn't stop her hand from shaking. She slopped chunks onto someone's sleeve, which earned her a grunt. She couldn't even raise her eyes. Most campers wouldn't do anything to her in front of the counselors, but pissing off the wrong person would catch up with her eventually. Right now, it was all she could do to stay standing.

"Hey, Spook," said a bright voice in front of her.

Spooky pulled her gaze off the floor and onto the heart-shaped face of Brianna Van Den Berg. Her cloud of curly yellow hair obscured the line behind her.

Brianna was the type of girl everyone knew, regardless of whether or not they'd officially met—which, before now, Spooky hadn't. The drab dress code and no make-up rule did nothing to diminish the number of eyes following her around the camp. She held court between bells and at meals with a circle of other attention-getting girls. They snickered and chattered like they were strolling between classes at high school, instead of across the dirt at Dodgson. Their antisocial, twitchy, greasy-haired peers looked all the worse in comparison. Her long eyelashes and pouty lips made Spooky want to tug the hairnet over her ears, as if the sparse threads would make a difference.

"Uh, hi Brianna."

"You can call me Bree."

"Okay. Hi Bree."

Bree scrunched her nose. "Oh, you're funny."

Spooky hadn't meant to be funny. She was too tired to think.

"Sit with me. I'll save you a seat."

Spooky's bar for strangeness was hovering somewhere near the edge of the universe, but Brianna Van Den Berg wanting to sit with her still qualified as weird. A counselor in line cleared his throat, jerking Spooky back into scooping oatmeal. She gave Bree her spoonful. Bree winked and strolled away.

After everyone else was served and seated, Spooky was supposed to join in on the "social benefits" of mealtime. For her first few weeks, figuring out which table to approach with her tray had been a daily ordeal; the open chairs weren't usually next to the most agreeable campers. Then she and Luke had started eating together. Somehow, she doubted he planned to have breakfast with her today. His platinum head was easy to spot at a table full of guys across the room. He hadn't visited the oatmeal bar and didn't look in her direction.

Bree, on the other hand, was waving and pointing at the chair next to her. There was never space at that table. The invitation probably held some joke at Spooky's expense. At least Bree seemed like your average mean girl, not someone who would lure you out back and beat you senseless. Then again, mean girls could be bad enough —rumor had it, one of the girls who sat at that table had seduced her sister's boyfriend, then cyberbullied her until she had a mental breakdown.

But that was just a rumor. Campers didn't talk about their reason for being at Dodgson. Only someone looking for trouble would ask.

Spooky approached the table with her tray.

"Hey! You've got..." Bree pointed at her head.

Spooky reached up and touched her hairnet. She pulled it off and shoved it into her sweatshirt pocket. Ears warming, Spooky glanced around the circle of girls. Everyone was watching Bree, waiting for their next cue. Even among the delinquents, she commanded.

"Sit," Bree said with a smile. Spooky sat. Bree reached over and smoothed a stray hair. "That's better."

The other girls at the table seemed to collectively shrug, picking up their foam sporks and continuing with their conversations.

"Another spectacular day at Camp Dodgson, right? It's like it's their mission to make everything as boring as possible. That's asking for us to get inventive, don't you think?" Bree talked like they sat together every day, without any reserve or preamble. "I hear Raquel got a hold of some matches."

"Uh..." Spooky eyed the counselor sitting across the table.

"Ignore Jeanine, she's hard of hearing. That's why we sit here."

Counselor Jeanine slurped the milk off her spork. If she had overheard, she clearly didn't care.

Spooky pushed her oatmeal around. Her stomach churned. She wasn't sure if she was starving or about to throw up.

Bree touched her arm. "You don't have an eating disorder, do you?"

"What? No," Spooky said.

"You're not eating."

Spooky spooned some oatmeal into her mouth and immediately wished she hadn't.

"Good," Bree said. "That would be tragic. They're not equipped to handle that kind of delicate issue here. But I'm curious, what is your story?"

Spooky stopped mid chew. You would get twenty-five scuffs for sharing the reason you were sent to Dodgson. According to Izeah, focusing on "why" reinforced the negative narrative of the past.

But Spooky wasn't only worried about the scuffs—"why" established pecking order. Campers here for more benign reasons became instant targets for more serious offenders. A few people had made the mistake of sharing their story in the first week. Spooky had seen firsthand how important it was that she keep her mouth shut.

The only apparent division between campers was the open cabins and the closed cabins. The highest risk campers slept under lock and key. Other than that, with a mean face and no questions asked, shoplifters and druggies blended in with bullies and budding psychopaths. There was a mutual understanding that asking someone what they did was as good as starting a fight. It was a challenge to a camper's reputation.

With one hand tucked under her tan chin, Bree didn't seem worried about forbidden questions. Spooky swallowed her oatmeal. Bree hadn't asked her why she was here, exactly, but it felt like she was digging.

"I work in the cafeteria," Spooky said, picking something innocuous.

"Maybe that's how you spend your days." Bree leaned in. "But I heard you found something else to do last night."

Last night? Spooky's heart kicked once. What had Bree seen? What did she know?

"I don't know what..."

"Oh please, I can see the bruises on Luke's balls from here, and you look like you haven't slept in a decade."

Oh. That.

Bree smiled, her straight teeth coming into view two at a time. "So, how was it? Fun?"

"Uh, no," Spooky said without thinking. She should have been mortified Luke had told anyone, but right now, any embarrassment was buried under layers of exhaustion. "I mean, I don't know."

"Ha! You're hilarious." Bree batted her arm and Spooky flinched. "But I'll get the juicy details later. What I really want to know is, how did you sneak out?"

Spooky opened and closed her mouth. Even to her clogged brain, explicitly admitting she had been out of bed last night seemed like a bad idea.

"Don't hold out. You made it in and out of the cabins without tripping the lights. Cher tried that and got caught two steps away from the cabin circle."

Bree gestured to a hunched girl in the far corner of the cafeteria. Her red nose and cheeks suggested recent tears. She must have been the one who'd activated the floodlights.

"She already had a lot of scuffs, poor girl. Always late. But, anyway, tell me..."

The end-of-breakfast bell clanged over Bree's next word.

"Bus your trays, campers," Counselor Jeanine croaked, looking up for the first time.

Bree's eyes narrowed like Spooky had been the one who interrupted her. But then she smiled.

"I'll find you later, Spook," Bree said, before the din of dragging chairs and clanking dishes drowned out any further conversation.

As soon as she was alone in the cafeteria, Spooky felt like she couldn't do enough things with her body at once. She ricocheted off the buffet, flinging tins of cold food onto a cart from the kitchen. She sprayed down tables with one hand and dried with the other. She started mopping before remembering she hadn't swept. Foam sporks and food fragments stuck to the wet strings.

It wasn't the threat of scuffs that made her fly. Sure, she'd get a couple if she couldn't finish cleanup. She had twice as many tasks to handle without Luke's help. But after what she had risked last night, a few scuffs didn't matter.

What she was really racing against was the silence that descended every time she paused to breathe. It left a gap for a low voice to sing in her ear: "grubs for the starlings..."

The broom just spread around the wet debris the mop had left behind. She let it clatter to the floor and slid into a crouch.

Her hips, knees, and shoulders burned. The fabric of her jeans was like a nail file against the skin of her left ankle. She hung her head and let it all ache, her gloved hands dangling between her knees.

She wasn't in trouble. No counselors seemed to know she had been out of bed after hours. No one had any idea she'd been outside the fence. She wasn't kicked out of Dodgson or her home. Everything was exactly the way it had been yesterday.

But she wasn't the same. There was evidence on her body that something had happened, but none of what she kept replaying in her head could be real.

Maybe she had spent too much time inhaling Dodgson's cheap cleaning chemicals. Maybe she had been exposed to a hallucinogenic fungus in the forest or black mold in the walls. Maybe the drudgery of Dodgson had pushed her to a psychotic break.

What if something was really wrong with her?

What if Carcass was real?

She wasn't ready for either possibility to be true.

"Camper Laurel," Trevor yelled from the kitchen. "Trash."

Spooky grabbed the broom and jumped up.

Trevor leaned out of the kitchen doorway as she jogged over. He handed her the bag from the kitchen and a ring with the keys to the back door and the dumpsters.

"We're doing some renovations down the hall, so the door out back is open. Put the keys in the slot when you're done."

She bobbed her head.

"Get going camper. You have two bells or you're late," Trevor barked. "Err, I'm *trusting* you to get everything done in two bells. Whatever."

He waved her off and shut the kitchen door.

Trevor was particularly unconvincing at delivering his lines about trust, but Spooky preferred his sincere sternness to the fake smiles of other counselors. She gripped the keys to her chest and stared at the closed door. She could still yell after him and beg him to take the trash out for her. He might even do it.

But as much as she didn't want to know the truth, she needed to find out what was back there. She didn't think she would make it through another bell otherwise.

Spooky held the trash bag up like a shield and marched down the hallway. She passed closed doors labeled as staff offices and storage closets, and numbered doors that marked holding rooms for short-term isolation. She rounded the corner.

A horned figure flashed in the shadows.

She shook her head. It was her imagination. This figment was nothing like the solid monster of last night.

Still, sweat prickled on her skin. Pieces of cardboard had been taped over portions of the walls. There was a square of it on the door of the counselors' break room. She peeled up the edge, revealing long gouges. Claw marks. Spooky felt like she was returning to the scene of her own crime. She ducked her head and hurried past the wired window.

The back door was propped open. Here, too, tape and cardboard concealed damage where the deadbolt had smashed through the frame.

Renovations, huh.

Still, there were explanations for this level of destruction that didn't have to be supernatural. In a psychotic state, it was possible she could have scraped herself up, broken into the lodge, and taken the phone and the scissors. Maybe the wood was rotting. She could have pushed a deadbolt through rotting wood. Even though it wasn't what she remembered happening, it was possible that she had used the scissors to maul the walls and the door.

Despite the contraband in her waistband, the bruises on her body, and the mess at the back of the lodge, there was only one thing that would prove she'd had an encounter with the beyond: the wires that went into another world.

The area behind the lodge appeared smaller in daylight. The mysterious dark shapes that might have extended on forever were now solid and finite. There were the blue dumpsters, a few trees, and the fence.

Everything looked normal, except for the mound of earth snaking from the foundation of the lodge to the dumpsters.

Spooky staggered down the steps and dropped the trash bag. She reached a shaking hand toward the disturbed ground. The dirt she had kicked into place a few hours ago fell away and the white cords came up in her loose fist. A glowing spot appeared between the dumpsters. The void.

It was real. It had all really happened. Carcass existed, and he was on the other side of the invisible door. Maybe he was beside his fire right now, surfing the internet.

Spooky fell to her knees and scraped more dirt and pine needles over the wires. Not many people came back here, but she couldn't leave a noticeable trace. If someone found the cords and unplugged them, Carcass might come back for her. This internet connection was what had freed her. It was her insurance policy against another visit.

When the ground was even, Spooky sat back on her heels. She stared at her dusty gloves. They went in and out of focus.

The bell rang.

She brushed off her hands and jumped up. She couldn't freak out right now. She still had three more trash cans to empty, and only one more bell until small group meetings. Adrenaline helped her lift the dumpster lid with one hand and heave the bag in with the other. She took one last look at the area from the top of the steps. No one would notice the wires now.

This time when she passed the counselors' break room, she peeked inside. The router was still tucked under the desk. They had cleaned up the chips. Two beige-clad counselors lounged on the couch facing the TV, completely unaware of who, or what, had sat there mere hours before. They were watching a news report on Office Shack.

Office Shack.

Spooky put her nose to the glass. "Local Robbery Rocks Solid Community" ran across the bottom of the screen. A reporter with a microphone stood in the parking lot. The storefront was wrapped in yellow tape, and plastic covered the missing front window.

One of the counselors on the couch turned his head and she ducked.

Whatever her adrenal glands had left to pump worked its way through her veins as she bolted down the hallway toward the cafeteria.

Trevor was waiting for her in the dining room with his hands on his hips.

"What took so long?" He furrowed his brow at the sight of her. "What's wrong? What did you do?"

Now that wasn't a Dodgson approved line. So much for trust.

"I need to go to the nurse."

Maybe it was the sweat beading on her forehead, or something in her expression, but he took the keys from her hand without argument.

"Don't throw up in here, or sick or not, you'll have to clean it up before lunch. I'll inform your small group leader."

Spooky peeled off her gloves, smock, and hairnet, and wobbled to the door. All of her attention had been on keeping it together. Somehow, it had slipped her mind that her supernatural encounter had ended in grand theft Office Shack.

# CHAPTER VIII
# CHECK-UP

Spooky swayed out of the lodge and onto the broad central thoroughfare. Other campers, outfitted in utility uniforms, criss-crossed the grounds between brambles, animal pens, bathrooms, and cabins. The daylight was too bright. The activity around her blurred. A boy jabbed a rake at her as she stumbled across his path. He glared but jogged away. Everyone only had one more bell to finish their work duties.

Spooky had never been in trouble with the law. She had never even received a speeding ticket.

But this morning, she had robbed an electronics store.

If she didn't get somewhere private soon, she would throw up. She pumped her legs and swung her arms, hitching her aching body toward the front gate.

The gingerbread-style administrative building had the cheeriest architecture in the camp, but there was no good reason for a camper to go there—you had to either be sick, injured, or scheduled to meet with Adam Dodgson. After her scuff level meeting on orientation day, Spooky had promised herself she wouldn't be back. But she needed time alone with the phone to look up the news story she had seen on the break room TV. She had to find out what the police knew. She could only hope the nurse would prescribe rest and isolation, or at least give her a few minutes of privacy.

Spooky pulled open the heavy door. Only the upper and lower deadbolts betrayed the image of a friendly reception area. Pictures of smiling campers and racks of informational pamphlets decorated the walls. Clearly, this building was designed to impress visiting parents. Campers in the photos stood arm in arm with each other, apparently unconcerned about the no-touching policy. There was even one picture of uniformed campers on the edge of a blue lake. Spooky had never seen those uniforms or that lake.

A white and cherry sign at the end of the corridor said "nurse" in block letters. A woman with a clipboard stepped out.

"Camper Laurel. You're one minute later than expected. Come in."

The nurse reported her arrival to someone on the other end of the radio. Even though the door to Adam Dodgson's office was closed, Spooky lowered her head as she passed. If he saw her face right now, he would know she was guilty of something. Spooky followed the nurse into the clean white office.

"I see this is your first time here. Before we begin, I should tell you there is a twenty-five scuff penalty for wasting my time. If there is nothing wrong with you, turn around now, and finish your work duty."

Apparently, the nurse didn't bother with lines about trust at all.

"I don't know what's wrong with me, but I feel terrible," Spooky said. Even though a bug wasn't the reason for her frothing stomach, the acid rising in her throat was real enough.

"Alright." The nurse made a note and guided Spooky to the sink in the first examination room. "Are you always this pale?"

For the first time that summer, Spooky looked at herself in a mirror. Her reflection was ashen, with purple circles bruising each eye. Sweat plastered her dark hair to her skull. No wonder Trevor hadn't accused her of faking illness. No wonder the nurse hadn't asked her twice if she was lying.

"Maybe I'm a little paler than usual," Spooky croaked.

"Right, okay." The nurse scribbled something down. "Sit here. What are your symptoms?"

Spooky sunk onto the padded bench, crinkling the paper. "My

heart is beating really hard. I feel hot. And nauseous. And like I might faint. And throw up."

The nurse stuck a thermometer under her tongue. "Did you eat breakfast?"

"Sort of," Spooky answered around the metal stick.

"How did you sleep last night?"

"Uh...not well."

"Mhm," the nurse muttered. "Are you on your period?"

"No."

"Drugs?"

"No."

"I'll test you anyway. For the drugs, not the period. And the flu. Camp protocol. Open."

Spooky opened her mouth and the nurse took the thermometer. She pulled out a cotton swab and scraped the back of Spooky's throat, then handed her a sealed cup.

"No temperature. Pee in this. You have two minutes in the bathroom with the door closed."

The radio at the nurse's hip crackled. Before she could pick it up, the door to the office swung open. A counselor dragged a boy in by the elbow. He had one hand clutched to his eye. Blood dripped through his fingers.

The nurse jumped up. "What happened?"

"Camper Lars," the counselor replied. "Camper Troy here was, apparently, 'asking for it all summer.'"

"What did he use? I don't know why they let these kids touch tools..."

"Lars is on maximum restriction. He found a stick."

"Honestly, next thing you know they'll have to get rid of the trees in the forest." The nurse pulled the counselor and the camper into another examination room. "Don't remove pressure..."

Spooky didn't hear the rest as the door clicked shut.

A few seconds later, the nurse burst back out into the main room.

"You." She jabbed a finger at Spooky. "I have to escort Camper

Troy into town. I'm assigning you rest until I complete your examination. Counselor Dave will be in the waiting area until I get back. Don't move. Don't touch anything."

She didn't wait for confirmation before grabbing the bleeding boy and swooping out the door. After a few minutes of silence, Spooky peeked out. Counselor Dave sat guard on the bench outside the office, the curly back of his head visible through the viewing window.

This was better than she could have hoped for. Spooky inched the door shut and lay down on the paper-covered exam table. She tugged the phone out of her waistband, pushed the "on" button, and held the glowing rectangle in front of her face.

The reception was as good in here as it was in the counselors' break room. The Western Colorado Tribune's website had the story on its main page. She pressed "play" on the first video.

"I'm standing in front of Office Shack, an electronics store located in downtown Root Park. Police were called to the scene this morning after the first employee arrived to open the store and found evidence of a break in..."

Spooky held her breath while the reporter covered the details of the scene. The cops had searched and secured the area. The break-in could have taken place any time between closing at the cafe next door and the first employee arriving today. Authorities suspected it had occurred late evening or early morning.

"Although the store is still assessing how much merchandise was taken, this crime is drawing attention because of the strange circumstances under which the perpetrators gained entry. The front window, which was designed to shatter safely, was broken with such force it was reduced to granules the size of table salt. While there are security cameras on premises..."

Spooky dropped the phone. Her heart thudded so hard she could feel each beat in her fingertips. She hadn't even thought about cameras. It was a podunk shop, but it did sell electronics. She had robbed a store, and all she had been thinking about was the orange god threatening her to do it.

She fumbled with the phone and clicked back to the point where she had left off.

"...we've been told the security system was destroyed sometime during the incident. It is unclear at this time if investigators will be able to recover footage that could lend more insight into this bizarre break-in."

At least Carcass had been annoyed enough by the burglar alarm to do some damage. She clicked on the next video segment. The thumbnail opened to an anchor sitting behind a desk.

"The town of Root Park is on edge this morning after a bizarre break-in that has businesses questioning if their security is up to snuff. Police have managed to retrieve footage from security cameras a few blocks away from the burglarized store. The video shows an unknown woman approaching the area around four a.m. this morning. We're going to play it for you now. If you have any information on the identity of this person, please contact authorities. It is possible she may have witnessed something that could help the investigation."

Spooky brought the phone an inch away from her nose as the black and white clip started. It began with an empty street. On the sidewalk across from the camera, a scrawny woman with dark hair shuffled into view. She had her face turned away, and she was gesturing. She crossed the screen and disappeared.

It was a little creepy.

It was her, of course, but the scene didn't match up with her memory. Her head had been turned because she was talking to Carcass. He had been walking right next to her.

Maybe cameras couldn't capture gods.

The important thing was her face wasn't on video. The paper rustled as she sagged against it. The figure could have been any woman with dark hair. And she would be the least suspicious dark-haired person in Root Park—she was locked inside the fence at Camp Dodgson, day and night.

Spooky scrolled through a few more articles. There were no updates on whether or not police had been able to recover video footage, or any other evidence, from Office Shack. She couldn't keep reading the same information. The phone only had so much charge. She switched it to battery saver and slipped it back into her waistband.

Spooky's whole body felt heavy. She closed her eyes.

She must have fallen asleep because when she opened them, the nurse was shaking her and telling her to pee in a cup.

The nurse took the sample. "Do you have any new or worsening symptoms?"

"No," Spooky said, even though she felt like a train had hit her twice. The few minutes of sleep had done more harm than good.

"Then get to your small group session. You've only missed the first half. I'm radioing over now. They'll expect you in your seat within ten minutes."

Her small group met in a multi-purpose room in the activity center. She would have to jog to make it.

Jogging hurt. Her joints were stiff, and her lungs ached. Even though the day was warm, and she was sweating, her skin felt cold. Up until this point, her worst-case scenario for the summer had been maxing out. Now she was facing arrest, a criminal record, and incarceration.

The police may not have any evidence yet, but that didn't mean there wasn't any for them to find. She hadn't covered her face or snuck around. She had strolled along the highway with bags of stolen property. No cars had driven by, but she had passed plenty of houses. Any early risers could have seen her from their windows.

Her hand twitched toward the phone. She wanted to research her legal options and potential outcomes. Was there any way she could defend herself if they had video evidence or witnesses? Would she go to jail or prison? For how long? Should she tell the police what really happened and let them conclude she had lost her mind? Then where would she go?

She couldn't risk using the phone in the open, but the internet wasn't her only source of information—plenty of kids at Dodgson had experience with the legal system. The camp marketed itself as the perfect follow up to juvenile detention to help prevent reoffending. It was in the pamphlet. Someone here should be able to tell her the consequences of robbing a store. Or at least give her a better idea.

Knowing what she was up against wouldn't change the outcome, but it would help her narrow down what to worry about. She just had to figure out who to ask without attracting too much attention.

Her small group meeting was her first opportunity.

# CHAPTER IX
# LESSONS FROM LISA

Camp life was conducted at five levels of interpersonal misery: all camp, cabin group, small group, work duty, and individual.

All camp gathered in the cafeteria for speeches and meals, and in the recreation area for outdoor therapy. Cabin groups split bathroom shifts and shared sleeping quarters. Small groups met daily for group therapy. Two to ten campers shared the same work duty assignment, which was a great barometer for how much Adam Dodgson wanted to punish them. And every other week, campers had individual counseling sessions in Izeah Dodgson's office.

These five levels of interaction were supposed to provide the perfect balance of individual work and community support to create the change Dodgson promised. Of course, promises flew from Izeah's mouth like spittle, with as much speed and as little meaning. Words like "counseling" and "therapy" were tacked onto any chore or punishment.

Although Spooky had never been to group therapy before Dodgson, she was fairly certain you were supposed to sit in a circle and talk about yourself and your feelings. Her small group did sit in a circle, but the "therapy" part was completely scripted. They reviewed the rules, recited pledges, and copied manifestos. Even though she met with the same fourteen campers every day, she knew almost nothing about them. Their identities before Dodgson were meant to be forgotten, buried, or ignored.

Which meant any of the campers staring at her as she walked in could have the information she wanted.

"Any of you rob an electronics store recently?" she imagined herself asking as she headed for the empty chair.

"I was at the nurse's office," she said instead.

"I trust you, and she radioed," Marie, their small group leader, replied. "Sit, sit. We waited for you so we could all write our weekly letters home together. We want to keep your parents up to date on your progress."

Marie passed out paper and numbered pens along with each camper's "suggested topics" sheet. Spooky scanned the bulleted talking points the camp recommended for her letter. They wanted her to emphasize her progress going into the second month: the friends she had made, the newfound feelings of responsibility for her actions, and the tranquility she had found in nature.

She couldn't stop an eye roll but started writing. She knew her parents didn't want to hear from her, but if she didn't write what the camp "suggested" the first time, she would be called in to redo it. Dodgson controlled all camper-parent communications; they couldn't have parents swooping in to pick up their little monsters early or asking for refunds. The weekly letters were ingenious, really—the campers were doing the camp's marketing.

"Okay, thank you for the pens back! I knew I could trust you all to use them for their intended purpose and return them." Marie straightened the stack of letters and tucked them into a folder. "Now, as Izeah mentioned at breakfast, we have an important announcement: we had another visit from a large animal last night. We believe it was a bear."

Of course the camp had made sure they had completed their letters home before announcing a bear was wandering the grounds at night. They didn't want to have to manage two hundred rewrites.

"None of this is anything to be worried about. The bear was just looking for food. Your cabins are being searched for anything that could attract wildlife as we speak. If any of you would like to be your best selves and admit to removing food from the cafeteria, now would be the time."

Marie bounced her gaze around the circle, making eye contact with each of them for a few seconds. The scissors had warmed to her skin temperature, but Spooky could still feel the rigid blades along her spine as Marie met her eyes.

She may not have thought about security cameras, but at least she'd had the foresight not to leave the phone and scissors in her bunk in case of a search.

A few campers squirmed, but no one spoke.

"Okay, I trust that none of you brought food into the cabins. I know you all respect the rules, but we need to make sure we can account one hundred percent for your safety. We have to ensure everybody stays in bed after lights-out. So we also have an update to our scuff board: anybody caught out of their cabin after the last bell will get one hundred scuffs and their maximum scuff level consequences."

Spooky blinked. She had to assume if counselors overheard whispers that she'd been out of bed last night, the rule change wouldn't be retroactive.

At least her ruse had worked. Clearly, the counselors believed a bear had scratched up the lodge and weren't looking for a camper to blame.

Marie licked her thumb and peeled two pieces of paper out of her binder. "We are going to role-play a few scenarios to prepare you all to be your best selves. Why don't you start us off...Camper Laurel!" Spooky flinched. "Take the role of yourself. And let's see... Camper Crystal, step up and read for us as the camper making the wrong choices."

Crystal took the script Marie passed her and swung her knees to face Spooky.

"'Hi camper name,'" Crystal began robotically. "'I have a...'"

"Please say her name," Marie said.

"What?" Crystal let the paper flop.

"In place of where it says 'camper name,' please say her name." Marie put on a forced smile.

"Okay." Crystal breathed in through her teeth as she flipped the paper back up. "'Hi Spooky, I have a cool thing I want to show you...'"

"Her name is Laurel,'" Marie corrected. "First names only, please."

"Do you want someone else to do this?" Crystal snapped.

"Three scuffs for talking back. You are one away from your next level. Camper Tom, take over."

Spooky ducked behind her paper. At the beginning of the summer, when campers asked her for her name, she'd automatically said "Spooky." They didn't have to know "Spooky Specki, Spooky Specki" had started as a playground chant because she was quiet and pale and creeped out other kids when she hovered at the edges of their games at recess. For all they knew, she had earned the nickname doing something sinister. It made for a much more intimidating introduction than "Laurel."

Besides, she wouldn't have responded to Laurel. Everyone at school called her Spooky. Her parents and Victoria didn't, but then, they didn't say her name often enough for it to count as a pattern.

"'Hi Laurel.'" Tom emphasized each syllable. "'I have a cool thing I want to show you. But you'll have to leave your cabin and meet me after dark...'"

Spooky only devoted half her attention to the script. She kept her eyes up and scanned the circle. Crystal had twitchy fingers. Sam liked to show off his extensive knowledge of the street names for drugs. Leo had a temper.

She didn't have any idea who might have had experience with the police, breaking and entering, or theft. But after considering each of the fourteen campers, she had identified the right person to ask —Lisa.

The Lisa she had met at the beginning of the summer was very different from the Lisa slumped in small group today. Week one, when they happened to pick folding chairs next to one another, Lisa had introduced herself with a smile. Spooky had extended a hand to shake, which felt stupid even as she was doing it, but Lisa had only giggled. They sat next to one another at lunch, and to Spooky's relief, Lisa did most of the talking. It was her first summer at Dodgson too. She found it all jarring too. She wasted no time explaining why she was there—her parents enrolled her when they found out she had an older boyfriend.

That was it. For Lisa's parents, an older boyfriend was all the justification required to send their daughter away to a camp to be reprogrammed.

In that moment, the summer ahead looked a little less scary. Maybe Spooky wasn't at camp with a group of soon-to-be axe murderers. Here was Lisa—a seemingly nicer and more normal girl than Spooky—who happened to have an older boyfriend and intense parents.

Her elation at finding a potential ally faded fast.

Spooky hadn't been the only person at the lunch table when Lisa told her story. Or maybe Lisa had been gabbing about her "older boyfriend" to anyone who would listen. Either way, the next day Lisa came to small group with a bruised cheek. The day after that, she had a bloody lip and torn clothes. The counselors didn't see what happened in every crowded room or on every empty path. What the counselors did see was a disheveled camper. Marie gave Lisa scuffs for a sloppy appearance. When Lisa's clothes were ripped or dirty enough days in a row, Spooky had to stop serving her specialty items like Jello, mashed potatoes, cinnamon, and salt. Apparently, decent food was one of the first things Adam Dodgson had on her scuff levels.

Lisa cried in her cabin every night. Lisa lost weight. Lisa started to smell. Someone must have been keeping her out of the showers. Or maybe they had stolen her soap.

And then there were the whispers—the comments campers made as Lisa walked by on the paths. Guys made passes. Girls called her "slut."

Lisa's tooth went through her lip. She had to go into town for stitches. Lisa got an infection. Lisa had to go into the holding cabins and live in isolation for three days so she could take her antibiotic regimen.

Spooky watched Lisa get broken down, bit by bit, in small group snapshots. The only thing Spooky could be grateful for was the fact that she had stayed quiet at lunch that day. She had wanted to tell Lisa her own reason "why." She had wanted to talk about how it felt to fall so short of her parents' expectations.

But thankfully, Spooky had always been the quiet type. And now she knew better—you didn't tell anyone why you were at Dodgson, and you didn't ask either. You didn't try to find friends in a school of sharks. You tried to keep out of the way and look too mean to eat.

Spooky didn't have to feel bad for Lisa anymore. After the infection cleared up, she started getting more bruises on her knuckles and fewer on her face. The wound on her lip was already a tiny pink scar.

Despite how the summer had changed her, Lisa was still the safest person Spooky could think of to ask for information. Besides, Lisa had encountered all the worst bullies here. She might know who was into what kind of trouble.

"Hey," Spooky said, sidling up to her as small group ended.

Lisa's eyes darted over Spooky's hands and then toward the exit. "I have to get to the showers. What do you want?"

She hadn't even made eye contact. The bubbly girl from week one was long gone.

Spooky picked her words carefully. None of the campers had access to the internet, TV, or even newspapers. No one would guess her questions were about a crime that had actually happened in Root Park this morning. Still, it seemed safer to obscure the details.

"I was wondering if you knew anybody here who got in trouble for stealing. Something big enough for the police to be involved."

Lisa's eyes flashed, then narrowed. It was no surprise she would be suspicious, on the lookout for a prank or a trap.

Spooky showed her palms. "I'm asking for someone else."

"What'll you do for me if I tell you?"

Yep, Dodgson had definitely changed Lisa. No need to feel sorry for her anymore.

"What do you want?"

Lisa started walking. "You work in the cafeteria, right?"

"Yeah." Spooky kept pace.

"I want double on bacon day. And an extra cookie on cookie day."

It was such an innocent request, Spooky could almost see the Lisa from the beginning of the summer, who had laughed and smiled as she admitted how harsh her parents were.

Still, cookies and bacon weren't in the buffet with the slop. They were controlled substances, and Spooky would lose her work duty in the cafeteria if a counselor caught her giving out extras.

But her skin itched and her eyes throbbed and she couldn't stop twisting her hands. She needed to know how much trouble she could be in for Office Shack. Not knowing what to worry about was somehow worse than worrying about a specific fate.

"Done," Spooky said. "I'll put them under your plate. Lift it up when you're first in line." That was the system she and Luke used when serving each other.

"Okay then. Reed. Reed Campbell. Talk to him."

Lisa stalked off without giving Spooky a chance to say thanks.

Spooky knew what Reed Campbell looked like. Reed was one of the guys Luke had cleaned cabins with before he joined cafeteria duty. And she knew where she could find him—at the next all camp activity, lunch.

When Reed was first in line for his scoop of Jello, Spooky held his bowl down with her serving spoon.

"Hey, I need to talk to you," she whispered. "Save me a seat."

Reed stared at her through his parted bangs like he didn't know she could speak. Talking to an unknown camper probably would have terrified her a day ago. But right now, she only cared about answers.

"If you help me, I can get you food." She plopped a heaping pile of Jello in his bowl as a demonstration of the partnership to come. Food bribery had worked on Lisa. It might work on Reed. "Just save me a seat. Move. Go."

Reed frowned, but he took his tray and got out of line.

Offering Reed a trade didn't just risk catching the eye of counselors; if other campers heard she was giving out extras, they might pressure her to give them the same. She would probably end up losing cafeteria duty.

But she was already out on a wire. What was a little wind?

When Spooky pulled off her hairnet and picked up her tray of food, there was an open spot waiting for her. Actually, there were two —one next to Reed, and one next to Bree, who caught her eye and waved. Bree pointed at the seat next to her and smiled, but Spooky couldn't afford to play whatever game Bree had in mind right now. She tried to pretend she hadn't seen the gesture. She might pay for snubbing Bree later, but Spooky only had about fifteen minutes, and she needed every second of it.

None of the guys at the table acknowledged her as she took the open chair. They were engrossed in their own conversations. The supervising counselor glanced at her, then looked away. Luke sometimes ate with this group, but Spooky spotted the back of his blond head a few tables over.

Reed started talking to her out of the corner of his mouth.

"I told my man Luke you wanted to talk to me. He said not to."

This was a bad start. Spooky moved her green beans around with her spork.

"But Luke doesn't work in the cafeteria anymore." Reed cracked his knuckles. "So you're in luck. I happen to need a new hookup for cookie day."

"Sure, I can do that," Spooky mumbled to her plate. She should have known Luke had given out extra food to other people. "But I want to know some things."

"What do you want to know?"

"A friend of mine broke into a...a furniture store...and I want to help her." Spooky glanced at the counselor. He was focused on two guys at the table who were on the verge of yelling at each other.

"Who is it? Somebody here?"

"Not important. She just wants to find out what will happen if she gets caught. I heard you might know."

"Yeah, I might." Reed crossed his arms. "Three cookies every cookie day."

"Two."

"Two, and they better be chocolate chip."

"Two cookies, chocolate chip if I have them. And no more questions from you, just answers. She wants privacy, so if I find out you told anyone we talked about this, no more cookies."

She knew she couldn't trust him on that last point, but it was worth a try.

"Alright." Reed nodded. "You have a deal. First of all, the police have to catch her."

"How did you get caught?"

Reed looked at her. "I didn't."

She should have known to stay away from questions about his past. She kept her eyes on her tray until he continued.

"A guy I knew did. He held up a truck making a delivery to a warehouse. They ID'ed his car and pulled him over a few blocks away. Did they catch her like that?"

"No."

"That's good. Usually, if they don't catch you at the scene, they don't find you at all."

"The police could have security footage."

Reed clicked his cheek. "Did she cover her face?"

"I said no questions," Spooky hissed. She was too tired for a lecture on her supreme lack of criminal foresight.

"Alright, alright." Reed put his hands up. "Security footage sounds bad, but it really isn't the worst thing. They still need someone to ID her from the tape." Reed shoved half of his sandwich in his mouth and talked around it. "And I do need to ask a few questions—did she carry a weapon?"

"No." Although she wasn't sure anyone would believe it, given the pulverized front window.

"Anybody get hurt?"

"No."

He swallowed the sandwich. "What'd she take?"

"Why?"

"You don't get the same punishment for stealing a keychain as you do for a car. The penalty is based on the cost. The theft could be petty, misdemeanor, or felony. The number of years she might get, and her record, all depend on the..." He rubbed his fingers together.

Spooky closed her eyes. "How much?"

"How much what?"

"How much does what she stole have to be worth for it to be a felony?"

"I'm not a lawyer." Reed shrugged. "Thousands, maybe? I hope your friend didn't get grabby. That felony shit will stick."

Between the computer, the accessories, and the property damage, Spooky was certain she had swung for a felony.

The bell rang, and she jumped.

"One last thing," Reed said as he scraped his chair back and stood. "If she's under eighteen, she probably doesn't have to worry about any of that. They'll send her to juvy, and she can get her record expunged."

"Yeah." Spooky felt like the chair was tilting back even though all four legs were on the ground. "Thanks."

Reed pointed at her. "I'll see you on cookie day."

Spooky nodded him off but stayed seated. She was over eighteen. If she was convicted for robbing Office Shack, she wouldn't just be a dropout with no home and no job prospects—she would be all of those things and a felon.

But Reed's answers had given her a reason to hope. In movies and books, it seemed like crimes always got solved. But in real life, the police weren't magically going to know it was her. They wouldn't just need a witness—they would need a witness who could actually identify her. The security footage they had could be of anyone. There would be a mess of DNA and fingerprints in the store, and she hadn't touched much. She hadn't touched anything, really, other than the items they took.

And unless they had definitive proof, she still had the perfect alibi.

Spooky jumped up to go put on her smock and gloves for post-lunch cleanup. Reed had given her hope. She wanted to pull out the phone and look up the latest news report. She wanted to put all this behind her.

Unfortunately, Trevor wasn't cooperating with her need for privacy. She directed the angry look she wanted to give him at the mop water as he strolled through the dining room for the third time on some stupid errand.

"Still sick?" he asked on his way back to the kitchen.

"No," she said through her teeth.

"Good. The trash is full."

"Great!" She almost threw down the mop before remembering to look casual. She swiped it around a few more times, rested it in its bucket, and trotted over to the kitchen door.

"Trash," Trevor said, handing her the bag. "Keys. Empty the dining room containers then bring these back. Don't be late this time."

Spooky almost pulled out the phone after the first bend in the hallway, but she would have more privacy outside. The trash bag hitting her knees was weightless as she trotted toward the back of the building.

The door to the counselors' break room was wide open. A man in a jumpsuit that said "Joanne's Repairs" crouched beside it, fiddling with a screwdriver.

"Hullo," he said. "This should be fixed in twenty or less."

She shrugged, unsure why he was telling her anything about his repair timeline. Maybe her dark circles, smock, and hair net made her look more like overworked janitorial staff than a camper.

Behind the man's back, Spooky saw herself on TV.

# CHAPTER X
# LEVERAGE

The sound was off, and the picture was in black and white. She was standing outside Office Shack in her sweatpants and flannel pajama top. She approached the front window and examined it. She turned her head to the side and said something. She took a phone out of her pocket. The store window exploded inward. The Spooky on screen jumped back and blocked her face with her arms. Then the camera went black.

It looked like she had set off a remote-control bomb.

The image switched to reporters behind a desk.

The police had security footage. They had her face.

All they needed now was someone to ID her.

Not all of the counselors here would know her by name, but she was going to get recognized within the hour if her face kept replaying on their break room TV.

Spooky strode into the room, jingling her keys. "Just need to grab something."

"Yes ma'am." The man working on the door didn't even glance up from his screwdriver.

She hesitated in front of the TV. "Suspect Caught on Camera in Local Robbery" was plastered across the bottom of the screen. She couldn't look at it another second without screaming.

She shut the set off, but off wasn't enough. She reached behind the TV, grabbed the power cord, and pulled until something inside the plastic set popped. The power button didn't light up when she pushed it. The screen stayed dark.

Face burning, she nodded at the man's back and dashed out the door.

She was totally screwed. As soon as she got outside, she dropped the trash bag and the keys in the dirt and sat hard on the wooden steps. Totally, completely, utterly screwed. She snatched the phone out of her waistband. It only took a few seconds to find the most recent news report.

"The police have just released new details about the bizarre break-in at Office Shack that took place earlier this morning," a man behind a desk said. "More troubling for law enforcement than the value of the stolen merchandise is what officers found on the checkout counter; for reasons unknown, the perpetrator left hundreds of counterfeit five-dollar bills in plain sight."

Spooky sagged back against the door to the lodge. She had thought leaving money would help. Instead, she had implicated herself in another crime.

"Although the fakes were able to replicate many of the five-dollar bill's security features, including weight, texture, and watermarks, they were distinguished from genuine bills because they each had the exact same serial number. Real bills of any denomination have unique serial numbers, while those left at Office Shack all had the same eight digits, in the exact same order.

"Police say they require further analysis, but these near-perfect fakes suggest a sophisticated counterfeiting operation, capable of duping even cautious inspectors. Are other local businesses and residents holding thousands in counterfeit? Is a counterfeiting ring operating locally in Root Park? More after the break."

She could have smashed the phone as a commercial for laundry detergent played, taking up a precious twenty seconds. The battery was low, and Trevor might come looking for her at any moment. Then the man behind the desk was back. This time, the camera was zoomed out to show both him and his female co-anchor.

"We're discussing the latest development in the Office Shack break-in—counterfeit five-dollar bills, left on the counter. With the sophistication of these fakes, it's clear the thieves could have purchased the stolen merchandise without attracting attention. Instead, they chose to expose their counterfeiting capabilities to the local authorities, brazenly leaving the evidence in plain sight."

"That's odd," the woman said.

"It is odd, Diane." The man stared down the camera. "And it gets even stranger—the lab has informed us that each of the fake bills bears an identical thumbprint over Lincoln's nose. Considering the unabashed placement of the counterfeit, the minimal merchandise taken from a store full of valuable electronics, and the intentional nature of the thumbprint, the police are now considering that this crime might be some kind of political statement."

"Now, that's asking for trouble!" Diane touched her neck-bow.

"Very bold indeed, Diane. An inside source tells us the thumbprint on each fake could represent the perpetrators 'thumbing their nose' at the police, the government, or perhaps, even the tech industry. Regardless, this crime is being treated as a taunt to local police. The police department has assured us it will be pursued with all their resources until a perpetrator is brought to justice."

Diane made some comment, but Spooky didn't hear it.

Her thumbprint was on the five-dollar bill she had put on the counter. Now it was on every single bill Carcass had copied from the original. Her thumbprint—a thousand of her thumbprints—were in evidence at the police station. She had never been fingerprinted in connection with a crime, but she didn't have to be. Just like every other driver in the state of Colorado, she had submitted her thumbprint to the DMV when she got her driver's license at sixteen.

Maybe if they only had footage of her outside the building, she could still argue she was a bystander. But there was no claiming she wasn't involved with her thumbprint on a thousand counterfeit bills found inside the store.

She was never going to get a chance to start over. She was going to prison.

Spooky wandered into the lodge in a daze, leaving the trash bag and the keys in the dirt.

The man was still working on the break room door. The blank TV screen taunted her from behind his back. It was only a matter of time before the police showed the footage to the camp administration, or a counselor saw it online somewhere. It was only a matter of time before they compared the thumbprint with the DMV's records.

All her plans after high school, all her effort to get through Dodgson—none of it mattered anymore. All because of a stupid, selfish god, who only cared about his own entertainment. The choice he had given her wasn't a choice at all—if she had refused to take the computer from Office Shack, she would still be his storyteller. Either way, she had no future. Either way, she would have ended up in a cage.

Before she could think twice about what she was doing, Spooky ran through the open door of the break room. She dove under the desk and yanked out the Ethernet cord from the router and the power cord from the wall.

If Carcass wanted the internet so badly, he could come back and get it.

As soon as she was out of the room, Spooky regretted having gone in. She meandered toward the cafeteria, feet placed at odd angles as she almost changed course with every step.

She had unplugged the internet. Carcass's internet. The internet she had risked everything to connect in the first place.

Trevor was waiting for her in the cafeteria with crossed arms.

"One scuff for being slow," he said. "I don't care if you were sick earlier. The nurse cleared you. It'll be four more if you're not done at the bell."

Spooky nodded, wide-eyed and numb.

By the time she ripped three black trash bags off the lips of their bins and dragged them down the hallway, the man from Joanne's Repairs was gone. The break room door was fixed, with a plate screwed over the claw marks, fresh hinges, and a pristine brushed-steel handle. She jiggled it. The ability to change her mind was locked inside.

Spooky had never considered herself to be impulsive, but she couldn't think of a better word to describe what she had just done. After everything she had gone through to get rid of Carcass, she had purposefully poked the orange bull. If he tried to log on and found himself facing a blank screen, who was the first person he'd come looking for? Then what would she do?

She had an inkling of a rationale—if she was going to escape conviction, she would need divine intervention. She needed a full do-over of the last twenty-four hours, memory modification, or some other magic. It was Carcass who had demanded the computer, broken into Office Shack, and created the counterfeit. He should help her escape the consequences.

The glaring problem was, of course, that he wouldn't care.

Carcass had made it very clear he had no investment in her well-being or freedom. He had been more than willing to threaten those things himself. So, if he liked the internet enough to come find out why it wasn't working, the only one he'd be here to help would be himself.

She heaved the trash bags into the dumpster and returned to the mop. She swung it around the room in a constant twirling stumble. It was the only thing holding her up.

On the other hand, if he really liked the internet, that gave her some leverage. He was eight thousand years behind the times. He wouldn't know why he had lost connection. She could help him troubleshoot. She could be his divine help desk. But, she could argue, only if she wasn't behind bars.

Carcass had proven he was capable of keeping a deal. He had said he would leave her alone when she gave him a computer with internet access, and he had. Maybe she could make a new deal. Not based on some concern for her he didn't have, or guilt he didn't feel, but based on his own interest in remaining entertained without interruption.

There were too many ifs for this sliver of a possibility to feel like hope, but Spooky turned it around in her mind like a precious object. If she could make a strong enough case that he needed her, maybe he could make it like Office Shack never happened.

"That's four more scuffs," Trevor told her as he collected the keys at the last bell. She still hadn't put away the mop and bucket or finished stacking the chairs. "I might have overlooked it given the loss of a shift mate, but you took your time."

Spooky nodded and made what she hoped was a remorseful face. She had too many things running through her mind to worry about five scuffs.

"Also, no outdoor therapy for you today."

"Really?" She was so tired her eyelids were hard to lift. Scaling, piling, and dragging tires for the next three hours sounded impossible.

"Really. You're going to have your individual meeting, ahead of schedule."

Spooky dug her nails into her arm behind her back. Her third individual meeting wasn't supposed to be until next week. Getting called in sooner couldn't be a good thing.

"Well, hurry up. Activity center, office 3A."

Outside, lines of campers trudged toward the recreation area. Spooky walked across the current. When she tried to pick the reason for her crawling skin or her knotted stomach, her mind flipped through a catalog of options that only made her feel dizzy and worse. At this point, she didn't know what to be more afraid of.

Maybe the local police had shared the security footage with the Dodgsons, and this "individual meeting" was a ploy to arrest her.

Maybe Carcass wouldn't show up.

Or maybe he would.

Luke's white-blond hair stood out in the crowd of down-turned faces. His light eyes shifted back and forth as his bow-shaped mouth moved. He was talking to someone in the subtle way campers did when they didn't want a counselor to notice, muttering a stream of words without looking at the listener.

Spooky had a million more important things to worry about than Luke, but for a moment she paused. Maybe he was saying something about her.

It seemed like a silly thought, until she saw Bree's telltale yellow curls floating next to him. Bree, who had all too recently asked Spooky about her late-night exploits.

Spooky backed up until she was in their path. Yesterday, she would have ducked away, deferring to his interest in a gorgeous girl like Bree. But today, she was embracing a new impulsive side. She didn't think she liked Luke, but she knew she didn't like seeing him talking to another girl less than twelve hours after they had kissed.

Plus, there was one other reason Izeah Dodgson might have moved up their meeting—Luke could have ratted on her for being out of bed last night.

The pair strolled closer, but neither of them looked at Spooky. She put her shoulders back.

"Hey," she projected when they were a few feet away.

Luke jumped.

"I'll see you later, Luke," Bree said.

Spooky kept her eyes on Luke as Bree swayed past. "Can we talk for a second?"

Luke recovered himself and scowled at her. "I have to get to outdoor therapy."

"I'll walk with you," she said, even though she should have been going in the opposite direction.

"Seriously Spooky, what for? Screw you." His thin nose and carved cheekbones seemed haughtier today, and his voice had a nasal whine. "I'm stuck cleaning toilets. My parents are selling my car."

"Sneaking out was your idea."

"Yeah, well, you weren't worth it. Just stay away from me."

Her stomach twisted. Whatever feelings had been building over the last two weeks had dissolved under his excessive use of tongue. It didn't matter if he didn't like her either.

She almost let him walk away but sped up to keep pace. "I will. I just need to know if you told anyone I was out of bed last night."

"Of course I didn't."

"You told Bree." It was a guess, but it seemed likely.

"I didn't tell the counselors, I mean." He glared at her. "Just stay away from me. Or I might change my mind."

It was a threat he probably wouldn't keep, but this time, she let him go. She pivoted and backtracked through the thinning campers toward the activity center.

She crept up the front steps. She couldn't stop herself from picturing cops bursting out of the multi-purpose rooms to take her down. It would do wonders for her reputation at Dodgson to be led out of the camp in handcuffs, even though she wouldn't get to enjoy the notoriety for very long.

But the hallway stayed empty. The only open door was the office at the end—Izeah Dodgson's office.

She hadn't known it orientation day, but Izeah and Adam were like the sun and the moon. Izeah made himself a daily presence for the campers, blazing with energy as he delivered speeches about trust and potential. Just as he could warm, he could burn—if smiles failed, he blustered and turned bright red as he screamed out scuffs.

Adam stayed in the background. After orientation day, he mostly existed in her peripheral vision, or as the occasional distant figure crossing the camp. He materialized to deliver punishment when trust wasn't enough, but with none of Izeah's heat. Spooky had never heard him raise his voice. The moon stayed calm, even as it brought wave after wave of the tide up to your neck.

While Adam Dodgson's office was in the out-of-bounds administrative building, Izeah's was in the center of camp. It was labeled "Office 3A," but it appeared to be a repurposed closet.

Izeah was alone in the room, reviewing papers on his half-sized desk. That was a good sign. If she was in big trouble, like getting kicked out of camp trouble, Adam Dodgson would be here too. He hadn't lifted his bald head, so she tapped on the door.

Izeah glanced up with a scowl on his face, then swapped it for a smile. "Camper Laurel! Come in! Come in!"

She sat on the edge of the plastic chair across from him.

"So! How the heck are ya?" His head bobbed like it was on a spring.

"I'm good, Mr. Dodgson."

"Oh please, Mr. Dodgson is my brother. Call me Izzy!"

"Okay," she said, resolving to never call him anything.

He opened a blue folder with her name on it, grinning. "You're a good camper, little lady! Your scuff trajectory is solid. Your name never comes up in our staff meetings." He raised his eyebrows and gazed at her over his glasses. "Which is a good thing." He threw his head back like they'd just shared the most delicious joke.

Even for Izeah, this was a weird level of exuberance.

She twitched a smile back at him. "I, uh, thought we weren't meeting until next week."

"Oh yes, we moved your meeting up a smidge." He closed her folder. "I thought maybe, after the day you've had, we should check in."

"The day I've had?"

"Well, for example, we just shuffled your shift mate. Don't worry, we are aware that cafeteria duty is not a one-camper job, even for a good camper like yourself! We just need to rearrange a few things. It might take another half a day, no biggie."

Campers changed work duties all the time. That shouldn't have warranted an early individual meeting. She waited.

He pushed the bridge of his glasses, even though they were so tight he had a permanent indentation in his temples. "And I heard you visited the nurse earlier."

"Yes."

"Well, so, how are you feeling then?"

"Fine."

"Good, good. Because I know while you were visiting the nurse, we had an incident. Just wanted to make sure that wasn't disturbing for you. And that you were handling it well."

He must have been referring to the camper with the bloody eye. "Um, yeah fine."

"Good, good." He touched his glasses and tapped the folder on his desk, even though it didn't need straightening. "And have you... mentioned it to anyone?"

There it was. That's why she had been called in today. Spooky wanted to melt back in the chair, but she was careful not to move.

She had witnessed the aftermath of one camper's bloody attack on another. Phone calls were supposedly "disruptive to rehabilitation," but occasionally, someone's parents insisted on talking live. Izeah wanted to make sure she wouldn't tell her parents or hadn't told anyone else who would worry theirs.

"No. Well, not yet...it was a little disturbing."

"Oh?"

"Yeah, I mean, there was a lot of blood. I got a few scuffs at lunch because I was distracted. I didn't finish my tasks on time."

"That's perfectly understandable." Izeah waved his hand. "Given how your day went, we'll just wipe away those scuffs from lunch, won't we?"

Spooky nodded and wrapped her arm over her stomach as if thinking about it made her queasy.

"Good, good. We want you to continue to be successful here. I know it's a juicy tidbit to talk about, but can I trust you to join us in respecting the privacy of those involved? You'll make sure if you want to talk to anyone about the incident, you come talk to me first?"

"Yes, sir."

"Izzy." He smiled and held it.

"Yes, yes I will, Izzy."

"Good!" He slapped the table. "Fantastic. I've got my next individual meeting in a few minutes, and I think we're done here. Now, where are you supposed to be..." He checked his watch and then rocked back in his chair. "You look a little tired. Why don't you just go have a nap in your cabin for the rest of outdoor therapy time? And we'll add it to the list of our little secrets!"

Now that was an allowance she hadn't expected. Maybe the boy had lost his eye.

"Thank you, Mr....Izzy."

"Sure thing. Keep deserving our trust now." He gave her a wink so pronounced, it would have knocked off his glasses if they weren't molded into his skull. He pointed a finger at her. "Or else! Just kidding, just kidding. Don't be late for dinner. Get outta here. Scoot."

He laughed her out of the room.

# CHAPTER XI
# WIN-WIN

As soon as she laid down on her bunk, Spooky wondered if she would make it to dinner at all. She wondered if she would ever be able to get up again.

She glanced at the phone, but the screen was blank. The battery had finally died.

It was alarming what a single night without sleep could do to a body. Her eyes ached even when she closed them. She never slept on her back, but she was too tired to roll over. All the things she might think about and worry about and plan for faded. The world fuzzed out as she sunk into darkness.

"Are you dead?" a deep voice said.

Spooky's whole body seized and her eyes snapped open. She whipped her head toward the voice. From curled horns, to rounded shoulders, to draped robes, the figure was unmistakable—Carcass was backlit in the cabin's open entrance.

"Apparently not." He glided into the cabin. "You were very still."

"Carcass!" Spooky swung her shaking legs to the floor. She could feel her pulse in every limb. He had come back. This was her chance to get his help. This was her chance to fix everything.

In the daylight, he looked like a CGI character in a movie. Her eyes couldn't interpret his massive frame and toady face and white horns and pumpkin skin as real. The figure before her had to be a hologram, a costume, or a video hoax. He took a seat on the counselor's bed, which creaked and moaned under his weight.

Even though she had invited his return, it was hard to breathe.

He could save her, or he could make everything worse. He had the power to crush her, kidnap her, or turn her into a bird feeder.

She shook her head. As long as she had leverage, they should be able to have a conversation.

"So, you're back," she said, as if a visit from a god was the most ordinary thing in the world. She picked at the thin comforter draped over the edge of her bunk. "Why are you back?"

"The internet stopped working," he said in a flat tone.

"I see. That can happen sometimes." She couldn't read anything in his expression. He didn't seem upset. "And were you...enjoying the internet?"

He nodded. "It is the greatest thing I have encountered since I was born in the void."

"Great! Great, great, great. Yes, it's very popular here too." She gripped her knees. This was her opportunity. This was her chance to make a trade. He loved the internet, and he didn't know she was the reason it wasn't working.

Spooky tapped her chin, making a show of thinking. "I might be able to fix it for you."

"Is that so?" He tilted his head.

"Uh, yes. There are a number of things that can go wrong with modern technology. You know, it's..." She wiggled her fingers in the air. "Complicated. But I can almost definitely figure it out."

"Mm. You can figure it out."

"Yep. But, in order to help you...there is something I need you to help me with first."

He blinked his glassy eyes. "Is that so."

"Uh, yeah. Yeah, now that I think about it. Yep."

"And what is it you need help with?"

"Well, the thing is..." She hadn't had time to prepare for this moment. She just had to keep talking and hope it would come out right. "You know how we stole the computer from Office Shack?"

"Stole?" He raised an eyebrow. "I recall legitimizing our acquisition with modern tender."

"You can't just break into a store and leave cash. And they could tell the money we left was fake."

"Fake? It was as real as anything in this world. Zero modifications, whatsoever, from the molecular structure of the original."

"Well, that's actually the problem. The bills should have had different serial numbers. The point is, you aren't allowed to make your own money, and they know that we did. It's a crime." She sighed. "What I'm saying is, I am going to get in trouble, big trouble, for last night. I'll probably be arrested and sent to prison."

"Is that so?" He tilted his head further. He seemed more curious than sorry for her, but she hadn't expected sympathy.

"Yes. And if I'm in prison, I won't be able to help you with your computer or the internet. So, I'd like to propose that we help each other—you use your godly powers to make sure I don't get blamed for anything that happened last night, and I'll help make sure your internet starts working again." She spread her hands. "What do you think?"

"Mm, you want to ensure you aren't blamed for stealing the computer?"

"...Or for leaving the fence, or for breaking the window, or for the counterfeit. Basically, anything that happened since I met you. And then I'm free to help you fix the internet! It's a win-win."

"And if I don't agree to this 'win-win,' the internet remains unfixed. And you...?"

"Will go to prison." Spooky inhaled a shaky breath. "You cared enough about stories to abduct me. All you have to do is help me this once, and you'll have the internet again. Isn't that worth it?"

The corners of his lips pulled up, revealing yellow-brick teeth. "Oh, it is, most assuredly."

"Whew." She exhaled and a giddy laugh rose in her chest. "Then let's just talk about how you're going to..."

"However." He raised a hand to silence her. "I have already plugged in the power cord and reinserted the Ethernet cable into the router."

"You...you did?"

"I did." His grin widened. "Isn't that fortunate?"

She hadn't taught him how to do that. So much for lording the mysteries of technology over him.

"Yeah," she said. "That's good, glad you fixed it. But there are a lot of things that can go wrong with technology. If I'm in prison..."

"I will visit and ask you for your advice as I require it." His smile stretched even further.

"You could. You could do that." Her heart beat faster. This was her only option. She had to keep trying. "But if I'm not here to help, anyone could find and unplug the cords."

"Besides you, you mean?"

Her mouth opened and closed. His glassy expression disappeared, and glee shone in every fold of his face. He had known she had been the one to disconnect the internet from the beginning of this conversation. She hadn't fooled him for a second.

She had no leverage, and now she was at his mercy again.

"How lucky for me that there are a multitude of doors between your world and mine," he continued. "Given the prevalence of the internet on Earth, I'm sure a great number of them open near similar points of connection. Not to worry, when you are in prison, I will find another router and electrical socket where I'm sure no one will unplug what I need."

He was enjoying this.

Spooky shoved her palms into her eyes. "If you don't need me, why are you even here? Did you just come to gloat?"

"Now, that is the crux of this delightful exchange, isn't it? Why am I here?"

She lifted her face off her hands and glared at him.

"Think about it, Spooky. If I knew how to reconnect the internet on my own, and do not require your help with technology now or in the future, then why did I come here to find you?"

"To make fun of me?"

"Not only that. I wanted to know why you interfered with my

internet connection. I thought perhaps you needed something. And indeed you do."

She hid her face again.

"Well, I have something that I need as well. And now I have a trade of my own to propose. A slightly different 'win-win.'"

Almost anything would be better than waiting for the police to come. She peeked up. "What is it?"

"Help me maintain continued access to the internet, and I will ensure you aren't held accountable for any of last night's events."

"What? Yes! I mean...what? That's exactly what I offered you!"

He shook his head. "No amount of cords between our worlds will keep me connected. But maybe there is a way, with the help of a human."

She narrowed her eyes. "What sort of help?"

"Do you remember when I told you that there was but one god of this world?"

"Yes."

"And that I told you Earth is a High Order world?"

"Yes. I don't know what that means, but I remember."

"The Orders describe general categories of creation. You might think of a Low Order world as a puppet show: beings exist in a physical space, but nothing happens without the constant hand of a creator. A Middle Order world is more like a play: the director could be sleeping and the show would continue, but the actors would only follow the cues and script preset for them.

"A High-Order world is life as you know it: it is a self-contained system of change, without the need for divine puppet strings or a director to step in to make new things happen. Every being on Earth comes into existence, lives as it will, and fades away without direct divine interaction." He paused. "There are shades of orders in between, but generally, that is the distinction—the level of intervention required for that world to, as you say, turn."

"Okay..." Spooky would have to set aside processing that there were enough worlds to require categorization. "What do world 'orders' have to do with me?"

"This information is relevant for two reasons: firstly, Earth does not require the constant attention or presence of its god. Nothing illustrates this better than your own unawareness. Your creator is so distant from your daily movements that you did not even know you had one."

"Is that normal on other worlds? To know your god?"

"Yes, you are uniquely ignorant." Carcass nodded. "Secondly, High Order worlds are attractive. Gods travel through the void to visit new worlds for entertainment, inspiration, and a bevy of other reasons. The most popular destinations are those of the High Order. Most gods pass through foreign worlds unnoticed, as this choice proves the most polite to the resident creator. Some gods may interfere, either with the originator's permission, or by avoiding detection. And, more rarely, one god may try to overtake the world of another.

"Ordinarily, such clashes for control do not take place. A world is remarkable because the god who created it is powerful. Although High Order worlds may be desirable, lesser gods cannot hope to claim them. The Lower Order worlds of weaker gods are simpler to conquer, but those who could overtake them can fare better with their own creations. These simple truths of hierarchy maintain order. Do you understand?"

"Yes, I think so. But why..."

"An impressive and complex world such as Earth would normally be impossible to take by force. But it would be all too tempting if left undefended. Which brings me to my problem." He looked as serious as she'd ever seen him, the lines on his face creasing in shadow as he inclined forward, tawny eyes unblinking. "No one has seen the god of Earth for a very long time."

"Did they...expect to?" Spooky rubbed her arms. "You said High Order worlds kind of run themselves."

"When visiting gods began meddling, yes, one would have expected Earth's creator to appear and annihilate them. When no creator appeared, ambitious and envious gods grew bolder. When those challenges also went unmet, word across the universe spread—Earth has been abandoned."

"Abandoned." Spooky repeated the word flatly. "Abandoned?"

"By your god."

"Right...but what does that mean, exactly?"

"It means it is free for the taking. Surely, you've noticed that things on Earth are changing? Humans cause themselves a lot of misery, but they are not at the core of every modern plague."

Spooky jerked her shoulders up and down.

"The temperature on Earth is growing warmer, is it not? That is helped along by Tultoti, a beast who lives in a world of fire, whispering hot breath into human ears. There is a god called Cannibal who eats all that he creates and loves delicacies from High Order worlds. I hear he has been at work in your food industry, filling your bodies with ingredients that will enhance your flavor."

"You can't be serious. How do you know all this?"

"The signs aren't hidden if you know what to look for. Tultoti, Cannibal, Yazerob, Leber—I have confirmed the presence of four disruptive entities. And I suspect at least three others as well." He waved his hand. "Let it be enough for you to know that other gods are here. Terraforming, altering, shifting, whispering...remaking this world into something they desire.

"Thus far, the manipulation has been subtle. Even I only took a human when she was alone, in the event that witnesses could attract the god of Earth's attention. No one is sure the god of Earth is really gone. No one has made an overt play."

Spooky couldn't ignore a troubling possibility. "And you?"

"Me what?"

"Are you here to 'make a play'? Bigger than kidnapping me?"

He scoffed. "No. Why would I tell you this if I were?"

"I don't know. Why *are* you telling me this?"

"I'm getting to that. Very soon, visiting gods will not show restraint. They will set this world on fire, or devour it, or switch the charge of atomic particles, or turn man against man and create a bloody battlefield. The territory that once fostered your flourishing will be twisted and almost definitely bring your destruction. And your brilliant inventions." His voice caught and his eyes raised toward the ceiling. "Will be extinguished forever."

"You're talking about the internet, aren't you."

"What else?" He looked back at her. "I am the god of a Middle Order world, Spooky. I am the director who is only able to watch his own play. The internet has exceeded my greatest aspirations for entertainment and joy. I thought the time Earth has remaining would be enough for me. But your little router prank showed me that every hour without connection will feel like another eight thousand years of boredom. And so, I have only pulled myself away from the internet now to find a solution."

Spooky twisted and untwisted her fingers.

"Okay. Earth is abandoned. Which is bad." She shook her head as if that could help all this otherworldly information find a place. "So how are you going to fix it?"

"I am not."

"Then what are you going to..."

"You are."

"...I am what?"

"This is the trade I am proposing—I will make it like last night never happened, if you do what I ask to save Earth."

"Um..." She scanned his face for the joke. "That doesn't sound very realistic."

"I have a plan."

"And why doesn't the plan have you doing the world-saving?"

"The plan requires a human."

"Okay, then go find a human."

"I already have."

"Me?" Spooky laughed. "You think I'm going to be able to stop evil gods from invading Earth? Really?"

He shrugged. "I could abduct another human, but I think it will be much more effective to send someone who is personally committed to the endeavor. Of course, all humans should have an interest in their species' survival, but with a new captive there is always screaming and crying, and less action than is required at this late stage."

"The fact that you even know that..."

"And besides." He gestured toward her with a nine-fingered hand. "Who better than you?"

"Who better than me..." She shook her head again. Now he was being absurd. "I can think of a lot of people better than me, actually. A scientist. An astronaut. A black belt. Somebody. I don't know... anybody. Literally, any functioning member of society, which, by the way, I'm not."

"Spooky, you are overestimating the importance of *who* you are, compared to *what* you are." He arched one pointed black nail and scratched his chin. "That may be the opposite lesson of every story humans like to tell themselves about personal qualities and special strengths. But in this case, it's true. You are human. That is enough."

"But there has to be someone better."

"Are you human?"

"Yes, but I'm not a..."

"Are you able to follow basic instructions?"

"Sometimes."

"Are you motivated to follow my instructions in exchange for freedom from prison, if not the continued existence of your species?"

"Not just freedom from prison," she said. If he was going to suggest nonsensical trades, she was at least going to get what she needed out of the impossible bargain. "I can't be held responsible for anything that happened last night—not leaving the camp, not breaking into the lodge, not anything that happened at Office Shack."

"Understood. And speaking of qualifications, any human bold enough to try to trick a god into helping her by unplugging his internet connection will be perfectly suited to the task."

Her ears burned.

He lifted a hand and shrugged. "But, if you refuse, I will engage another human to assist me. And, assuming we're successful, you can enjoy the resulting longevity of your world from prison."

He shifted like he was going to stand up.

"Hold on," she said. He smiled. She hated that smile. "Let's imagine I was willing to help get rid of the evil gods, or whatever. What would I have to do?"

"You would need to send a message to the god of Earth. With a single appearance, all of these opportunists would flee back to their own Lower creations."

"And how would 'I' get him a message?"

"I don't have time to explain the plan to one who will not undertake it."

"This is suddenly so urgent you don't even have time to explain?"

"As soon as one god makes a public move and goes unchallenged, the others will strike. Earth will be torn apart in days. I had only hoped to enjoy a few evenings of entertainment by the fire and get out before the end began."

"So, last night, you knew the world was ending."

"And now, at the point of this happy reunion, I am unwilling to let it happen. You have but one god in the universe that is both here and on humanity's side. I suggest you accept my help. But you have to act."

"Well, I need to know if I can even do anything about it before I say yes."

"I told you the objective: send a message to the god of Earth."

"And I asked you how."

"For one truly committed to a goal, there is no possibility that could stand between her and success."

"That...definitely is not true."

"Spooky, think on what I have said. There are preparations that require my attention. I have a role to play as well." He opened his wide left hand. "If we have a deal, and you are willing to do as I say, come through the door between our worlds before the sun disappears from the sky." He presented his right. "If you are unwilling to act on behalf of your world, I will leave you to your imprisonment, and find another who is." He closed both hands. "I will search until humanity is either lost or has its champion."

He floated up to his full height and settled on the ground.

"Think hard, Spooky. What is your world worth to you?"

Carcass disappeared.

# CHAPTER XII
# SUNDOWN

After a few more seconds staring at the spot where Carcass had vanished, Spooky's shoulders sagged, and she melted back onto the bed. She was, by all appearances, alone in the cabin once more.

That hadn't gone according to plan.

Was the world really in danger from a fire beast or a cannibal god? She pictured a ball of flames and a gaping mouth full of teeth. The images were fuzzy, and maybe even a little funny. They didn't feel real. At the very least, they felt far away.

She turned onto her side and swiped a hand to brush her bent ear flat.

But then, Carcass was real. If someone had tried to tell her about Carcass a day ago, she would have laughed or rolled her eyes. Other gods being here and wanting something from life on Earth was no stranger than Carcass kidnapping her or surfing the internet for stories.

The world felt big, but what if there was something bigger? What if other beings, shadowy and mountainous, emerged from the woods? Hungry, with feet the size of houses, and heads that blocked out the sun? Beings that could overtake any boat or plane or escape car? Beings with abilities that could wipe out any human army?

Her bones tingled. It was like she was crossing the dark field again and looking up at the stars. On the other side of that awe and wonder was the sister sensation—fear. What if they really were abandoned? What if gods descended to tear the world apart, and there was nowhere safe to hide?

If there really were monsters shuffling at the edge of the world, waiting to strike, it was too big a problem for any one human to handle.

She shook her head, nuzzling into the scratchy mattress cover. She couldn't be the only one who knew about this. If gods were here, trying to influence nations and industries, scientists must have picked up some sign. Entire governments might be aware of the "gods on Earth" problem. That was exactly the kind of thing to conceal from the public and resolve quietly, like aliens, or a comet collision. There were probably task forces working through the night, with bombs at the ready.

Even if no one else knew, and Earth was about to become a battlefield, what exactly was she going to be able to do about it?

She jerked as the next bell rang. She had about five minutes before the cabin would flood with sweaty, grumpy girls. This was her cue to wash up and rush off to dinner service. She considered playing sick, but after her surprise session with Izeah, she didn't think she would get more rest without unwanted attention.

It was absurd how the world kept expecting her to participate when everything was falling apart.

Somehow, she staggered to the cafeteria. All the bruises from the last twenty-four hours reminded her they still existed under her clothes. The sun hovered above the tree line. By the end of dinner, it would be setting. By the time she finished post-dinner cleanup, it would be dark.

And Carcass would be expecting her.

Trevor greeted her as she entered the lodge. "Camper Laurel. Meet your new shift mate, Camper Elliot." A guy with wavy brown hair and rosy cheeks stood to one side. "For tonight, he is going to shadow you on all duties. I'll split up assignments tomorrow."

Trevor left her alone with her new shift mate.

"I'm Elliot Hall."

"Spooky."

His ready smile and raised eyebrows made him look like a kicked puppy. He was tall enough to avoid being targeted physically, but with an expression like that, she didn't wonder why he had a bruise on one flushed cheek. He was looking her over too. His eyes lingered on her ears. She reached one hand up to adjust her hair and turned away.

Ordinarily, Spooky would be anxious about turning her back on a new camper, but tonight she didn't have any nerves to spare. Besides, they only trusted nonviolent campers to be near the kitchens and food. If this guy wanted to psychologically torture her, he'd have to get in line.

She put on her smock and gloves and pointed him to his gear. She started unstacking chairs, and he did the same. He might have said something else, but her mind was on the setting sun.

There were only a few hours left.

Carcass had said he needed a human, but what did he need a human to do? It couldn't be as easy as say, praying, or he would have just told her that. Contacting the god of Earth was probably difficult or dangerous. Like, "stop your heart so you can talk to god," dangerous. He had outmaneuvered her in negotiations. Now he was trying to trick her into saying yes before learning about her end of the bargain.

She finished the setup and serving and scooped this and that onto a tray. She sat in the first open chair she saw and ignored the sideways glances from other campers at the table. She spooned whatever into her mouth and kept an eye on the hallway that led to the back door. It was locked now, but at the end of dinner, Trevor would give her the key.

Carcass would only help her if she went down that hallway and didn't come back.

From one perspective, her impulsive plan had worked. Carcass cared about the internet enough to come back. He had agreed to help her in exchange for continued access.

The minor kink in her plan was that continued access meant she had to go on a mystery mission to stop evil gods.

She snorted into a scoop of mashed potatoes. It would have been even funnier if he wasn't serious. She stabbed her foam spork into the pile of starch and wiped her face.

If she didn't accept Carcass's trade, she was going to prison. After two months at Dodgson, she felt like she could imagine that outcome in all too much detail. Every day, she would slog through sweat and fear. Every day, she would count the hours. It was the end of any kind of aspiration for something better.

Spooky pushed away her tray and closed her eyes. She was sitting in the cafeteria of a penitentiary. The voices around her were the other inmates. After dinner, she would go back to her cell. She could feel the receiver in her hand as she waited for her one phone call to connect. She could hear the click after her parents told her not to call back. She could see herself standing in a courtroom. The seats behind her would all be empty.

As much as prison sounded like the end of a future, at least she could picture it.

She rubbed her skull through her hair. Prison she could imagine. But strolling out back, opening a door to another world, and putting herself at the mercy of Carcass? Her image of herself went off the map. Like she was agreeing to disappear. Like dying. She didn't even know what to envision, plan for, or be afraid of.

Izeah said some words she didn't hear. Everyone shuffled and stood. One girl with pigtails whacked a taller girl across the face with her tray. Spooky retreated toward the kitchen as the counselors swarmed.

She searched for the sun through the window. The trees were dark against the graying sky.

What if she had to follow some ancient map or solve riddles? What if she had to outmaneuver or fight a god? Even if all it took to reach the god of Earth was prayer, she still wasn't the best humanity had to offer. She didn't know any special words or rituals. No matter what the mystery mission required, there was someone else out there who was more likely to succeed.

Carcass hadn't listened to her numerous valid points about being unqualified. He didn't care what happened to her. He only cared about getting a human to do what he wanted.

She had barely escaped Carcass the first time. He might have refused to let her return to Dodgson to get the phone. He easily could have lost patience with the hunt for a computer and taken her back to his house in the clearing. If things had gone a little differently, she would still be there right now, hungry and hoarse, curling up to sleep with the birds in his aviary. Engaging in another bargain when she had even less control over whether or not she succeeded was unthinkable. This time, she at least had the choice to stay on Earth.

She started cleanup, barely registering Elliot trailing behind her. Soon, Trevor would pop his head out of the kitchen and offer her the key to take out the trash.

She had no way of checking the news to see if the police had a suspect, but there was still hope she had overestimated their chances of finding her. Maybe the DMV wasn't allowed to share fingerprint data, or the camp administration would never see the tape. Maybe the police would bungle the evidence. Maybe she could just get through Dodgson and go home, like she had planned.

If she went out to the dumpsters now and didn't come back, they would think she found some way off the grounds. She would max out. They would probably contact the police to search for her. Everything would come crashing down that much faster.

But maybe everything would be fine if she stayed.

She clutched the table she had just wiped and leaned against it, as if it could anchor her in this world. She wasn't going anywhere.

By the time Trevor held out the keys and the trash from the kitchen, it was the wrong side of sunset. The deadline had passed. Carcass had said he wanted her to come willingly, but if she went near the dumpsters, alone, he might change his mind. It seemed unwise to get close to the door.

"Umm, Elliot, right?" She held out the trash and the keys. "Luke, my last shift mate, always took the trash. I know we haven't split up duties yet..."

He smiled. "Sure, I'll do it."

"Great! This key is for the back door, this one is for the dumpsters. Make sure you lock them after. There are three cans in the dining room, plus this. And hurry, there is never much time to do it before the last bell."

She spit out the words so fast she wasn't sure if he had understood, but he nodded and put out his hand. She almost held onto the keys at the last second. Her fingers flailed and they dropped into his open palm. He turned and walked down the hall, leaving her alone with the mop.

She closed her eyes and breathed in and out through her nose. It was done. She wasn't going through the door between the dumpsters. She wasn't going to accept Carcass's deal.

She finished putting away the mop and bucket as the last bell rang. She returned her smock and threw her gloves and hairnet in the garbage.

Her feet dragged on the way to the cabins. Her body did a poor job of shivering off the nighttime chill. She took her five-minute shift at the sink. The toothpaste foamed and she closed her eyes. A black and white image of her outside Office Shack flashed on her lids, and they snapped open again.

She fell into bed. She curled into a ball under the covers. Visions of Carcass silhouetted at the cabin entrance blurred into dreams.

SOMETHING JOLTED her out of deep sleep. It was light. She had no way of knowing if it had been ten minutes or ten hours. She rolled over and shielded her eyes; floodlights lit the ring of cabins. Across the circle, she could see other girls shifting in their bunks.

"Line up, campers," Cabin-leader Lucy called. She was already standing, with a radio at her hip. "Headcount."

Spooky dragged herself up, feeling like she had been punched in both eyes and the back of the head. She managed to stand, swaying, until Lucy counted her off the list.

She hit the bed and fell asleep before she was even sure whether or not it had been a dream.

ANOTHER BELL RANG, and Spooky opened her eyes to soft morning light. Blanketed bodies around her groaned and rustled.

She wiggled her toes in the cold mountain air. Nothing else had disturbed her in the night. Carcass hadn't come to steal her away. It seemed he had kept his word and let her choose whether or not to help him. That also meant he would leave her to whatever fate awaited her here on Earth. That fate was still in question, but waking up on a new day, she felt as if a spell had been broken. Maybe she had finally passed the last of the tests from the other night.

Spooky sped through her morning routine and headed for the main lodge, ready for a boring, predictable day at Dodgson. She wore a long baseball t-shirt to cover the contours of the dead phone and scissors. Carrying them around presented a greater risk than benefit at this point, but she couldn't leave them in her bunk in case of another search. She would slip them into a trash bag during cleanup.

She was halfway through breakfast prep before she remembered the new guy was supposed to help her. Trevor hadn't mentioned it, so she kept working. His absence wouldn't be her scuffs to worry about. She finished putting chairs around the final table as the breakfast bell rang. She took her position beside the oatmeal station and held up her serving spoon.

After a few moments, she lowered the spoon. No hungry delinquents had filed in. The cafeteria was empty. She crossed the room and peeked out the double doors.

Across the grounds, campers stood motionless, facing away from the lodge. A police car drove up the central thoroughfare, followed by a golf cart. Campers on the center path shuffled out of the way as the caravan rolled past.

Spooky stumbled onto the porch.

The car stopped. Uniformed cops got out. Izeah and Adam Dodgson climbed out of the golf cart.

The bell to begin breakfast announcements rang. As if shaken out of their stupor, no less than five campers took off running. But the police weren't here for them. Adam Dodgson pointed toward the lodge. Toward her. He pulled out his radio.

Spooky dropped her spoon and ran.

She jumped down the stairs and launched herself around the side of the building. She glanced back as Trevor burst out of the double doors, holding up a crackling radio.

"Laurel!"

If he caught her, she wouldn't have any choices left. She rounded what felt like an endless corner, hugging the lodge's boarded foundation.

A screeching alarm blared. One of the fleeing campers must have gone through the fence. The sound blended into the screaming in her head. Panic seized her chest and the hairs on the back of her neck rose up. Trevor was faster than her. He could tackle her to the ground at any moment.

The corner of a blue dumpster appeared. She pumped her legs harder and skidded into the area behind the lodge. She leapt between the bins, scrambling the rest of the way on her hands and knees. She clawed through the dirt and grabbed the wires.

Trevor's voice was close enough that she could hear him yelling to her over the alarm.

Spooky yanked the wires apart and threw herself into the void.

# CHAPTER XIII
# INTO THE VOID

The void caught her in its cloudy embrace. The piercing alarm still rang in her ears. She twisted her body, half expecting to see Trevor jump in after her.

The only thing floating behind her was the cords.

Even if he saw a glowing white line between the dumpsters, he wouldn't run toward it. He was probably still sprinting around the building, chasing her ghost.

Still, now that she had knocked the dirt off the wires, someone would notice them eventually. Carcass had told her he didn't need to stay connected to this particular router. She grabbed a plug between extension cords and pulled it out of its socket. The Ethernet cable didn't have a convenient breaking point, but she still had the scissors in her waistband. Touching only the rubber grip, she snipped through it. She threw the ends back toward Earth. They floated further and further out of reach, until they vanished.

Now no one could find any evidence of where she had disappeared to. They would assume she had run through one of the emergency exits and into the woods.

She shivered. Being chased made her want to throw up. The disorienting whiteness and bobbing motion weren't helping. She managed to breathe past the vomity feeling, although the pulsing in her ears didn't slow.

She hadn't planned on running. She hadn't brought any food or water, or even taken a jacket. The only extra clothes with her were her smock, gloves, and hairnet. The only tools she had on her were the dead cell phone and the scissors.

But prepared or not, now she had no choice but to help Carcass.

She had left Dodgson. She had run from the police. They would find the stolen wires, which would add to the overwhelming evidence against her. If she wanted to go back to a world where she had a home and a future, she couldn't just return to Earth. She needed a divine do-over.

The void released her, and she spilled out into gray light and dirt.

The clearing was silent. The round house puffed smoke.

"Carcass!" she called, shedding her work duty gear. "I changed my mind, I'm here now! I'll do whatever you want me to!"

She stalked up to the arched entrance and banged on the door with the side of her fist, releasing the sweet smell of cedar. The birds inside chirped and squawked.

"Carcass!"

She listened, but only the birds replied.

She hammered on it again. "I...am...ready...to...accept... your...deal!"

This had to work. He had to help her. She would break down the door if she had to. She switched to kicking, her foot bouncing off the boards.

A boom reverberated through the house.

"What are you doing to my door?" Carcass's deep voice called from above her.

He was crouching near the conical point of his roof, like a lump of chewing gum. He flattened against the planks and leapt into the air, robes billowing as he soared over her. He landed with a thump, his face spreading and chins rippling with the impact.

He popped up, softball eyes fixed on her. "Well?"

"I was...knocking."

"With your foot?"

"You weren't answering!"

He sniffed. "Not only do I come upon you beating my house, I see you have destroyed my internet connection."

Spooky glanced at the cords beside her. "I...had some people following me. You said there are plenty of doors between your world and Earth. You can find another."

"I have already implemented additional points of connection, but you interrupted some downloads. More importantly, you are very late."

"Yeah, well. I had to think about it." She shifted. "I couldn't have done anything without a night of sleep anyway."

"Hmm. And what have you decided?"

There was only one path forward now. She stood up a little straighter. "I'll accept your deal. If you make sure I'm not blamed for anything that happened the other night, running away from the police today, or going missing for however long this takes, I'll help you."

"Very well. But you must complete my plans first. You have wasted some of the limited time remaining to save Earth. Once you succeed, there will be plenty of time to vindicate you."

"Fine."

He grinned. "Then we have a deal."

She sucked in a breath. She had just made an agreement with a powerful being she didn't trust to do something she didn't even understand.

She exhaled and closed her eyes. In another month, she would leave Dodgson. She would go home and work hard her senior year. Then she would be off to a distant college and a new life.

She opened her eyes. "What do I need to do?"

"As I told you before, we need the god of Earth to make an appearance to scare off the would-be usurpers. You need to notify your god of the urgency of the situation and ask for help."

Spooky still didn't consider herself the best choice to go before any god for anything. "What makes you think he'll come when I ask?"

"My assumption is that he does not know of Earth's plight. I have been observing your world closely. So far, meddling gods have been subtle. If he is occupying himself elsewhere, presuming his creation is ticking along as usual, he may sweep back with a vengeance when you tell him of the interference."

"Okay, but what if he does know and just doesn't care?"

"In that case, I'm hoping you might move him to pity. Some gods do feel such things for their creations." Carcass shrugged. "If nothing else, you'll prove how far from his original plan Earth has strayed. He didn't inform humans he existed, much less let you travel between worlds. If not pity, your presence off Earth may move him to annoyance. And therefore, action."

"I don't know if I love the idea of annoying...god."

"I think you'll agree your other options are much worse. Your god's specific motivations are a variable, but my plan plays to the most possibilities. If you deliver the message, I will consider our deal complete. Regardless of the outcome."

"Okay, fine then." It was on Carcass whether or not his plan worked. "So where do I find him?"

"You cannot find him, because there is no way of knowing where he is. You need to seek the help of a god called Axonaphis. He has the power to communicate with any being in the universe. Visit his world, and he can get your message to the god of Earth."

"Okay. So how do I find...that guy?"

"Axonaphis," Carcass said.

"Ax-on-a-phis, right."

"The trick is to find the door. His world is through the mist that separates all worlds—through the void. Here beside my house, there could be fifty tunnels that would take us to Axonaphis. There could be thousands. There could be none. We have no way of knowing because tunnels to other worlds aren't detectable by any of the common sixteen senses." He pointed a black-tipped finger in front of her face. "Even if someone told us the passageway we need was right here, it wouldn't help. You have to find the exact particle of the universe that will open. You have to find the door."

Spooky couldn't help but contract her neck as the long finger arched toward her nose. "So how do we find the door?"

"There is but one god who can see the doors: Geyegorg of the Extraordinary Sight. He labels the doors with beacons, so that others may see them too."

Carcass pointed at the air above the wires. A spot of yellowish-green light appeared. He dragged the spot and drew a symbol, which looked like a lowercase "e" that had its crossbar interrupted by an uppercase "L" layered overtop.

"Can you see that?"

Spooky nodded at the glowing green emblem.

"That is a beacon. You might think of it as a visible knob on an invisible door. This is the specific beacon marking all the doors that lead to Earth." He reached out a hand as if to stroke it. He shook his head. "I haven't been able to see this for eight thousand years. I knew a door to Earth was here the whole time, but I couldn't see the knob to open it."

"How do you lose the ability to see something? No wait, how do you gain the ability to see something?"

"If you make a contract with Geyegorg, he infuses your eye with the light and visual blueprint of the beacon, granting you sight of it. If he wishes to end your contract, he removes it."

"Does that hurt?"

"It sizzles." Carcass shrugged. "Regardless, it's the only way. Once he gives you the beacon to Axonaphis's world, it will be a simple matter of looking around for the nearest door and going through. The only question is what you will have to pay."

"Pay? To have something put in my eye?"

"Pay for the ability to traverse the universe! Being closed off in one world is," Carcass shivered, "stifling. You must go and ask Geyegorg what the beacon to Axonaphis's world will cost. Geyegorg sets prices, and changes them, depending on the popularity of each world.

That is why I was able to return to Earth for the first time in eight thousand years—the price for the beacon just plummeted. There isn't much demand for access to Earth now that it's about to become a war zone. We must hope Axonaphis's world is similarly unpopular, so Geyegorg accepts an easy trade."

"Can I just stop you here and point out that maybe you should be the one to go ask him what the price is?" Spooky wasn't thrilled about the prospect of anything sizzling in her eye or visiting a world as unpopular as a war zone. "You're the one who knows him, and you're both gods. It just seems like it would be easier if you did it."

"On the contrary, you will fare better than I. Geyegorg is always looking for new business partners, and he's always more generous when he hopes to build a lucrative relationship. Perhaps he'll even grant you a goodwill beacon for your first deal."

"I don't know. It seems like something I could screw up. Maybe you should go pay for the beacon." Spooky put her hand to her chest. "And then send me to Axonaphis so I can play the sad human to the god of Earth."

"First of all, there will be no role to play; you *are* a sad human. And secondly, I cannot go in your stead. I have other matters to attend to."

"More important than saving Earth?"

"Someone has to give you enough time to save Earth," Carcass growled. "I need to put things in motion to delay whoever is going to be bold enough to make the first move. If the first attack is successful, and the god of Earth doesn't show, the rate of destruction will increase exponentially. I give it a matter of hours before there is irreparable slaughter. Possibly, extinction."

"How long will it be?" Spooky bounced on her toes. "Until the first attack?"

"It's impossible to say, but I am going to do my utmost to give you one news cycle."

"Huh?"

"I am going to inspire humans to do what they do best—tell

stories." He flip-flopped his hand. "A miracle here, a miracle there, and humans will spread rumors about god's presence on Earth across every media outlet. It should give the invaders pause. Although, as you well know, airtime will depend on other global events."

"You think news reports will be enough?"

"With the fervor with which humans spread these stories, it should buy you a few days."

Spooky thought back to the last time there was a report about the face of a saint appearing in cream cheese. "Well, could that solve the entire problem? If everyone's saying the god of Earth is back, maybe the other gods will all just leave."

Carcass shook his head. "Some might leave, for a time. But if a single city comes under siege or mountain is leveled and no god appears in direct challenge, it won't be enough. It's a tactic that will fold under scrutiny. I just need to give you enough time to make the stories of his return come true."

Spooky twitched her closed mouth back and forth. She wasn't responsible for whether or not the plan worked. She had to remember that. She just had to follow the steps Carcass gave her, and then everything would be fine.

"Okay. I get it. So how do I get to that guy with the doors?"

"Geyegorg."

"Right, Geyegorg."

"There is a door you can use to reach him on the other side of the forest, near my winter home." He looked her up and down. "Walking on those little sticks, it will take you half a day to get there. Perhaps more."

Row after row of straight, gray trunks blocked any view of the horizon. "Is that really the easiest way? Isn't there a closer door?"

"If there is, we cannot see it. Geyegorg doesn't like visitors. He only likes business. He typically only labels a single passageway to and from his world for each trading partner."

"So I'm supposed to walk through the woods for half a day to— what was it?—your winter home, and then negotiate with a god to pay for a beacon that will get put in my eye. So that I can visit another god...who will let me talk to the god of Earth."

"Correct."

Spooky blinked at him. "That is a little more complicated than you made it sound when you asked if I could follow instructions."

"Nonetheless, it is the only way. But good fortune! You won't have to go alone."

Spooky could have done a cartwheel. "You're coming?"

"Weren't you listening? No." He pointed behind her.

# CHAPTER XIV
## THREE'S COMPANY

Spooky looked over her shoulder. There was nothing behind her but the swamp. Even though it was full daylight, the gnarled trees blocked all but a glimmer on the dark water.

Vines lowered from the canopy, suspending two figures. Loops covered them from head to toe. Although the coils obscured most of her face and body, the cloud of blonde hair was unmistakable—Brianna Van Den Berg. With her was another, longer body in a gray Dodgson smock and striped sneakers.

Bree's eyes found Spooky's and they opened wider. She made a strained sound and bucked against the vines. Both figures were pulled back up into the treetops.

"Carcass," Spooky said, gritting her teeth. "What was that?"

"I set a trap for one and caught two! Isn't that fortunate?"

Spooky raked her nails through her hair. "Why are they here?"

"You didn't appear at the designated time." Carcass shrugged. "So I decided to take volunteering out of the equation."

"Okay, but I'm here now."

"Earth's champion!" He spread his hands in front of her. "I do believe the mission will be more successful with you at the helm, motivated as you are to receive my help. But these other humans are already here. Why not take them with you? The presence of others might protect your delicate psyche from fear, doubt, or fatigue. Humans are pack animals, after all."

Spooky opened her mouth, but Carcass continued, "I leave that decision to you. I do have to address the challenges of your delicate physical being, however."

He lifted his left hand, examining the wrinkly joints and sharp, black tips of all nine fingers. He touched the smallest finger to his eye. It looked like he was removing a contact. When he pulled it away, she could have sworn the pad of his finger blinked at her.

"I cannot transfer the sight of Geyegorg's beacon, but I can lend you a part of myself to do the seeing."

Carcass grasped the blinking finger with his other hand and lifted. Sinewy orange tendons wriggled like worms under his skin as he yanked the finger up, up, up, until she could see his house through stringy, stretching pieces of flesh. The finger detached completely with a sucking sound.

Carcass held the appendage toward her. "You will have to borrow this."

Spooky shook her head and backed away.

Carcass raised an eyebrow. "Do you think every world in the universe offers a breathable atmosphere? Do you think every god speaks your language? Stop fussing and do as I say."

Spooky extended a shaking hand toward the wriggling thing. Tendrils enveloped her palm and wrist, forming a hideous orange bracelet of flesh and bone.

"Tuck it behind your ear."

Spooky grimaced. She wanted to keep her entombed hand as far away from her face as possible. She guided the digit around the back of her left ear. She was glad, for once, that her ears stuck out; it may have been his smallest finger, but it was half the length of her forearm. The joints molded into the space, and the black nail scraped the edge of her cheekbone. She could feel the distinction between the gummy, lukewarm flesh and the inflexible bone. The stretchy bits let go of her wrist and wrapped around the base of her skull.

"Ouch!" The tendrils dug into her hair and skin. She touched the back of her neck and brought away red-tipped fingers. She resisted the urge to rip the disgusting thing off her.

"Thank you would be appropriate. I don't know if the obvious needs to be stated, but that is a godfinger. A powerful tool. I have limited its powers, so you don't instantiate every whim. It will grant you four things:

"The first, oxygen, for you and your comrades. You can breathe here, but not in the world of Geyegorg. It will produce continuously, so you need not ask for it.

"The second, food. I took the liberty of sampling some items from the cafeteria at Dodgson. Request one of them, and it will appear.

"The third, communication. Geyegorg can see the meaning of your words, but he does not speak English. The finger will translate spoken languages for you, enabling perfect understanding. It will also allow me to confer with you, and track you, on your journey."

Spooky blinked as the finger's joints cracked and flexed next to her ear.

"And the fourth, it has my sight of Geyegorg's beacon and can open the door for you. All you must do is command it. Do you understand?"

"Uh, sure," Spooky said. "I will be able to talk to you if I need help, right?"

"I will be preoccupied on Earth. Only ask for my attention if you get into serious trouble."

"Will I be getting into serious trouble?"

"You will be safe in my world, as long as you stay on the path." He bobbed his head in a way that wasn't quite a nod. "I am giving you the best chance I can on short notice. If there is trouble to be found, you must hurry and find it. Now go. The path will lead you directly to my winter home."

Spooky glanced around the clearing. "Erm, what path?"

Carcass's mouth tugged down. "Mm. Well I did take care of most things, did I not?"

He took his hands out of his sleeves and motioned as if he were pushing something in front of him. Behind the house, trees rustled and cracked. The earth buckled like a giant mole was burrowing through the forest. The ground where it passed settled into a clear lane of fresh-turned earth.

"The path is before you." Carcass dusted off his unbalanced hands, then gestured toward the swamp. Vines lowered from the canopy and deposited the captives in the mud.

A single vine snaked across the clearing and up into Carcass's waiting hand, like an obedient pet.

"I'll leave this holding the door to Earth open, in case you don't want to keep the other humans as company." Carcass glided past her and gave her a slight wave. A glowing line appeared, and he melted into it, outlined in white. "Best of luck."

He disappeared. The whiteness shrank around the vine until only a curl of mist leaked out. Then all was still.

Geyegorg and Axonaphis. Air, language, food. Carcass's instructions swirled in her head. Following the path was the first task. She just had to focus on one thing at a time.

"Hey!"

Spooky turned. Bree was limping across the clearing toward her, teeth bared.

"What the hell is going on?" Bree's eyes were wild, and her pajamas were twisted. She winced with every step but didn't slow down until she was right in front of Spooky.

"What the hell is going on?" she asked again.

"Uh, hi Brianna...Bree..."

"Where did that big guy go? The guy in the mask?"

"Mask?" She must mean Carcass. "He went...away."

Bree grabbed Spooky's shoulders. "Is he coming back?"

"I don't think so." The words came out in bites as Bree shook her.

"Where are we? What are we doing here?" Bree leaned her face close enough that Spooky could only focus on one eye or the other.

"Uh, well..."

The other captive was on his feet. The uniform made her think of Luke, but the wavy brown hair didn't fit. It took her a few seconds to recognize her new work duty shift mate—Elliot. Her mysteriously absent work duty shift mate.

The one she hadn't seen since she sent him to take out the garbage after the sun went down.

"I saw you talking to that guy. That big...guy." Bree didn't seem to know how to describe Carcass. She let Spooky go and stepped back. "Are you helping him? Are you involved in whatever's going on here?"

Spooky realized too late she shouldn't have paused.

"You better start talking, or I'll find a new use for your mouth." Bree's raised fist clarified what violent use that might be. Spooky hadn't guessed Bree was at Dodgson for violence, but she couldn't rule it out.

"Where are we?" Elliot staggered over to them. He was still wearing his gray smock and disposable gloves from dinner service. His flushed cheeks were paler than when she had seen him yesterday. "Ow." He sat down hard.

"Are you okay?" Spooky asked.

"Yeah. Just numb."

He took off his gloves with shaking fingers and lifted one pant leg. His calf was covered in red welts. They were just like the marks the vine had left on Spooky.

"Were you here all night?" Spooky asked.

"Shut up," Bree said. "I don't trust you. And you." She spun on Elliot, who squinted up at her. "I don't trust you either."

"I was in that tree hours before you were." He got to his feet and scanned the clearing. "What's going on? Where are we?"

"You already asked that." Bree crossed her arms. "I already asked that. The only person who hasn't asked that is her."

They both looked at Spooky.

"Um, well...it's hard to explain..."

She couldn't think of anything to say that they would believe. It wasn't her fault Carcass had kidnapped them, but having more information than they did made her feel jittery and guilty.

Then again, she'd sent Elliot to take out the trash after Carcass's deadline. She'd had a sense it might not be safe to go back there. She glanced at his face. He was watching her with wide blue eyes, but his expression wasn't accusatory.

Bree's scowl told a different story. "When you've finished staring, we're still waiting for an explanation."

"It's just...not simple." Spooky had been intimidated enough when Bree was being nice to her. Now talking at all was difficult.

"Well make it simple. That big guy could come back any second. I'm not going to get murdered out here."

"How about one thing at a time." Elliot put his palms out. "Do you know where we are?"

"Yeah. Kind of."

"How far are we from Dodgson?"

"Uh...far."

"How do we get back? I know there are mountains west of Dodgson, but I don't see them."

He searched the horizon for mountains that probably didn't exist in this world. Unlike Bree, he seemed focused on solutions rather than blame or threats. Unfortunately, he was seeking Earthly solutions for an off-world problem.

The door to Earth was right there. The vine was still propping it open. All she'd have to do to send them back would be to lift and push. They'd probably be accused of drug use if they told their story, but they'd be back at Dodgson. They'd be fine.

But what would happen to her?

"Come on," Bree said. "She's just going to stare at us and give us one-word answers. Let's get out of here before that weird guy shows up again."

Bree pivoted and marched toward the tree line. Elliot held Spooky's gaze a second longer, then shrugged and followed.

Spooky jolted and took a few steps after them. "No, you can't!"

They both turned.

"Who's going to stop us?" Bree put her hands on her hips. "You?"

Us. They were already an "Us."

"No, I mean, you can't just walk off. You'll never find your way back to Dodgson."

Bree scoffed. "I told you she's not going to help us."

"Well," Elliot scratched his chin, "we need some kind of landmark, or we'll just get lost…"

Spooky barely listened as they went back and forth on navigation. Elliot brought up cardinal directions and started searching for the sun.

Elliot didn't seem like the Dodgson type. If anything, he was acting like a boy scout. There was something in his flushed face that seemed a little sad, even when he smiled. But overall, from the cafeteria until now, he had been cooperative. Friendly, even.

Still, there was a reason he was at Dodgson. Drugs? Strict parents? Maybe some bad luck that had landed him in the wrong place at the wrong time? She was being generous with her guesses, but even in this strange situation, he hadn't lashed out.

Bree, on the other hand, was almost shouting. She looked like she was about to rip someone's head off. She was confident, self-possessed, and at least a little mean. She wasn't going to do anything just because Spooky said so.

But despite the fact that she had been hostile and clearly didn't trust Spooky, Bree hadn't actually punched anyone or stormed off into the woods. Whatever her reason for being at Dodgson, she at least had some degree of impulse control.

Spooky was pretending to mull it over, but deep down, she knew what she was justifying. It didn't matter who these two were. They could have been the most violent, foul, and psychopathic delinquents from Dodgson. More than anything, she didn't want to have to go on that path alone. The idea of walking through the woods with only silence and her doubts made her shudder. Visiting a strange god in another world by herself was unimaginable.

Besides, Carcass had a better idea of what lay ahead than she did. He had recommended she bring them with her. Even if she so much as twisted an ankle, she would wish she had someone to link arms with. It seemed much more likely the mission would be successful if she had help.

"We need an idea of where we're going," Elliot said. His tone was still light even though Bree had been snapping. "Getting lost in thousands of acres of wilderness would be more dangerous than staying here."

"Well, then what do you suggest? You couldn't find the sun. You can't see the mountains. We'd have to wait all day for you to navigate by the stars. I spent the night in a tree, I'm really not in the mood for this!" Bree crossed her arms and sat in the dirt.

Elliot pivoted toward Spooky. "You seem to know where we are. Can you at least point us in the direction of civilization?"

"Um. No. You can't walk back to civilization. We're too far away." She averted her eyes. "There's somewhere I have to go, though. You could come with me."

"Come with you?"

"Yes. On that path over there."

His gaze followed her finger. "Where does it lead?"

"Through the woods."

"Through the woods to where?"

"It's hard to explain." Spooky fidgeted. "There's something I have to go do."

"Well, that's mysterious." He ruffled his hair. "Is it illegal?"

"No."

"Dangerous?"

"I hope not," she said truthfully.

He tilted his head back and forth. "How long will it take?"

"I don't know. But maybe it will go faster with your help. And after we're done, I'll help you find a way back to Dodgson."

"I'm not going back to Dodgson." He said it so plainly, a bit of steel showed through his kicked-puppy expression. "But I would like to make it back to civilization in one piece, if you can help with that."

"Sure, okay, after I'm done I'll help you get back to civilization."

Spooky realized how bizarre her offer sounded. She should have at least tried to be convincing. Unfortunately, she didn't have any more time to stand here talking.

She put her hands up. "But it's up to you. You can come with me. Or you can wait here for me to get back. But what you can't do is wander off. You'll never find your way out of this place on your own. Never."

Elliot looked at the path and back at her. "Okay. I'll come."

"Really?" A grin spread over her face before she could quash it.

"What?" Bree jumped to her feet. "You can't be serious."

Elliot shrugged. "It's the only path out of this clearing. And it's not like I have somewhere else to be."

"I'm not going anywhere until she tells us what's going on," Bree said.

She wasn't wrong to be skeptical, but the way Bree kept talking past her made Spooky's face warm.

"I know you want answers," Spooky said through her teeth. "But I have to go. Stay here if you want."

She turned her back and strode toward the path.

She jumped when Elliot appeared beside her. He smiled, and the corners of her mouth twitched up again.

"Are you crazy?" Bree called. "I'm not waiting here by myself!"

"Well then, come with us," Elliot said over his shoulder. He might have been out of his mind after all, but Spooky could have kicked her heels together.

After a beat, Bree huffed along after them. "Fine, but I want answers. And if I'm about to get murdered, I'll make sure you're first."

It was, at least, less of a threat. "I'll tell you everything I know on the way," Spooky said. "It just...might be a little hard to believe."

"It's been a strange night," Elliot said. He stretched out his chest. "I'm feeling open."

Spooky's feet connected with the freshly churned path. She was barely into the woods, but it already smelled different, like old leaves and dust. Every step left a footprint.

Spooky set a pace she hoped would cut down on Carcass's time estimate and began to tell her story.

# CHAPTER XV
# WALK IN THE WOODS

Silvery gray trees framed the straight path. There was a uniformity to the forest that felt unnatural, like the trees had been planted on a grid. Radiating branches covered in rust-brown needles couldn't break the illusion that she was walking through a colonnade instead of a forest.

The repetitive columns made it easy to lose track of time as she talked. It was easier to look straight ahead than at Bree or Elliot's faces.

She explained, as simply as she could, what had happened to her —sneaking out, the vine, and the house in the clearing. Her attempt to tell Carcass stories, before introducing the internet. The break-in at Office Shack. The danger Earth was in. The trade he had offered her. And finally, where the path led—to the door to Geyegorg. Who could give her the beacon to visit Axonaphis. Who could send a message to the god of Earth. Who would return and scare off the invading gods.

"That's it," she said. "That's everything I know."

Neither of them spoke.

She risked a sideways glance at their expressions. Elliot's brow furrowed as he gazed off into the trees.

Bree's eyebrows arched halfway up her forehead. "Well, that was elaborate."

"Huh?"

"I didn't peg you for it yesterday." Bree shook her head. "But you must be full-on pathological."

"I'm not lying." Spooky wouldn't have believed her own story either, but being called a liar still made her cheeks warm.

"Okay, then you're psychotic."

"You saw Carcass yourself!"

"I saw a weird guy in a mask. It's been a weird night. That doesn't mean we are on another planet."

"World," Elliot said.

"Who cares what she called it?" Bree rolled her eyes. "We're in a forest, on the only path in sight, with someone who either suffers from massive hallucinations or thinks we are stupid enough to believe a story about a carcass who loves the internet so much he decided to save the world."

At least she had been sort of listening. Spooky glanced at Elliot again, but he looked off into the trees and said nothing.

Elliot and Bree were still an "Us." An "Us" who didn't believe her. An "Us" who currently had nowhere else to go but would leave her alone with her unbelievable mission as soon as they had another option.

"I can prove it," Spooky blurted. "Well, kind of." She pulled her hair back from the godfinger. "Carcass gave me this."

They both stopped walking and stared at her.

"Ew." Bree gawked at the side of her head. "That is disgusting."

"Yeah, it is," Spooky agreed. She finally seemed to have reclaimed Elliot's attention from the trees. He came up to her and examined the side of her head so closely, she had to lean away. "It...it can do magic."

"Really." Bree's tone dripped with acid.

"Um, yeah." Now Spooky really wished she had tested the finger's powers before Carcass left. "It can...make air."

"How magically convenient," Bree said. "Proof we can't see."

"And..." Spooky tried to remember what Carcass had told her. "It can translate languages for me."

"Languages, huh? *Can you understand what I'm saying?*" Elliot asked.

"You asked if I can understand what you're saying."

*"The chair is big and ugly."* His mouth wasn't forming the words she heard, like a dubbed movie.

"The chair is big and ugly," Spooky repeated.

"So she speaks French." Bree shrugged. "who cares?"

"That was Danish," he said.

"Thanks for showing off, but use your head. We don't know what languages she speaks. That doesn't prove anything."

*"Not very nice,"* Elliot mumbled. His mouth didn't match the words again.

Bree crossed her arms. "We should go back. We can't trust her, and her story has done nothing but confirm that. We have no idea where she's taking us."

There it was again. "Us."

There was no point in telling them she could use the finger to talk to Carcass, or that it could open a door to another world if they just walked with her another half a day.

"Oh!" Spooky flapped her hands. "And it can make food!"

"Like, cooking?" Her features were doll-like, but Bree's face was never soft. Exaggerated eye rolls, mouth pulls, and cocked brows let Spooky know exactly what she thought of her.

"No, it can make food appear. I think."

Elliot raised his eyebrows. "That would definitely be hard to fake."

Carcass had said all she had to do was ask for what she wanted.

"Give me cookies."

Nothing happened. Spooky's cheeks burned.

"Right, I'm out of here. See ya." Bree pivoted and stomped back the way they had come.

The finger had worked to translate Danish, which she definitely did not speak. What had gone wrong? Spooky tried to recall Carcass's exact words. He had said he sampled food from the cafeteria yesterday. What had she served yesterday? She had been too preoccupied thinking about why Bree wanted to sit with her, and what Reed knew, and what evidence the police had, and the setting of the sun. She hadn't paid any attention to what she had been serving, or what was on her plate.

Elliot watched her. She couldn't stand his pitying expression.

"What did we eat yesterday?" she demanded.

"What?"

"What did the cafeteria serve yesterday? I need to know."

"There was a sloppy joe bar at dinner..."

"Right! Sloppy joes!"

Two sloppy joes appeared in front of her face and dropped, buns and beef spilling in the dirt. She pointed at them and gaped at Elliot. His blue eyes widened.

"Ha! Sloppy joe!" she said again. The magic repeated. Apparently, all the finger needed was the right words. No wonder Carcass had limited the finger's powers—she would have to be careful what she said otherwise. "Sloppy joe, sloppy joe, sloppy joe!"

Elliot grinned at the mess of bread and fillings growing between them. It was the biggest smile she had seen on his face so far, and she glowed back. It felt so good to be believed.

"Ha, amazing! Bree!" He called. "Bree, come back!"

"What?" Bree snapped.

"She wasn't lying! You weren't lying."

"Sloppy joe!" Spooky said. This one she caught in the air and held out to Elliot. He accepted it.

He examined the bun. "Is this safe to eat?"

"It should be." Carcass had given her the finger to sustain her, after all.

Bree trudged over. "She could have been hiding that."

"Mashed potatoes," Spooky blurted, remembering that's what she had been scooping at dinner. Beige mush slopped into the dirt. Elliot laughed.

Bree scowled at the pile of potatoes, then at Spooky. "This isn't possible. I don't believe you."

"I do," Elliot said through a bite of his sandwich. He had Worcester sauce on the corners of his mouth.

"You do?" Spooky bounced on her toes.

"Hold on," Bree stepped between them. "You can't seriously believe her entire insane story based on one magic trick. We didn't check her sleeves. We don't know what she set up ahead of time."

Spooky shook her arms. "How much do you think I can hide in here?"

"It's not just because of the food," Elliot said. "The vines were moving."

"No...no." Bree stuck her chin up. "That guy tied us up."

"He wasn't anywhere near us."

"It was some kind of pulley system."

"What about the whiteness? The floating? That's exactly what happened to me by the dumpsters."

A twinge of guilt nudged through the giddiness in Spooky's chest. She was the one who had sent Elliot back there.

Joy at being believed bubbled over it.

Bree raised her hands and shoulders. "We were drugged!"

"Then we must still be." Elliot shook his head. "Because we've already passed this tree at least fifty times."

"Huh?" Spooky inspected the one he indicated on the left side of the path. It had a big knothole at face height.

He pointed ahead. "The next one has a split branch."

Most of the trees' branches extended straight out, like spokes on a wheel. But the next tree leveled a branch shaped like a "Y" over the path.

"And the one after that has six knotholes."

Spooky jogged toward the next silvery trunk. It had a constellation of six knotholes.

"How did you know that?"

"I'll show you." He beckoned her to stand beside him. "Look."

Spooky followed the line of his finger with her eyes. At a diagonal from where she stood, she could see another tree with six knotholes. And at an equal distance further, there was another trunk with the same pattern. And a ways further, another.

"Oh. So...?"

"This isn't a real forest. Or, at least, not a natural one. There is a pattern. I've counted about twenty different variations that repeat."

"Carcass did say he copies things from Earth." Spooky met his dark blue eyes.

"Well then, seems like he made some copies of those copies."

Her chest warmed. It felt so good to be believed, and even told something, about this strange world.

"Aren't you supposed to be trying to convince me?" Bree stalked over and peered through the trees, positioning herself to see the same angle.

"Do you still need convincing?" Elliot asked.

"Whatever." She tossed her hair. "Like I'm going to trust a closed cabin kid anyway."

Spooky took a moment to register that she meant Elliot. Closed cabins were reserved for the most violent, uncontrollable campers. She hadn't imagined for a second that Elliot might fit into that category. He worked in the cafeteria, where you had to be trusted to handle both food and cleaning supplies. And then there was his dopey, sad smile.

But he didn't correct Bree. Suddenly, the fading bruise on his cheek looked less like evidence of an attack and more like the aftermath of a fight.

She wanted to ask him what he'd done to get himself locked up at night, but she held the question in her mouth. They had just crossed an important threshold—he believed her. She didn't want to destroy progress with dangerous questions. She would rather have company she couldn't quite trust than be alone. She just couldn't drop her guard entirely.

"I'm glad you believe me," she said to Elliot, then turned to Bree. "And I don't blame you for not. But it's all true, and Carcass said there isn't much time. Now that you know the truth, you can decide if you want to come. But I have to keep going."

"Come on, Bree," Elliot said. "You can't get back to Earth anyway. We might as well help."

Spooky's ears blazed. She hadn't mentioned that a vine was holding the door to Dodgson open in the clearing. "We should uh, keep moving."

Bree grumbled, but shuffled forward.

Now that Elliot had called her attention to it, Spooky couldn't unsee the repetition in the forest. Even the steely bark was too uniform, cut deep with swirling grooves in too-few patterns. There were none of the messy signs of unordered life. She couldn't see any ground vegetation or hear any animal sounds. The lack of blue and green was almost irritating to her eyes, like she should be able to blink away the brown and gray and reveal even one waxy, vibrant leaf.

The clothing they had brought on their backs from Dodgson didn't add much to the color palette; Bree's pajamas were so faded it was hard to tell what color the stripes once were, and Elliot had removed his cafeteria gear to reveal a heather shirt and worn jeans. His rosy cheeks and blue eyes added a spot of freshness, and Bree's yellow hair and tan skin glowed. Spooky imagined her own pallid face and dull hair blended into the background perfectly.

"Speaking of getting back," Elliot said. "How will we get back to Earth?"

"Um, well." Spooky cleared her throat. She stuck to a partial truth. "There is a door to Dodgson in the clearing. Once I've given Axonaphis the message, Carcass will open it and let us return." She coughed, eager to change the conversation. "So, how exactly did Carcass get you here? Did a vine grab you and pull you in?"

"No." Elliot wiggled his shoulders in an exaggerated shiver. "The vines came later. When I was taking the trash out, there was money on the ground between the dumpsters."

"Money?"

"A stack of five-dollar bills."

Spooky hadn't mentioned the counterfeit Carcass had made at

Office Shack. Apparently, he had found another use for modern tender—bait.

"I went to look closer and everything turned white. I thought..." He let out a short laugh and shook himself again. "I was very relieved when I landed in the clearing. Until the vines dragged me up into the treetops."

"I shouldn't have sent you back there," Spooky said. "I didn't think Carcass would take someone else that quickly."

"It's okay, it's not your fault." Elliot gave her a half smile, then chuckled. "I'm sure Adam Dodgson is pulling his hair out trying to figure out how I escaped."

"That makes two of us," Spooky muttered. "I disappeared in broad daylight while being chased by cops."

"Three of us," Bree said. "They must have noticed my bunk was empty by morning."

"There was a headcount last night." Spooky had almost forgotten. "Was that for you?"

"Maybe. When you wouldn't share how to get past the motion detectors, I had to ask Luke. He was more than happy to arrange to meet at the dumpsters."

Bree said it in the most casual of tones, but based on the way she flipped her hair and swung her hips, she seemed to know exactly how this information would land. Spooky blinked a few times and tried to remember that Luke was a jerk who she didn't even like.

Still, him being a jerk didn't make Bree any less of one.

"I was waiting for him," Bree continued. "And I saw a white light, like a penlight, shining on a stack of cash between the dumpsters. I went to pick it up, and the next thing I know, I'm being dragged into the treetops and tied up. I thought I was going to die."

Spooky glanced at Bree's face again. Her tan skin was paler than usual. Her freckles stood out through the dirt and crusty salt of old tears. Spooky's chest squeezed. Bree and Elliot had just spent all night in captivity, with no explanation as to where they were or what was going to happen to them. And she had told them they couldn't go home until they walked twelve hours and completed a mission across worlds.

If she hadn't been allowed to return to Earth the night she met Carcass, she wasn't sure she would still be standing.

"Hey." Spooky stopped. "You seriously must be hungry."

"Ugh, yes," Bree said. "I need food."

Elliot smiled. "I'm already hungry again. And thirsty."

"The finger makes food they served in the cafeteria yesterday."

Bree scowled. "I said *food*. Nothing served at Dodgson fits that definition."

Hungry or not, she'd still found the energy to make a snide comment. Bree sure did make it difficult to sympathize with what she'd been through.

Spooky spoke slowly to avoid snapping. "That's all it can do."

"Why couldn't yesterday have been cookie day." Bree sighed. "Alright, give me a sloppy joe."

Spooky said the magic words and handed out two sandwiches, then conjured one for herself.

"What about water?" Elliot asked.

"Water," Spooky said. A full plastic glass appeared in front of her face and sloshed to the ground. It appeared that Carcass had sampled more than the edible items from the kitchen.

"Green beans?" Bree asked.

They spent the next half an hour trying to remember the full menu. Nothing appeared from breakfast or lunch, but they got every item they remembered from dinner, plus service ware. They snacked on what they wanted and left a trail of what they didn't—mashed potatoes, glasses of water, trays, foam sporks, and napkins.

They didn't talk much while they ate, except for the call and response of any new food requests. Elliot zigzagged, examining things on either side of the path until he fell behind. Spooky found herself walking alone with Bree.

The words spilled out of her mouth before she could stop them. "So. You snuck out last night."

"Yeah. That's right. To meet Luke."

"Right." Spooky knew she shouldn't have said anything. "Wait, they just changed the rules. Both of you could have been kicked out for that!"

"I wish." Bree snorted. "No amount of scuffs can get me kicked out of Dodgson."

"Oh, right." Everyone had a custom punishment waiting for them at one hundred scuffs. "But weren't you worried about maxing out?"

Bree twirled her hair. "I was bored. I didn't think I would get caught. And hey, I was right. I didn't get caught... I got kidnapped."

"So there is nothing you could do to get kicked out? What if you hurt someone?"

"If I could punch someone and get sent home, I would punch someone."

"Would your parents take you back?"

"I mean, they would have to. Until they found somewhere else to send me." Bree shrugged, her freckled face smooth and carefree at the presumption her parents would have to welcome her home and take care of her. "But again. Not one of my scuff levels."

Of course campers would try to get kicked out of Dodgson if they could. Being "sent home" just meant the opposite for Spooky.

"But Dodgson can't keep you there no matter what." Spooky thought of the camper with the bloody eye. "What if you stabbed someone?"

Bree narrowed her eyes. "If I stabbed someone, I would go to jail, not home to my family."

"Oh right. Right, that wouldn't work."

"Okay, creepy." Bree slid her eyes up and down Spooky. "Good talk." She sashayed away.

Even though Bree's springy hair was nothing like Victoria's sleek locks, and Victoria didn't swing her hips, for a moment, Spooky felt like she was watching her sister's retreating back.

If Bree was an electric magenta, Victoria was a pale pink—different versions of feminine perfection, both disapproving of

Spooky's sullen, awkward presentation. Victoria wouldn't call Spooky creepy. She had an image to maintain, and name-calling wasn't part of it. But Victoria still found ways to communicate what she thought of her younger sister. A long sideways glance and a firmly shut door could express more than words.

That was Victoria's way—no open conversation, just shut doors. Victoria invited the best and brightest into her circle, but if grades slipped, appearances cracked, or voices rose, Spooky never heard that friend or boyfriend's name again. Despite the attention and praise her parents lavished on Victoria, Spooky knew their relationship was like that too. Neither side could introduce embarrassment or struggle. Closeness was always conditional.

Even for her accolades and achievements, Spooky didn't want to be like Victoria. She didn't want to pretend to like people who bolstered her image. She didn't want to use people to get ahead and be used in turn. She would rather wait in the shadows than fake it in the sun.

Despite Bree's prickly attitude, Spooky found herself preferring Bree's style to Victoria's. At least Bree said the awful things she thought out loud. Spooky would rather know Bree didn't like her than have her pretend to be a friend.

Fast footsteps made Spooky look over her shoulder. Elliot jogged toward her, glancing back every few paces.

"Hey," he said. "I saw something in the woods."

# CHAPTER XVI

# THE FALL

Spooky scanned the trees. The scenery was exactly as it had been the entire walk so far—silent, gray, and still.

"You saw something?" Bree backtracked to join them. "Something like what?"

"Something yellow and gray. It was fast—I only caught a glimpse as it moved through the trees. It might have been an animal." Elliot watched the woods behind them. "Are there animals here?"

"Carcass has a horse," Spooky supplied. "And chickens. There could be other things. But Carcass said the path would be safe." She spoke with more conviction than she felt.

"Well, I'm not walking last." Bree shrugged and strode away, swinging her fists.

Elliot shrugged too. "Shall we?"

Spooky nodded and fell in step with him, not wanting to be last either.

They walked in silence. She snuck glances at his profile. Long lashes danced as he kept his eyes roving over the trees and sky and path in turn. If he was searching for the animal, he didn't appear nervous. In fact, he had a slight smile on his lips.

"You're handling all of this remarkably well," she finally said.

He met her eyes and his smile grew. "What do you mean?"

"Well, you've been so calm. And weirdly okay with everything."

"What would I be doing otherwise? Spending another day at Dodgson?" He tilted his head back and gazed up through his bangs.

"At least this way I'm somewhere new. Somewhere no one else has ever seen before."

How could he be so cheerful? "That is a very positive way of looking at it."

"Last night was terrible, if that makes you feel any better."

"Sorry, again, about having you take out the trash."

"It's okay. It was a much more hardcore first night than I expected from cafeteria duty."

"How did you get that work duty anyway?" Spooky asked before she could stop herself. "I mean, it's just, they don't usually let...some people...work with the food."

"Closed cabin kids?"

She winced. "Yeah."

"No it's okay, it's true—I sleep in one of the locked cabins."

"But then, how is it that you're so...so..."

"Normal?" he asked, with a lopsided smile.

"I was going to say nonviolent."

"That's not really how they decide who goes in there."

"No? What about Ralph Jones?" Spooky had seen Ralph swing lunch trays and fists at campers and counselors alike.

"Okay, sometimes that's why people are there," he conceded. "But not everyone. Remember when the alarm went off week two?"

"Yes." The alarm on the fence had gone off during lunch. According to repeat campers, someone made a run for it at least once a summer, despite Adam Dodgson's warnings.

"That was me. They put me in the closed cabins after that."

"That's all?" There was no way a closed cabin sleeping assignment was all he got for maxing out.

"I also spent two weeks in isolation and got re-enrolled for next summer."

"That doesn't sound so bad." Spooky would happily have spent the whole summer in isolation. She wouldn't look forward to another stint at Dodgson, but she could accept it as long as her life outside didn't suffer.

He didn't say anything for a few paces. "Do you know why Dodgson works? Why kids follow the rules, when no one could get them to at home?"

"Um, because they trust us?"

"It's because Adam Dodgson knows what each of us is and isn't willing to lose." His eyes were shadowed. "It's easy to break the rules if you aren't afraid of getting yelled at, or grounded, or even expelled. But tell a kid whose best friend in the world is his dog that you'll give it to the pound? Suddenly, he'll do anything."

"Is that someone's real maximum scuff level?"

He nodded. "Another violent inmate of the closed cabins, brought to heel because Adam Dodgson figured out what really matters to him."

Spooky opened her mouth to say something else, then closed it. She flushed. She had basically just told Elliot that something he cared about losing was no big deal. No matter how manageable his maximum scuff level consequences seemed to her, it was the type of pain that mattered to him. That was how Dodgson worked.

From the moment she had walked into his office, Adam Dodgson had known exactly how to motivate her. True, the ultimatum had been her parents' idea. But he had come up with the eighty-scuff punishment revoking her access to their cars, which meant no job at the yogurt shop to save money. And the ninety-scuff punishment dictating they wouldn't cosign on a college loan. Somehow, he knew all she wanted to do was start her life after high school. If she didn't follow his rules, he would chip away at her chances for The Change. She could put up with a lot of pain, but that, she couldn't accept.

Of course, it was The Change that had gotten her in trouble in the first place.

Up until junior year, a passing grade had been a passing grade in Spooky's eyes. But second semester, when she concluded her life would only start after high school, her priorities had shifted. She needed to make sure a four-year residential college would take her.

She and her parents had wanted the same thing. They wanted

her to leave home with a diploma. They wanted her to attend whatever college would have her. They wanted to launch her into the world, then exchange holiday cards until they died. That's the relationship they maintained with her grandparents in upstate New York, and her one aunt in Oregon. She may have been a disappointment, but they didn't want her to be a disgrace.

But then she had inflicted the kind of pain they couldn't tolerate.

Halfway through second semester, Spooky met with the college counselor. He made it clear her track record of mediocrity wasn't good enough for most admissions departments. She had to get her grade point average up. And if there was one thing that could help pull off a miracle in time for finals, it was Victoria's notes.

That same night, Spooky snuck into her sister's room. Even though Victoria hadn't been home for months, the space still smelled of lilac and pepper. The clothes she hadn't taken to Harvard hung in an ombre of taupe, salmon, mauve, and camel. Pictures on the wall showed Victoria at prom, Victoria arm in arm with smiling girls, and Victoria accepting her diploma.

Spooky crept to the bookshelf, where Victoria had accumulated a complete collection of college prep materials. She ran her finger over the spines of books promising help with admissions essays, tests, and school selection. After finals were done, she would raid this shelf. She flipped through one of the university's brochures; she could see The Change on every page.

Spooky picked through the notebooks, labeled by subject and year. She selected the one labeled English Three, and pulled out a binder labeled Physics One. The book next to it rattled. Behind The Canterbury Tales, she found the tin.

Spooky hadn't even intended on taking one. She couldn't be sure of the contents or the dosage. But she was fairly sure they were part of Victoria's study routine, and she put them in her pocket—just in case she couldn't raise her grades with notes alone. And from her pocket to her backpack. And from her backpack to the floor of the classroom, where the little orange dots were unmistakably not mints.

If she had only been caught with the pills, the incident might have blown over. She would have been in trouble with the school, but as long as they didn't flunk her, she could have continued improving her grades and working toward leaving town.

But at that moment, sweating under the shame of the first trouble she'd ever really been in, she panicked.

They weren't even hers, she said.

Then whose were they?

And she answered truthfully.

Victoria had awards all over the high school. A feature for her acceptance to Harvard Law had just run in the school paper. When the administration told her parents their second daughter had blamed their first for abusing pills, they did an impressive job of hiding their reaction. They assured the school this was exactly the sort of thing their youngest would do. They said they were confident Victoria had nothing to do with it. They encouraged the school to bestow any punishment they felt was necessary onto Laurel.

It was the first time they'd said her name in what felt like months.

At first, when Spooky realized how much more she could have been doing to demand their attention, how much trouble she could have caused to really earn their sighs of disappointment, it had almost felt good. They were saying her name every day.

But she also learned their eyes could squint instead of glazing over. Their voices could raise instead of murmuring. Her parents didn't have to pretend she didn't live in their house. They could send her away.

She had pushed them past the limit of their tolerance. She was determined to scandalize them. She had involved herself in things they couldn't have in their household. Worst of all, she had dragged her sister into it.

But they were willing to give her one more chance.

If Spooky had tried to tell anyone at Dodgson about the pills she didn't take, she would have ended up like Lisa. So she had never asked anyone else "why," and she would never tell. Even though she, Elliot, and Bree were outside the camp, camp rules still applied.

Bree brought her out of her thoughts with a request for water. The conversation came and went in waves as they took turns leading and following. Spooky found herself repeating portions of her story. Now that they believed her, they both had more questions about what Carcass had told her.

"What about angels?" Bree asked.

"Angels?"

"Yeah, I mean, we are talking about god here, right? If he's real, angels could be too. Couldn't they protect us?"

"Uh, Carcass didn't mention that."

"Does this mean there aren't any aliens?" Elliot asked. "Carcass only talked about gods invading Earth, but there's a whole universe full of other planets and solar systems."

"Maybe Earth is the main feature," Spooky said. "I don't know."

"Didn't you say High Order worlds work without divine intervention?" Elliot's eyes were bright. "Maybe all the other stuff—space dust, galaxies, stars—was planned to create Earth in a self-contained chain reaction. That would be amazing!"

Even if she didn't have the answers, it felt good to discuss the possibilities. The strangeness of all this wasn't just in her head anymore. Elliot believed her. Even Bree believed her. They were each contributing questions she hadn't thought of asking Carcass. She wasn't alone with the wondering.

Bree stopped in the middle of the path, facing back the way they'd come, eyes wide.

"What's wrong?"

"There was something there."

A chill ran over Spooky. "Where?"

Bree pointed. "Next to that tree."

"What did you see?" Elliot asked.

"It looked like a big guy, not an animal. But it was yellow and gray, and it moved fast."

Spooky's heart thumped as she scanned the forest. Each of the trunks was at least three feet thick—wide enough to conceal a fairly large threat. A monster could easily dart between the evenly spaced trees, following the path the whole way.

And if it was the same thing Elliot had seen earlier, it was following them.

"What do you think?" Elliot muttered to Spooky.

"Let's just stay together. And hurry."

They rushed along the path, glancing back at intervals. Their scrambling kicked up dust, distorting the sharp lines of the trees. Spooky strained to peer through the haze, desperate to see, but terrified to spot something running up the path behind them. Something colossal and quick, that had finished with its silent game, and was ready to get what it came for.

Just as her breath began to get short, and her legs began to ache, the path steepened for the first time.

"Hold on, hold on." Elliot held up his hands. "Has anyone actually seen anything move?"

"Nothing," Bree said.

Spooky shook her head. "Wait here. Let me get a better view."

Spooky backed up the hill. She stared into the distance, challenging the silent trees to give up what, if anything, they concealed. The dust cleared, but all she could see was the straight path and repeating trunks. Maybe Bree had seen some creature that had inadvertently come upon the path. Maybe they had all gotten too used to the idea of being alone in the woods. You were never really alone in the woods, were you? She shuddered, not sure her own thoughts were making her feel any better. She scanned the trees as her elevation changed, putting one foot behind the next.

"I don't think anything is there," she called.

She reached her foot behind her again, but it didn't connect with anything this time. Her stomach lurched as she fell backward.

# CHAPTER XVII
# JAGBI

There was a loud crack, and something grabbed her wrist, stopping her fall. The hill had ended in a cliff. All she could see out of the corner of her eye was black. Only her arm and the ball of one foot kept her suspended above oblivion. Spooky whimpered.

The lumpy form above her almost looked like... "Carcass?"

But the figure was too small, and the hand gripping her forearm only had three fingers and a thumb. She focused on that hand as the thing pulled her up, grunting with the effort.

As soon as her weight was back on her feet, she stumbled down the slope and flattened herself on the ground. She took a few shaky breaths, clinging to the dirt.

The thing that had saved her could have been Carcass's distant cousin. Like Carcass, he was broad and hunched. Instead of deep orange, his skin was rosy yellow—the color of marigolds. His physique and posture resembled an old man's, but his skin was as smooth as a baby's, folding in big shiny rolls rather than fine lines. His golf ball-sized eyes were light and watery. They matched the gray cloth wrapped around him, held up by knots in half a dozen places. On top of his head, he had two nubs for horns.

Bree and Elliot ran up the slope to join her.

"Are you okay?" Elliot asked.

"Yeah, I'm okay," she said without taking her gaze off the creature. "Who are you?"

The creature's eyes widened. With a sound like a bat hitting a ball, he disappeared. Another crack echoed in the trees. Down the hill, off the path, he peeked out from behind one.

"That's the guy I saw!" Bree said. "Friend of yours?"

"I've never seen him before."

Elliot helped her to her feet. "Should we be worried?"

"I don't think so." Spooky brushed the dirt off her shirt with shaking hands. "He saved me."

If she hadn't been walking backward, she would have seen that the path veered to the right at the top of the slope. It skirted a black crater the size of a stadium. The dark color in her peripheral vision had made her think she was hanging over the edge of an abyss, but it was only about a four-foot drop. The fall would have hurt, but she wasn't in real danger.

The surface of the crater looked like wavy black glass, covered in lumps and bumps that rose no higher than her knee. Spooky crouched and reached toward it to check if the texture was smooth like obsidian or sticky like tar.

A crack sounded next to her. The marigold cousin grabbed her arm and yanked it back. He lifted her, revealing the strength in his burly form.

"Hey!" Spooky shouted, heart racing. She wouldn't be able to get her arm back if he didn't want her to. Maybe she'd misjudged the harmlessness of this new creature.

"Don't touch it!" he croaked. He grasped his throat, then glanced to and fro.

He let go of her arm and hobbled toward the trees.

"What the hell is wrong with that thing?" Bree whispered.

"Let's not be rude until we're sure it isn't going to try and kill us," Elliot whispered back.

Spooky rubbed her arm, now twice grabbed, and neither time gently. Was this creature trying to help her, or just protective of this black crater?

Another snap sounded, this time due to breaking wood. The

thing waddled back, dragging a six-foot tree branch. He held it toward Spooky.

She leaned away as he waved it at her. "Yes, that's a branch."

He made a guttural sound and dipped one end into the crater.

As soon as the first needles made contact, the slick surface bubbled. Globs of black goo shot up, arched over the branch, and wrenched it down. Another layer of liquid erupted, enveloping more of the branch and pulling it out of the yellow monster's hands. As each new needle or twig connected with the shiny black, wave after wave of goo layered overtop. In a matter of seconds, the bubbles settled, and the branch was gone. All that was left was a half-inch bump in the tarry surface.

If she had fallen, she would have been buried alive. Spooky's eyes roved to the larger lumps distorting the crater. She would be one of them.

She looked the yellow thing in the eyes. "Thank you."

"Lead-ther," he croaked.

"What?"

"My throat... I haven't..." He coughed and his gray eyes watered. "Talked in..."

"It's okay, take your time. I'm Spooky. This is Elliot, and this is Bree."

Elliot waved, wide-eyed. Bree scowled and crossed her arms.

The yellow thing rubbed his throat, humming.

"Leber," he said with better diction.

"You're Leber?"

"No. This," he gestured to the crater, "is where Leber arrived."

"Oh. Okay." She wasn't sure what he was talking about, but the name sounded familiar. "I think Carcass might have mentioned a Leber. Do you know Carcass?"

"Car-cass?" he seemed to be trying the word in his mouth. "Carcass..."

"The god of this world," Spooky supplied.

"Oh! Do you mean Inanimate-Body-Filled-With-The-Living-Blood? That's Father!" His words came faster now. "He made me. He made this world."

"Uh, okay. We only know him as Carcass. Is that the same god?"

"That would be a shortened version of his proper name. I call him Father."

Spooky hadn't realized she had been calling Carcass by a nickname. "And what's your name?"

He beamed at her, revealing teeth the size of eggs. "My father calls me Jagbi."

Bree stepped forward. "Okay, Jagbi, so happy we're all friends now. But since no one else is, I have to ask, were you following us?"

Jagbi shifted his eyes back and forth as if searching for a place to disappear to.

"It's okay if you were," Spooky offered. "We aren't mad."

Bree's face told a different story.

"I was counting rocks when I saw you pass." He fiddled with one of the knots on his makeshift toga. "Yes, I followed you."

"Why?" Elliot asked.

"For observation. I thought you might do something interesting. You are so much more animated than rocks!" He smiled again.

Elliot shrugged. "Okay."

Bree scoffed. "You're just going to accept that explanation?"

"Come on, Bree," Spooky said. "He saved me. Twice. Although, I will have to have a chat with Carcass." She shouldn't have needed saving in the first place.

"Oh!" Jagbi's light eyes stretched into vertical ovals. "Is Father here?"

"No, but he said I can talk to him through this." Spooky pointed to the finger behind her ear.

Jagbi's lips parted. He shuffled over and cupped the air around the side of her face. Then he looked down and shook his head. "Don't tell Father I'm here with you. He'd be so upset. You mustn't!"

"Uh, why?"

"I'm supposed to be counting rocks," Jagbi wailed. He jumped from foot to foot. "He won't be pleased I stopped to help you! You mustn't tell him!"

"I'm sure he'll be glad you helped us; we're actually doing something important for him. But, fine, I won't tell him. I won't, okay? Just, calm down."

Jagbi curled his four-fingered hands against either side of his shaking head, doing a poor imitation of calm. "I must get back. I mustn't dawdle."

With a pop, he disappeared.

"Well, that was weird," Bree said.

"Thanks again!" Spooky called, just in case Jagbi was within earshot in the trees. She wasn't sure how to use the finger to reach Carcass but making the food had been simple enough. "Um, Carcass? I want to talk to you."

"Yes?" The gravelly drawl echoed in her ear.

"It's working! I can hear you!"

"Of course it's working. Is that all?"

"No." Spooky crossed her arms. "When you said your world was safe, did you forget to mention the pit of black tar that sucks things in at the slightest touch?"

A pause.

"That seemed rather obviously dangerous."

"Not obvious enough!" Spooky said.

"The path clears you of it, does it not?"

"Yeah, but there is nothing to stop one of us from falling in." She wasn't about to admit that she had been walking backward.

"Did one of the other humans fall in? There is nothing that can be done for them now. Best to hurry on your way, or this and worse will happen on Earth."

"No one fell in, thanks for your concern." Spooky rolled her eyes. She wanted to ask him about Leber, but she couldn't bring up the name without mentioning Jagbi. "What happened here?"

"Keep moving, and I'll tell you. You don't seem to grasp the severity of your world's situation. Perhaps this will help motivate you."

"Alright, I'm walking." Spooky waved for Bree and Elliot to follow her on the path around the crater.

"In the past, my world hasn't been a popular destination for travelers. It's a Middle Order world. Nothing to flock to, nothing to fight over. Geyegorg didn't sell many beacons. I didn't get many visitors.

"As you know, I enjoy imitating things from Earth. After I was shut out eight thousand years ago, I continued to use the examples I had copied to populate my forests. It gave me the feeling of Earth, even if I could no longer visit."

"We noticed the repeating trees."

"Trees are hard to digest." Carcass sniffed. She heard the sound like he was standing right in front of her. "But I wasn't the only one who lost access to Earth when the price of the beacon went up. A god named Leber did as well. He took notice of my little corner of the universe. He liked my imitations. And he thought he might try to claim it."

"Leber tried to take over your world?"

"Indeed. He is also Middle Order, but less interested in what he is creating than in what he is vomiting black goo over to destroy. Somewhere above the center of the damage you see is a door between our worlds. That is the door he came through when he first launched his attack.

"At the time, my world was the closest imitation of what he truly desired. Now that the god of Earth appears to have abandoned his creation, Leber is among those waiting for the auspicious moment to strike."

Spooky hadn't spent much time imagining what would happen to Earth if she failed. The consequences that had weighed on her mind were the legal ones. The threat of invading gods hadn't felt nearly as tangible as the police chasing her.

This was proof of a greater threat. Proof she would have

preferred not to see. She didn't want to be the only thing standing between this kind of destructive power and lives on Earth. Carcass had been right about motivation—she had been walking faster ever since he started his story.

"But your world isn't covered in this stuff. You fought him off."

"I did not. That crater is a graveyard of my creations who tried and failed to do just that."

The lumps on the tarry surface gleamed. Graves. Spooky swallowed, her throat dry. "But you stopped him somehow, right?"

"Not through any method that will work on Earth, Spooky." He had guessed what she really wanted to know. "I went to Geyegorg and bought the exclusive sight of my own beacon. The few others who could see it lost it, Leber among them. When I opened a door and pushed him through, he could not find the tunnel to return. And so, his attack ended."

"But can't we just do that for Earth?" Spooky asked. "Buy the exclusive beacon so only we can see it and shut everyone else out?"

"We can barely hope to afford passage to Axonaphis, and you want to buy out everyone else's contracts for the beacon to Earth?" Carcass laughed. "I gave up half the blood in my body for that trade, and my world wasn't even popular."

"Geyegorg wanted your blood?" She didn't like the image forming in her mind of the god she was traveling to visit.

"My blood is my power, Spooky. It was in the form of two children. You will never see me at my full strength because of the price I paid."

"I just want there to be a plan B. In case I fail."

"There isn't one. At this late stage, only the god of Earth has the power to protect humanity."

"Then what about time travel? Or maybe we could get the help of a different really powerful god. We could make a deal with them to be the new god of Earth..."

"Just do as I say," he growled. "And hurry."

There was no signal their conversation had ended, but it was clear he was done talking. Spooky's skin itched. She wanted to discuss every other option in the universe before concluding she was humanity's only hope against a god who vomited smothering goo.

At least if she was sitting in prison, she wouldn't be responsible for any of this.

Spooky relayed Carcass's story to Elliot and Bree as they rounded the crater. They reached the opposite side, where the path descended and continued into the trees.

Bree paused and looked back. "Is this really going to happen somewhere on Earth?"

"I hope not, but Carcass said it will," she rubbed the outside of her arms, "if I don't get the message to the god of Earth in time."

"'We,'" Elliot interjected. "If *we* don't get the message to the god of Earth."

Spooky couldn't hold back a smile. She looked down to avoid his eyes.

"I was there when Leber arrived," a voice behind them said.

Spooky jolted. Jagbi peeked out from behind a tree.

"Were you following us again?" Bree snapped.

He shrank back.

"No, it's okay! I want to hear." Spooky held her hands out between them. "Walk with us."

She waved him forward as they walked down the slope and back into the trees.

"Were you really there?" She wouldn't put it past Carcass to conceal some important detail or change events to serve his agenda.

"Oh, yes. I remember it well."

"What really happened?"

"I will tell you the story." Jagbi put one hand across his stomach and the other behind his back. He drew in a breath. "There were thirty-six large rocks and seventy-eight small rocks in the area. Leber's landing generated a force which moved all one hundred and fourteen rocks. Ninety-two struck dirt, sixteen hit trees, and one hit a chicken. The other five were never accounted for."

Jagbi stopped speaking. Spooky gaped at him.

"I can tell you are skeptical of my story." Jagbi wagged a finger at them. "And I understand your confusion—I assigned the rocks a subjective adjective defining their size." He spread his arms. "That's the storytelling part! Who's to say whether or not a rock is large or small? I passed judgment on the size based on whether or not they were larger, or smaller, than my own hand."

"Oh, uh, okay." Spooky looked at Elliot and Bree. Elliot's eyebrows rose halfway up his forehead. Bree's mouth hung open.

"Father created me to tell him stories. My special interest in rock-related stories developed over time."

"Isn't that why Carcass kidnapped you?" Elliot muttered. "To tell him stories?"

Spooky nodded. "That's pretty much the whole reason he wants to save Earth."

"Yes!" Jagbi said. "Father was so impressed with the stories told on Earth, by the humans, he made me to do the same. Have you ever heard a human tell a story?"

"Err, yeah," Spooky said. "We are humans."

Jagbi stopped walking. He squinted at each of them, twisting his head to and fro to get a better angle.

"Humans!" he exclaimed, clasping his hands. "It was such a long time ago that Father took me to Earth to observe you. You look so different now! No wonder you're so interesting!"

He leaned in closer to Spooky, studying her.

She backed away. "We should probably keep moving."

"Would you like to hear one of my first stories?" Jagbi waddled after. "A rock rolled. It flipped over three times. It stopped at the trunk of a tree."

Spooky waited for him to continue, but he just beamed at her, the corners of his eyes crinkling.

"I know, not very good, right?" He laughed but then raised his eyebrows like he hoped one of them would say it was. "Anyway, that was what I would have said, before Father sent me to Earth to learn more about the storytelling style of the humans. If I were to retell the story now, I would tell you if the rock is large or small. And I might say something like, 'the rock fell into water.'" He barked out a laugh and Spooky jumped. "But that didn't happen, you see! That's embellishment for a more dramatic ending. Humans tell stories of things that aren't true all the time. But you know that—you are humans!"

"Uh, yes." Spooky felt a sudden, deep sympathy for Carcass's desperation for entertainment. If this was the best storyteller he could make for himself, even her shoddy version of Romeo and Juliet must have been revolutionary.

"Well, did you like the story?" He hopped up and down.

"Very nice," Spooky said.

"Great story." Elliot nodded.

Bree looked too horrified to say anything at all.

"I haven't had an audience in so long." Jagbi's face sagged. "Father decided...Father decided he wanted to give me a break from telling him stories all the time. So he sent me to the forest to count rocks. And he demanded I not return, or speak to him, until I could provide a full account of every rock in the world."

And Spooky had thought being sent to Dodgson with an ultimatum was bad. Carcass's method of expressing parental disappointment was a life sentence.

"I was counting rocks when I saw you passing by, and I thought maybe you would do something that would make a good story. And maybe...maybe I could bring that story back to Father, and he would be pleased with me. Might I continue to accompany you?" His goldfish face was hopeful. "Just to observe?"

"He did save me. Twice," Spooky said to Bree, who looked like she was about to say no. "And he knows this place better than we do."

"He just wants to observe," Elliot added.

Bree huffed, but she didn't object.

"Alright," Spooky said. "You can come with us."

He jumped and clapped. "Hurray! I will continue to learn from you and practice the art of storytelling!"

"Practice in your head," Bree snapped. "I don't want to hear another word about rocks."

# CHAPTER XVIII
# THE CAVE

With his favorite subject matter off-limits, Jagbi mostly stayed out of sight. It was easy to forget he was even still with them, except for the few times when he inserted his face a little too far into the conversation. Occasionally, Spooky glimpsed him in the distance, eyeing a pebble.

The straight path and repeating trees went on for what felt like forever. The only change in the scenery was the sky, which had begun to turn darker shades of gray and orange. Sweat and dirt caked her from head to toe. Spooky asked the finger for water. She handed a glass to Bree, then made one for Elliot.

"Thanks." He downed half of it between breaths.

"How much farther?" Bree asked.

"I don't know." Spooky stared into the distance. "How long have we been walking?"

"Like ten hours," Bree said.

"We should be close." She really hoped they were close.

They ran out of light before they reached any kind of destination. With no moon or stars, Spooky couldn't see the path in front of her. Even if they reached the winter home, they might pass it.

"Carcass, I need to talk to you," Spooky said.

After a pause, he responded, "Yesss?"

"It's too dark to see where we're going. Can you make the sky light again?"

"I will not impact the internal causality of my world! I would have to give up my place in the Middle Order." He sniffed. "Even for this crucial quest, you ask too much."

"Okay, fine, then we need to stop. And we need sleep, anyway."

"Mm, I had hoped you would be there before dark. But there will be no opportunity to rest once you reach Geyegorg, so better to address this physical limitation now. Sleep until the beast with the glowing tongue opens its mouth again."

"Um, okay. How long is that?"

"It usually takes about four hours for its tongue to remoisten to its satisfaction."

"Where should we sleep?"

"Where you are. I have an agent obtaining some options to offer Geyegorg in trade. He will meet you at my winter home tomorrow. Sleep now."

Spooky turned in the direction of the dark shapes she hoped were Bree and Elliot. "Sounds like we'll be spending the night here."

"In the middle of the woods?" Bree whimpered. "In the dirt?"

"What other choice do we have?"

"But we're out in the open."

It wasn't cold, but Spooky didn't want to stay out in the open either. She didn't think she could sleep in the middle of the wilderness, unguarded on all sides.

"There is a place that isn't open," a voice behind them said.

Spooky tensed, before realizing it was just Jagbi. "Really? Where?"

"It is a place that is not made of dirt, but rather, made of...oh." Jagbi stopped. "I'm not allowed to talk about that anymore."

"Is it made of rocks?"

"That's right!" Jagbi said. "All around you!"

"Like a cave?" Elliot asked.

"Yes, a cave."

"How far away is it?" Now that she had stopped walking, Spooky's legs trembled.

"You could throw a you-know-what at it," he said. Apparently, he had taken Bree's no rock-talk ruling to heart. "I can take you there."

"I'm in," Bree said. "Lead the way."

Spooky followed Jagbi's footsteps. She kept her hands up to avoid smacking into any tree trunks. After a few moments, Bree grabbed the back of her shirt. Elliot bumped into her, so she took his sleeve and dragged him after. She couldn't see any better than they could, but she still felt responsible for getting them where they needed to go.

After ten minutes of stumbling, she hit her shin on a boulder. "Ow."

"It's up there." Jagbi's voice came from her right.

Spooky felt her way up a rocky incline on all fours. The mouth of the cave was only visible as an even deeper onyx. She moved hand over hand along a smooth wall, then sat against it. Bree crawled around her to the far side, while Elliot settled closer to the entrance. Having a wall at her back felt much more secure than being exposed on the path.

She was glad Jagbi had stuck with them. He was a little eccentric, but aside from making them listen to a few of his stories, he had offered practical assistance that Carcass wasn't here to provide. Jagbi lived in the woods, and if there was one thing he seemed to be an expert on, it was the local rock formations. Between the crater and the cave, that counted for a lot.

"Thank you, Jagbi," Spooky mumbled into the blackness. Her voice echoed. She hadn't heard him climb up after them; she didn't know if he needed sleep or if he spent all of his nights counting pebbles.

Her eyelids drooped. "Anyone need food or anything?"

"All I want is sleep," Bree murmured.

"Same." Elliot's voice was rough.

Spooky curled against the cool rock. "We'll rest until it gets light."

Exhaustion and total darkness took care of any awkwardness she might have felt about sleeping next to Bree and Elliot. She slipped into sleep.

SPOOKY CRACKED HEAVY EYELIDS. She was clutching soft fabric that smelled of dirt and sweat. She blinked and refocused on a strange back. Elliot's back. She uncurled her fingers and sat up. He had his nose tucked down toward the rock, and his long lashes were pressed against his flushed cheek. Spooky scooted away, glad he had slept through her unconscious advance.

The cave was a single rounded chamber. It was about the size of one of the cabins and scattered with brush and sticks. Bree's pouf of hair was silhouetted in its mouth.

Spooky tiptoed over to join her. "Hey."

"Shhh!" Bree said. "You'll scare the deer!"

In the distance, Spooky spotted the long legs and bent heads of a grazing herd. The morning wasn't cold, but the charcoal-gray light made everything feel chilly and fragile. The trees were still too evenly spaced, but Carcass was right—his imitation did feel like Earth.

Spooky sat down next to Bree and dangled her feet over the edge. It was remarkable that they had been able to scale the rocky slope in the dark. The boulders were jagged, and while it was only about ten feet down, it was steep.

Spooky asked the finger for two glasses of water and handed one to Bree. The cave floor had left imprints on Bree's heart-shaped face.

"How long have you been up?" Spooky asked. "Have you seen Jagbi?"

"Five minutes. Haven't seen him." Bree shrugged. "I would say good riddance, but I have to give him credit for the cave upgrade. I actually managed to sleep."

Spooky poured some water in her hand and rubbed her eyes. "We shouldn't stay long."

"Why don't we let your cuddle buddy rest just a little bit longer," Bree said with a smirk.

"We weren't...I mean, I wasn't..."

"You're blushing." Bree raised her eyebrows. "Careful now, or I'll question the rumors about the girl who handed Luke his ass the other night."

"That was an accident."

"Well, it helped your reputation. Now you're dangerous and mysterious. And creepy. People still think you're creepy."

At Dodgson, she wouldn't have turned away a spare bit of notoriety. A reputation was protection. But it felt silly to act tough now. "That was actually my first time meeting a guy. For, anything."

Bree looked at her, mouth open. "Are you saying Luke was your first...anything? Kiss?"

Spooky nodded, ears burning.

"Crush?" Bree squealed. "Hand hold?"

"Not crush. But yeah." If under the table to pass a note counted.

"Eee! I can't believe it!" Bree batted at her shoulder. "Did anything else happen?"

"Just a kiss. With a lot of tongue."

"Yeah, Raquel said he is a horrible kisser. Not to upset you, but just, like, so you know. For the future. It's not always like that."

There was no snarkiness in Bree's voice, for once. "Thanks."

"Shhh!" Bree flapped her hands and pointed. "The deer!"

The herd had ventured closer, their noses to the ground, searching for something to graze on. There were six of them, appearing and disappearing between the trees.

"I snuck out a few times." Bree looped her arms around one knee. "At a different camp. A regular camp, with real silverware and arts and crafts, and no fence. We would sneak off into the woods all the time."

One of the deer had white stripes through its fur, like a fawn.

"I didn't know until I was home and school had started that it wasn't a scare."

"A scare?" Spooky asked.

"Are you being funny?" Bree narrowed her eyes. "A pregnancy scare."

"Oh! Oh."

"Did you escape a cult? What other kind of scare is there?"

Spooky tapped her toes for a few moments, then glanced at Bree's face. "So, what happened?"

"I left school in April, came back for finals in May, and was shipped to Dodgson the day classes ended."

"What happened to the...scare?"

"A healthy baby girl. Ten fingers, ten toes. I named her Angela. Thank god I got to name her, at least."

Spooky stared at the rock between her feet. She never would have guessed that Bree—beautiful, cutting, popular Bree—had a baby. It seemed inappropriate to say either "sorry" or "congratulations."

"What's it like? Being a mom."

"Oh, I'm not a mom." Bree's voice was sharp. "My parents tell me that all the time. I haven't cared for her a single day. They don't want me to get too attached. I'm going to an all-girls boarding school after Dodgson. I'm going to be her older sister."

"It doesn't sound like that was your idea."

"My parents want to 'protect my future.' They don't care what I want. I think I can get a lawyer or something, claim parental rights... but I couldn't figure it out in time." The corners of her mouth tugged down. "All I want to do is see her."

"That's why you can't get sent home. In your scuff levels."

"If I had any way to visit her, I would take it." Bree cupped her hands like she was holding something. "You don't know what 'missing' is. She's so sweet, you can't imagine. Her eyes were blue. I wonder if they've changed by now."

Spooky blinked a few times. "What about the dad?"

"Who cares." Bree leaned back on her arms. "He's not anywhere like Dodgson or going to boarding school either. I'm sure he's having a great summer."

"There's this girl in my small group who's only at Dodgson because she had an older boyfriend."

"I bet her older boyfriend is having a great summer too." Bree kicked a rock down the slope.

The deer with the stripes swiveled its head in their direction as the stone clattered to the bottom. Its ears twitched.

"But whatever." Bree shook her curls. "If I can't be her mom, officially, I don't want people knowing. She doesn't need to be confused, or have people talking about her, you know?"

"I won't tell anyone."

Spooky wished she could go talk to Bree's parents and tell them they were wrong. That getting pregnant may have been an accident, but sometime during the nine months, Bree had become a mom. They couldn't undo that just by sending her away.

Bree was prickly and snippy, and even hostile at times. But she had a good reason to be mad at the world. For her, Dodgson wasn't a steppingstone to get back to normal—it was irreplaceable time away from her baby. It was the start of a lie that, eventually, she would tell her daughter herself.

Even now, sitting in the cave, Bree looked every inch the confident, popular girl. But for a moment, something else had been on her face—grief.

The striped deer trotted closer. It stopped twenty feet from them and raised its head.

"Oooh look," Bree cooed. "It's not even afraid!"

The deer's nose twitched.

Its jaw unhinged and dropped open, revealing rows of pointed teeth.

"What the hell!" Bree shrieked.

"Ahhh!" Spooky scrambled to her feet.

The deer hissed. The rest of the herd perked up their heads and swiveled them toward the cave.

"Elliot get up!" Spooky yelled. "Get up, get up!"

He jerked and raised his head, his eyes half open. "What's wrong? Oh, look, a deAAHR!"

All at once, the five remaining deer's faces split from ear to ear, revealing their own mouths full of white shredders.

Predators.

The striped deer bent its legs like a spider's, dropping its body low. It scuttled toward the base of the incline.

Spooky's chest went cold, then flooded with heat. She needed something, anything, to put between her and those teeth. She grabbed a rock and hurled it at the deer. Bree threw another and hit its flank, but it didn't slow down.

It scrambled up the slope, snarling and snapping at their projectiles. Saliva swung from its jaws as it leapt into the mouth of the cave.

It collided with Elliot and bowled him over in a tangle of limbs. The deer thrashed, trying to sink teeth into flesh.

"Dinner tray! Give me one!" Spooky yelled.

One of the plastic Dodgson trays fell into her hands. She swung it at the deer as hard as she could, knocking it to one side. Before it could get its spindly legs under its body, Bree ran at it with a screech. She booted it over the lip of the cave.

The striped deer tumbled to the bottom of the slope. It shook its head and got to its feet. It looked every bit the innocent fawn, except for its murderous mouth. It sauntered over to join the rest of the herd.

"What the hell are those things?" Bree wailed.

Elliot groaned.

Spooky helped him to his feet. "Are you okay?"

"Yeah." He grimaced. Blood ran down his arm.

"Carcass, we need you! We're in serious trouble!"

There was no reply.

The six deer fanned out in a semicircle. They were slight, no more than seventy or eighty pounds each, but their mouths were vicious. A single bite would be decisive.

"I need to talk to Carcass!" Spooky shouted again. "Deer are trying to eat us! We need help!"

"Get back!" Bree yelled, throwing rocks. "Stay away!"

The deer's formation tightened around the base of the slope. They took their dainty steps with care. They knew their prey wasn't going anywhere.

Spooky scanned the cave for anything they could use. She reached into her waistband and pulled out the scissors. The blades were warm. She gripped them together like a knife. Bree picked up a jagged rock. Elliot cradled his bloody arm. She handed him the tray for defense, then made one for herself and one for Bree.

They retreated to the back of the cave.

Where the hell was Carcass?

"Carcass if you don't help us right now, we are all going to die, and we're taking the internet with us!"

Six graceful heads appeared in the entrance, long ears perked up. Spooky lifted the scissors and tray like a sword and shield. She looked at Elliot and he nodded. He held his tray up with his good hand. Bree danced back and forth like a boxer.

The deer's black tongues lolled around their needle teeth as they lined up, one by one. The striped deer was the last to take its position. It bent its leg joints the wrong way, tightening into a low crouch.

Spooky didn't want to die. She wanted to live. She had to fight.

Before the deer could pounce, she leapt forward and swung her scissors as hard as she could.

# CHAPTER XIX
## KRU

One moment the deer was in front of her and the point of the scissors was arching toward it, and the next Spooky slammed into something so hard her ribs compressed. She bounced back and fell to the cave floor, the tray and scissors clattering out of her hands.

For the second time that morning, she found herself staring at an unfamiliar back.

An eight-foot-tall figure stood between her and the herd. He held the striped deer by the neck.

Two of the other deer swiveled their legs and leapt at the newcomer. The man's core barely moved as he knocked one into the cave wall, and swung the striped deer down onto the other, smashing them both into the rock. They whimpered.

The three remaining deer charged. While two of them snarled and nipped at the man's legs, the third skittered up the cave wall like an insect. It scurried past him and launched itself at Spooky. The man whirled and snatched its tail. Its jaws snapped inches from her nose, spraying her cheeks with spittle. He yanked it away from her.

Hands grabbed her arms and pulled her backward. Elliot and Bree dragged her to the rear of the cave. They huddled together, crouching behind a plastic tray.

The deer took turns feinting and falling back. The man stayed motionless unless one of them tried to get by him, which he blocked with a blurred arm or foot. The whole pack lunged forward in unison, and a deer sunk its teeth into his leg. Shiny liquid pooled around its mouth. He didn't make a sound, but grabbed its neck and squeezed until it crunched. The deer slumped, its gory mouth lolling open.

The striped deer hissed. It took a few steps toward the entrance, then galloped out of the cave. The others closed their jaws and scrambled after it.

The man kicked aside the broken predator, then squared his broad shoulders toward the cave's mouth. Spooky gripped Bree's and Elliot's hands.

"Carcass, I need to talk to you," she whispered.

"Did Kru arrive in time to avoid fatalities?" Carcass responded at a volume that made her jump.

"Yes...no...maybe. A man came and saved us and killed a deer."

"Insolent child!" Carcass roared in her ear. "He was not to kill them!"

"He's still here." The figure didn't flinch or turn at the sound of her voice. "Is it safe?"

"Hold on. I am discussing the use of excessive force with the blood of my blood."

Bree whimpered.

"Just hold on a minute," Spooky whispered.

Elliot squeezed her hand.

"Now, as for you," Carcass's voice growled in her ear. "Why are you in that cave, when I expressly told you to stay on the path?"

Spooky's cheeks heated. "Are you kidding? You said your world was safe! We were attacked! If we hadn't been in the cave, we would have been eaten alive!"

"Except for the fact that my deer wouldn't have attacked you had you not been in one of their nests!"

"Oh."

"Yes. 'Oh.' And now my deer is dead. Humans," Carcass snarled. "They don't follow instructions and then act surprised when things go wrong."

"You could have warned us," Spooky mumbled.

"No more excuses, you've delayed your progress enough already. And distracted Kru from his errands. Keep walking."

The man next to the dead deer still hadn't moved. He blocked their exit.

"That tall guy is still here. Is it safe?"

"Kru won't hurt you."

Spooky didn't budge. "You said Kru wasn't supposed to kill the deer."

"Yes, but he has countered that, apparently, in my haste to save your lives, I didn't communicate that explicitly."

"Well, have you told him, explicitly, not to hurt us?"

"You flatter me with your unreserved faith. He has been instructed to protect you. Now go! You are wasting tongue-light. And follow my directions in the future, or you will most assuredly die. And worse, fail."

Spooky gestured for Bree and Elliot to stay back and tiptoed to the middle of the cave. Like Jagbi, Kru was humanoid, but he wouldn't be mistaken for a human. He had a blockish head, with no hair, ears, or nose. His mouth cut a straight line across his face. Only his dark eyes showed awareness of her presence as they followed her. All eight feet of him were naked, although there was no discernable part worth covering. His joints popped out like hinges, and muscles coiled in elaborate patterns beneath his skin. He was a similar color to Carcass but deeper, like rust. There were splashes of shiny claret blood on his calf, but she couldn't see any teeth marks.

"Um, hi. I'm Spooky. This is Elliot, and this is Bree. Carcass said you have been instructed to protect us." It couldn't hurt to reinforce the message.

Kru looked at her but showed no other indication he had heard her words.

"Okay, so that's us. We need to get going to reach Geye…"

There was a burnt-orange blur and a rush of air. Before she could say "gorg," they were alone in the cave with the body of the dead deer.

"Is it safe now?" Bree asked.

"I think so," Spooky said. "Carcass sent him to save us. I guess we don't need saving anymore."

"Elliot!" Bree squealed. "You're bleeding!"

Elliot peeled back his shredded sleeve. A series of long gashes marked the path of the deer's teeth on his forearm. The cave got darker around the edges as Spooky stared at the red. She reached out clumsy hands that didn't feel like her own.

"Woah," Elliot said. "Blood." His rosy cheeks paled.

Somehow, seeing Elliot rattled calmed her. If he was freaking out, she had to keep it together.

"Elliot, sit down," Spooky said. "And don't look."

He took a knee and sat hard, but he didn't take his eyes off his arm. It was hard to tell how deep the wounds were. They kept filling with blood.

"We have to apply pressure." Spooky asked the godfinger for napkins and pressed them into the wound. She had Bree hold them snug while she used the scissors to cut up his ruined sleeve. She tied strips around the napkins to keep them in place.

His arm looked like a mummy's, but no blood leaked through. "Thank you."

"I'm so sorry," Spooky said. Now that she had nothing to do with them, her hands shook. Elliot's pink cheeks were pale, and he was sweating. She felt like crying.

"For what?" he asked. "You were the first one to leap into battle."

"Yeah." Bree grinned, and nudged her. "If that guy hadn't shown up, you would have been the first to get eaten, for sure."

Spooky shivered, but a smile crept onto her face.

"You know," Elliot said. "You're handling this situation pretty well, yourself."

He echoed the words she had said to him yesterday. It turned the fizzy feeling in her chest into acid.

She was here because she had made a deal with Carcass.

Bree and Elliot were here because she had lied to them.

She could have sent them back to Dodgson, but she hadn't wanted to go on alone. Elliot was pale from blood loss because of her. Either of them could have died because of her.

The cave was too stuffy. Spooky couldn't get a deep enough breath. She stalked toward the entrance, inhaling again and again. She clambered down the rocky slope on weak legs.

"I need to speak to Carcass," she said. "Carcass!"

"If the matter of imminent death is resolved, could you handle things on your own for a few minutes? I'm a little preoccupied."

"Are there any more deer out there?" She hugged her arms, staring into the trees.

"Yes. But they won't harm you if you stay out of their nests."

"Are you sure?"

"Yes, I'm sure. I made them. Simply stay on the path."

"Okay." She closed her eyes. "Is the vine still holding open the door to Dodgson?"

Carcass paused. "Yes."

"I'm sending Bree and Elliot back the way we came. I'm continuing on to meet Geyegorg alone."

"As you wish, but do not dawdle. Kru is collecting offerings for Geyegorg. Saving you has put him behind schedule, but he will meet you at my winter home in a matter of hours. Be there when he arrives."

"I'll hurry," Spooky promised.

"Hey, what's wrong?" Elliot staggered down the slope, holding out his injured arm. Bree climbed down the other side and beat him to the bottom.

Spooky drew an unsteady breath. "I'm sending you back. I never should have brought you with me."

"Is this about my arm?" Elliot asked. "It was our choice. We could have stayed behind."

"No, I...I could have sent you back to Dodgson."

Elliot's blue eyes widened. Bree's narrowed.

"I didn't know Carcass would kidnap you! But once you were

here, he said I should take you with me, and I didn't know it would be dangerous. I just thought I would get there faster if you helped me."

Words were coming out of her mouth, but none of them changed the expression on Elliot's face.

"Did Carcass make you bring us?" His eyebrows pulled together. His blue eyes were sad, as they often were, but this time they were fixed on her.

Why was he making this so much harder? She wanted to say yes and smooth things over. "No, he gave me a choice. I could have sent you back."

"So you dragged us," Bree articulated each word, "on a twelve-hour hike, made us sleep in a cave, and risked our lives for nothing?"

"Yes, but..."

"But what?" Bree crossed her arms. "Those deer could have torn us to pieces. Elliot's arm is shredded."

"I didn't know..."

"What? You didn't know, what? I opened up to you. You know what I have to get back to, and you still didn't tell me I could go home to my family?" Bree's eyes were bright, and she was almost shouting. "I thought you were a loner by choice. Now I see why no one wants you!"

Spooky's eyes hit the ground and wouldn't lift. Bree's words were like a punch in the chest.

"Just follow the path back to the clearing," she mumbled. "There is a vine on the ground. Lift it up and walk straight into the white stuff, and you'll get back. I'll leave some food and water for you." She struggled to clear her throat. "Okay, good...good luck getting back. Sorry. I'm sorry."

Spooky bolted. Her eyes blurred as she ran through the trees. It only took her a few minutes to reach the path. The soft dirt still held their footprints from the day before.

She asked the godfinger to make eight sloppy joes, twenty glasses of water, and extra napkins for Elliot's arm. She added a few trays to help them carry the supplies.

They would be fine. They had a path. They had food and water. They had each other.

They would make it back just fine.

With nothing else to contribute, and not wanting to face them again, Spooky turned left and started on the unmarked expanse toward Geyegorg.

# CHAPTER XX
# THE STORYTELLER

The duplicated trees seemed more like steel bars than a living forest. There were no rustling branches or birds chirping. The only sounds were her own breath and plodding steps. She could have been walking through a painting, repeating the same section of path forever. She didn't know if any of the afterlife options she'd heard of were real, but this felt like a purgatory.

She wanted to curl up in a ball and go back to sleep. She wanted to wake up and forget. She kicked the dirt, and gritty pieces slid into her shoe.

Taking Elliot and Bree with her wasn't an accident or a bad split-second decision. No one—not Carcass, not Adam Dodgson, not her parents—had threatened her with any consequences. Elliot and Bree had asked her how to get back, and she had lied to them. And she had kept lying, every minute the journey continued and she didn't tell them they could leave.

Her shoes made long troughs in the dirt. Every part of her ached. Her chest hurt, her legs burned, and her stomach felt empty in a way food would only partially help. Elliot's blood stained the edges of her fingernails.

Spooky had always taken solace in the idea that, while she may not measure up to Victoria in any external capacity, she wasn't fake. Victoria was better at everything—school, sports, making friends. But Victoria was an actress. She took pills to stay perky. She picked friends that would make her popular. She did charity work to fill out her resume. Victoria hustled to look generous and caring, but when there was no upside for her, she didn't lift a finger for anyone.

Spooky had believed that if she made a friend, it would be genuine. If she helped someone, it wouldn't be for a college resume. If she pursued something, it wouldn't be for the accolades. She had believed that if the stars aligned and gave her a chance, she would be ready.

But all Spooky's potential accomplishments had stayed "ifs." Every year, she had been waiting for The Change.

And now it had turned out she was just as good as Victoria at one thing—using people. She had justified bringing Elliot and Bree with her in case she needed their help, but she was on a journey to negotiate with gods. Three humans were just as easy to maim, squash, or eat as one. She had put their lives in danger, just so she could feel more comfortable.

Was that the kind of person she was? Someone who only pretended to care about others? Spooky could only imagine she hadn't seen this side of herself before because she hadn't been ambitious. What lies would she have told, and what people would she have stepped on if she'd had the drive to be like Victoria? What path of bodies would she have left behind if she had been determined to get her parents' admiration, ivy league admission, or a high-powered career? She didn't know she could be just as self-centered as Victoria with none of the accomplishments to show for it.

When she'd had the power to make a selfish choice, she hadn't even hesitated.

"Let me speak to Carcass. Carcass? Are you there?"

"Spooky," he groaned. "Has another emergency befallen you already?"

She ignored his tone. "Can you turn back time?"

There was more than one thing she'd like to undo. She would send Elliot and Bree back to Dodgson right away. She would make it so they had never been kidnapped at all.

"Time does not 'turn.' And no, I cannot change past events."

"Then, can you erase memories?" At the very least, she could make Bree and Elliot forget they'd ever left Earth.

"Not without significant damage. Meddling would just as soon break a mind as achieve any specific goal."

"But then, what about our deal?"

"What about it?"

Spooky stopped walking. "How are you going to make it like Office Shack never happened if you can't change the past or erase memories?"

"I assure you, I will not honor any deal if you do not keep moving."

"I'm not going anywhere." Spooky locked her knees and crossed her arms. "Not until you tell me exactly how you're going to keep up your end of the bargain."

"Well, since you asked." His cool tone raised her temperature. "I needed more equipment to increase my download speed, so I already fixed your little problem. I robbed a few dozen electronics stores."

"How does that help? They know Office Shack was me."

"Human accounts are nothing if not flexible."

"They won't just forget! They have video! They have my finger-prints!" Spooky almost laughed. Maybe this was what she deserved—to come all this way, only to be tricked by Carcass.

But there had to be a magic reset button. She needed a second chance now more than ever. She couldn't be sent to prison knowing all she had ever done with her freedom was wait for change and hurt two people who had trusted her.

"Spooky, how do the police determine who is guilty of a crime? Can they 'turn back' time and attend the act in person?"

"No, but they have evidence."

"Evidence tells a story. I've incorporated what they already think they know into a new narrative that has a happier ending for you."

Carcass and his stupid stories.

"This isn't a story. This is my life."

"Your view of reality is not as fixed as you think."

"Carcass, if you don't..."

"Was there ever a bear at Dodgson?"

"What?"

"You asked me to claw the doors and walls of the building housing the router. Why?"

"So...the counselors would think a bear broke in."

"You didn't destroy the evidence of a break in. You did not erase memories. You added new information to change the narrative in their minds. And they accepted it, did they not?"

"Yes. But we're talking about video and fingerprints..."

"And yet, I have already absolved you."

"How? What's the 'narrative'?"

"The police currently believe you are a victim of someone else's crime spree. A criminal ring has been robbing electronics stores, leaving counterfeit money, and impersonating the police. They've taken you and the two other humans as hostages."

"How could the police believe that? That's so far-fetched..."

"You are young, and you are female. Other humans will believe you're a victim more easily than a villain. Besides, there is video."

"Video?"

"Security footage, showing a group of shadowy criminals breaking into other stores."

"You could have opened with that!"

"You can hardly hold me accountable for your lack of curiosity up until this point."

"Well, I'm curious now!" Spooky shouted. "They could still think I'm an accomplice. I went back to the camp. I ran from the police. Why would I have done that?"

"It's all mentioned in the ransom note."

"Ransom note?" Spooky rubbed her temples.

"That's what I understand one leaves behind when one has taken a hostage. And they absconded with you not once, but twice! You'll have to come up with the story of how you escaped temporarily. I look forward to hearing it."

Getting taken hostage for a night, escaping, spending the day at Dodgson, and then disappearing again? Carcass's solution was messy and full of weak points.

But what other explanation could the police come up with? How could she have gotten out of the camp, broken into Office Shack, made the counterfeit, and disappeared with two additional hostages otherwise? The nine-fingered hands behind it all would never be considered. The truth was impossible. They would have no choice but to believe the explanation provided in the videos and note Carcass had manufactured.

"So if I went back to Earth right now..."

"You would be welcomed as an innocent. Now, I warn you," Carcass growled. "I will undo all I have done and then some if you turn back now."

"Alright, alright, I'm walking." She shook out her knees. "I'm going."

"I have collected batteries and hard drives and started as many downloads as I can in case the worst happens. But these tactics won't last me another eight thousand years. So if you would stop bothering me, I'm going to continue working on giving you the time you require. The media has lost interest in the scientific team I saved in the Arctic. I need to perform another miracle."

"Okay, I'll be quiet. And Carcass? Thank you."

"Do your part," he grumbled. "Kru will join you at my winter home."

Spooky stretched out her legs, taking longer steps.

It seemed like Carcass had solved her legal troubles. But the police weren't the only threat to her future. Did her parents believe she'd been kidnapped? More importantly, did becoming a hostage make her a bigger burden? She was supposed to stay out of trouble for the summer. There was no stipulation in their ultimatum for a hostage situation.

But her parents did care about public perception. They wouldn't be able to kick her out if there was any kind of media attention. The poor young hostage, returned after days of captivity, thrown out on the streets by cold-hearted parents? They were lawyers, officers of the court. That wouldn't look good for them.

They just needed to see the cost-benefit-analysis of letting her continue to live in their house for one more year. It seemed likely they would.

Another factor would be Bree and Elliot. She didn't deserve to go to prison for Office Shack, but she wasn't blameless either. Her stomach still felt empty in a way she didn't know how to fill. Hopefully, they would play along with their status as returned hostages. Hopefully, they wouldn't tell the police she had cooperated with their kidnapper.

She couldn't deny the accusation, but she still really wanted her second chance.

Something gray and yellow moved in her peripheral vision. She flinched, but it was just Jagbi.

"Oh. Hi," she said. "Where have you been?"

"Observing rocks. And now you." He smiled at her, his baby-face open. He waddled in step beside her. "Where are the other two humans?"

"They went back home."

"And you?"

"I'm continuing on."

"Why?"

"To try to save Earth."

"Oh." He touched his chin. "Did the other two not want to save Earth?"

"No. I mean, yes, I'm sure they did. But it's dangerous."

Something in the distance was different. After hours and hours of the same straight trees, the brush ahead was denser. She started to jog, not bothering to see if Jagbi would keep up.

An invisible line divided two forests. The gray, bare trunks gave way to what looked like forty-foot-tall squirrel tails. They were stuck in the ground close enough together that they made a fur wall on either side of the path. Spooky had learned better than to touch anything, but the dappled gray and white fluff tempted her.

She felt lighter as she trotted through the plush trees. The fibers waved in the breeze she made as she passed. She only wished she was experiencing this new part of the world with Bree and Elliot. She wanted to hear Bree's reaction. Elliot would have pointed out something she hadn't noticed or asked a question she hadn't thought of.

The squirrel trees opened up to reveal a clearing. In the middle of the clearing sat a structure as big as the wood house. It resembled a teardrop-shaped blob of honey, with walls that were translucent but thick enough to distort dark shapes inside. It wasn't what she would traditionally think of as a house, or even a building, but the path ended here. This had to be Carcass's winter home.

She had made it.

The beacon marking the door to Geyegorg was somewhere nearby. She only had to ask the godfinger to reveal it to her.

"Open the door to Geyegorg."

A crack in her ear made her jump. Jagbi appeared next to her.

"Woah! You scared me."

"Are you going to be Father's storyteller when you get back?"

"What? No. He doesn't need me to."

Jagbi touched her arm and she jumped again. His water-gray eyes met hers. "I'm so sorry."

"No, no, don't be." She laughed. "It's a good thing. I don't want to be his storyteller. He has the internet now."

"In-ter-net?"

"It's like...a storytelling machine. From Earth," Spooky said. "That's why he brought me here. So he can keep using it."

"Will he be able to keep using it?"

"If I succeed. Just, hold on one second, Jagbi." She looked at the house. "Open the door to Geyegorg."

On the far side of the structure, near the fur tree line, a glowing fissure appeared in the air.

Wherever it led, she would go through that door alone. This was what she had signed up for. The unknown.

"And what if you fail?" Jagbi asked, trotting along beside her.

"Hm? Oh, then I guess Carcass will be bored and Earth will be destroyed." She squared off with the line. "I have to go through there."

"Then this may be my only chance." Jagbi sighed. "It's worth a try."

"What's worth a try?"

Jagbi hooked his hands into the sides of his mouth and pulled. His eyes grew round and wild, the stretching skin revealing too much white around the gray centers.

"Jagbi, what are you doing?"

He let go of his mouth, but it stuck a little wider. "Eating you."

She laughed but her heart clenched. "What?"

"I said 'eating you.' If you keep going, Father will have an in-ter-net storyteller. But if I stop you, he might need me again." He looked her up and down, then grabbed his jaw and resumed tugging. "And if I consume you, maybe I can absorb some of what he likes so much about you humans."

"That won't work." She took a step toward the glowing doorway. "And he'll be furious. He wants me to keep going."

"I know what he wants!" Jagbi snapped. "He wants storytellers from another world! If you're the last human here, I have to try. Otherwise, I will always be alone, accounting for rocks. That's not what I was made for!"

His words were pitiable, but his stretched mouth revealed every single blunt tooth in his head. Spooky's heart thudded and her legs tensed.

He looked her over once more. "Do you think if I hit your body with rocks it can be broken into smaller pieces? That's what happens when I hit small rocks with big rocks."

Spooky leapt for the white line. With a crack, Jagbi teleported in front of her.

"Carcass, I need you!" she shouted.

Jagbi clawed at the side of her head. He grasped the finger and yanked it away from her skull. She screamed as the tendrils ripped out of her skin.

He wagged the appendage at her. "None of that."

He gazed at it for a moment, his eyebrows drawn together. Then he threw the wriggling thing across the clearing.

Spooky watched the godfinger fall. She had no way of reaching Carcass. The glowing white line was gone; the door to Geyegorg had closed. She couldn't even materialize a tray to smack Jagbi over the head with.

"Jagbi, don't eat me!" She searched for some hint of the baby-faced creature who had saved her from Leber's pit. She backed away from him until she bumped into the smooth wall of the honey structure. "I don't want to die!"

"Die?"

"Yes Jagbi, die. If you eat me, I'll die!"

"Oh, yes. 'Die.' Rocks don't die you see. But I remember now. Humans die." Jagbi paused. For a second, she thought she might have swayed him. "Is that why you threw so many rocks at the deer? Because if they ate you, you'd die?"

"You were there?"

"I wanted you to sleep in their nest," Jagbi said. "I was hoping when they found you, it would make a good story."

He gave his lower lip another yank, then released it. His jaw hung halfway down his body, and his tongue rolled in the empty space. He lumbered forward and reached for her.

Spooky snatched the scissors from her waistband and swung. She sunk the double blades a few inches into his shoulder. Her cheeks were wet. She didn't know when she had started crying.

Jagbi furrowed his brow. He yanked the scissors out and threw them into the trees. His shoulder leaked pinkish blood.

"You seem upset."

"Yeah!" Her breath hitched. "Because you're trying to kill me! I don't want to die!"

"But you will. I remember now." His loose mouth garbled his words. "I don't think the lives of humans turn out any other way."

Spooky dashed around him. She didn't make it two steps toward the tree line before Jagbi was in front of her, her wrist in his four-fingered hand.

She screamed again, jerking and thrashing, but she couldn't free herself from his grip. He seized her shoulders, and his hanging mouth filled her vision. His throat was ribbed and shiny.

"Please, Jagbi, don't do this." She shook in his grasp and let out a sob. "I will teach you how to tell stories. I don't want to die."

"Whether you want to or not, you will. Right now."

Jagbi swung her into the air. She stared straight down his throat and screamed.

He let her drop.

# CHAPTER XXI
# OFFERINGS

The warm sides of Jagbi's throat were closing around Spooky's head when the world went sideways. Her hip hit the ground, and she tumbled out of his mouth and onto her back. She lifted her head in time to see Elliot roll off Jagbi. He jumped to his feet and stood over the larger being.

"What were you doing to her?" he shouted.

Bree was a few paces behind, fists clenched.

Jagbi lumbered to his feet. He stalked toward Elliot, his jaw swinging.

"Your stories about rocks are boring!" Bree shouted.

Jagbi turned away from Elliot, his brows lowered.

Jagbi was too burly for the three of them to overpower, and Spooky doubted there would be as much preamble before he tried to eat another human. She jumped up and scanned the ground for the godfinger.

"That's right! I said it!" Bree taunted. "I wouldn't even call them stories! They're boring, idiotic, repetitive, and...ah!"

Jagbi took Bree by the shoulders. Spooky spotted the orange appendage and dove for it, grasping it against her ear.

"I need to talk to Carcass!" She screamed.

At the word "Carcass," Jagbi rounded on her, eyes wide and fearful.

"Jagbi is trying to kill us!"

Jagbi let go of Bree and appeared in front of Spooky. He tore the finger from her grip and pulled her to her feet with one hand around her throat.

He didn't lift her toward his mouth. Instead, he squeezed.

"If you kill me like this," she managed to wheeze out, "you won't get to absorb my stories."

"Any way I kill you," Jagbi gritted his teeth, "at least you won't be telling them."

Bree and Elliot were yelling. He didn't seem to notice their blows.

Spooky's head felt like it was going to burst. She scratched at his hand. She couldn't get a breath. Her lungs strained.

The world darkened.

Jagbi bellowed and let go of her. Spooky dropped to her knees. She coughed and wheezed, clasping her throat. The new air escaped her lungs as fast as she could draw it in. She tried to take slower breaths, focusing on the dirt.

When she looked up, Jagbi was thrashing and swinging his arms. Kru towered over him, holding him captive by his two nubby horns. Jagbi was wider, but Kru's grip didn't give even when Jagbi kicked his feet off the ground.

"Let me go!" he twisted and swung at Kru's torso. "Let me go, brother!"

A loud crack sounded; Jagbi's body twitched, but it didn't disappear.

"Spooky, are you okay?" Elliot helped her to her feet.

"Yeah," she rasped. Her throat was on fire. She avoided his eyes.

Kru's mouth hinged open like a puppet's. Unlike Jagbi, he had no tongue or teeth or gullet. His mouth was smooth, like the inside of a polished wooden bowl.

"Spooky!" Carcass's voice boomed out of the hole. "What has happened?"

"Carcass! Jagbi," she coughed, "he tried to eat me."

"Jagbi!" It was like a speaker was embedded in Kru's throat. "What is this insolence?"

If Jagbi had the power to melt, Spooky thought he would have. His eyes rolled and he sagged against Kru's grip.

"Please, Father, don't be angry," he whimpered.

"You cannot even be left to a desolate corner of my world," Carcass hissed. "You still find a way to disappoint me."

"I only meant to become better for you, Father." Jagbi's stretched mouth curved downward. "You made me to become better at story-telling. I was only doing what you wanted."

"And yet you are still worth less than nothing to me, child. A waste of my blood. And so, you shall return it to me."

"Brother, let me go!" Jagbi screeched.

The air around him snapped again, but he didn't teleport.

Jagbi's gray eyes sunk back into his skull. His hanging mouth closed and shriveled around his cry. His arms retracted into his torso. His horns popped off in Kru's hands as his head sank down into his knotted robe. The garment deflated with his decreasing mass, until it dropped to the ground. A tangerine worm the size of a baguette wriggled out of the pile of rags.

Kru dropped the disembodied horns.

The worm was a deeper version of Jagbi's marigold hue, but that was the extent of the resemblance. Spooky didn't know if Jagbi was dead in the familiar sense, but he was definitely gone. The worm flopped. It didn't seem distressed, but Jagbi sure had been before the transformation.

"Spooky, put this unfortunate encounter behind you," Carcass said out of Kru's mouth. "Jagbi was the most unpredictable child I ever managed to create, in hopes that he would learn to tell me new stories. This interference was not the intended outcome of that free-dom. I should have undone him a long time ago."

Even though Jagbi's attempts to please Carcass had involved her almost dying, she still felt a little sorry for him.

"Now," he continued, "do you have the godfinger?"

"Jagbi threw it," she croaked. "I'll get it..."

"We shall communicate like this for now. Have you located the door to Geyegorg?"

"Yes."

"Good. You must press on. While you were travelling to my winter home, Kru was crisscrossing the universe, accumulating offerings for Geyegorg. It is my hope that he will accept one of them in exchange for the beacon to Axonaphis. Kru, fetch the offerings."

Kru blurred out of sight. Only the rippling fur trees gave a clue as to which way he'd gone.

Spooky was left alone with Bree, Elliot, and the worm that had been Jagbi.

"So, is this what you hear when Carcass talks to you through the finger?" Elliot asked.

"Oh, uh, yeah."

She couldn't look at his face. His makeshift bandage was stained brown. The amount of dried blood made her heart skip a beat, but hopefully, the color meant the bleeding had stopped.

"Thank you. For saving me from Jagbi. He was going to kill me... he actually led us to the cave on purpose, so the deer would attack us."

"Oh wow," Elliot said.

Bree crossed her arms. Spooky glanced at her scowl and could guess what it meant—it didn't matter what Jagbi had done. It mattered what she had done.

Kru zoomed back and deposited five bundles in front of her.

"These items are all I could acquire within a limited time frame," Carcass said through Kru's unmoving mouth. "Perhaps it would be a better assortment if Kru hadn't had to come save you. Twice. Open them."

Spooky untied the first bundle, revealing two stacks of five-dollar bills. She couldn't imagine why Earth money would be valuable to a god from another world but moved on to the next one. It contained a top hat. The third and fourth offerings seemed a little more special—the wrappings fell away to expose a glowing orb and a pile of golden sticks. The last parcel held a jar of something that looked like gritty pudding. It was moving. The little pieces scattered and swirled in shifting patterns.

"This is what you think he'll want?" Even though she hadn't touched the stuff in the jar, Spooky wiped her hands on her shirt. "Money, a hat, a glow ball, sticks, and living oatmeal?"

"Finding things to offer Geyegorg is not as easy as you may think; you cannot offer something in trade that you have no authority to give. I could have sent Kru to steal some valuable artifact, but Geyegorg would know you had no right to trade it. He can see rights over property, like you or I can see the sky."

"Oh," Spooky said. "So these are...your things?"

"I have the authority to give them, and I must extend it to you. Spooky, I give you this money, this top hat, this borderlight, these scrying sticks, and this slangslorn. They are now yours to offer in trade."

He said it with such seriousness, she felt like a spotlight should have shone on her. "Okay...but why would he want cash? Or a top hat?"

"He has something of a fascination with how business is conducted on Earth. I thought he might enjoy accepting Earth money in trade or wearing a formal Earthly hat."

"Well, then, what about a cellphone?" Spooky pulled the dead phone out of her waistband. "That seems like a more interesting thing to offer him."

"Do not!" Carcass barked. Kru lunged forward and snatched it out of her hand. The muscles of his arm rippled as he slung it into the trees. "That is not yours to give! He takes offense at being offered illegitimate trades."

"Okay, alright. You didn't have to throw it." She lowered her empty hand. She wasn't sure which camper's phone was now lost in the forest of another world. "But you could go buy me a different phone and give it to me to trade."

"You misunderstand my meaning. Just because something is

considered personal property in your world, that doesn't make it yours to trade on a cosmic level. I created that cash and top hat. I was gifted that slangslorn. The creator of the particles in that phone gave you no authority to trade them."

"Remind me why you can't be the one to go handle the negotiations?" Spooky scratched her head. "You know all the rules."

"I have already given Geyegorg the best of what I can offer. He might not even take an audience with me for another hundred years or so. But you have an advantage. You are a human. He will immediately know you belong to the god of Earth. A powerful god, who owns many treasures Geyegorg would covet. It is my hope that he will assume you are an emissary of this powerful new business partner and open the relationship with an easy trade. Perhaps he will even give you the beacon to Axonaphis for free. Just follow my instructions, and you'll have little to fear."

Little wasn't nothing.

"You must conceal that I am the one who sent you to him and the reason you want to visit Axonaphis. Do not reveal that you've had no contact with your god, or you'll hurt your chances for an easy negotiation. And you must hide my godfinger carefully—if he catches sight of it with his third eye, he will see that it belongs to me. Perhaps you can put it under your skin?"

"Um. How about I hide it in my hair?"

"Very well, just keep it near your ear so it may translate for you. No need to call for me; I will be listening the whole time. Repeat back my instructions."

"Pretend like I don't know you. Try to pretend like I do know the god of Earth." Spooky bounced on her toes. "Don't offer him anything that's not mine to trade. Hide the godfinger. Got it."

"And Spooky, do not leave this negotiation without an agreement. There is no time for a second chance. My intel suggests the first attack will begin in the middle of the Pacific, tomorrow."

"At least it isn't going to be on land."

"Whether it is in the ocean or the most populous city, if an attack is successfully completed with no direct challenge from the god of Earth, the rest of the invading gods will strike. The damage will spiral into something irreversible in a matter of hours."

"So we have a day."

"Yes, but you must hide your desperation from Geyegorg, or he will exploit it and demand a higher price. Make your request casually, display your offerings one at a time. Remember, in his eyes, you represent the god of Earth, so you have nothing to fear. Recover the godfinger and go through the door."

With that, Kru's jaw and head converged, closing down on Carcass's voice. Kru bent and scooped up the rags, horn-nubs, and worm that used to be Jagbi, and zipped away.

Spooky was alone with Bree and Elliot once more. She fidgeted and kicked the dirt. When she finally looked up, they were staring at her.

"So...what are you doing here?" Spooky wished she couldn't hear the emotion in her own voice.

"You don't deserve our help," Bree snarled, pointing in Spooky's face. "You lied to us. If things were different, I would never talk to you again. We're not here for you."

"No, we're not," Elliot said. He wasn't snapping, but he wasn't smiling either. Spooky expected bite from Bree, but even frank words stung coming from Elliot. "We just couldn't pretend, after all we've seen and heard, that this is only about you. Or about us."

"I need to make sure nothing like that tar pit comes near my family." Bree narrowed her eyes. "But I want to be clear—we are not good. Don't talk to me like we're friends, and don't expect me to be yours."

Elliot ruffled his bangs and looked away. "Carcass said we only have a day, right? So we should probably get moving."

Spooky nodded. She should be grateful they were going to help her. She should be glad that she didn't have to go face Geyegorg alone.

But when she had raised her head after Jagbi's attack and saw them standing there, she thought maybe they had come back for her. Maybe they had forgiven her.

She was being selfish again. Of course they had their own reasons for not wanting evil gods to overrun Earth. Of course protecting Angela was more important to Bree than whether or not she hated Spooky. Elliot probably had people he wanted to protect too.

"Okay. Are you both clear on what we have to do?"

"Go visit Geyegorg and offer him these items for the beacon to Axonaphis," Elliot said.

"Pretend like we are in with the god of Earth, instead of trying to find him," Bree added.

"Right. I just need the godfinger."

Spooky limped over to where Jagbi had tossed it. With the adrenaline of Jagbi's attack fading, the pain in her hip throbbed. As Spooky passed Elliot, she almost looked up, but stopped herself. She wasn't quite ready to see how he would look back at her.

The appendage still felt warm and alive, even though it had been disembodied for over a day. She lifted her hair and positioned it low on her head, so the fingernail curved behind her ear. It was gross, but she was relieved to have it back; it felt like a lifeline. The bones clicked as it formed into place. The orange tendrils squirmed down her spine, gripping and digging into her skin. She clenched her teeth, determined not to ask for any sympathy.

"Let me check it." Bree arranged Spooky's hair over the finger, pulling a bit harder than necessary.

Elliot circled her a few times. "Can't see it."

"Say something in Danish," Spooky said.

"*Let's get going,*" he replied.

"Good. I don't think you'll be able to understand Geyegorg without this, so I'll have to do the talking."

She had signed up to do this alone. Any help she received from them was a bonus. As long as she remembered that, it shouldn't ache too badly, no matter how they looked at her.

They retied the packages. Spooky took the oatmeal and the orb.

She asked the finger to open the door to Geyegorg. The misting line appeared.

"All you have to do is walk straight at it." She hesitated. "I don't know what's on the other side of this door. It could be dangerous. Are you absolutely sure you want to come?"

"Shut up," Bree said.

"Right, okay, here we go." Spooky strode forward and stepped into whiteness.

# CHAPTER XXII
## GEYEGORG

The endless whiteness enveloped Spooky. It was a new door, but the void was the same—infinite and mind-numbingly blank. She twisted to face back the way she had come, strands of her dark hair dragging across her vision. For a moment, she wondered if anyone would follow.

But then Elliot's arm appeared in the nothingness, followed by his shoulders and head. He tipped in and rotated. He laughed, his wide smile clear even though the sound was muffled. His brown hair drifted up like he had just jumped into a pool.

A second later, Bree stepped into the void with her eyes squeezed shut. When she opened them her mouth opened too, and she kicked her legs like she was trying to swim.

Spooky let her knees float up toward her chest, enjoying the gentle bobbing. She focused on the emotions playing across Bree's and Elliot's faces. She wished they could stay in this weightless place for a while longer.

Then she fell in darkness. She landed in a half-crouch, clutching her parcels. She stood and moved to the side. Elliot emerged a few seconds later, outlined in white. Bree kicked him as she tumbled out after.

"Ow," Elliot said. "But wow. That's a lot more fun when you do it on purpose."

"You have a weird idea of fun." Bree straightened her nightshirt and smoothed her wild hair.

Spooky blinked away the auras the bright blankness had left in her eyes. They were standing on one end of a platform the length of a football field. Everything up was black, but it didn't look like sky; something about the dispersion of light made it feel like an enclosed space, even though any walls or ceiling were lost in darkness.

The flat expanse was elevated above a shining honeycomb that stretched to the horizon. Spooky meandered to one side and peered over. Each hexagonal cell was outlined in rough stone and filled with liquid gold. It was at least a three-story drop. Her limbs tingled, and she backed away from the edge.

The soft glow from the honeycomb illuminated the length of the platform, but the far end was spotlit. A figure slumped in a huge stone chair.

"Walk toward the throne," Carcass said in her ear.

She beckoned Elliot and Bree. The commotion at the end was loud enough to overhear as they approached.

"Please!" called a thin, wheedling voice. "Please! I need her back! Please, give her back to me."

"Give her back, give her back, I want her back." The voice from the throne was mocking. "Why should I give her back to you when you have a beautiful beacon to guide you from hither to thither whenever you please?"

"Take the beacon! End our contract! I need her!"

The creature hunched before the throne was made of what appeared to be hundreds of layered moth wings. They fluttered in waves as the creature spoke.

The being glowering down from the stone seat had a smooth, oval face, and no nose. His mouth was low, almost at the edge of his jawline. On his head sat a cylindrical hat, like the kind Spooky had made in kindergarten with a rolled piece of construction paper.

It had to be Geyegorg, and based on his frown and slouch, it did not look like he was in a very good mood.

"No ho ho, my dear, that is not the way this works. We made a trade, and the contract is mine to maintain or to end. Why would I give back something that still pleases me, without any incentive?"

"I'll give you anything!" The creature fluttered. "I've offered you everything!"

"Your offers bore me, as does this conversation."

"Can you understand what they're saying?" Elliot whispered in her ear. "What is happening?"

"Obviously," Bree muttered. "The butterfly thing is mad at King Tut."

"Yeah," Spooky said. "That's about right."

"I wasn't talking to you," Bree hissed at her.

Apparently, Bree had meant it when she said Spooky couldn't expect her to be friendly.

"If you will not give her back to me..." The moth creature's voice grew shrill. "I must do what I must do!"

"How very vague." Geyegorg tucked his chin into one hand. "But that does sound like a threat. I do not recommend taking that tack with me."

The creature's wings rose up like the strings on a spinning mop. It trilled a higher and higher note. All at once, it snapped its layers shut and launched itself at Geyegorg.

Two burnt-orange blurs zoomed out from behind the throne and caught it mid-flight.

Bree gasped. "Hey, isn't that..."

"Kru!" Spooky breathed.

The moth creature was immobilized in the hands of two exact replicas of Kru. They had the same blocky heads, oversized joints, and long limbs rippling with the contours of coiled muscle. Even their impassive facial expressions were exactly the same.

"Silence," Carcass hissed in her ear. "Revealing you know Kru would reveal you know me. Plus, I may have sworn up and down to Geyegorg I could only make two such children with the blood in my body. He doesn't know a third exists."

"Kru-clones?" Bree asked.

Spooky put her finger to her lips and shook her head. "We don't know them, because we don't know you-know-who. Our orange friend."

As nervous as she was to talk to Bree, she was more afraid of ruining their chances with Geyegorg before they had even started. She glanced at Elliot to make sure he understood. He nodded. They were only halfway down the platform. It was unlikely Geyegorg could have overheard them whispering.

Plus, he was occupied.

The two Krus held the winged creature in place as it undulated and flapped, squealing.

Geyegorg hadn't even flinched from his slouch. "You know the rules, my codes, my standards. Violence it is, then. Bought with violence."

Strands of golden light rose up from either side of the platform. They climbed high over the throne, then arched downward toward the captive moth. The two Krus assumed identical stances, lunging back from the flapping creature. The strands of light moved at a steady pace, converging at the center of the wings. They pierced straight through the layers and came out the other side, unimpeded by the moth's mass.

The creature let out a sound for which the finger had no translation. Its wings stiffened, then crumpled.

The glowing filaments withdrew from the moth's body, then looped around it. The Krus released the limp form and faced each other. The light lifted the creature and carried it over the length of the platform. Spooky craned her neck as it passed above their heads. Near where they had arrived, the mess of wings lit up in a white halo and disappeared.

The moth creature had been ejected into the void.

The empty golden strands retracted and vanished beneath the platform.

Spooky had to force herself to loosen her grip on the bundles before she crushed the offerings. Even though Bree and Elliot hadn't been able to understand the conversation, their pale faces showed they had understood the violence.

Getting stabbed with rays of light was definitely not what Spooky had signed up for in her deal with Carcass. But Bree and Elliot weren't here for any deal—they were only here to protect Earth. She couldn't be the one to seek comfort or turn back now.

"Our orange friend warned us not to break Geyegorg's rules," Spooky whispered. "If we stick to them, we should be fine."

"Do we know all the rules?" Elliot asked.

"We know the first one—no bad trades." Spooky shook out her shoulders. "And now we know the second—don't attack him."

She forced herself to walk toward the throne.

"Halt!" called a voice at her feet.

Spooky almost dropped her parcels and leapt off the platform.

A figure that only came up as high as her hip stood in her path. Spooky wasn't sure if it had appeared there or if it had just been below her field of vision. It looked like an upright, aging lizard. Its pinched face struck her as more pompous than threatening, but after the black goo, Jagbi, and the murderous ropes of light, Spooky wasn't ready to assume anything about anything.

The creature wore a much shorter version of Geyegorg's hat. It held a tablet in one hand and used the other to keep the hat on as it stared up at her.

"Please select your language. Please select your language. Please select your language. Please select your language. Please select your language."

Spooky could see that the movement of its mouth changed each time, even though the words she heard kept repeating.

"Please select your language?" Its pinched face twisted. "Please select your language?"

"Um, English?" she said.

"English!" It repeated back, its mouth at last matching the words she heard. "Language selected. Welcome to the world of Geyegorg of the Extraordinary Sight. First-time visitor or returning?"

"Err, first-time," Spooky said.

"Are you familiar with the rules of engagement?"

"Uh, no." Carcass had told them the basics, but he was a need-to-know kind of god.

The little lizard-man looked at his tablet. "To reduce wait times and increase servicing speeds, we have compiled some frequently asked questions into a presentation. Following this presentation, you will have the opportunity to ask questions before being queued for an audience with Geyegorg of the Extraordinary Sight. Thank you for your patience and cooperation."

It took a deep breath.

"Geyegorg of the Extraordinary Sight is the savior who has opened the wonders of the universe to all." Its voice was monotone. "Through his singular power, he sees the unseeable doors between worlds. Through his ultimate benevolence, he will grant you the ability to see them too, using a marker called a beacon.

"Most of our beacon packages begin at the worldwide, multiparty access level. You can also request custom beacons for specific portals or pay for private access points. Pricing varies. Do you know what you'd like to buy today, or can I walk you through some popular options?"

It lifted its fine-boned face from the tablet.

"We know what we're here for. We want to know the price for the beacon to Axon..."

"No representative can negotiate on behalf of Geyegorg!" The creature said, holding up a hand. "When you get an audience, make your request clearly and concisely. He will determine the appropriate fee. If you cannot come to an agreement on an exchange, return to your own world. If you do not have a beacon to return to your own world, a door of Geyegorg's choice will be opened for you."

"He has been known to eject gods into strange and terrible worlds if their offers displease him," Carcass added in her ear.

"Oh," Spooky said to both of them. Of course Carcass hadn't mentioned that until now.

"Don't interrupt." It sniffed, returning its attention to the script. "Geyegorg represents the pinnacle of civil business practices. He does not condone or support the sale of stolen material. As such, he will only accept collateral in trade from those with the rightful authority to grant said collateral, as outlined in section A-13.

"If you do come to a verbal agreement, a written contract will formalize the details of your arrangement. Your contract begins as soon as the agreed upon collateral is collected by Geyegorg. Geyegorg may terminate any contract, at any time, for any reason. At such time, you will lose sight of the associated beacon, and the collateral will be returned to you at a predetermined location. If you wish to regain sight of a beacon, return here to seek an audience and negotiate a new contract.

"And finally, this is a combat-free zone. Any being interrupting business in this world will be terminated.

"If you wish to observe negotiations, wait on the white line. When you are ready to seek an audience with Geyegorg of the Extraordinary Sight, wait on the red line. Geyegorg accepts negotiations in any spoken or written language, and he negotiates in Clrechnv. Will you require translation to English for an additional fee?"

"Uh, no," Spooky said.

"Very well. It is your great honor to be in the presence of Geyegorg of the Extraordinary Sight."

The thing clapped its board to its chest and stepped to one side.

Spooky took a deep breath and continued past the creature. The cloth packages in her hands felt pathetic, like she was bringing her lunchbox to a fancy restaurant. Not that she wanted to think of the living oatmeal as lunch.

"So, there are a few more rules than we had been told," Spooky whispered.

"At least the way they do business is familiar," Elliot said.

"Aside from the 'we murder you if you interrupt it' part," Bree added.

"Shh, we don't know how good his hearing is." Spooky glanced at the figure on the throne. Geyegorg hadn't stirred from his slump.

"He's got super sight, not hearing." Bree still lowered her voice. "This game is rigged. Did you hear the part about needing a beacon to leave? Contracts end whenever he wants them to. He will kill us if we try to mess with him. He put that in his welcome presentation!"

"I guess when you're the only one in the universe who can provide something, and everyone wants it, you get to make the rules," Elliot said.

Spooky reached the white line for observers and stopped. A dozen feet ahead, the red line for negotiators encircled the bright area around the throne. Geyegorg's eyes were closed. He had his elbow draped over one blocky armrest, and his chin in his hand. Murdering a moth creature had barely interrupted his nap. On either side of the throne, just outside the light, the Kru-clones waited. They were perfect copies of the Kru who had protected them, but their blank expressions and straight mouths looked sinister.

"Bree is right. Negotiating with him is dangerous and completely on his terms," Spooky whispered. She wiggled her toes on the white line. "You both should stay here and watch. You won't be able to understand what he says anyway. If I mess up, or something else happens, you can take the finger or pay for translation and try again. We can't leave here without a trade."

"Sounds good to me." Everything from Bree's shrug to her pursed lips screamed 'I don't care what happens to you.'

Elliot's brows pulled together. "I guess we can't help much if we don't understand what he's saying."

"We're here for the mission," Bree said. "Having back-ups in case she fails just makes sense."

"Right, okay." Spooky hoped they would see her offer, at least in part, as proof that she wasn't going to use them again. "Give me your bags."

Spooky locked her knees so her legs wouldn't shake. She gathered the five bundles against her chest and turned toward the throne. She stepped over the white line.

# CHAPTER XXIII
## BARGAIN BEACON

Spooky crept toward the red line. She stopped at the edge of it, teetering. Geyegorg remained motionless, his eyes closed.

She heard panting and tapping steps behind her. The little lizard-man ran around to stand in front of her.

"You may now step forward and begin your negotiation." The thing paused to gasp. "With Geyegorg of the Extraordinary Sight!"

Spooky stepped over the line. She set down her five cloth bundles. Still, Geyegorg didn't move.

"Um, hello," she said. "I'm here to..."

His eyes opened halfway, then sprung wide. He raised his chin from his hand.

"You! Come here! Come, come, come!"

Wanting nothing more than to run the other direction, Spooky shuffled closer. She thought it would be warmer here under the bright light, but goosebumps prickled on her arms.

"Now let me see you..."

Geyegorg grabbed the top of his hat and lifted it off his head. She had assumed the cylindrical hat was adding height, but it revealed an equally tall forehead beneath. His eyeline was actually in the middle of a symmetrical oval face. A circle of light shone from his elongated brow. It looked like a lantern behind his skin.

Now that it was exposed, she could hear a faint hum.

Geyegorg sat up so fast he practically left his seat. Spooky jumped back in alarm. His hat bounced down the steps in front of the throne. The creature with the tablet ran to fetch it.

"Oh ho ho ho, if I didn't trust my third eye, I would think I was seeing things." He perched on the edge of his chair, straining and weaving. His low mouth curved up. "I thought it too late to dream of adding a human to my collection. Whoever has brought you to me shall have a prize indeed. Secretary! Where is the being who has brought me this morsel?"

The lizard rushed forward. "She came with two others."

"Bring them before me."

It nodded and dashed away. Panting, it reappeared, shoving the back of Bree's and Elliot's legs into the pool of light. So much for keeping them in the shadows as back-up. They looked just as nervous as she felt to be standing where the moth creature had just been skewered.

"No. No, no, no!" Geyegorg pounded the armrests of his throne. "Nothing on you, no part of you. None of you have the right!" He leaned down toward them. "Where is your creator? Who am I to do business with?"

"It's just us," Spooky said. "For today! We're the ones who are here to do business with you. For now."

She tried to stand straighter. She was an emissary of the god of Earth, after all.

He sat back. The pair of eyes in the middle of his face squinted. His third eye stayed round and bright.

"Secretary!" he said again. "Confirm there is no one else present who may witness."

"There are no other visitors here at present, but your Extraordinariness..."

Geyegorg held up a hand and the delicate creature closed its mouth.

Elliot tugged Spooky's sleeve and tipped his head toward the side of the platform. Golden ropes made of light were poking up over the edge. The same ones that had just pierced through the moth's body like a needle through a ball of yarn.

Was he going to kill them? Or would he just capture them for his collection? He wasn't supposed to accept stolen offerings, but did that apply if he was the one doing the stealing? She bit her tongue to stop herself from calling out to Carcass.

The threads hovered and Geyegorg stared at her. Somehow, she felt like the light in his forehead was staring at her too.

Then his low mouth cracked into a smile. His oblong head fell back as he let out a wild laugh.

"Oh ho ho ho, no," he cackled. "I wouldn't dare. I wouldn't dare." He half stood and then sat three times, arranging the way his weight was distributed. He wagged his finger. "It's things like you, missy, creations like you, that tempt me to less than honorable business practices. What I wouldn't give to see you three wrapped up tight, arching into one of my pens for safekeeping. What I wouldn't give."

He leaned forward again, all trace of a smile gone. Spooky barely stopped herself from stepping back. She felt every heartbeat as she waited.

"No, ho ho, oh no." He smiled and shook his head. "The number of gods I would have charging in here to reclaim their property if I broke protocol. The claims of fraudulent trades I would have to manage...not to mention your god, if he came banging on my door! No, no, no, best to stay above reproach. Above reproach all around." He tilted forward. "It's hard making the rules, isn't it? Just because I made them doesn't mean I like them."

He settled into his chair. The tendrils of light disappeared below the edge of the platform.

"I based my system on Earthly business centers, you know. The combination of contractual clarity, politeness, and violence seemed like the best way to build a business empire. Did you notice? Did it measure up?"

"Uh, yes." Spooky half bowed. "Very much like Earthly business centers. And like in Earthly business centers, I appreciate that you follow your own rules. Very, um, consistent."

"Pishposh, you flatter me." He waved a hand, smiling behind the other. "Now, why have you come to see me? Surely not to torture me with temptation, surely not!"

"Um, no," Spooky said. "And it's just me here to negotiate today. The others are just observing. For our report."

She waved for them to return to the relative safety of the white line. She wiped her forehead.

"I have come to ask for the beacon to Axon...Axonaphis."

"Have you now?" Geyegorg said. "A human from Earth seeking the beacon to visit Axonaphis's world. A useful beacon for those with a need to send a message. Not much else to Axonaphis's realm beyond that. But," he tapped his fingers on his armrest, "I find that those with a need to visit usually have no choice but to pay."

He paused. Spooky tried to keep a straight face.

"I don't suppose someone will materialize to offer you to me? Even just a finger or a toe? I'd take a cell sample, perhaps from your brain? I'd give you more than the beacon to Axonaphis for that..."

"No, sorry, not today." Spooky suppressed a shudder, but she couldn't quite control the waver in her voice. "I've brought you some other options I'm authorized to trade."

He flapped his hands. "Come come, let me see them."

Spooky peeked at the oatmeal then decided to start with the cash. She unwrapped it and held out the bills.

"Money. This is what we use for trade on Earth."

He tapped his fingers against his chin. "And what else?"

"Um." She opened the next one. "A top hat. Also from Earth."

He looked down at it, then at her. "Is this mockery? You bring me inanimate objects? Something that any low god could have spun together?"

"Uh." Spooky blinked and breathed in deeply. "These things are very authentic for how we do business on Earth. But okay...how about these?"

She untied the bundles containing the orb and the golden sticks.

He shook his head.

She held up the living porridge.

"Gah!" He scoffed and twisted so far in his seat he wasn't even facing her anymore. "I already have slangslorn. A whole pen of it. This is an insult. I want an Earthly life form. I won't take less!"

"Tell him no, not for your first trade," Carcass said. Spooky twitched. "My animals only resemble Earthly creatures. We can't fool him with them if he looks upon them with his third eye, and we can't gain authority over the real thing without the god of Earth."

Spooky cleared her throat. "The, the god who sent me would like to start with a simple trade. Just to test things out."

"On no ho ho, no no no." He shook his head. "Don't expect a deal after dangling such a treat in front of me. You've made me feel very greedy, very greedy. Such a tasty dish paraded in front of me, and you can't even serve it? What about...a flower? A honeybee?"

"Uh, no. Nothing living from Earth, this time. Next time."

"Gah! You have no shame. No shame!" He struck his armrest.

So much for Carcass's plan to get an easy first trade out of him. She rubbed the goosebumps on her arms. "So, so then, will you accept these for the beacon to Axonaphis?"

She gestured to the open bags in front of her.

"If I can't have what I want from Earth, I must have a living being of another High Order world." He tapped his chin. "There is something else I have long awaited, almost as long as a creation from Earth." He raised a finger. "You must bring me a living creation from Targa."

"Is, is that a place?"

"Targa is a god, and a rotten one. A selfish one. He says he has no use for my beautiful beacons and keeps all of his creations for himself." Geyegorg shifted in his chair again. "And I won't have it. Or rather, I must have it—something he won't give me but might give you. I want one of his creations." He held up a fist like he already had something in his grip. "His daughter has done business with me, but that isn't good enough this time. Oh no, I don't want a creation of his creation. I want something Targa has made with his own power." He slapped the side of his leg. "You must convince him to let you have one of his Targytes, and then you can give it to me. Then I will give you the beacon to Axonaphis. You understand?"

"Uh..." She wasn't sure she did.

"I know of Targa," Carcass said in her ear. "I myself have the beacon to his world. He is known to be a gentle god, neither violent nor cruel. I don't know if he'd be willing to give you a Targyte, but it is possible, while acquiring a living being from Earth is not. Accept the trade."

"I accept," she parroted.

"I will even give you passage to visit him in exchange for these things you've already brought me, yes? See? Tell your god that I am generous, generous. And oh so ready to make many deals." He clapped and rubbed his hands together. "A bargain beacon, just for you! Do we have a deal? These five little gifts in exchange for the beacon that will take you to visit Targa?"

"Say yes," Carcass told her.

"Yes," Spooky said to Geyegorg.

"Excellent! Now, for some minor logistical details to complete our contract."

He waved his hand and the little lizard in a hat ran forward. He flipped his slab over and began to read:

"Thank you for doing business with the seer of doors, unlocker of the universe, Geyegorg of the Extraordinary Sight. This contract is initiated upon the receipt of your payment, henceforth referred to as 'the collateral.' You have agreed to provide the collateral in exchange for the beacon marking all doors leading to world 317, henceforth referred to as 'the beacon.'

"The collateral is now the property of Geyegorg, and any attempt to reclaim it will justify retaliation, up to and including deadly force. If Geyegorg were to become incapacitated, a coalition of entities listed in section B-2 would be activated to carry out retaliatory action on his behalf."

Spooky glanced at the money, the hat, the orb, the sticks, and the slop. "I won't try to reclaim them."

"Your verbal consent is not required for each section." The creature's annoyance was clear on its pinched face. It cleared its throat. "Should Geyegorg choose to nullify your contract, the only notification informing you of this change will be the absence of the beacon in your visual field and the return of the collateral to your seat of power.

"At such time, any doors held open to world 317 will be shut, by force. You are welcome to return to his Extraordinariness and renegotiate."

Spooky had no intention of renegotiating anything. Her visit to Targa would be a one-time trip.

"Please confirm you understand the terms of this contract, and the beacon will be provided to you."

"Yes. Yes, I confirm."

"Laborious." Geyegorg smiled. "But necessary. Now, for the fun part."

The golden ropes of light emerged and stretched upward into the dark. They curved over the platform like a map of the magnetic fields around Earth. Spooky flinched as they arched down toward her, but they aimed at the bundles at her feet. They encircled the five offerings and bore them out over the honeycomb. Each strand of light dipped into a golden hexagon and retracted with nothing.

"Okay," Spooky said. "So, what do I do now?"

"It is not what you do. It is what I do." Geyegorg nestled his chin into one hand with a smile. He raised the other straight up with his fingers spread wide.

A swirling cyclone descended from the blackness. Thousands of glowing symbols, in all the colors Spooky could think of and many she had no name for, rotated above the throne in a tornado the size of a skyscraper.

A single yellow pictograph drifted down from the whirling mass and into Geyegorg's palm.

He brought it to his lips and blew it toward her like a kiss. She put up her arms to block it on instinct, but it passed straight through them and into her left eye, where it sizzled and filled her vision with yellow light. It didn't hurt, but she cupped her face and doubled over anyway. When she blinked her eyes open, her vision was normal.

The yellow symbol floated back into the cyclone. Geyegorg pointed behind her.

"Now you can see them. The doors I have labeled from my world to Targa's."

Spooky turned around. Two identical, luminous symbols had appeared at the far end of the platform. One hovered on the left side and the other on the right. It looked like a pair of stacked "u's" with a line down the middle or a rudimentary drawing of a branch.

He gestured to the one on the right. "That door will take you to Targa's seat of power. I have waited so long for him to pay me a visit. But we will have a much better relationship, you and I! Much better!"

"Sure, of course."

"As the very first emissary to visit me from Earth, I would like to give you an important gift—the beacons you require to travel to and from my world. Free of charge, so you may come back and visit many times, yes? Yes."

Spooky clenched her jaw and nodded. She would just about rather jump off this platform than visit this lunatic again.

"The beacon to come and the beacon to go. The beacon to access my world and a beacon to return to your seat of power. Two sides of the same passageway between us. Where is your seat of power?"

"Um, my seat of...?"

"He means your house," Carcass said in her ear.

"Oh, uh, it's at 531 Pullman Drive, Diamond Springs, Colorado," Spooky said. "On Earth."

"I see, I see." His third eye thrummed. "There it is. Just there."

The glowing orb in his forehead pulsed. A circle of light transitioned from beneath his skin to outside it. It grew in front of his face until it was roughly the size of his throne. It displayed a translucent picture, like a projection on a wall.

It was of her house.

Slate roof. Gray bricks. Green grass. The leaves on the tree in the front yard swayed in the breeze. It had been over a month since she had seen it in person. She felt like she was so far away from Earth her old life barely existed.

She raised her hand, as if she could touch it. Things had been hard for her there, but they had been simple. She wanted to go back very, very badly.

"Is this the right spot? It's onerous to read house numbers through the void. The finer details, you know."

"Yes."

The image faded, and she snapped back into her body. She was trapped in a dark cavern across the universe, with no easy way home.

"Is that what you see?" Spooky asked.

Geyegorg smiled. "The void is nothing but a veil of gauze to me. There are several doors between here and that general area. I will make you a beacon to label the closest."

He raised his hand and drew in the air. He traced an incomplete green "e" with an uppercase "L" intersecting it, then added an "x" at the top.

It floated above his hand. "This isn't the beacon to all of Earth's doors, mind you. I'm not so generous as to give you that for free. It's a new beacon, just for the door from here to your seat of power. Do you like it?"

"Yes!" A way home. Even though Geyegorg had questionable motivations for giving her this, gratitude bubbled in her chest.

"No need for a contract, as this is given freely from me to you. Now, to label the appropriate door..."

Geyegorg pushed the symbol forward. Spooky followed it with her gaze as it flew between Elliot and Bree. It reached the end of the platform and flashed.

"And then, to give it to you..."

The symbol zoomed back down the length of the platform. It whooshed into her right eye, blinding her with green light. She shook her head and blinked, wishing the sizzle didn't sound so physical.

The tornado of symbols descended, and the new beacon sailed skyward to join the others. Spooky lost track of it in the swirling kaleidoscope. Another symbol broke away and glided down—a blue eye with an "x" through it.

"And now for the beacon that will let you visit me anytime you wish. Any door you take to leave my world, this will guide you back to me. I'll add it to the door near your seat of power." It flew to the end of the platform, then back toward her. Her left eye flashed blue.

The blue symbol and the tornado retreated into the darkness.

"When will you learn to say thank you when you receive a gift," Carcass hissed in her ear.

"Thank you," Spooky stuttered. "For your gift."

"Ah very good, very good." Geyegorg smiled. "A wonderful start to our partnership." He pointed at her. "But don't return without something to trade from Targa, or I will take back my beacons, and you will not be trading with me for another thousand years."

"I won't come back without it," Spooky said, and she meant it. She wasn't going to rely on his self-control to obey his own rules again. She would come back with something to offer him that wasn't one of her body parts, or not at all.

"Hurry, hurry!" He bounced in his chair. "I can hardly wait."

Spooky gave him an awkward half bow and dashed over the red and white lines. She grabbed Elliot and Bree and dragged them with her.

"Wow, that was incredible," Elliot said. "Did it go well? He accepted the offerings. Did you get the beacon to Axonaphis?"

"No," Spooky said. "He didn't accept the trade. But he told me what he wants for it." Her head buzzed with details about which beacons labeled what door. "We have to go get a creation from a god named Targa. He wants a Targyte."

"Is that a good thing?" Elliot asked.

Spooky shrugged. "Our orange friend approved it. He says Targa isn't so bad."

Three symbols now decorated the end of the platform—two yellow, and one green. They stuck in the air like glow-in the-dark stickers, as sharp and clear as anything else in the scene around her.

On the right side was one of the yellow branches—the door that would take her to Targa's seat of power.

On the left was the modified green "e"—the door that would take her back to Earth.

All she had to do was open it, and she would be somewhere near home. No more creepy, manipulative, or hungry monsters. No more uncertainty and pain and falling on her ass. No more doubt and failure and shame. She could climb into her bed and put the covers over her head. Her eyes ached at the thought of burrowing into smooth white sheets and drifting off. She would sleep forever.

Or at least until Carcass framed her as the head of a crime ring. Until her parents kicked her out onto the streets. Until something worse descended on Earth. Something she could have stopped.

It wouldn't be a very long nap.

This mission had turned out to be a lot messier and more dangerous than Carcass had advertised. But she couldn't go back now. They had faced so much danger, and they had come so far. If she went home now, no one else would get a second chance at this.

She wouldn't quit, but she couldn't live with herself if she made the same mistake twice. She faced Bree and Elliot.

"Geyegorg gave me three beacons. The one to Targa, the one to his world, and one back to Earth."

Elliot tilted his head. "To Earth? Why?"

"So I don't get trapped here when I come to negotiate, I guess." Spooky took a deep breath. "Thank you both for saving me from Jagbi and coming here with me. I never would have made it this far without you. But our orange friend said Targa isn't dangerous. You can go home now. You'll be back on Earth. Probably in Colorado. Somewhere near my house."

Elliot opened his mouth, but she spoke over him.

"Before you decide, I should also mention that our friend made the police think we have all been taken hostage by a gang of electronics-store thieves. So, when you get back, you won't be in any trouble for disappearing. Just find a police station, and pretend to have amnesia or something."

Bree scowled. "That's just...what?"

"No," Elliot said. He looked into her eyes. It was the first prolonged eye contact they'd really shared since the cave, and her chest tingled. Fear, she decided, over what he would say next. "I'm not going back. Our orange friend may have said it would be fine, but we have never seen the danger coming."

"I really don't think it will be dangerous," Spooky said.

"Just like Jagbi or the tar or the deer?" Bree said. "Or Geyegorg..."

"Well, if it is dangerous," Spooky argued, "what are three humans going to do against a god anyway?"

"Are you stupid?" Bree put her hands on her hips and leaned forward. "What if Targa gives you something too big for you to carry on your own? What if you need a boost or a hand or three pairs of hands? You don't know what's on the other side of that door. You have no idea, and I wish you'd stop pretending you do. You're not making the way you lied to us any better by trying to be a martyr, and you're not equally likely to succeed if you send us home. You need back-up. You should accept all of the willing help you can get. The key word being willing."

Spooky flinched. Bree's delivery was sharp, but she was right. Spooky should accept all the help she could get. She should stop having this weird argument with them and be grateful they were willing to come.

Maybe it was just that she was still hoping for something more like forgiveness.

"We're coming with you," Elliot said. "And why not bring more than human back-up? Can our tall friend help us?" He raised his eyebrows and tipped his head in the direction of Geyegorg.

"Huh?"

"Oh yeah!" Bree said. "If we could bring someone ridiculously strong and fast, we wouldn't have to worry so much about safety. See? You already desperately need our help."

Spooky had thought Elliot meant Geyegorg, but he'd been gesturing to the Kru-clones who stood sentinel in the shadows behind the throne.

"Oh! Ahem, for anyone listening." She covered her mouth and whispered. "You said you had the beacon to Targa. Can you send Kru to join us as a bodyguard?"

"I can't imagine that being necessary," Carcass replied. "Targytes are without claws or teeth or the malicious will to use either. But if it will end this foolish sedentary conversation, I will send Kru to meet you. After he finishes collecting more electronic equipment for me."

Spooky gave Elliot and Bree a thumbs up. "There might be a delay, but we'll have back-up."

"Well then, what are we waiting for?" Elliot said. A smile spread on his face and crept halfway onto Spooky's. "Let's go see Targa."

# CHAPTER XXIV
# THE TUNNEL

Spooky approached the yellow symbol. It had a three-dimensional quality, like the glass tubing on a neon sign. It was hard to imagine Elliot and Bree couldn't see the radiance reflecting on her face.

"Um, hey...uh..." Spooky hoped Carcass was still listening. "I'm looking at the beacon to Targa. How do I use it?"

"It doesn't require telekinesis," Carcass replied. "Beacons act as a visible doorknob. Now that you have it, you can move it with your hand."

She reached for the glowing emblem. Her fingers didn't connect with anything tangible, but the symbol flared as if she had turned up the wattage. She moved her arm down, dragging the beacon. A misting white line followed its path. It was like a zipper opening the fabric of the universe, revealing the stuffing behind.

As soon as she let go, the beacon floated back to its original position. The line shrank away to nothing.

"We should hold hands, so the door doesn't close behind me." She put out her hand. Bree ignored it and took Elliot's. He accepted the one Spooky offered. "Let's go."

Spooky opened the door again and stepped through, pulling in Elliot who pulled in Bree. The dazzling white of the void illuminated the dirt on his face and the dust in his hair. Even Bree was disheveled, although on her it looked grungy and chic. Spooky didn't want to imagine what the lighting would show on her face, so she twisted away.

As usual, the trip ended without warning. Spooky was getting better at keeping her knees bent and ready. This time, she only had to take one extra step to keep her balance as she landed. Elliot bumped into her back, and they stumbled out of the way for Bree.

The sky here was bright, and the air warmed her skin. They were standing in a structure made of what appeared to be sandstone. Geyegorg's beacon, an electric blue pictograph of an eye, hung in the air next to Bree's shoulder. If she could revisit Carcass's winter home, Spooky guessed she would see this same symbol floating nearby.

"I can see the door to return to Geyegorg," Spooky said. "After we get what we need from Targa, we can go back through here."

"So, where are we supposed to go?" Bree asked.

"Do we know what Targa looks like or where to find him?" Elliot asked.

"This is his 'seat of power,' which is like his house." Spooky scratched her head. "I guess that doesn't mean Targa is here at this exact moment."

Spooky peered through the structure. She couldn't tell if it was a work of architecture or a natural formation. Walls and ceilings of rough, beige material intersected at random corners and middle points. They stacked up at least four stories, but she could see the sky and the horizon through the gaps.

At first glance, the material appeared to be a desert tan, but as she got closer and changed angles, she could see hints of purple, green, and orange. From an inch away, it looked woven—not like the predictable hatched pattern of mesh, but more like a funnel cake, with curling, interlocking tubes. The weave was so small that when she leaned back, it resembled sandstone once more.

"Spooky, that's a wall," Bree said. "Do you know where we're supposed to go or not?"

New world, same prickly attitude. Elliot was examining one of the walls too, but of course, Bree had only picked at Spooky.

She sighed. "I'll see if Carcass knows anything. I want to talk to Carcass."

"What is it you need?"

"It doesn't seem like anyone is here." Spooky paced in a circle. "Any tips on how to find Targa or what he looks like?"

"I cannot say for certain," Carcass said. "Targa is a shapeshifter. As are his Targytes. That is part of the reason why Geyegorg is so interested in them. If you encounter any being, I suggest you simply ask where to find Targa."

Spooky chewed her lip, uneager to go up to any strange being they might encounter. "And how long until Kru can meet us?"

"I will open a door for him, but the one I am familiar with will not deposit him near Targa's seat of power. He will track the godfinger and move at top speed to meet you, but you do not need his protection, so do not wait for it. Find Targa, quickly."

Carcass did sound a little more harried than usual.

"Okay." Spooky faced Bree and Elliot. "Carcass said he doesn't know where Targa is. We're just supposed to find someone to ask. And we're supposed to hurry."

"Should we split up to search?" Elliot asked.

"We are not splitting up," Bree scoffed. "That's how we get picked off, one by one. And we can't leave without her."

Spooky really wished Bree would stop talking past her.

"Let's just stick together," Spooky mumbled.

She followed Bree and Elliot through the formation, glimpsing bits of the open landscape beyond. They separated to peek around corners before converging and picking the next direction to go. It was like a vertical maze. Despite its skeletal frame, they couldn't walk in a straight line for long.

Spooky stepped around a wall and found herself looking out over a vast expanse. It reminded her of a desert, but it was too flat and perfect to be made of sand. Only a cluster of spheres in the distance broke up the plain.

"Should we go investigate those?" Spooky asked as Bree came up behind her.

"Those are boulders," Bree said.

"Well, what do you suggest we do?"

Bree shrugged.

"Let's go back to where we started," Elliot said. "Then we can explore the other side of this place."

Elliot led the way. He strode around the barriers without pausing; he seemed to have memorized their path, even though Spooky couldn't tell the difference between one sandy wall and the next. She trotted around a corner and almost ran into him. He had stopped walking.

She couldn't see Geyegorg's beacon, so they weren't back where they had started yet.

"Those weren't there before." He pointed at four mini slabs of sandstone. They had the same texture as every other part of the structure, but they were smaller and disconnected, like shells stuck up in the sand.

"Are you sure?"

"AHHHH!" Bree ran forward, shrieking.

Spooky jumped a foot in the air, then whipped around, searching for the threat.

Bree put her hands on her hips and turned in a slow circle.

"What the hell was that for?" Spooky yelled.

"Just trying to scare any threats out of hiding." Bree flapped her eyelashes. "Better that we scare them than let them scare us."

"You almost gave me a heart attack!"

"That rock moved," Elliot said. He indicated the rock on the far right.

Spooky stared at it, her heart still leaping. Something about it was changing.

"Does that one have..."

"...eyes?" Elliot leaned in.

The sandstone slab shivered. Before Spooky could blink, it transformed into a creature with no arms, two legs, and a tail. Its head looked like a peeled almond, with vertical lines running down it. Its eyelids slid over perfectly round black eyes. Its only other facial feature was a hole at the tip of its pointed chin.

The thing squeaked a few times before Spooky could understand any words.

"Are you of Bagoula?" it trilled.

"What did it say?" Bree asked, fists raised.

"Um, I'm not sure," Spooky said.

Another stone undulated and reformed into the same sort of creature, but a little taller.

"If they were of Bagoula," this new creature said to the first, "you would already be dead."

The first one shook. "Thank goodness! It isn't her."

The remaining two sandstone shapes wiggled and transformed into almond-faced creatures. They were almost identical, except one was missing an eye, and the other had a bent leg. The tall one had scars across its belly.

"Um, hello there," Spooky said. "We're looking for Targa. Do any of you know where we can find him?"

"Yes, we're going to join him now!" One-eye said.

"You're lucky," the tall one said. "We're some of the last to arrive."

"Soon the tunnel will be closed forever," Crooked-leg muttered.

"Are you sure they are not of Bagoula?" The first one shivered again. Its legs turned back into the stone substance.

"If they were of Bagoula, we'd be dead," the tall one declared.

The first's stubby legs reformed, but they quivered.

"Okay, seriously, what are they saying?" Bree asked.

"Um, I think they're going to show us where Targa is. They're going there now. You're going to take us to see him, right?"

"Follow us!" three of them said. The first changed into stone and back again, and squeaked.

Spooky waved Elliot and Bree to follow her. She trailed the tail of the creature with the bent leg. The four beings marched around one wall, then another, their armless torsos swaying from side to side.

Spooky hoped Elliot was doing a better job of keeping track of their position than she was. With every turn, she became less sure where they were in relation to the blue eye.

A few minutes later, the creatures circled a symbol stamped into the ground. If the creatures hadn't stopped, Spooky wouldn't have noticed it; it was the same tan color as everything else and only a few inches deep. It was shaped like the branching pattern electricity left after it flowed through wood.

"I'll open it," the tall one said.

It put its foot in the center of the shape and began to melt. It filled the indentation like batter poured into a mold, flowing into every twist and turn until it coated the symbol. Only its eyes retained their original round shape, floating in the widest part of the branch.

"We aren't too late, are we?" the first one said.

"Targa would never abandon us," said One-eye.

They stared at their puddled friend. The floating eyes blinked.

The center of the symbol began to sink. The ground liquefied and swirled away, like water going down a drain. It dragged the symbol and the creature into the earth, leaving behind a dark hole. The hole widened until it was bigger than Spooky could reach across, then the edges solidified.

"Come on!" The melted creature squeaked from below.

One-eye jumped into the black pit. The one with the crooked leg limped to the edge.

"This is where Targa is?" Spooky asked it.

"Yes!" It answered.

"Is it safe?"

"It's safer down there than up here! Quickly, join us, before it closes!" It hopped into the hole.

"Hurry, or you'll be left to Bagoula!" the quivering one said. It squeaked and leapt into the darkness.

Spooky knelt at the edge. The symbol had opened a tunnel, which curved to the right and descended into the earth. The footsteps and shrill voices of the creatures echoed, but they were already out of sight. A red light glowed from somewhere further down.

"They said Targa is down there," Spooky said.

Bree raised her eyebrows. "That looks like the literal mouth of hell."

"Yeah." She took a deep breath. "But they said it will close if we don't hurry."

"Are you kidding me?" Bree said. "I don't want to get sealed in the ground! Let's wait for our bodyguard to show up."

"Carcass said not to wait for Kru." Spooky glanced at Elliot.

He was staring into the hole and frowning.

Every moment he didn't speak made her a little more nervous. "Elliot, do you think we should stay here?"

"Hm? No. No! I think we have to go down there if that's where Targa is."

He grimaced and didn't move.

"Okay, alright." Spooky examined his face another moment, but he didn't meet her eyes. "Well, if you both want to wait here, I understand. I'll come back and meet you after I talk to Targa."

Her body hummed with nervous energy. They were so close. They had to finish this.

She couldn't bring herself to jump into the hole as the creatures had, so she sat down on the rim. When she put her feet over the edge, it felt like they were being pushed back out. She lifted her knees up and down.

"It feels almost like...I'm stepping on something."

She flipped onto her stomach and extended her legs further into the hole, but they didn't dangle. Instead of falling, her legs slid along the opposite side of the ground. She kicked for the bottom but stuck to the tunnel's ceiling.

She scooted further in and found herself on her hands and knees on the other side of the earth. Her whole body tingled as she looked down at endless open sky. She glanced behind her. She knew the tunnel burrowed further into the ground, but from her current perspective, it sloped up.

Beneath the surface of this world, gravity had reversed.

Elliot kneeled and leaned over the hole. Their faces could have been reflections in a pool.

"Wow," he said. "How does it seem down there?"

"Um..." As far as she could see, the passageway was smooth, round, and deserted. The creatures that had gone ahead of them were out of sight and earshot. "It seems fine, I guess. Are you coming?"

"Fine," Bree said. "Move."

Spooky backed away as Bree's sneaker poked through the entrance, pointing straight up before it fell and found the new down. She clambered around the edge.

She sat up and scanned the tunnel. "It still looks like the way to hell."

For a second, Spooky wasn't sure if Elliot would follow, but then he crawled in headfirst. He stood.

The entrance swirled closed, cutting off the light.

"What the heck!" Bree grabbed Spooky's arm. "Is this a trap?"

"They said it would close," Spooky said, even though her heart hammered.

Elliot let out a shuddering breath.

She waited for her eyes to adjust. After a few moments, the red glow was enough to see by. Elliot was leaning against the tunnel wall with his hand over his face.

"Elliot?" She took a few steps toward him.

It looked like he was crying.

"Yeah, yeah. Let's just get going." He moved his hand. There were no tears, but a sheen of sweat reflected off his forehead.

Maybe he was claustrophobic. The tunnel was big enough for Spooky to swing her arms in all directions, but maybe that wasn't good enough if he was afraid of small spaces. Spooky tried to make eye contact, but he blinked and stared straight ahead.

"Uh, sure. Okay."

Spooky started up the incline, her shoes gripping the rough surface with ease. It didn't take long to reach the source of the red glow—a trail of eight-pointed red stars floated near the tunnel's ceiling. She brushed a hand underneath one but didn't feel any heat. The color had appeared sinister from far away, but up close, they looked magical, like a string of fairy lights.

She used the extra illumination to sneak another glance at Elliot. He was a dozen steps behind, and his mouth was a tight line. She slowed her pace. Had it been a mistake to come down here? Was he worried about the plan but just not saying it? Had she offended him?

"This is actually kind of nice, isn't it?" Bree said. She cupped her hand near one of the lights. "Pretty."

"Yeah," Spooky said, relieved to hear anything out of her mouth that wasn't negative.

"So what was it you were saying about a crime ring kidnapping us? I feel like that deserves a little more explanation."

"Uh, well, I don't know all the details...but remember how Carcass and I broke into an electronics store to get him a computer, and they caught me on camera?"

"Vaguely." Bree swung her arms. "That part of the story kind of took a backseat to everything else."

"Sure. Well, in exchange for getting a message to the god of Earth, he agreed to make sure I wouldn't be blamed for the robbery."

"Right, because you agreed to be here from the beginning."

"Yeah." Maybe that's why Elliot was upset. Maybe he was mad because she had lied to them.

"So? And?"

"Right, anyway, so, he made the police believe I am the hostage of the true thieves. There's a note and more thefts and security footage." Spooky shrugged. "You're both fake hostages too."

"Huh. I wonder if there could be a movie deal in this."

Spooky snorted. "About your fictional kidnapping?"

"Oo, oo! I know who I want to play me!"

"Uh, I don't think a movie deal is a good idea. If we try to explain the details, there's more risk the story will fall apart. It's probably better if we all pretend to have amnesia. Or that they kept us in a dark room and wore masks."

"You can say that if you want." Bree tapped her chin, a smile spreading across her face.

"Seriously, we shouldn't..."

Spooky looked for Elliot's support, but he had fallen so far behind he was just a dark red shape in the distance.

Spooky left Bree with her dreams of Hollywood and backtracked down the slope to join him.

"Hi." She fell in step beside him. "What about you? Are you going to go for a movie deal too?"

"Hm?"

"Oh, uh, I was just talking to Bree about when we get back. I think we should pretend to have amnesia."

"Oh." Elliot gave her a half-smile that faded quickly.

"Sorry." Spooky twiddled her fingers behind her back. "I can leave you alone."

"No, I'm sorry. Being here just reminds me of something. Talking would actually be nice."

"Okay. Who would play you in a movie?"

"I don't know." He chuckled. "Who would play you?"

"Uh." She couldn't think of a single actress. "I have no idea. Sorry, I'm not that good at small talk."

"Any kind of talking is good. Ask me something else."

"Okay. Can I ask..." She stopped herself.

"Go ahead," he prompted.

"I was going to ask why you were at Dodgson."

"Sure. It's because I ran away."

"From home?"

"Yep. For three weeks. Not that long, really. But when I came back, my parents didn't believe I wouldn't do it again. And they were right."

"Why?" Most of the stories she had heard about kids on the run involved neglect or abuse. She bit her lip. She had asked a forbidden question. Now the conversation was out of her control, leading wherever the dark tunnel took them.

"Because I wanted to see the world." He shook his head. "That's so cheesy, I know. But it's not as romantic as it sounds. It wasn't that I didn't want to wait. I actually can't wait."

In the stilted way he talked, she could almost hear him debating himself. She was aware of every step and breath she took in the silence.

"I'm being vague," he said finally. "I don't usually talk about this."

"It's okay. You don't have to."

"But I want to." He paused again. "I have something. I have Stargardt's." He breathed out as he said it. "It's a degenerative eye disease."

Spooky glanced at him. In the red glow, his features were shaded. But she had seen his eyes in the daylight. They were a beautiful, deep blue.

"Don't worry," he said. "It's not contagious."

"I wasn't thinking that. What does that mean?"

"I'm going to go blind." The word filled the round space. "Legally, anyway. Probably by the time I'm twenty. I might retain peripheral vision, but no one knows for sure. And there is nothing anyone can do to stop it."

"I'm so sorry. I've never heard of it."

"Neither had I until my mom's cousin's son—my second cousin—got diagnosed last year. Someone on my dad's side had it too, so my mom took me to get tested. I hadn't even noticed the blind spots. They're still small. But the doctor did, and when I got my diagnosis, it changed everything for me."

"How so?"

He shrugged. "I didn't use to worry about how I spent my time. I did whatever my parents said. Or my friends suggested. Which was pretty much just school and hanging out at each other's houses. But as soon as I found out, I just..." He squeezed his hands around nothing. "I couldn't waste days doing the same things over and over. I started going new places and doing new things. Like watching plays in the park. And biking. And going to museums. I was filled with this anxiety about what I might not be able to do and see.

"My parents were worried. I skipped a lot of school. They grounded me." He tilted his head back. "But I couldn't stay put. Every day I went farther, for longer. And one day, I went far enough that I didn't go home that night. Or the night after. And I just kept going."

"You really did run away to see the world."

"Yeah, but when I came back, my parents panicked. They signed me up for groups. They bought me books and name-dropped every vision impaired person who has ever achieved anything in the history of the world.

"And I know, I know there's a whole world full of people who live amazing lives after vision loss. But," he shook his head, "maybe I'm weaker than them. I'm just not ready."

"That doesn't make you weak," Spooky said softly.

"My parents knew I would probably leave again. And they were right. I was planning on it. I wasn't trying to punish them or worry them, but I couldn't stay to make them happy either. If I want to see certain things or do certain things—go mountain biking, go scuba diving, see Paris—" He sighed. "I might not be able to if I wait."

"So they sent you away to Dodgson?"

"Yeah. Which was the worst thing they could have done to me."

Spooky viewed her time at Dodgson as a kind of hibernation. It was a temporary stasis in exchange for her life blossoming senior year and beyond.

But for Elliot, every day at Dodgson represented something permanently lost, something he might never have a chance to see or do in the world. Dodgson was built around repetition and monotony.

"It must have been torture," she said.

"I almost lost my mind the first few weeks." He let out a breathy chuckle. "I stayed in bed all day. I broke all the rules. I left the camp... so Adam Dodgson made it worse."

Spooky gasped. "I'm so sorry. Back in the woods, when I said isolation didn't sound that bad..."

"It's okay. How could you have known?"

He shouldn't have had to be the one comforting her right now. Adam Dodgson had shut Elliot in a room where there was even less to see and experience. He had pre-enrolled Elliot for next summer, sentencing him to more months trapped inside the fence.

Her chest burned. Elliot was right. Adam Dodgson did understand what each camper cared about most. And he exploited it.

"And it got better. Once I got out of isolation, I had to look for smaller worlds, but I found them." He was talking more smoothly now, in the lighter tone she was used to. "I know all the trees and ant hills at Dodgson and the constellations that come out before the last bell." He paused. "I think that's why it's been easier for me to forgive you for not telling us we could go back."

"What?" She didn't dare to repeat the word "forgive," in case he would hear it and take it back.

"I forgive you," he said. "If you had given me the option to return to Earth, I wouldn't have taken it. I had been trying to make the most of Dodgson but invite me on an adventure? I would have run off with you to parts unknown in a heartbeat. Right now, I'm seeing things and doing things no one else has before."

She couldn't help but mirror his smile, but it fell off her face.

She kicked the ground. "I was so selfish. I don't fully understand how I let myself get so...so wrapped up that I didn't think about what I was doing to you."

"Hey, I said I forgive you."

"Well, I don't think I deserve it." Her heart swelled. "But I'm so glad you're here instead of Dodgson."

"Me too."

"And thank you for telling me about everything."

"I don't usually tell people," Elliot said. "But being down here...

my eyes don't transition well in the dark. And it just got me thinking about how I might see the world one day. And I just kind of...spiraled."

"Well, I'm really glad you told me. And next time, I'll know."

This time, Spooky was comfortable with the silence. Their shoulders brushed, and the light contact sent tingles through her arm. She felt so many things—guilt, embarrassment, sorrow, relief—but for one second, that one little touch was enough to chase all the other feelings away.

"Hey!" Bree called from further up the slope. "I think we're here."

# CHAPTER XXV
## TARGA

Spooky's calves ached for somewhere flat to stand, but she jogged up the incline. Bree was waiting twenty feet further up. Red light reflected off her curls.

"There's a group of those little things ahead," Bree said. "Listen."

Faint chattering drifted down the tunnel.

"Let's go." Spooky took a step, but Bree grabbed her shoulder.

"We should wait here for Kru."

"They were harmless. And Carcass said we don't have to be afraid of Targa either."

"The deer looked harmless, didn't they?" Bree hissed. "Carcass isn't here. Think for yourself."

"I am." Spooky shook off Bree's grip. "We only ran into the deer because we didn't listen to Carcass and followed Jagbi off the path."

Bree raised her eyebrows. "Don't even get me started on Jagbi. That was your fault too!"

"Carcass said Earth has less than a day," Elliot interjected. "We don't have time to argue."

Spooky clenched her hands. "You can wait here if you want, but I'm going to find Targa."

Spooky's confident words trapped her into marching up the tunnel. Her cheeks flushed, and she swung her fists. She never argued with her parents or teachers, or anyone really. But Bree's constant insults grated on her. Every time she suggested a plan or even offered to do something herself, Bree took the opportunity to throw something back in her face.

The chatter rose to a din. The tunnel opened onto a larger chamber ahead. The entrance was packed with the almond-faced creatures, bobbing and milling. One of them turned. Its shiny eyes found her, and it started to shiver and squeak.

Before she could sneak back down the passageway, twenty more of the critters spun their heads to look. They all had the same almond faces and round, black eyes. She couldn't distinguish the ones they had met above ground from any of the others, but a number of them had crooked tails, scars, or bent legs.

"Bagoula?" Whispers started and spread. "Bagoula? Bagoula?"

Spooky was taller than them, but she was also massively outnumbered. Bree had made a good point about the deer, but it was too late to admit it.

"What are they saying?" Elliot asked. Spooky jumped, surprised to see that both he and Bree had followed her to the top. Bree lagged in the shadows with her arms crossed.

"They're saying 'bagoula,'" Spooky translated. "But I don't know what that means."

"It sounds like 'bagoula' to me too," he said.

"If this goes badly, I will outrun you," Bree snapped.

Spooky turned her back to hide her eye roll.

Silence chased the whispers of "bagoula," and after a few moments, the crowd was quiet. All eyes were on them.

"Ahem." Spooky cleared her throat. It echoed. "Excuse me. We're looking for Targa."

A voice that seemed to come from nowhere, and everywhere, and maybe just from inside her head said, "Targytes, move aside."

The creatures at the entrance parted, leaving a corridor of free space into the chamber.

"Approach," the voice called.

"He said..."

"'Approach,'" Bree repeated. "Yeah, we heard."

"Targa speaks English?" Elliot asked.

"I wish to be understood, and so I am," the voice resounded. "I wish to understand your words, and so I do. But please, speak up. And come closer."

"Oops." Elliot lowered his voice.

"Come on," Spooky said. "Let's go."

She trekked up the last bit of the incline and entered a huge cavern. Thousands of the little creatures filled the space, and each set of inky eyes was trained on her. In addition to the throng on the cavern floor, sandstone balls clung to the walls like sparrows' nests. One, two, or three tiny almond-heads poked out of the top of each. They looked like babies.

A tangle of roots the size of a truck hung from the ceiling, cradling a huge almond face. Its eye sockets held glowing red stars. More of the eight-pointed lights floated around the structure, casting complex shadows on the walls and the creatures below.

"Approach," the voice said again.

The Targytes had squeezed enough space out of the packed room for the three of them to pass. The ones on the edges weren't just close together—their bodies had shrunk until they were only as big around as soup cans.

Spooky walked to the center of the chamber and stopped in front of the root chandelier. Elliot and Bree trailed after. It didn't escape her notice that they were surrounded.

She took a deep breath and projected. "Are you Targa?"

"I am Targa. You are no Targyte." The red eyes glittered as the face tilted down.

"No, we're humans, from Earth."

"Then you've traveled far." As with the smaller almond faces, the round mouth at the tip of his chin didn't move when he spoke. His face looked like a carved wooden mask. "I'm sorry I could not receive you in my palace."

"That's quite alright." Formal speech felt appropriate. This was only the third god she'd met, and so far, he was the only one who didn't seem interested in kidnapping her.

"I welcome you, but I do not recommend you stay." The whole

contraption of roots shook as if he took a labored breath. "These are troubled times. I cannot ensure your protection."

"Of course he can't," Bree muttered.

"We won't stay," Spooky said, speaking over her. "But our world, Earth, is in trouble too. To save it, we came to ask if you would give us one of your creations."

"You said he wanted a Targyte," Elliot whispered.

"A Targyte!" Spooky repeated.

A shudder went through the crowd. The little creatures twittered and shifted.

"I am sorry for Earth's plight," Targa said. The red eyes twinkled. "But how is it possible that one of my Targytes could help you? My creations are good people, but they are not powerful."

"It's not for us." Bree stepped forward. "It's for Geyegorg. He..."

The coral structure vibrated again, this time intensely enough to shake the cavern floor. The Targytes bobbed and squeaked. Even though it had felt like they were scaling a mountain, it reminded Spooky just how deep in the ground they were.

"Geyegorg!" Targa said. "You dare come to me for Geyegorg?"

Bree flapped her mouth. Spooky glanced between her shocked face and the god looming over them. Maybe there was a good reason Geyegorg had never been able to get Targa to trade with him. Maybe there was a good reason he had sent a third party to do his negotiating.

"We're sorry," Spooky said. "We aren't here for Geyegorg, exactly..."

"Geyegorg has taken enough from me already." Targa's rigid face showed no emotion, but it clacked back and forth in the root structure. "I will give nothing to you meant for Geyegorg's hands."

"If we don't bring him a Targyte, Geyegorg won't help us," Spooky said. "Earth will be destroyed."

"Although you speak his name, I can tell you do not know him, child. Help does not come from Geyegorg." The star eyes blazed. "Only sorrow."

"But please, there has to be something we can trade. We'll do anything…"

"I love my Targytes. I will not give you one for Geyegorg. You are free to leave the way you came."

The face creaked upward. The Targytes returned to their chattering.

It seemed their audience with Targa was over.

Spooky's heart sank into her stomach. There was no opportunity to go back and pick better words. She didn't blame Bree for mentioning Geyegorg. Whatever Targa's issue was with him, they hadn't been briefed. She would have said it herself, eventually.

Bree sulked to one side. She glowered down at the closest group of Targytes, who shrank back and squeaked. Based on her narrowed eyes and clenched fists, she might need a reminder that they couldn't just grab a Targyte and run. They needed Targa's permission. And now it didn't seem like they were going to get it.

They were here. They had made it this far, but for what? Without Targa's help, they would have nothing to offer Geyegorg. Spooky seriously doubted he would entertain a second negotiation if they showed up with nothing. She shook her head and looked at her empty hands.

"Hey," Elliot said in a low voice. He took her arm and led her a few steps away. "Keep trying."

"He won't give us something now that he knows it's for Geyegorg," Spooky whispered. "He clearly hates him."

"That doesn't mean we can't convince him."

She glanced up at Targa. The impassive face stared straight over the crowd. "He isn't like Carcass or Geyegorg. He doesn't want anything from us."

"You don't know that." Elliot turned her to face him. "Remember what we talked about?"

She didn't know if it was the adrenaline or the dim lighting, but she couldn't break eye contact. What had they talked about? She couldn't remember a single conversation before this one.

"Think about Dodgson." His voice was barely above a breath. "Adam Dodgson gets us to do things we don't want to all the time because he understands what we care about most. There has to be something Targa cares about more than he hates Geyegorg."

"Sure. He said he loves his Targytes. But what are we supposed to do with that?"

"It's a place to start. He also said these were troubled times. Whatever is going on here, it doesn't seem like he's got it under control. Maybe there's something we can do to help."

"Maybe." The cavern full of injured Targytes chattered, but they didn't seem very happy. They seemed scared. "Maybe, if his Targyes are in danger, we can offer him a safe place for them on Earth? Or... something else."

"You won't know unless you ask." Elliot took both her shoulders and turned her back toward the center of the room. As soon as his palms lifted, she felt cold, but heat ran through her when he leaned close to her face. "Put on your Adam Dodgson hat," he said into her ear. "And keep trying."

Spooky raised her chin up toward the god. She wasn't Adam Dodgson. She wasn't an expert manipulator. And Adam Dodgson controlled most aspects of their lives. She didn't have that kind of power, to either help or hurt Targa and his people.

But Elliot was right. Just because Targa didn't want to give them something for Geyegorg didn't mean he wouldn't. There might be something that mattered more to him. Maybe she could even right the wrongs between them. She had to try.

She opened her mouth, hoping the words would come.

"I'm sorry." Spooky projected up to Targa. "We didn't mean to upset you. You said you couldn't guarantee our safety, and that these were troubled times. What is going on, exactly? Please tell me."

The face did not turn down toward her. "The one you come here for, Geyegorg, is the source of all the strife in my land."

No wonder their request had gone over poorly. "What did he do to you? Maybe we can help fix it."

"You seem kind, child, so I will tell you, if only as a warning against him. Geyegorg is the reason for Bagoula's successful conquest on the surface of my world. I have brought what is left of my people down here so they may survive Bagoula and her armies."

A murmur rippled through the crowd, echoing the name. Spooky exchanged a glance with Elliot. "Is Bagoula another god?"

"No." The almond face tipped down. "Bagoula is my daughter."

Long strands of what looked like taffy pulled out of the root structure, lowering Targa's face toward the floor. The Targytes opened a circle as the ribbons pooled to the ground. They twisted together and formed a teardrop body, like a pile of spaghetti twirled up on a fork. The wooden face loomed over her, bobbing at the top of a coiled neck.

"My daughter. A creator in her own right, whom Geyegorg corrupted."

Spooky thought of the moth creature, begging for his loved one back. "What did he do to her?"

"When his invite came to do business, I sent her in my place. I was not interested in what he had to offer, but he enticed Bagoula into a few deals. She was satisfied with her life here before she bought his beacons." Targa's body shivered. "On other worlds, she learned greed. She learned war. She learned violence. She traded her own creations for more beacons and trained the ones she kept to grow teeth and claws and fight in her armies. Now she has overtaken my world." He shuddered again. "Now, she is a monster."

"But, if you made her, can't you stop her?"

"There were no words she would hear. And even to give my people a life on the surface, I will not fall to violence. I will not counter flesh with flesh in battle. I will not become a monster." The strings of spaghetti undulated. "I have created a haven here, rather than watch any more of my people be slaughtered. When the last arrive, I will close the tunnels, so we may live down here, untroubled. Even her clawed creations will not be able to dig this deep."

Targa looked impressive and powerful, looming over her. But

Spooky had to wonder what the little Targytes thought of their god. He had called this place a haven, but it was a crowded hole in the ground. He had said he loved them, but he was going to trap them in the dark. He had let them die, rather than fight his daughter. Spooky didn't get the impression that he couldn't beat her, only that he was unwilling to.

Targa wanted to end Bagoula's reign of terror and save his people, but he wasn't willing to be the one to fight Bagoula himself.

Electricity buzzed through her limbs. "What if we could help do something about Bagoula for you?"

"You?" Targa said.

"Yeah. Isn't there anything we could do to stop her? What if we could, I don't know...capture her? Defeat her? So you don't have to 'fall to violence.' And so your people won't have to hide down here."

Targa's form stretched, arching his head closer to Spooky's face.

"You do have some teeth and stubby little claws," Targa said. "But Bagoula is a warrior. I don't think you would be a match for her in battle."

"But if we were..."

"We can't fight armies!" Bree blurted.

"Her armies are not the problem," Targa said. "Her creations do not engage in battle unless she commands them to. Without Bagoula, there would be no more calls to violence. If she were gone, my people could return to the surface."

"Good!" Spooky said. "Perfect. Alright then."

"Spooky!" Bree hissed. "Seriously, what are you thinking?"

"I'm thinking," Spooky said to everyone and no one. "That we have a very strong, very fast friend, who will give us a good chance of winning any fight."

She locked eyes with Elliot, who nodded, a smile tweaking up the corners of his lips. This was their chance.

"Targa, we only want to protect our home. And I think you want to protect yours too." Spooky fixed her gaze on Targa's face. "If we can stop Bagoula, so that she can't command her armies or attack your people, will you give us a Targyte?"

Targa's body coiled tighter. All the glittering black eyes in the room were on him.

"If you incapacitate Bagoula in such a fashion, I will give you a Targyte to take to Geyegorg so you may save your world. The cycle of destruction can end with he who began it."

The crowd gasped and babbled, although whether in appreciation or fear, Spooky couldn't tell.

"What if Kru kills her?" Elliot whispered.

Spooky didn't want to think about it, but Elliot was right to bring it up. If a battle with Kru ended the way it had with the deer, they still needed Targa to follow through on his end of the bargain.

"Targa, what if we have to seriously hurt Bagoula, or even kill her, to 'incapacitate' her?"

"I will not fall to violence, but I cannot protect her from a violent end." Targa's head jerked from side to side. "You may do whatever you wish with her. Her fate is up to you. I do not wish to know it."

"And you'll still give us a Targyte?"

"As long as you stop her from her conquest, I will give you a Targyte."

"Okay. Then we have a deal." Spooky stuck out her hand on instinct.

Targa's mask of a face tipped down toward it. A section of his abdomen twisted out. It congealed into a human hand that was an exact mirror of her own.

"We have a deal."

The twin hands hovered for a second. Targa didn't move his hand to shake, and Spooky was too surprised to take it. She dropped her arm to her side, and his was reabsorbed into his body.

"Great," she said. "How can we find Bagoula?"

"Her encampment is on the plains. She is quite territorial. Once you reach the surface, I'm sure she'll find you."

"Okay," Spooky said. "And what does she look like?"

"Like me, she is accomplished at taking many forms."

Spooky would keep an eye out for any piles of spaghetti. "Alright."

"I will create a tunnel for you to travel to the plains."

Targa's tendrils reformed into a hand and reached over the crowd. The limb stretched over hundreds of heads and pressed into the cavern wall, leaving an indentation of a handprint. He retracted it into his coils.

"Your hand will be the key. Press it into the lock to open the tunnel and follow it to the surface. If you succeed, return here the same way, and I will give you a Targyte. Targytes, move aside."

The Targytes created a path to the handprint on the wall. Spooky and Elliot walked toward it. Bree stomped after. Whether it was because of what Spooky had just told Targa she would achieve, or that they were no longer afraid, the Targytes left less space for them to pass this time, chattering and tilting their almond heads. Spooky picked out a few words: "surface," "return," and "hope" among them. She was glad Bree and Elliot couldn't understand the number of times "Bagoula," "destroy," and "fail" repeated through the chamber.

Spooky pressed her hand into the mark on the wall. After a few seconds, the handprint sank backward. The rock liquefied and swirled away, like a whirlpool. A black hole appeared. A new tunnel descended into darkness.

A hiss behind her made her glance back. Targa's coiled body expanded and then contracted. A trail of glowing red stars flowed out from the hole at the bottom of his chin. They flew into the new tunnel like fireworks streaking across the sky.

The stars were beautiful, but facing a group of creatures who were going to entomb themselves, the red glow seemed like a tragic substitute for a bright, wide sky. The huddled Targytes needed help. Spooky felt like a mercenary from another world, offering to save them. Or, at least, offering for Kru to save them.

Targa's face betrayed nothing. She wondered what he wished for more—their safe return at the expense of his daughter, or their failure at the expense of his people. He may have been the most civil of the gods they had encountered, but there was something disturbing about his priorities. He was willing to let Bagoula die or his creations die, but he wasn't willing to get his own hands dirty. He would hide rather than fight.

"Don't worry," she said to the Targytes. "We'll be back."

# CHAPTER XXVI
# SURFACING

Spooky entered the tunnel, followed by Elliot and Bree. The circular passageway sloped downward. She glanced back at the crowd of Targytes and the star-eyed megalith that loomed over them. Before she could even turn away, the entrance to the cavern swirled shut, cutting off most of the light.

"Elliot?" If her eyes needed time to adjust, his would take longer. "Are you okay?"

"Yeah," he said. "I just need a few minutes."

"What the hell is wrong with you?" Bree snapped. She was silhouetted in red.

"What?"

"You literally just promised we would go fight a monster who scared an entire civilization into hiding. And you didn't think you needed to consult us about that?"

"I...I didn't know what to do. It seemed like the only option."

"I told her to keep trying," Elliot said.

"Don't cover for her." Bree stalked over to Spooky. "You made another choice for us."

"We had to get something from Targa. I'm just trying to get what we need..."

"Get what you need, you mean? As long as you get out of jail free, you're good." Bree scoffed. "Who cares what happens to us in the process?"

"That's not true." Spooky balled her hands into fists. "At least I was able to get him to agree to something."

"And that's all that ever matters to you, isn't it? At least you got what you wanted, right?"

"That's not fair." Elliot stepped around Bree's back. "We're all in this together."

"Really?" Bree glared at him. "What do you and I get if we succeed? Do we get our problems fixed for us? What's our reward?"

"It's not a reward!" Spooky sputtered. "It's just...not going to prison!"

"We all agreed to finish this," Elliot said. "We're on the same side."

"No, we're not. She doesn't care what happens to us," Bree said to Elliot. "She made that clear enough."

The red stars felt hot on Spooky's face. "I do care! I didn't know what to say to Targa, but I did the best I could!"

"Well, the best you could do sucked!" Bree snapped. "You volunteered us to track down, and maybe kill, the daughter of a god? You don't know how strong Bagoula is! You don't know if we can win!"

"At least she's trying," Elliot said. "Do you care if we succeed? Because we agreed to help, and this isn't helping."

"I care." Bree jabbed her finger at her chest. "I actually have something at home to protect. Just because I want to survive to get back doesn't mean I don't care!" Bree narrowed her eyes at Elliot. "You've been following her around like a puppy ever since we left Earth. You probably don't even care that she tricked us into coming with her."

"I forgave her." Elliot's voice was even.

"Then you're an idiot who deserves whatever mess she leads you into."

The red stars burned like heat lamps now. "Stop talking about me like I'm not here!" Spooky's voice echoed in the tunnel. "I messed up before, but I didn't lie to you with Targa. I made a decision. For me. Not you. Whether you help or just sit here is up to you!"

"That would be great, except I can't get back without you!" Bree yelled.

"You could have gone back so many times! I wish you had!"

"Me too!" Bree swung around and stalked down the incline.

The sound of her stomping feet faded until all Spooky could hear was her own heavy breaths.

Elliot reached for her. "Hey..."

Spooky didn't wait to hear what he had to say. She took off down the tunnel. Her nerves were singing, and her mind rang with all the things she could have said.

They had all stood together on that platform and chosen their door. They had all chosen to go see Targa.

And Bree'd had a nasty attitude since the beginning. Spooky was tired of it. Maybe she could handle all the picking and berating if Bree offered a solution now and then. Instead, she just sat back as Spooky made the decisions, then criticized her for it.

Still, under her pounding blood, Spooky itched. Maybe she had only been acting less selfishly to prove something. Maybe Bree was more right about her than she had ever been about herself.

The doubt rose through her, pushing out the heat and leaving behind shaky cold. Had she thought about Bree's and Elliot's safety when she made the deal with Targa? Had she ever really thought about what was best for them? Or had everything she'd done since they found out she'd lied just been a performance to convince them they could trust her? Hadn't she just offered to send them home to reassure herself?

Wasn't she still just faking it?

She wanted to think down the doubt, but she couldn't. And she couldn't just reduce her selfishness to the one lie. All she had thought about since Carcass arrived was protecting herself; from scuffs, from her parents, from prison time, from danger. And who was she even protecting? Before that, all she'd done was wait.

Fast footsteps echoed behind her.

"Hey." Elliot skidded into view. "Hey, wait up."

Spooky wrapped her arms around herself. "I don't want to talk."

"You don't have to talk. But I'm going to." Elliot matched her pace. "Bree is probably just upset because she's the one who brought up Geyegorg and derailed the conversation. You didn't do anything wrong with Targa."

"Didn't I?" Spooky mumbled. "I just volunteered us as mercenaries to chase down his evil daughter."

"You found an option, maybe the only option, to keep us moving forward."

"I could have talked to you both about it first though."

"Maybe, but I don't think so. If you stopped the conversation, you might never have gotten Targa talking again. He might have reconsidered. The point is, we all agreed to continue without knowing what might come next."

"But I still made the decision for us. I have the godfinger and the beacons. It's not like the two of you can walk back to Geyegorg and take the door to Earth without me. I knew we would all have to go forward if I offered to fight Bagoula. I was only thinking about getting what I wanted."

"What you wanted? You're trying to save Earth! That's worth fighting for!" Elliot said. "You're viewing this all wrong."

Elliot's confidence in her was misplaced. Getting better at tricking people into thinking she wasn't selfish only made her more like Victoria.

"You don't know me." Spooky whirled on him. "I sent you to take out the trash instead of me. I tricked you and Bree into coming with me. I would have given up anyone else at camp to be Carcass's storyteller. I wasn't even going to try to save Earth until Carcass gave me a personal incentive!"

"Spooky, those aren't normal circumstances."

"Well, I wasn't that great in my regular life either! Do you know why I'm at Dodgson? I took pills from my sister's room, and when I got caught, I told everyone they were hers. I didn't think about what she had to lose, I just thought about keeping myself out of trouble." Spooky didn't want Elliot to know any of this, but she couldn't stop herself. The words came faster and faster. "I have no friends, my parents wish I didn't exist, my grades will barely get me into college, I don't have any talents, my ears are huge, I've only had one terrible kiss from a guy who didn't even like me, and I'm selfish. I didn't realize I could only think about myself and still be a total failure."

"You've only had one, terrible kiss?" Elliot asked.

She gaped at him. "That's what you took from that?"

"Well, that's the only part I can fix." He stepped closer to her. He was taller than her, but he was standing lower on the slope, so their faces were level. She froze and tingles ran all over her body. He leaned in slowly, keeping eye contact. Her face warmed.

She closed her eyes and he kissed her. Her head went fuzzy. The red stars twinkled on the inside of her eyelids. She wanted to pull him closer, but he stepped away and took her shoulders in his hands.

"Listen to me—every door we've opened, every risk we've taken, you've always gone first. You ran at the deer when we were backed into a corner. When you saw how dangerous Geyegorg was, you made us stay back and faced him alone. You didn't go home when you had the chance, and you practically begged us to. You've had to balance all this absurdity and danger and make decisions really fast. And because of you, we're farther than I think almost anyone else would have made it.

"Do you even hear yourself right now?" She managed to take her eyes off his lips. "Bree was way out of line—no one can say that you could have done better negotiating with Targa. But you haven't even mentioned that. You're upset because you are so afraid of being self-ish. Selfish people don't usually end up shouting about not caring enough."

"I wasn't shouting," Spooky muttered. The warmth of his hands on her shoulders anchored her in this moment. She could barely even remember why they were there.

"Well." He cleared his throat. "You were. A little."

He let go of her shoulders and backed down the tunnel away from her. She felt chilled.

"Let's get to the surface and see what's out there." He smiled up at her as he walked backward. "If we don't think Kru can handle Bagoula, we can ask Carcass for more reinforcements."

"Yeah...yeah," Spooky said. She watched the way his shoulders moved as he walked away. "Reinforcements."

Spooky had almost lost sight of Elliot by the time she remembered to follow him. Had that really just happened? The strange lighting made everything feel dreamlike. She put her hands where Elliot's had been on her shoulders. Had he been trying to fix the fact that she had only had one, terrible kiss? Or had he been trying to fix the fact that she had only had one, terrible kiss from someone who didn't even like her?

Was she even likeable right now?

He had been generous with his assessment of her—she had been selfish. But maybe she was being a bit unfair, too. Sure, at first she had only been motivated to get herself out of trouble. Back in the clearing, back when none of the gods except Carcass had felt real, the only thing on Spooky's mind had been the police on her heels. And for a long time, too long, she had been thinking like a bystander, waiting for change.

But when she had gotten the chance to go home from Geyegorg's platform, she hadn't kept going because of her deal with Carcass. And even her own safety hadn't crossed her mind while she was trying to negotiate with Targa. She wanted to finish the mission. She wanted to contact the god of Earth. She wanted to do whatever she could. She may not have been humanity's best choice, but she was the one who was here. She had finally accepted that.

What she did now mattered. She couldn't pretend like she was waiting for anything anymore. Spooky hugged the outside of her arms.

"Spooky." Carcass's voice startled her. "What is your status? Did you get a Targyte?"

"Right, hi, uh, not yet." Spooky was very glad Carcass couldn't see her face. "We're working on it. Targa only agreed to give us a Targyte if we stop his daughter, Bagoula. My plan was to have Kru fight her—he can capture or even kill her if he has to. We're going to find her now."

Carcass paused. "Unexpected, but very well. Kru will be able to best almost any opponent in physical battle. If you point Kru toward Bagoula, he can end this very quickly. He is nearly at Targa's seat of power. He should catch up to your current location soon."

"Good!" The fact that Carcass hadn't insulted her plan made her hold her chin up a little higher. Bree wasn't the authority on dealing with gods. Maybe Spooky had a budding talent after all.

And maybe she could continue to put it to good use.

"Carcass..." Spooky spoke slowly as the idea formed. "I know we have an arrangement, and you've already kept your side of the bargain, but Bree and Elliot have helped me a lot."

"Who?"

"Bree and Elliot. The two people you kidnapped?"

"What about them?"

Spooky rolled her eyes. "Well, when your plan failed to account for the killer deer or Jagbi trying to eat me or world hopping to track down a god's evil daughter, they stepped up to help. A lot. It wouldn't take much effort for you to reward them with 'modern tender.' They deserve it."

Maybe Carcass didn't have the power to erase Bree's parents' memories of their original plan for their daughter or the time-turning power to stop Elliot from losing his eyesight, but at the very least, he could give them money. Money for Bree to hire a lawyer and set up a life for herself and her daughter. Money so Elliot could fly anywhere he wanted to.

"Fine, yes, a reward for the other humans. As long as it gets you to hur..."

The voice in her ear went silent.

"Carcass?" She reached around her head to tap the finger through her hair. "Carcass?"

"The first attack. It happened. The humans think it's a natural disaster, but it's not. The Earth is under..."

"Where? What happened? Carcass? Carcass!" Spooky spoke louder as if that would help.

The finger stayed silent. Spooky's body turned cold. Carcass had told them if the first attack was completed and the god of Earth didn't interfere, it would be the confirmation the other invaders had been waiting for. A chain reaction would be set off. All the others who wanted a bite of Earth would sink their teeth in.

Their countdown toward widespread destruction had just gone from a day to hours.

Spooky tore down the slope. It only took a few seconds to catch up to Elliot.

"Come on." Spooky grabbed his elbow. "First attack, have to hurry."

It took another few moments to catch up to Bree.

She must have heard them coming, because she turned her head and glared.

"Bree!" Spooky yelled. "We have to go. The first attack started."

"Where?" Bree snapped. They passed her. "Where was the attack?"

"I don't know," Spooky called back. "Come on!"

The tunnel was getting lighter. Spooky's knees almost buckled with every bounding step. She skidded to a stop a few feet short of the tunnel's exit—a hole that opened onto the sky.

"Hey!" Bree wrenched Spooky's arm, breathing hard. "Where was the attack?"

"I don't know. Carcass stopped responding."

"I'm hungry, I haven't slept in like twenty hours, and you just told me gods are attacking Earth. I need to know what's going on!" Bree's face contorted and her voice broke.

Bree was yelling at her again, but Spooky felt the tightness in her chest loosen. In the daylight, there was no missing her wild eyes smeared with dried salt. Her fingernails were chewed, and her lips were dry and cracked. The most important thing in the world to her was in danger. Now wasn't the time to worry about who had said what.

"I'm sure it wasn't in Colorado." Spooky pried Bree's hands off her shirt and squeezed them. "And it's not over yet. We can still stop this. Kru is coming here to meet us."

Bree nodded, but she looked like she was going to throw up.

"We can wait in here for Kru," Elliot said.

Spooky cleared her throat and turned away. "Yeah, we won't be able to do anything to Bagoula until he gets here."

She wasn't ready to make eye contact with Elliot yet. She was afraid to see some hint of disappointment or pity or even apathy. And she didn't know what her face would show him either—discomfort or nerves or overeagerness. Or even an expression she didn't mean, something that would deter him from kissing her again.

She shook herself. She didn't have time to think about that right now.

Bree crouched down at the side of the hole. "How long until Kru gets here?"

"Carcass said soon."

Bree laid down on her stomach and poked her head through the opening. Spooky gasped and pounced on her foot. It looked like Bree was dangling her head over the edge of a cliff.

"Relax," Bree said, nudging Spooky off. "I just want to see if I can spot him coming."

"What's out there?" Elliot asked.

"There are some gray things. Let me just get a better view." Bree put her arms through and pulled more of her torso onto the other side. "There! I see..."

Bree shrieked as something dragged her out of the tunnel.

# CHAPTER XXVII
# BAGOULA

"Bree!" Spooky and Elliot yelled.

Spooky scrambled to the edge of the hole, dropped onto her stomach, and stuck her head out into the light. Elliot grabbed her arm and half sat on her. The hole was surrounded by a cluster of vertical stones that blocked her sightline in most directions. She couldn't see any sign of Bree or what had taken her. She swiveled her head around and caught sight of a curl of blonde hair and a hand. They vanished behind one of the tall rocks.

"Bree!" she shouted again.

A beige pointed face peered at her from between two stones. It was a bigger version of the Targytes' faces or a smaller version of Targa's. It disappeared.

It had to have been Bagoula.

"Elliot!"

He seized her shoulders and heaved her back into the tunnel.

"What is it?"

"I think I saw Bagoula." Spooky's hands shook. "She had Bree."

"Any sign of Kru?"

"No, but I couldn't see very far. Can I talk to Carcass? Carcass, are you there?"

She listened to her own breathing as she waited for a voice to reply. Whatever was happening on Earth, he wasn't sparing her any attention.

It didn't matter if Bree was difficult or didn't like her. Spooky wasn't going to sit here and let her get dragged away where they would never find her. Spooky was the one with the finger on her head. She was the one Kru was tracking.

She locked eyes with Elliot. "We can't wait for Kru. We have to help her."

He nodded.

Spooky crawled around the edge of the hole, reaching with her arms and kicking her legs to pull her body over the dividing line between one gravity and the other. Elliot followed and stood beside her. The tunnel closed after them, filling in like a hole on the beach near the surf. The only proof it had ever been there was an indentation in the shape of a human hand. Just like the lightning-branch pattern, it was only a few inches deep and the same tan color as the ground. It would be easy to miss if they didn't remember their way back to this exact spot.

Smooth, cylindrical rocks surrounded them. They were all made of the same oyster-gray material, swirled into a shape that resembled soft-serve ice-cream. Some only came up as high as her hip, while others reached over her head. It gave Spooky an eerie feeling, like being judged by a silent crowd.

"Which way?" Elliot asked.

"She was over there." Spooky started in the direction she had seen the hair. If they found Bree, Spooky would latch onto her until Kru arrived. She wasn't sure what she would do if they encountered Bagoula. The columns were wide enough and dense enough to block her view of any approaching threat.

Bree screamed.

"Bree!" Spooky whirled toward the cry.

Bree leaned out from behind a tall column. She reached for Spooky with both hands, then slipped around the edge, pulled away by something unseen.

"Come on!" Spooky took off after her.

Spooky darted around the stones, doing her best to keep track of the spot where Bree had disappeared. The pillars got closer together, forcing her to squeeze between them, pushing with her hands as she angled her shoulders and hips.

Then the cluster thinned out and opened onto a flat landscape, which stretched to the horizon. Only a few scattered spires broke up the expanse. She must have gone too far. With all the twists and turns, she could have passed right by Bree and not even known it.

To her right, about fifty feet away, something glowed blue. It was a blue eye with an "x" through it—the beacon to Geyegorg. Targa had said Bagoula traded with Geyegorg. Maybe he had given her this to mark her seat of power—a separate seat from Targa's.

"Hey, I can see a..." She looked behind her. "Elliot?"

The forest of stone stood silent and still. Spooky backed further into the open area, heart pounding. Bree and Elliot were in there, somewhere. But in among the swirled columns, anything could be hiding a pounce away. That blank, flat face, could emerge from behind any pillar.

"Elliot?" she called again, as loudly as she dared. She wished she still had the scissors. "Lunch tray," she whispered to the finger. She caught it and held it up like a shield.

Spooky took another step backward and shrieked when she bumped into something soft. She clutched her chest and coughed out a laugh. It was Elliot.

"I thought I lost you!"

He smiled. "I'm right here."

"Any sign of Bree?" Spooky faced the cluster and stood on her tiptoes, searching for another glimpse of blonde curls among the rocks. Maybe she could balance on a shorter spire and see further in.

"Nope," he said.

She turned and found him only a step away from her. His head was tilted and he had a strange expression on his face. Was he going to try to kiss her again?

"Um, now isn't a good time..." she stuttered.

"A good time for what?"

Was he trying to be cute or playing dumb? Was he going to pretend, in the light, that the kiss had never happened?

Spooky felt a sting in her chest and turned away. "Never mind."

It wasn't important right now. What was important was finding Bree, Bagoula, and Kru. Hopefully not in that order.

The hairs on her neck stood up. She glanced over her shoulder and jumped. Elliot was inches from her, and he was smiling. She thought of Luke pressing her against the dumpster after she'd tried to push him off.

Then the smell hit her.

It brought her back to the seventh-grade girls' locker room. It smelled like bodies and stale blood.

"Ugh." She jerked back. "What is that?"

Elliot's smile didn't change. Something wasn't right. Spooky's chest seized.

The smell was coming from him.

A chill ran through her.

"You're not Elliot, are you?"

The smile got bigger, warping into one she didn't recognize.

"And you are not of Targa," the thing across from her said. "You're of Earth's god. You're human."

She had seen Targa and his Targytes change shape—shrinking smaller to let them pass, or when Targa mirrored her hand—but she hadn't imagined shapeshifting like this. Head to toe, the imitation was perfect. She never would have known anything was off, except for the odor. She didn't have a name for it. It smelled like life and death, somehow all in one.

"Are you Bagoula?" Spooky whispered.

"You know my name. How did you know I wasn't your friend?" Bagoula cocked Elliot's head. "I stretched the vocal cords to match his tone. Eeeeee." She sang a note, which became shriller and shriller, beyond the range of a human voice. "Is this better?" Elliot's voice deepened.

Spooky shook her head, backing up.

"No," Bagoula purred in Elliot's exact tone. "I got it right the first time, didn't I? Ah! I know what I forgot." Bagoula leaned in Spooky's direction. "I forgot to adjust for how a human boy smells."

The stench dissipated, but Spooky backed away further, holding up the dinner tray.

"What did you do with my friends?"

"Aw, sorry. They're gone." Bagoula used Elliot's face to pout. "How about I introduce you to some of my friends instead?"

Elliot's hand gestured with two fingers.

A dozen creatures emerged from the forest of stone. They all had tan skin and springy, yellow hair. It took her a second to realize they all resembled Bree—or funhouse reflections of Bree that distorted her shape and features.

One had stubby arms and three-foot fingers. Another limped along on legs that kept buckling due to extra knees. Double-size ribs, missing or multiple mouths, long bones that connected at odd angles —Spooky couldn't move as they lined up, forming a semi-circle behind Bagoula. Although many of them had elongated bodies and limbs, most were only able to stand a few feet tall.

"Ugh." Bagoula surveyed them with an expression of disgust that Spooky had never seen on the real Elliot's face. "You examined the girl for how long, and this is the best you can do?"

Spooky stumbled back until a column blocked her retreat.

"Look! Did you see how she moved?" Bagoula barked at the group. The crowd of Brees watched with undersized, milky white, and misaligned eyes. Several of them nodded and shuffled backward. A few sprouted darker hair and bigger ears. Misplaced curves straightened, as limbs grew and shrank. They were trying to imitate her.

"None of you are ready for assignment. Pay attention, or I will unmake you." Bagoula shook Elliot's head, then raised his blue eyes to meet Spooky's. "I didn't expect three young models to stumble into my camp. Are more of you coming?"

"Where are my friends?" Spooky swatted the tray at one of the monsters who had inched closer. Its tan face became thinner and pale, then reverted back. "We don't have anything to do with your fight against Targa, so just let us go."

"Scouts, search the area," Bagoula barked, ignoring her. "I would prefer a set of pairs. Two male types and two female types would be ideal. Do you have another boy with you? A living boy? Moving models are so important for practice."

Spooky glared, not loosening her grip on the tray. She didn't know what Bagoula wanted with them, but she wasn't going to reveal her intentions either.

"Could you move around a little bit while you grovel in fear?" Bagoula tilted Elliot's head and smiled. "Wiggle your fingers? They always have trouble with the fingers. Oh, well done you!"

One of the monsters walked forward, navigating a bipedal gait better than the others. As Spooky watched, it changed the length of its torso and limbs until they matched Bree's proportions. The eyes were still too wide, and the mouth sat crooked, but it could have been Bree's cousin. Every minor adjustment that played on its face brought it closer to its mark. Watching the subtly shifting face made Spooky queasy.

"You," Bagoula barked at it. "We still have yet to replace two humans in key households in sector nineteen. Report there now for final appearance adjustments and assignment."

The Bree nodded its recently settled chin. It was still too square compared to Bree's true heart-shape.

"Has your friend been to Oak Harbor?" Bagoula asked Spooky. "Oak Harbor, in Washington State?"

"I don't know..." It was a simple question, but Spooky couldn't make sense of what she was hearing. Why was Bagoula, a monster from another world, asking where Bree was from? How had she ever heard of any city or state? Why did she care about models for a pair of girls and boys?

"No matter." Bagoula addressed the calibrating Bree. "Wait at the pickup point. Don't let anyone see you until the general makes contact and assigns you a new appearance."

The Bree spun and crossed the flat expanse, her newly formed back straight, if not a little too stiff. Bagoula raised Elliot's hand and a white line appeared in the air in the distance. The Bree continued toward it, flashed in white light, then disappeared.

The creature had gone through a door. But a door to where?

"You're one of them." The words were out of Spooky's mouth before she had time to reconsider. "You want Earth."

Bagoula blinked Elliot's long eyelashes at her. "It seems Earth is so eager for my dominion that its inhabitants have started coming to me. Who am I to deny them?" She clicked Elliot's tongue. "Not long to wait now. You'll all be mine very, very soon."

Leber had been a shadow of a threat. Spooky had only seen the scar he left behind on Carcass's world. But now, one of Earth's would-be invaders was right here in front of her. If Bagoula's creations could learn to imitate as well as she could, they could replace anybody, anywhere. Already, in Oak Harbor, some people weren't what they seemed.

She had to stop Bagoula. Not just for Targa, but for Earth too. She needed to keep her distracted until Kru arrived.

"Don't. You can't," Spooky said lamely.

"'Don't?'" Bagoula spread Elliot's arms wide. "I already rule over everything my father has. This place is a monument to the limits of his imagination. He's never even left. I deserve another world. I deserve more."

"No, I mean you can't win." Spooky forced her shoulders back. "The god of Earth will crush you."

"You may hope so, human, but my scouts have informed me otherwise."

"I'm just warning you. Besides," Spooky tried to keep her voice from shaking, "your creations will never pass as humans. If that's what they were even trying to do."

"My children on Earth are ready." Elliot's gaze stayed fixed on

Spooky's face. "You won't be able to tell a human from one of mine until they are clawing your eyes out."

"You say that, but you couldn't even fool me." Spooky managed to shrug. "I knew you weren't Elliot."

Bagoula stared a second longer. "I had already decided to kill the blonde, but you are making a strong case for it to be you."

"You said you wanted moving models for practice," Spooky stammered. Her bravado slipped away.

"Well," Bagoula shrugged. "Sometimes there's a benefit to a model staying still."

Elliot's face began to melt.

# CHAPTER XXVIII
## BATTLE OF THE BREES

Elliot's face sagged, and his mouth reformed into a gray hole. His head fell back, then hurled forward, sending a glob of something toward Spooky. Spooky dove to the right, and whatever Bagoula had spat splatted onto the column that had been behind her.

"I need to talk to Carcass!" Spooky shouted. "I need Kru, now!"

At this point, she didn't expect him to reply. She just hoped he had received the message.

Elliot's face grew long and lost its eyebrows, nose, and hair. His arms and clothes disappeared as he rose up on two knobby, ostrich legs. His torso rotated until it was parallel with the ground and stretched into a serpentine body, connecting an almond-shaped head with a four-foot tail. Flexible tubes, similar to the ones that made up Targa's twisted form, whipped at the top of the grooved face like hair.

Spooky hovered at the edge of the cluster, keeping a medium-sized column between her and Bagoula. As much as she wanted to run into the maze of stone and hide, she wasn't sure she would have the advantage. Bagoula and her minions had stayed out of sight and picked off Elliot without trouble.

"What did you do to my friends?" she shouted.

"Oh there, there." Bagoula's true voice whirred out of the hole in her chin, in high and low tones a human couldn't hit at the same time, if at all. "You won't have to worry about them long. Grab her, hold her still."

The strange versions of Bree advanced, their movements proving to be just as imprecise as their features. They hopped and galloped on unexpected combinations of elbows and fingers and feet.

One of the monsters pulled ahead of the others, running on all fours like an animal. Its face was as wide as its shoulders, and Bree's fluffy hair only grew out of the very top of its head. It lunged and snatched her foot. Spooky yelled and whacked its face with the tray as hard as she could. The creature snarled and backed away, growing pointed teeth through its cheeks and turning the humanoid face into something out of a nightmare.

Spooky whirled and found herself nose to nose with another Bree. This creature had captured Bree's heart-shaped face perfectly, but it had sprouted needles at the end of its wrists. Spooky knocked it to one side with her tray, but it swung back and slashed its needles across Spooky's thigh. She screamed.

"No spines! No claws!" Bagoula whirred in a din of voices, high and low. "You'll ruin her skin!"

The creature's spikes retracted. Spooky took the opportunity to smack it in the head with her tray.

She ignored the blood streaming down her leg and threw herself into the thick of the columns, bouncing off them like a ball in a machine. Blonde hair and reaching hands flashed between them. If she slowed down, she would end up surrounded.

"Give me a tray! Another tray! Another tray!" She hurdled the plastic sheets at anything that moved.

Spooky tore around a column and skidded back into the open, barely changing direction in time as Bagoula spat something gray out of the hole in her chin. The ball of goo whooshed past Spooky's head and struck a Bree coming up behind her. The pearlescent glob swirled over the monster, covering it completely, then congealed into a spire of the same height.

Spooky blinked at the new formation beside her. It was indistinguishable from the other stone columns around it, as if a snarling monster hadn't just been trapped inside. The gray stuff had solidified so fast, if she hadn't been watching, she never would have noticed a new column had appeared there.

Maybe she hadn't lost Elliot in the maze. Maybe he'd become a part of it.

Spooky pivoted and rammed her shoulder into another column. She bounced off, but she had felt it waver. She threw herself at it again. This time, the base cracked, and she fell over with it. It broke like a clay pot against the tan ground, revealing the pointed face of a Targyte. Its round eyes stayed closed.

"Grab her and keep her still! Before she damages her bone structure."

There was nothing natural about this stone cluster. It was a prison. It was a graveyard. Hopefully, if Elliot and Bree were trapped in this stuff, they could survive long enough for her to find them.

Spooky scrambled to her feet and almost slammed into a wall. Not a wall—a burnt-orange torso, roped with muscle.

"Kru!" Relief welled in her chest. She could have hugged him, but monsters seized her legs and held her in place. "Fight Bagoula! You have to beat her!"

Spooky pointed at Bagoula. Kru followed her finger with his impassive gaze.

In a blur, he dashed over and punched Bagoula in the almond face. Bagoula shrieked and stumbled. She swiped at him with her serpentine tail, then whirled and spit. Kru didn't even tried to dodge. The glob of gray hit him in the chest. It swirled up and down over his body, pinning his arms and rooting him to the spot. Spooky shouted as it closed over his face.

The eight-foot column towered above the rest. Without Kru, she had no hope of defeating Bagoula or finding Elliot and Bree. Soon she would join them in her own stone tomb. Bagoula rounded on her, the tendrils at the top of her head whipping.

"Now, as for you..."

Kru's arms exploded straight out of the column, throwing dried gray stuff everywhere. He unhinged his mouth and roared. He sprung out of the stone remnants and onto Bagoula's back.

She shrieked out a horrible sound, like one thousand voices screaming all at once. Her powerful legs buckled as she swayed under his weight and rapid blows.

The Bree monsters emerged from the forest of stone and rushed toward Bagoula and Kru. They grew spines and spikes and razor-edged bits. The grooved skin of Bagoula's face peeled back, exposing a circle of needle-teeth.

The two Brees holding Spooky kept their grip, but they were distracted watching the battle. Spooky had to use every second Kru bought her to try and find Elliot and Bree. She body slammed the one to her left and kicked the one on the right. With a few more whacks of a new tray, she scrambled out of the pile of limbs and ran.

The only clue about what each of the rocks in the formation might contain was their size. There were dozens of columns that matched Bree's height but fewer that were as tall as Elliot. It narrowed down the possibilities.

She threw herself at the first one that looked about right. It cracked and fell, splitting open to unveil another Targyte. Its black eyes snapped open and she leapt back. The Targyte convulsed and squeaked.

Maybe it wasn't too late. Maybe not every creature that went into the stone was doomed.

"Are you of Bagoula?" the creature whimpered.

"No," Spooky replied. "But those two are. Run!"

The two Brees didn't even glance at the freed Targyte as they ambled toward her. Their imitations of the human body were gangly and uncoordinated—one's elbows and knees didn't bend and the other had a spindly right side and a squat left. Without any sharp bits, they only had the advantage of numbers. Spooky asked the finger for more trays and hurled them like Frisbees. She caught the first Bree in the face and fled from the second, heading for the next column that was Elliot's height.

She crashed into that one. Then the next one. Then the next one. Each stone broke open to reveal a face, but not the right face—there were Targytes and some other creatures with green patterns and blue webbed protrusions. Some moved. Others didn't. She didn't look long after confirming that each wasn't Elliot.

Spooky's ribs, shoulders, and arms throbbed. She tried to ignore the pain and switched sides when she couldn't. She ran at another and another and another, each blow turning aching to agony. The cuts on her leg left a trail of red, and her eyes blurred with tears.

She fell to the ground with a column that was probably too tall. The still face inside was pink and feathered. As she tried to rise, hands grabbed her. The two Brees had caught up. She struck out and twisted, but they were heavy enough to prevent her from rising. They snarled and forced her down.

Immobile, cheek pressed against the tan earth, Spooky tried to focus her bleary eyes on Kru. At least a dozen monsters battled in full fighting form, with teeth and spikes and claws coming out of every misshapen part of Bree's body. Kru punched and kicked and threw one after another, but every time he knocked away one, another took its place. His burgundy blood splattered the stones. Bagoula herself dove in and out, wriggling through the chaos like a snake through water and taking swipes at him with her needle teeth.

Bagoula jumped onto Kru's back, gripping his torso with her feet, and sunk her needle-mouth into his shoulder. Spooky shouted. Kru stumbled. Wine red ran down his side.

Kru couldn't help her. He might not even be able to save himself.

A heavy feeling flowed through Spooky, spreading from her chest out to her limbs, weighing her down as firmly as the monsters. She would die here. She would be held still and killed now or left to suffocate or starve with the other creatures entombed in the stone. Kru had been strong enough to break out of Bagoula's trap, but she wasn't. She couldn't even stand. Bagoula was a conqueror with an army. She was just a nobody who had been a dotted outline in her own life. A placeholder that took up space and waited for the person she would be to show up.

*That's the only part I can fix.*

Elliot's face filled her head. His eyes and his smile lit up her mind. Bree appeared next to him, laughing loudly. What about Elliot? What about Bree? They had families who needed to see them again. They had things they had to make it back to Earth to do. Bree had a daughter who deserved to have her mother to cherish and protect her. Elliot still had to see the world.

And he was trapped in the dark right now.

He was trapped in the dark.

She couldn't leave him there. She wasn't done. Even if she couldn't beat Bagoula, she had to fight until she was in darkness too.

There was a spire ahead of her. It was the right height.

One more. She had to break one more.

She elbowed the monster on her back and rolled. The creatures grappled for her arms, but she was able to get her feet under her. They each hung off a wrist as she dragged them toward the next spire. She leaned against it, pushing her filthy cheek into the rock. With her two captors yanking her back, she couldn't generate enough force to push it over.

Bagoula shrieked a different tone this time, with more high-pitched notes. The monsters squawked and released her arms. Kru must be holding his own if she was calling for more reinforcements.

Spooky put both hands against the spire and pushed. Her feet slid backward on the smooth ground, and she sobbed as she slipped on the blood dripping down her leg. She ran six more steps in place, backed away, then launched herself at it. The base cracked. It hit the ground and revealed another Targyte.

One more.

The only thing to do now was break one more.

This time she forced herself to jog, using her hands to brace the impact as much as she could. She had to back up and run at it again before it started to give. The column toppled, and Spooky fell to all fours beside it. She cried out when she saw brown hair and rosy cheeks.

"Elliot!" she sobbed.

He started coughing. His pupils were pinpoints as he squinted.

She cupped his face and smelled him. He smelled sweaty and like a boy, and totally human. She collapsed in the wreckage beside him and took a few shuddering breaths.

Her arms shook as she helped him out of the broken column. He stood up and swayed. She caught his elbow and was almost pulled down as he collapsed onto his knees.

"Are you okay?" she asked.

"I couldn't move. I couldn't...catch my breath," Elliot muttered. "What's happening? Where's Bree?"

"I haven't found her yet," Spooky said. "But Kru's here."

She glanced toward the fight. Kru picked up an entire spire and slammed it into Bagoula, who staggered back. Black spots had bloomed on her body and tail. The plain was scattered with her broken minions. Kru's skin was stained with dark blood, but he was still standing, fists curled. A monster scrambled forward, and he booted it.

"Kru!" Spooky helped Elliot stand. "You have to beat her. We need to end this and find Bree."

Kru didn't turn at her words, but he lunged toward Bagoula. He landed a few punches on her almond face, and she crumpled.

"Bagoula!" Spooky shouted. "Where's our friend?"

"Human girl," Bagoula whirred, her voice weak. She climbed back up onto knobby legs and staggered into the cluster of columns. "If you want your friend so much, I'll give her to you."

Her shape went molten and shrank behind a stone. She was transforming.

"Kru, don't let her get away!" Spooky called.

Kru dashed toward the spot where Bagoula had disappeared, but stopped.

Bree stepped out in front of him, perfect in her symmetry and beauty, every freckle and curl in place. The ruse wouldn't work a second time. Spooky knew it wasn't Bree.

But Kru didn't.

"Kru, that's Bagoula!" Spooky ran toward him.

"No, Kru, she's Bagoula. Not me." Bagoula said in Bree's voice.

Kru didn't move.

Spooky skidded to a stop. If Kru wouldn't know who to defend, she couldn't get close to Bagoula. She would ordinarily consider it a good thing that he wouldn't attack someone who looked like Bree, but in this case, she really needed him to.

Bagoula smiled. "Scouts, answer the call of your mother."

Two more Brees appeared from behind stone pillars. Their imitations were almost as flawless as Bagoula's. If they hadn't been standing next to each other, Spooky never would have noticed the lighter eyes on one and the higher cheekbones on the other.

"Kru, she's the one on the right!"

Kru stared.

Bagoula put up Bree's arm. A glowing white line appeared in the middle of the open expanse. "Report to the general that I'm engaging forces to clean up a mess here. Tell him to await my order to begin the attack on Earth."

The two new Brees dashed toward the door, then disappeared into the void.

Spooky couldn't let Bagoula give that order. Carcass had said Kru had been instructed to protect them. "Kru, you don't have to hurt her, just cover her mou..."

"Answer the call of your mother!" Bagoula shouted in Bree's voice. "Summon your siblings!"

A deafening and terrible noise filled the air, drowning out Spooky's words. The monsters who had survived Kru's onslaught put their heads back and let out a screech so loud, it could have reverberated all the way down to Targa.

"Kru!" Spooky tried to outmatch the chorus of voices. "Just grab her!"

It was no use—she couldn't even hear herself. Elliot curled against a pedestal, his hands over his ears. Spooky clutched her head, waiting for the ringing wail to stop.

Bree's face smirked. Bagoula touched the spire next to her, which exploded into dust. Spooky coughed and waved away the debris.

The screeching ended and the dust cleared. Two identical Brees lay on the ground next to each other with their eyes closed.

"Bree!" Spooky yelled, although her voice sounded muffled.

The two Brees were indistinguishable, like twins curled in the womb. Their skin was ashen. Spooky couldn't tell if either of their chests were moving. She tightened her fists. The real Bree was just unconscious. She had to be.

"Spooky!" Elliot called.

He pointed across the flat landscape. A horde of strange creatures filled the horizon. They screeched out a battle cry as they raced to join their mother. These creatures weren't trying to imitate any human—they had spikes and horns, plates and scales, and appendages that could be used for nothing except maiming. No wonder the Targytes hadn't stood a chance against Bagoula. She had built her army to represent the collective traits of all monsters. And it was charging to her aid.

They needed a quick exit.

"We have to get back to the handprint!"

Even as she said it, Spooky realized they wouldn't make it. The monsters were covering the distance at an alarming speed, and she doubted she could find her way back through the maze of stone even if she had time to spare. Besides, if she opened the tunnel, there was nothing to stop Bagoula's army from pouring in after them. Even Kru couldn't take on hundreds of enemies at once. Spooky scanned the area for shelter.

Then she saw it. The glowing blue eye. The other escape route from Bagoula's seat of power—the door to Geyegorg.

"Kru, pick both Brees up and follow me, we have to get to safety!"

Spooky said. Kru bent down and scooped up the limp blonde forms. "Elliot, can you run?"

He nodded, his hands on his knees.

"Come on!" Spooky seized his arm and raced toward the eye.

He had to make it. They all had to make it. If they could get to Geyegorg, she could go through the door to Targa's seat of power one more time. They would find some way to make Bagoula reveal herself. Kru would be able to subdue her—without her army, she was no match for him.

Targa would have to keep up his end of the deal. He would have to.

They were ten steps from the beacon, but thundering footsteps shook the ground as the wall of monsters closed in on their flank. A purple creature charged ahead of the horde, black teeth bared. His clubbed hands swung back and forth like wrecking balls.

Spooky lunged for the eye and dragged it down to open the door. She shoved Elliot into the void.

"Kru, through here! Come on, come on, come on!"

Kru sped into the glowing line. Wrecking ball let out a battle cry as he swung for her. She flung herself into whiteness.

# CHAPTER XXIX
# THE TRADE

A purple club swung into the void and whiffed past Spooky's face. The blunt instrument completed its arc and disappeared. The space behind her stayed blank. The whiteness muffled everything except for her pounding heart.

Spooky swiveled toward the others. Both of the unconscious Brees listed in the loops of Kru's arms. Elliot made eye contact, his brow furrowed. Spooky wished he was close enough that she could take his hand. They were going to figure this out. They would get the real Bree some help and get the fake Bree to Targa in time.

As soon as they landed on the dark platform, Spooky took one of the Bree's wrists and raised it to her nose, then the other's. They both smelled like salt and dirt and skin. Bagoula hadn't forgotten to adjust her scent a second time. Kru stared down at her as she checked them with her hands and her eyes. From their clammy palms, to their slack pouts, to the dirt on their cheeks, the Brees were identical. Thank goodness they were both still breathing.

Three beacons hung in the air around them; two yellow branches for Targa's world, and the modified "e" that could take them back to Colorado. Spooky intertwined her fingers as she looked at the yellow symbol marking the door they had just come through. One little motion, and she could open the tunnel back to Bagoula's seat of power and her army of monsters.

She faced the yellow branch on the right—the original door they had gone through to reach Targa. It was easier to transport Bagoula while she thought her disguise was keeping her safe from Kru, but Spooky was sure they could figure out a way to make her reveal herself once they got in front of Targa. She waved for Elliot to follow her to the correct beacon.

"My new friends!" A voice called from the other end of the platform. "Come, come, come, show me what you've brought me! I won't wait another moment to see!"

Spooky froze. She could pretend not to have heard him and dash for the door. But he had the power to take away her beacons. She couldn't make him angry.

"Geyegorg! I can explain." Clenching her teeth, Spooky pivoted toward the spotlit throne.

"Come here! Come here! Let me see!"

They didn't have time for this. She swept toward the throne. Real Bree needed a hospital. The world needed saving. She blew past the short assistant, who held up a finger and his tablet in protest. She crossed the white and red lines and entered the circle of light. Elliot and Kru's steps echoed behind her.

"We just need to talk to Targa one more time, and then we'll have a Targyte for you..." Spooky paused.

Geyegorg's eyes were narrowed, his chin low. He had told her not to return without a Targyte, but she didn't expect him to look this angry. He pulled his hat off with one hand, revealing the orb on his head.

He couldn't call off their deal now. Not when they were so close. "We're going to get you a..."

"I knew that orange slug was lying!" Geyegorg shouted, almost jumping out of his chair. "He promised me, swore up and down, left and right, that with all the blood in his body he could only give me two!"

Spooky stepped back. "What? Who?"

"That slug, Carcass! I gave him exclusive gifts, the sole sight of his world's beacon, and what does he give to me? The only two

Krudors in existence, he said. The only two. And now what do I see? A third striding toward me, casual as you like! Accompanying my new friends from Earth, like it's nothing! That liar!"

Geyegorg wasn't mad at her for returning without a Targyte. He was furious at Carcass for having another Kru. Spooky tugged at her hair, making sure all parts of the finger were covered.

"Oh... Are you talking about this guy?" Spooky said. "We just met."

Kru looked down at her. It was a thin lie, but Geyegorg seemed distracted.

"This blatant affront, what is it doing in existence? What is it doing here? I wonder if I might claim it as my own, as recompense for his lies." Geyegorg ran his eyes over Kru. Then he froze, and a smile spread across his face. He leapt out of his seat. "Oh my, oh my, how wonderful. Simply splendid."

"What?" Spooky couldn't follow Geyegorg's moods. Now he was grinning and clapping.

"Give her to me, give her to me!" He beckoned with two hands. "You've brought me Targa's one and only daughter! And I see you have the right to give her to me, so give her to me!"

"I have the... I what?"

"I accept! I accept the trade! Give me Bagoula for the beacon to Axonaphis! Forget the Targyte, I don't want one anymore, now that you have brought me something better! A simple yes will do!"

"Ye...yes?" Spooky stuttered.

"Yesss," Geyegorg hissed, settling back on his chair.

Strands of light appeared from either side of the platform and arched up and over Kru. They descended upon the Bree in his right arm and began encircling her. Elliot started forward but Spooky put up a hand.

Geyegorg could see things they couldn't. If he could see this Bree was Targa's creation, he must be right.

Before she had a chance to second guess herself, the body in the coiling light began to change. It melted and morphed into Bagoula's serpentine form, then back to Bree. Then it splayed into spaghetti, trying to escape the light's grasp. Bagoula flailed and cried out in her many tones, but the beams took her over the edge of the platform. The light dipped down into the golden honeycomb. After a few moments, the screeching tones stopped.

"In a prized place near my throne." He nodded at Spooky. "Closer than I would have placed a Targyte."

Spooky blinked at the still honeycomb. "Is she...dead?"

"Of course not!" Geyegorg scoffed. "What good is she to me dead? She is preserved, frozen in time. She will never die now that she is in my collection. Mine forever, if I choose to keep her."

Spooky didn't see how she was good to him either way but didn't say anything. Even though Bagoula had tried to kill them, Spooky still felt queasy.

At least she would never give her army the order to attack Earth.

"My new friend." Geyegorg leaned forward and slapped his knee. "I was right about you! We are going to be good friends. Good friends. How did you get Targa to agree to this? He won't do a single deal with me, then gives you permission to trade his only daughter?"

Spooky wasn't aware that Targa had agreed to this. She didn't think Targa had meant to give her the right to offer Bagoula to Geyegorg.

But Geyegorg could see things, things she couldn't. At one point, Targa had given her permission to do anything to Bagoula, including kill her. Apparently, that was approval enough to offer her in trade. Putting her in Geyegorg's time-juice was definitely one way to put an end to her path of destruction.

She had kept up her end of the bargain with Targa, even though she no longer needed him to fulfill his.

"I traded with her for years and had to watch her come and go, come and go," Geyegorg was still talking, his hand flapping at the wrist. "Never to be mine. Her shoddy shapeshifters—a poor excuse for her father's work, a poor excuse for herself—were all she could offer me. I'd cover my third eye and watch them go into my collection, then take them out again, just to watch them pretend to be things I couldn't have—humans, slargos, festicorps, Targytes. But even with my first and second eyes, I knew they were nothing. Cheap imitations by the hundreds that could not satisfy me."

Geyegorg's third eye pulsed with light. He leaned back in his chair, gazing up.

"But now I have the real thing. Barring a few logistical details."

He waved his hand and the little lizard in a hat came forward. It flipped its slab over, and began to read:

"Thank you for doing business with..."

"Hold on!" Spooky said. "I just need a few minutes."

The small creature gawked at her like she had walked up and slapped it. She ignored it and focused on the Bree curled in Kru's arms. The real Bree.

Spooky addressed Kru loudly. "It was nice to meet you, sir, thank you for helping us carry our offering to Geyegorg. Could you please help take my friend back to my seat of power?"

Kru stared at her with his usual unchanging expression.

She slid her eyes over to Geyegorg, but he was still leaning back in his chair, smiling to himself. The joy of adding Bagoula to his collection seemed to have curbed his concerns about the existence of Kru. For now, anyway.

"Come on," she said to Elliot. "Let's get Bree back to Earth."

She and Elliot ran to the end of the platform together, and Kru trailed close behind. In the green light of the beacon Elliot couldn't see, she turned to face him.

"Elliot, you have to take Bree to a hospital. I'll go talk to Axonaphis."

Elliot shook his head. "Kru can take her. You don't have to do this alone. You don't have to prove anything."

"I'm not," Spooky said, and she meant it. "We don't know how badly she's hurt. You have to go and make sure she gets whatever help she needs."

Elliot stared at her a second longer. Then he nodded. "I know you can do this."

"I...thank you. I never would have made it this far without you."

He smiled. "Yes, you would have. I know you would have."

She shook her head. She didn't have time to tell him all the ways he was wrong. She would have been a meal for Jagbi. She would have turned around before she made it to Geyegorg. She would have given up with Targa. She never would have found the strength to keep fighting Bagoula.

She thought the words as she looked into his eyes, hoping he could see how much him being with her had made all the difference. He grasped her hand, sending sparks up her arm.

She took a deep breath and smiled. "This is the easy part."

She used her other hand to drag the door to Earth open.

"This will put you somewhere near my neighborhood," Spooky said. "Just knock on doors and yell until someone calls you an ambulance."

They stood one more second. Neither of them let go.

"See you later," he said with a smile.

"Yeah."

His hand slid out of hers and into the whiteness. Kru stepped forward, Bree dangling in his arms. It made Spooky's heart seize to see her face so wan and lifeless. She never would have made it this far without Bree either. She squeezed Bree's hand, too, before Kru carried her into the void.

She had to finish what they had started.

Spooky jogged back to the throne. She felt the lack of food and sleep in every step, but she didn't have time to waste. An hour or so had passed since Carcass had told her the first attack had begun. Bagoula had seemed confident the god of Earth wouldn't intervene. She had been preparing to give her general the order. Others planning their own invasions were probably feeling just as bold, and bolder by the minute.

Whatever the god of Earth was doing, whatever corner of the universe had his attention, she had to get him to come back now, or there wouldn't be anything to come back to.

"Okay, I'm here," Spooky said to the lizard-thing. "What were you saying?"

"Ahem." The little creature took its time finding its place on its tablet. "Thank you for doing business with…"

"Can we hurry this up please?" Spooky bounced on her toes.

"You walk away from your contract phase and now you want to rush it?" The thing adjusted its little hat. "Make up your mind."

Geyegorg still didn't seem to be paying much attention. He had put his hat back over his third eye, but he was still gazing over the side of the platform where Bagoula had disappeared.

The lizard traced its finger down the tablet.

"You have agreed to provide the collateral in exchange for the beacon marking all doors leading to world 176, henceforth referred to as 'the beacon.'"

"World 176… That's where Axonaphis is, right?"

"I don't know where he is, but that is his world, yes." It gave a haughty sniff. "If you don't want to hear the contract, please confirm you understand the terms, and the beacon will be provided to you."

"Yes. Yes. I confirm."

"Laborious but necessary." Geyegorg smiled. "Now, for your prize."

He raised one hand toward the black sky, fingers spread wide.

The swirling tornado of symbols descended toward his outstretched hand. A single symbol, a red triangle with a "u" on top, floated down to his palm. He extended it toward her. It flew into her eye and her vision flashed and fizzled.

"The beacon to Axonaphis. Our contract is complete," Geyegorg said.

A red glow that hadn't been there before shone from the end of the platform.

Spooky bounded toward it. This was the thing she had been striving to get all along.

She just had to go to one more world and ask one more god for one more favor.

Then she could make her plea to the god of Earth.

# CHAPTER XXX
# TELEPHONE

The whiteness gave way to shape and color, but this time, Spooky didn't fall out of the void. Instead, she floated into the center of a glimmering, golden belly. It took her a moment to realize the fluted shapes and tubes surrounding her were metal phones, stacked and layered so densely they covered any hint of walls. They weren't cell phones or digital handsets. They were older, like the phones she had seen in old movies, with elegant curves and separate pieces to hold in each hand.

It was beautiful, but it was a little claustrophobic.

Spooky hugged her arms. The space felt smaller than when she first arrived. It wasn't her imagination—the room shuddered and contracted. The phones squeezed in a foot. Then another. The room shrank to the size of a van. Then a car. The devices jostled on top of one another and pressed in, in, in, until she had to curl into a ball to avoid the metal.

"Help!" She squawked.

"What you're seeing," a voice with a tremor said, "is not real."

"What?" Spooky clutched her arms around her knees.

"What you see can't touch you. There's nothing there but light and void." The voice was soft, like too much air escaped with each word. Like an old man's voice. "Picture a little more space for yourself."

As if on command, the phones drifted away from her. The chamber expanded into its original shape. But there was no chamber. He had said she was still in the void. Bits of white leaked between the golden curves. The phones separated further, like an explosion in slow motion, revealing the endless whiteness behind. They spun away into empty space. The only anchor was the blue beacon to Geyegorg stationed beside her. Spooky flapped her arms, wishing she had something to hold on to.

"Well, that's distracting," the voice said again. "How about you picture something a little less constricting, but a little more solid? Like a curtain, perhaps."

As if on command, the phones zoomed back to a formation the size of an ordinary room. A red curtain unfurled around them, wrapping the space like a present, until all the metallic shapes were nestled in velvet. Spooky felt like she was dreaming. She wasn't sure if the images appeared when she thought of them or after the voice described them, but the longer she sat with the current scene the more solid it became. The phones gleamed, and the red fabric looked lush and permanent.

"That's better, isn't it?"

"Are you..." Spooky regained her voice. "Are you Axonaphis?"

"I am." A portion of the curtain in front of her parted and revealed an old man. He wore high-waisted green pants and a collared shirt with rolled sleeves. He resembled someone from a movie she'd seen—the old-timey gentleman who operated the town telegraph. As she recalled the scene, it became apparent it was, in fact, him. As he floated into the main chamber, he adjusted a gray news cap on white hair. Spectacles perched at the end of his nose. The gold frames shone as bright as the phones around them.

"There aren't any defined visual properties in my world," he said. "The whole place looks like whatever you think it will. It's interesting to get a little taste of everyone's preconceptions about you." He glanced down at himself. "Not bad!"

That explained the weird dream-state she felt like she was in, where her surroundings chased her thoughts. She wasn't aware she'd had a preconception about Axonaphis's world; all she had known was that his world was devoted to communication. And his voice had sounded like an old man's.

But now that the scene was stable, each second corroborated its appearance. This was what she thought Axonaphis's world looked like now.

"So then." He ran an arthritic thumb along a suspender. "What can I do for you?"

"I'm here because I have to send a message to someone. I was told you could help me with that."

"I can indeed." He stared at her. She stared back. "Well?"

"What?"

"Are you going to give me the message and tell me who to deliver it to?"

A grip on Spooky's chest loosened. With every god so far, she had been hiding things, scheming, negotiating, and arguing. Now, here was a god who had just asked for what she needed. And when she told him, he would help her.

The feeling was completely unfamiliar, perhaps from long before she had met Carcass.

She breathed out and her shoulders relaxed. "Oh, right. I have a message for the god of Earth. Do I just...tell it to you?"

"I prefer something less distortable than sound waves. Can you transmit a telepathic package? No? Alright then, what about this?" He held out a paper, and a red fountain pen. "Write down the message."

"Okay!" Talking to the god of Earth directly seemed like a lot of pressure. A pen and paper gave her a moment to collect her thoughts. "Will I be able to get his answer?"

"Yes. If the god of Earth has a reply, I will receive it and deliver it directly to you."

This experience was proving to be more like snail mail than a phone call.

One by one, all the phones in the room transformed into golden mailboxes with their little red flags down.

Spooky took the paper and pen from Axonaphis's wrinkled hands. The paper had fine gold curls embossed around its edges. It already had *To: The God of Earth* written at the top. As she touched the tip of the pen down, she realized how little she had prepared for this moment. Even after all she had gone through to get here, it felt like it had arrived suddenly.

She fiddled with the pen and glanced at Axonaphis.

"Should I give you a moment?" He put his hands in his pockets.

"Uh, yeah. Thanks."

Axonaphis nodded and floated back through the curtain.

Spooky tapped the pen. Maybe if they could have a conversation face to face, she'd ask him "why." Why he'd abandoned Earth, why she had to come all this way to get his attention, why he hadn't taken responsibility for the safety and security of his own creation. Or maybe, why he'd created Earth, humans, and her, in the first place. But those answers wouldn't help her solve anything. Whether he knew what was happening on Earth or not, and whatever his reasons for any of it, all she could do now was ask for his help.

> *Dear God of Earth,*
>
> *My name is Laurel Specki, and I am a human. I left Earth to get you this message.*

Carcass thought if a human sent him the plea, he might be moved to pity. Alternatively, he might feel annoyed that a human was off Earth. The idea of annoying a god had scared her a lot more a few days ago. But now, after having annoyed several, she was aligned with Carcass's priorities—she needed to motivate action.

There was no delicate way to put the rest, and she didn't have time to waste on careful wording:

> *Other gods believe you've abandoned Earth and they are trying to take it over. If you don't come back right now and face them, Earth will be destroyed. Please return to Earth and save us.*

Axonaphis reemerged from behind the curtain. She nodded and held out the message and the pen. As soon as he took them from her, she wondered if she should have taken more time with the phrasing. She hoped it had been clear.

Axonaphis drifted over to one side of the chamber. He opened a mailbox and popped in her note.

They waited. Axonaphis bobbed, his hands folded, watching the mailbox. He noticed her staring and smiled.

Spooky tried to return it, but she dug her nails into her palms. "How long does this usually take?"

"It depends on the recipient. Some don't respond... Ah!"

The red flag on the mailbox sprung up. Axonaphis gave her a nod. He opened the metal door and took out a paper within.

He drifted back to her and presented it. It was on the same stationary she had just used, but at the top it said: *To: Laurel Specki* (*Spooky*). The note was written in an unfamiliar script. It was so perfect, it looked like it had been typed with a pencil.

Spooky held it in shaking hands and read each evenly spaced word.

She looked up from the paper. "Is that it?"

Axonaphis nodded. "That's his reply."

"That can't be it." Spooky read it again. "Are you sure this is really from the god of Earth?"

"Yes, that message came directly from the god of Earth." Axonaphis didn't seem flustered by her question. "You'll find that gods with specialized powers are usually more adept at our one skill. I am almost nothing except a messenger. I am confident in that."

Spooky's face heated. "Where is he? I'll go talk to him. I have to make him understand."

Her skin was crusted with dirt, sweat, and blood. Elliot was hurt. Bree was unconscious. Earth was under attack. She was finally here, and that couldn't be the answer.

"I'm sorry," Axonaphis said, his brows pulling together. "I can't help you with that. Finding someone is quite a different matter. I can send another message, if there's more you'd like to say?"

Spooky crumpled the paper and threw it. "Send him another message. Tell him that it's his fault we exist, and it's his fault we're in danger. None of us were given a choice. And if he's going to abandon us when we need him most, then maybe we're better off without him."

"Did you want me to try to use your sound waves, or...?"

"I don't care." It wasn't Axonaphis's fault, but she couldn't help herself from snapping the words at him. "And I don't care if he gives you a reply. Tell him if he has something else to say, he can say it to me in person."

Spooky turned her back and touched the blue eye. She dragged it open and made it into the void before the hot tears started.

She landed on the platform in Geyegorg's world. Only twenty or so minutes had passed, but everything had changed. She squeezed her fists over her eyes. There was nothing she could do now. It was over.

Shouting drew her attention down the platform toward the circle of light. Geyegorg was standing in front of his throne, his third eye glowing, waving. She couldn't handle his creepy weirdness right now, and in a few seconds, it wouldn't matter if he got mad and erased her beacons. She turned and bolted for the door that would take her back to Earth.

# CHAPTER XXXI
# RETURN

Spooky stepped out of the void into a sunny Colorado day. The sunlight filtered through the swaying branches of a maple tree. She didn't recognize this block, but the row of white, gray, and beige homes resembled the ones in her neighborhood. A car rolled by. The smell of garbage reached her nose. Behind her, a set of cans waited for pick up. It must be Sunday. Garbage day. The only thing out of place was the electric blue eye suspended next to the compost bin, marking the door she had just come through.

The nearest intersection was labeled Birch and Fourth. She was only a few blocks away from home. She walked toward her street in a daze. The sun warmed her skin. Geyegorg, Targa, and Carcass fuzzed like last night's dream. Even Dodgson felt like a distant memory.

She reached her driveway. Both of her parents' cars were gone. A face in the front yard made her jump.

It was a black and white version of her junior year class portrait, pinned to the tree on the lawn. Beneath the picture was a jumble of flowers, candles, stuffed animals, and paper signs that read "come home soon," "we're praying for Laurel," and "we miss you Laurel." She couldn't think of anyone who would have put this shrine together. No one at school called her Laurel. Probably people she'd never met who'd heard her name on the news. There were a lot of teddy bears and pink ribbons for an eighteen-year-old, but the pile was substantial. She could see more flower stems and the edges of cards sticking out of the garbage cans on the sidewalk, waiting for pick-up.

Spooky snorted. Her parents must hate this. They hated kitschy mess. They wouldn't have chosen that photo, either—her shoulders were slumped, her eyes were too wide, and her smile looked small and nervous. But appearances were paramount. If the community wanted to support their missing daughter with a pile of junk and her most recent class picture, they wouldn't want to appear heartless.

It was probably all they could do to avoid taking a match to the front lawn. Their spooky daughter, who'd had the audacity to go missing, was now on full display.

Three days ago, every dream she'd had for the future started with a return to this house. And for three days, she had been faced with constant reasons why she might not make it back. Between getting abducted by Carcass, kicked out of Dodgson, sent to prison, stranded in another world, or killed, the odds had been against her. And at every turn, she had fought to make it back here to restart her life as she had envisioned it.

She should be running for the front door.

Clearly, she would be received as a victim, not a criminal. They didn't even have to send a cab to pick her up from Dodgson. She could go inside right now. She knew which rock they kept the spare key under.

But she didn't move. There was something heavy in her core. No, not heavy—solid. Something that made it easy to hold her back straight and chin up.

If she walked in that door right now, her parents would look at her the way they always did—as a burden. As a failure. As a disappointment. But she had gone on an impossible journey and done impossible things. She had negotiated with gods and fought monsters. She could see doors to other worlds. The idea that she couldn't survive without their approval or accommodation was laughable.

Maybe, even if they opened the door for her, she shouldn't walk through it. Maybe she could do better than being an unwanted daughter in their home for another year. She hadn't had time to make new plans, but for the first time, she wasn't so afraid to let go of the old ones.

A face appeared in the window. She thought it was her mother at first, but after another second, the features softened into Victoria's. Her oval face and long shiny hair made her look like a ghost behind the glass.

She should still be on campus for her summer research intensive. Spooky watched Victoria settle onto the loveseat by the window and rest her chin on her crossed arms. She got a strange feeling Victoria was waiting for her.

Spooky took a step toward the door. She wanted to tell Victoria what she'd gone through. She wanted to tell Victoria the mistakes she'd made, how selfish she'd been, how passive in her own life so far. She wanted to ask how it had been for Victoria, growing up with parents who'd treated her like she was only worth what she accomplished.

She wanted to tell Victoria there was more behind the world.

"Did you succeed?" Carcass said in her ear.

And suddenly, the world was still in danger, and what she and her sister would say to each other became a question for another time.

"I made it to Axonaphis. I sent the message." Spooky shook her head even though he couldn't see her.

"What was the response?"

"Not good."

"I am with the other humans at St. Mercy's hospital. I've sent Kru to collect you. He will run slowly to avoid damage, but cover your eyes to block small particles."

"What?" Spooky's hair blew over her face. She brushed it back to see all eight feet of Kru standing over her. "Oh, hi..."

Before she could finish her greeting, he scooped her up in his arms and started running. Her cheeks flapped as the neighborhood blurred by. She squeezed her eyes shut and covered them with one hand. The wind was so strong it was hard to draw breath.

She peeked through her fingers. Her neighborhood had disappeared. They were racing through downtown. They were moving faster than the cars, but it wasn't like the constant movement of a car —the scene blurred and sharpened in intervals as Kru sped up and slowed. Her head reeled as her eyes tried and failed to follow the motion. She covered her face again.

A few moments later, they decelerated into the hospital parking lot. News vans crowded the front entrance. A few reporters were speaking into cameras. Behind their backs, a red beacon glowed—the beacon to Axonaphis. No one turned as Kru rushed Spooky around the side of the building and into the ambulance bay. He zipped her through swinging doors, down a linoleum hall, and up three flights of stairs. He deposited her in an empty waiting room.

As soon as her feet touched the ground, Spooky clutched her stomach and bent over. She took slow breaths while the room spun. She hadn't eaten anything to throw up, but that didn't mean her body wouldn't try. She swallowed a few times.

"I wasn't sure what acceleration you could tolerate," Carcass said. "We didn't have time to experiment."

His voice wasn't in her head this time. She jerked up and saw his toady face.

"Carcass!" She ducked again. "Ugh."

After a few more breaths, she rested her back against the wall and faced him. He had his usual stance and expression, with his arms folded into his sleeves and his eyes half-lidded, but something had changed. The last time she'd seen him, she'd wished he was just a nightmare. But in the intervening days, his voice had become a lifeline in her head. He could tell her what she needed to do next.

"Won't someone see you?" she asked.

"No one can see me unless I wish to be seen," Carcass said. "And given the hubbub around your two human friends, I will make it so no one can see you either. Hold the edge of my robe and walk with me. I can't have doctors making off with you before our business is finished."

Spooky pinched the rough fabric. Carcass led her out of the waiting room to a bricked garden terrace with a few trees. He settled himself onto an iron bench. Spooky leaned against the railing across from him.

"How are Bree and Elliot? The other humans."

"Your companions are receiving medical care," Carcass said. "They were welcomed as returned hostages."

"Thank you."

"A bargain is a bargain. The local news has picked up their return, although the international news cycle is focused...elsewhere."

"What's happened?"

"Flooding and earthquakes on the surface, tunneling beneath the seabed. But it's still only the first attack. It's not too late. Tell me, what did the god of Earth say? Is he going to return?"

"No." She squeezed her hands into fists. "I told him I was a human, I told him Earth was in danger, I asked him to come back, and he said 'no.'"

She paced back and forth. She gazed down at the reporters and vans in the parking lot. They thought a few lost teens were news. They had no idea what had happened today and what was at risk. They didn't know that a door to another world was only twenty feet behind them.

Their god had kept them ignorant and then abandoned them.

She whirled and slumped onto the bench next to Carcass. "Why did you think he would care?"

"I had hoped he did not know." Carcass sighed.

"If he cared, he would have been paying attention."

"Not if he thought his plans were in motion. The High Order sort pride themselves on noninterference."

"So he just created Earth and left us to fend for ourselves? No help, just..." she waved her hand around. "Good luck?"

"You have abundance here. So I wouldn't go so far as to say humanity had to rely on luck."

Spooky kicked the bricks. "But he abandoned us."

"So it seems." Carcass watched the sky. "I didn't believe that something so complex, so beautiful, so terrible, could be anything less than a project of intention and passion. Perhaps my own affection for this world clouded my judgment."

"Well, nice to know someone cares."

They sat in silence.

"There's a beacon to Axonaphis in the parking lot," Spooky said. "Isn't there someone else we can contact? An army for hire, maybe? A god of protection?"

"I have considered many possibilities, Spooky, but I can think of no other path forward to save Earth."

Carcass didn't sound angry, he just sounded sad.

Carcass not having a plan made her skin prickle. She had to find something to do. She wasn't ready to just wait for the end.

"I should go check on Elliot and Bree." She jumped up. "Will you help me stay out of sight?"

Clutching one of the many folds of Carcass's robe, Spooky walked through the waiting room and down a hallway. Two nurses passed them without glancing in their direction. Carcass led her to a door and stopped. Spooky peered in the window.

A woman with blonde hair and a man with dark skin and tight gray curls sat beside a bed. In the bed was Bree, her cloud of curls fanned out, her face slack. A tube was taped onto her nose, and more plastic came out of her arms and off her fingers. Her eyelids looked so delicate. She looked so frail.

"Is she going to be okay?" Spooky asked no one.

The woman swiveled toward the door. A tiny head poked out of the bundle of blankets in her arms. Baby Angela. Angela was there, and Bree didn't know it. Spooky wished she could burst in, throw off the tubes and plastic, and wake her. She wanted to see Bree's smile when she realized Angela was right in front of her. To see her face when she held her baby in her arms.

But the machines beeped, and Bree didn't open her eyes.

Spooky tightened her grip on Carcass's robe and turned away. "Where's Elliot?"

Carcass led her back the way they had come and down a different corridor. He stopped in front of the door of another room. The only person in this one was Elliot. He was lying in the bed, staring at the ceiling. Spooky opened the door and Elliot glanced up.

"Elliot!" She dropped the edge of the robe.

"Spooky!" He bolted upright.

"If you'll excuse me," Carcass said. "I don't have much time left to savor Earth. I am going to watch TV in the waiting room."

"Sure. Thanks," Spooky said.

"Was that...?" Elliot asked as the door swung shut. His eyes were wide. Apparently, Carcass had let himself be visible.

"Carcass, yeah."

Elliot's injured arm was mummified in bandages, and the other was connected to an IV. Spooky ran to the bed and hugged him. He caught her, despite the constraints. She buried her head in his shoulder. He smelled like disinfectant.

She wanted to hold on longer, but she let go. She scooted back to the edge of the bed.

"I'm so glad you're okay," he said.

"You too." She looked him over again. His pink cheeks were pale, and his eyes had dark circles under them. "I mean, are you okay?"

He lifted his arms. "This is mostly cautionary. The police are waiting until we've been medically evaluated to question us."

"And for Bree to wake up."

Elliot's brows pulled together. "She hasn't woken up yet?"

"It didn't look like it." Spooky picked at the blanket. "Her family is with her. What about your parents? Do they know you're back?"

"They're on the way now. But what happened after I left? How did it go with Axonaphis?"

"Well," Spooky scratched her head. It had been hard to tell Carcass. It was even harder to tell Elliot. "Axonaphis was nice. I gave him the message."

"Did you talk to the god of Earth?"

"It didn't really work like that. I wrote him a letter. Axonaphis sent it and gave me the response. It...wasn't what we hoped for."

"What did he say?"

"He said 'screw you,' that's what he said!" She couldn't even think about it without her face getting hot. Especially after seeing Bree.

"The god of Earth said 'screw you'?" Elliot frowned.

"Basically! I asked him to return and save us, and he said: '*No. You are free to do whatever you will.*' That was it! After everything we went through, that was his response!"

"Oh, wow." Elliot rubbed his forehead.

"He threw it back in my face!" Spooky couldn't stop her voice from rising. "He basically said 'you're on your own, but have fun in your final days!'"

"Why would he say that...is he referencing free will?"

"Probably, but who cares! Carcass said High Order gods pride themselves on not interfering, but every other god in the universe is about to show up and interfere! He can't put aside his pride to help us? He'd rather see us all die than step in?"

She covered her eyes.

"Spooky, I'm sorry. Now what?"

"I don't know. I don't know what's next."

He lifted one of her hands off her face and held it. They sat in silence for a few moments. Maybe if they didn't move or speak, this beige and plastic hospital room would stay frozen in this moment. Maybe evil gods would never come here, and everything would be fine. Spooky was willing to stay here as long as the world would let her.

"Spooky, I..." Elliot's eyes went past her and his mouth opened. "Mom!"

"Elliot!" A woman flew to the bed and hugged him. Spooky crawled off and retreated to the corner of the room. "Oh, sweetie, I'm so sorry! We were so worried! Are you okay?"

The man who came in after had Elliot's same thick brown hair.

"We were so worried," were the only words he managed to choke out before he put his arms around Elliot.

"It's okay, Dad, I'm okay." Elliot patted him on the back. "Really."

"We thought you ran away again," his mom said. "But then the police found the note, and the two other kids were missing...oh. Hello there." She had blue eyes, like Elliot. She gasped. "You're Laurel! You're one of the others who was missing! I thought they hadn't found you yet!"

Elliot's mom came toward her, and Spooky shrank back. Before she knew it, she was wrapped in a hug and being rocked back and forth.

"Laurel, sweetie, I'm so glad you all made it home." His mother pulled back, her eyes even bluer with tears. "Thank goodness!"

"Mom, this is Spooky," Elliot said. "We were together, for the whole thing."

His dad was crying too. Spooky's heart swelled.

"I should let you catch up." She started for the door.

"Oh, your leg! Have the nurses seen you?" his mom said. "You don't have to wait alone."

"My parents are in the other room," she lied, covering the dried blood on her jeans. "It was really nice to meet you. Bye Elliot."

He sat up. "I'll see you later."

He looked like he wanted to say more, but whether personal or otherworldly, now that his parents were here, it wasn't the right time.

Spooky walked back down the hallway toward the fork, and chose the corridor that didn't have nurses at the end of it. Luckily, it happened to be the one that led her to the waiting room.

Carcass didn't glance at her as she approached. His back was hunched, and his huge eyes were glued to the TV, tracking the movements of the players in a sitcom. She stood behind him for a moment.

"Can we turn to the news? Just for one second."

Carcass grumbled, but the screen flashed over to an aerial view of a flooded coastal city. Waves buffeted office buildings. From the height of the camera, Spooky couldn't see the men and women who had been swept away to drown.

"These metropolitan centers are lucky," Carcass said. "It's the ones the tunnels open onto that will experience true bloodshed. I imagine when the horde of Yazerob reaches the surface and starts ransacking cities, that will be the moment the invaders will decide Earth is truly abandoned."

It was hard to reconcile images of destruction from across the world with the beige walls and bleach smell of the hospital waiting room. Everything here was so civil, sterile, and well kept. How long would it be before there were no hospitals to turn to? When there was nowhere safe for anyone to go?

"How long until the tunnels reach the surface?"

Carcass shrugged. "Long enough to finish this episode, I hope."

The TV flipped back to the sitcom. Spooky didn't think she was going to be able to get the remote out of the orange hand that held it.

Should she try to go home and warn Victoria, or her parents? They would never believe her. Even if they did, there was nothing they could do.

Oddly, when it came to company for the end, she would rather stay here with Carcass. When Elliot was done catching up with his parents, they could talk again. When Bree woke up, Spooky wanted to talk to her too.

With nothing else to do, she sat down to watch TV.

"What will you do now?" she asked.

"Mourn. Maybe this was the cost of having something wonderful. If the god of Earth's absence achieved one thing, it was humanity's fervent need for self-defining stories. I won't find that somewhere else." He took in a deep breath that expanded his face like a bullfrog's and let it out. "Too bad his absence also led to your destruction."

He looked deflated. She both wanted and didn't want to pat his nine-fingered hand.

"You'll find something else to entertain you, on some other world."

"Not likely, now that Geyegorg has seen Kru." Carcass shook his head. "I doubt he will be willing to make another trade with me for a very, very long time. I shall count myself lucky if he does not end the contract I gave him Kru's brothers for."

"Which contract?"

"The contract I made to protect myself from Leber. Although I suppose Leber will be too busy on Earth to try to take over my little imitation."

Spooky had a sudden urge to call home and tell Victoria if she came across any black goo, not to touch it. But there were too many threats to offer a meaningful warning. If it wasn't a tarry pit, it would be a member of Bagoula's army, or whatever the horde of Yazerob was supposed to be.

Carcass chuckled.

"What?"

"Geyegorg craves most that which he does not have. Perhaps I could convince him to trade me the two Krudors he has for the one he doesn't."

She shuddered. Geyegorg and his priorities. The way he talked about Bagoula coming and going as a business partner, all the while hoping to add her to his collection, was disturbing. Spooky knew he viewed her the same way. Even as she had passed by on her way back from Axonaphis, he had been shouting for her.

Some idea wanted to become conscious. Spooky's exhausted brain wasn't processing fast enough. She sat upright and waved her hands. "Wait, what did you negotiate with Geyegorg again? How did you protect yourself from Leber?"

"I purchased the exclusive sight of the beacon to my world, nullifying all other contracts, including Leber's."

"But how did that help? Wasn't Leber already there?"

"He didn't know he'd lost the beacon until he left and couldn't see the door to return. I suppose he didn't leave so much as I opened a door and pushed him through...but I imagine he would have resisted more if he had known he wouldn't see a beacon to guide him back."

"But what if he had propped a door between your worlds open? Like we did with the wires."

"Geyegorg closes any open doors when he ends a contract." Carcass waved his hand at her. "Spooky, as much as I have enjoyed educating you on life beyond your world, we have reached the end of the opportunities for my words to be useful to you. So shh, I'm trying to watch."

He leaned toward the screen.

But Carcass hadn't seen the way Geyegorg had called to her. Something had changed. Something that might give Earth one last chance.

# CHAPTER XXXII
# THE FINAL BARGAIN

"I have to go."

Carcass didn't reply as Spooky dashed for the stairwell. She bounded down three flights and out into the parking lot. Most of the reporters had put down their microphones. Camera crews and vans stood by. Only one, a woman in a purple suit, seemed to be live.

The triangular red beacon was stamped in the air just twenty feet past her. Spooky walked as casually as she could behind the woman's back.

"We at K4 are giving you the most continuous coverage of the hostage situation unfolding in Colorado. Two of the missing teens turned up in the Diamond Springs community this morning. We haven't received any details yet on their condition, but we do know they are being treated here, at St. Mercy's..."

"There's someone in your shot, Marianne," the camera guy interjected.

"Oh? Hey...wait! Hey!"

Spooky glanced over her shoulder. The reporter was wobbling after her as fast as her pencil skirt would allow, heels clacking.

"Hey, Laurel! A word! Gary, camera up, that's her!"

Spooky bolted for the beacon.

"Gary, why aren't you filming this?"

She unzipped the symbol and jumped into the void.

The whiteness spit her out in Axonaphis's chamber of golden mailboxes. He had his back turned. He lowered the red flag on one of the units, then faced her.

"Oh, you're back!" His eyes crinkled and his spectacles flashed.

"I'm just passing through." Spooky drifted toward the neon blue eye she had come here to find—the door to Geyegorg.

She paused.

"Actually, could you send one more message for me?"

"Of course." Axonaphis gave a floating bow. "Who would you like to send it to?"

"Elliot Hall. He's a human, on Earth, at St. Mercy's hospital," Spooky said.

"It doesn't matter where; I only need to know who." Axonaphis held out a paper and a fountain pen. "I'll get it to Mr. Hall."

Her hands quivered. She did her best to make the words legible:

*Dear Elliot,*

*I'm sorry for leaving without saying goodbye. There isn't much time, but I think I have found a way to help Earth. I have to try.*

*If this fails, I'll come back and say sorry in person, and we can watch the end together.*

*Tell Bree to get better.*

*Spooky*

She wanted to write more, but every second counted. She handed the pen and paper to Axonaphis, who took them and nodded.

"I don't need a reply," Spooky said. "Sorry I was rude before. Thanks for your help."

She opened the door to Geyegorg.

*You are free to do whatever you will.* Could that really be enough? Could those words, written to her by her creator, have changed something? With direct permission from the god of Earth to do whatever she chose, maybe she could choose to offer herself in trade. And maybe, if she could offer Geyegorg the human he craved for his collection, she could buy private access to Earth.

It wouldn't be nearly as neat a solution as the god of Earth returning. There was still a risk of widespread destruction. But, if others like Bagoula were off-world waiting to see the outcome of the first attack, they wouldn't be able to strike. Armies would stay locked away across the void. Gods who left Earth wouldn't be able to return.

If she could give Earth any chance at all, she had to try.

She landed on the end of the platform and strode toward the throne. Her eyes adjusted to the darkness. The honeycomb glittered. Bagoula, and who knew how many thousands of creatures, slept beneath the golden surface.

"Geyegorg," she called.

He raised his head at her approach and smiled. He removed his hat, and his third eye shone.

"Ah." He opened his arms to her. "You've returned."

"I have."

"You've changed! Something is different! You're positively glowing!" he squealed. "You have the right to offer yourself, I can see it!"

Spooky's pulse surged. She had been right. The god of Earth had given her his permission to do whatever she willed—and that included trading herself with Geyegorg. Targa's permission to do what she wished with Bagoula had been just as offhand, but offhand words from a divine authority were apparently enough. Whether the god of Earth had intended his response as a rebuff or an opportunity, she couldn't know. But if she could seize this opening, she could use her will to save Earth.

"I'm disappointed your god wouldn't come to me directly. I suppose he is becoming known for being a bit absent, isn't he?" Geyegorg gave her a wicked smile. "Still. Aren't I a lucky boy? It's all because I decided to be so generous, to build up these good relations." He leaned forward. "Now, what must I give to have you?"

The strands of light peeked up on either side of the platform as Geyegorg bounced in his seat. Now wasn't the time to be afraid. It was time to put her Adam Dodgson hat on. Elliot had given her the words to describe it, but she'd had an instinct for motivating people and gods ever since she first met Carcass.

Maybe she had a knack for telling stories after all.

She stood straight.

"I want to be the only one who can see the beacon to Earth."

He paused.

"Not what I expected." Geyegorg sat back and squinted his eyes. "And a very expensive request. Do you know how many gods have given me treasures in order to visit Earth? Do you know how many of my pens would be empty with just that one trade? Thousands and thousands of years of deals, poof." He spread his fingers. "Returned. Gone."

He hadn't said no.

"Earth is under attack. I think you know that." Carcass had told her the reason he'd been able to return to Earth after eight thousand years was because the price of the beacon had dropped. "The beacon to Earth is about to become worthless. No one will give you anything to visit a war zone."

"True." He tapped his armrest. "I wasn't expecting any new buyers. But the current contractors have given me so much already."

"Well, if you miss any of that old stuff, you can make new deals for different beacons and get it back. The one thing you can't have any other way is a living being from Earth. And I'm not offering you a honeybee, or a brain cell. I'm offering you a human."

Carcass had mentioned that Geyegorg valued the things he lacked more than the things he had. She could only hope the allure of a new addition to his collection would be strong enough.

He leaned forward. "Do you even understand what you're asking, errand girl? If only you can see the beacon, even your own god won't be able to go to and fro. You would be both the contractor and the collateral. You'd be the only one who could find the doors. Tucked away, safe in my collection."

"I know." She took a deep breath. "But think about it—if no one can visit Earth, you will have access to the only human. No one else will be able to see one, much less have one."

He tapped his chin and smiled. "You would be quite the rarity indeed."

"In fact, the god of Earth is prepared to commit to never give anyone another human again." It was a lie, but no one would ever make the trek to Axonaphis to get the same permission. The god of Earth's absence would make it true. "I am the only one he will ever offer. For this deal. Right now."

"Oooo, you drive quite a hard bargain. A one-time exclusive offering, for an exclusive beacon?" He curled his hands over the armrests. His smile widened. "How can I resist? I accept."

The little secretary ran forward with its tablet.

"You don't have to read me the whole thing," Spooky said. "But I want to confirm a few points."

If she was going to do this, she had to make sure it would make a difference.

The lizard sniffed. Geyegorg gestured for her to continue.

"I want to make sure the gods who have the beacon now don't get warning that they've lost it." Her voice shook.

"I don't give warning." Geyegorg wrinkled his face. "Gods tend to camp out when you let them know a contract is up. They won't sense the removal. They simply won't be able to see the beacon, if they are off Earth and looking."

"What if they've propped doors to Earth open? I want—the god of Earth wants—to make sure no one can come and go."

"Oh no no no, I don't allow that. I make sure all open doors are closed, by force if necessary. My representatives are very fast and very persuasive." Geyegorg gestured a hand toward one of the Krus behind his throne.

Spooky fidgeted. She couldn't think of anything else. "Alright then."

"Proceed with the binding part of the agreement," Geyegorg said.

Spooky barely listened as the small creature read her the end of the contract—in exchange for the exclusive sight of the beacon marking the doors to Earth, she would give herself. As long as she was in Geyegorg's possession, no one else would be able to see the doors to Earth.

"Do you accept?"

Spooky's heart stopped. She would never get her chance to start over. She would never go to college or see what Elliot had meant by that kiss. She wouldn't get to find out what it was like to belong somewhere, have true friends, or fall in love. Her body shook, and her throat tightened. What was she doing? She couldn't do this.

Spooky closed her eyes. All that had mattered to her a few days ago was getting the chance to start over. She had been desperate for The Change to come into her life. But over the last few days, everything had changed. Everything she believed about who she was, who she wanted to be, and how she was going to get between the two had changed.

She didn't have to be the spooky girl waiting for an opportunity to do something or be someone.

She already was someone.

And the person she wanted to be would only make one choice.

Spooky opened her eyes. "I accept."

"Then we have a deal. Before I can give you the exclusive sight of the beacon, I must nullify the past contracts. Secretary, mark all the contracts for the beacon to Earth nullified. Remove the beacon from the contractors' eyes."

Cold sweat raised goosebumps on her arms, but Spooky blew out a shaky breath. She had done it. Any god that wasn't on Earth already wouldn't be able to make the journey. Hopefully, the majority had been preparing from afar.

"Secretary, return the collateral." Geyegorg slumped back in his chair and shoved his hat over the glowing orb on his forehead. "Eek, I can never bear to watch this part." He covered his two remaining eyes and squirmed. "My beauties."

Light unfurled from under the platform. Ten, fifty, then hundreds of glowing strands arched over the honeycomb. The filaments dipped into golden hexagons across the expanse. One emerged from a nearby cell encircling a creature made of eyes. The light carried the blinking ball over the platform and pushed it through a door.

Each rope of light that entered the golden liquid fetched some combination of wings, legs, tails, hands, heads, and appendages she had no name for. Others didn't look like living things at all. Some growled and screeched, while others sailed by silently. According to Geyegorg, no time had passed for them at all. They had been frozen since the moment Geyegorg accepted them in trade.

Hundreds of doors opened and closed around hundreds of beings. Returned to their contractors' seat of power.

Would she wake up to the same experience? Would Geyegorg change his mind, nullify their contract, and send her through the door at the end of the platform? Would she wake up in Colorado, under the maple tree, on some future garbage day? She couldn't even wish for that. If he ever released her, it would mean the end of their contract. It would mean Earth was vulnerable again.

Spooky covered her mouth with a shaking hand and turned away from Geyegorg.

"Carcass," she whispered. She still had the finger under her hair. It was too late to try to give it back. "Are you there?"

"Yes, Spooky," he said in her ear. His voice was sad. Maybe he'd been listening the whole time.

"You can't leave Earth, or you won't be able to return."

"Do not worry about me. I have contingencies."

"And please, when I'm gone, try to trick the invading gods into leaving. There are reporters outside the hospital. Maybe Elliot can help you talk to them about the god of Earth returning. I don't want to do this just to have it destroyed anyway."

"I will employ every trick I know to push the invaders out. I will stay and defend it."

"Will it hurt?" She shook harder. The beings soaring over her babbled, bayed, and shouted.

"No. You won't feel anything at all. You will be suspended in time, unharmed and unconscious."

"Okay." Tears slid down her cheeks. "Goodbye, Carcass."

"Goodbye, Spooky."

The last ropes of light retracted from the end of the platform, empty. It was almost her turn. Her tears streamed now.

"I do hate that part." Geyegorg uncovered all three of his eyes. "Now then, it's time to give you your prize."

Geyegorg lifted one hand and the swirling tornado of symbols descended. The colors were beautiful, but at that moment, all Spooky wanted to see was blue sky. And Bree awake. And Elliot smiling. And even Victoria.

A single green symbol floated down—the "e" with an "L" through it that Carcass had traced for her days ago. Geyegorg cupped it and pushed it toward her eye. It sizzled there, the verdant light reflecting off her tears in a thousand green stars. She blinked to clear them as best she could.

"And now," Geyegorg purred. His third eye thrummed. "For my prize."

Spooky locked her knees so hard she thought they might crack. She wanted to run for the nearest door and jump through. She wanted to forget this contract and go back to Elliot and Bree. Even Victoria. Even her parents. Even Dodgson. Everything that had made her life on Earth terrible and great, she wanted it. She wanted it so badly she could barely stand. Her heart pounded and her breath came quick. How could she let it all go so soon?

But there was no going back. This was the only thing she could give the world—its own second start.

The strands of light came for her. Arching over the sides of the platform, they seemed to draw their patterns with extra care. As they encircled her, she found they felt soft, and neither warm nor cold. As they lifted her up, tears rolled down her face and dripped onto the stone. The contract was signed, nothing she could say or do would change it now. So she cried and hummed her silent goodbyes, and the light lifted her up, up, and over.

For a second, the platform and the hungry eyes watching her

faded away. She focused on her own two hands. They were so beautiful and intricate and strange. The lines on her palms and the pads of her fingers were the sweetest things she had ever seen. She wanted to kiss them. She wanted to hug herself. She watched as her palms reflected gold. Then she saw nothing at all.

# EPILOGUE

Inanimate-Body-Filled-With-The-Living-Blood didn't have the power of foresight. Or at least it only seemed to be through scheming and detailed planning that the future formed itself to his will. But as he watched the girl's back retreating down the stairwell, he felt a strange prickling sensation behind his eyes and a curiosity if he would ever see her again.

Perhaps he wouldn't have, if he didn't already have a plan.

The boy sat on the end of the bed, holding a note from another world. He moved it between his eyes as if he had some trouble reading it. Maybe that was because he was crying.

The god let himself be seen.

The boy jumped and yelled, which were the most common human reactions. But he calmed down faster than most, because they had met before.

"Human, I am the god known as Carcass," he said. "I will strike a bargain with you."

# ACKNOWLEDGMENTS

Strange Gods is my first novel, and for most of the time I spent writing it, few people knew how I spent my nights (hunched over a keyboard) and weekends (staring at the ceiling filling plot holes). Therefore, there were many contributors along the way who didn't know I was writing at all, but accepted me, supported me, laughed with me, danced with me, and made all the difference.

This past year, as I moved toward publication, I have needed more support from my community than ever before. I would like to acknowledge the people who helped me on that journey:

First and foremost, I would like to thank my husband, Spencer. From the beginning, he has been my biggest supporter, secret keeper, cheerleader, and safe harbor. From ceding the living room in our tiny apartment to writing time, to giving up evenings for workshops and writing group, to late nights offering synonyms and input on the natural sound of sentences, he has treated my dreams as his own. No one could ask for a better partner, and I'm so grateful he's mine.

I would like to thank my family:

Mom, for always believing in me. Truly, I am who I am today because of your love and support. Your pride and joy have propelled me through some long nights as I worked to complete this book. (I hope you are still proud after having read it. I can hear you saying "oh, Alison..." when you get to the creepy bits. And now I know you are saying "Of course I am, I couldn't be prouder!!!" very indignantly. Thank you, Mom.)

Pop, for giving me your best counsel at every stage, checking in, and showing up with doggies and Costco hotdogs in crucial moments. It means so much to have your care and support, every time.

Anne, for dropping everything to help me and giving me the perspective I desperately needed. You helped me get in touch with my main character in a way that made this book much, much better. And you jumped in again when I was out of my depth with the symbols; thank you for helping me, even when you were so busy yourself.

Jonathan, for always supporting me and asking how the writing is going, for buying me books and always looking out for my dream, while inspiring me with your pursuit of your own. I am so lucky to have you to lean on and look up to.

Sarah and Beth, for caring and rooting me on from afar every Sunday, and for offering long-distance assistance in the form of readers, shares, likes, and ideas. The glorious seven are always more powerful together!

I would like to thank my friends who read pages and provided feedback at various stages of the writing process: Reggie, Brenda, Laura, and Amrita. I would especially like to thank Amrita, who read the entire work as a beta reader and gave me the absolute joy of hearing my first fantasy nerd's reactions.

Thank you to Beth Buck, for picking Strange Gods out of the ether and giving it a home at Immortal Works. I had put it in a drawer to write the next thing, and your faith in this story made me pull it out again, dust it off, and polish it until I could see my face in it. If not for this process, I would never have progressed as much as I have as a writer. You made my dreams come true, and I hope the finished work makes you proud.

I want to thank Holli Anderson, for being so supportive throughout the editing process. Thank you to Ruth Mitchell, for partnering with me and guiding me—you gave me the path to get this book into readers' hands and made me feel understood, supported, and motivated. And thank you to the entire Immortal Works team, for helping me bring Strange Gods to the world. I am honored to be among your wonderful community of authors.

Thank you to Marc, for lending your hand and being my advocate. Your support and perspective helped me launch with confidence.

I want to thank my writing group, Anthony, Bobby, Marlow, and Naihobe, who for three years were the only people who read and weighed in on my words. Our every-other-Wednesdays were a joy that both energized me and offered crucial feedback on this novel. We all wrote very different things, but somehow, fit together as our own little writing community!

And finally, thank YOU, strange reader, for reading Strange Gods. I hope you enjoyed the weird and wild ride. Please leave a review, even a few words or thoughts, on Amazon or Goodreads. I read them all, and that is how other readers will discover Strange Gods!

# ABOUT THE AUTHOR

Alison Kimble began writing because she loves stories and believes in their power to shape our world and ourselves. Her writing blends the real and the fantastical and crosses genres of horror, fantasy, and sci-fi. Now that her debut novel, Strange Gods, is in your hands, she is working on her next novel and a short story anthology. She lives in the Greater Seattle Area with her husband and spends her time walking in the woods, going to the movies, and seeking adventures large and small.

This has been an
Immortal Production